Previous Titles by Caro Ramsay

The Anderson and Costello series

ABSOLUTION
SINGING TO THE DEAD
DARK WATER
THE BLOOD OF CROWS
THE NIGHT HUNTER *

* *available from Severn House*

KT-514-528

05004786

THE TEARS OF ANGELS

THE TEARS OF ANGELS

Caro Ramsay

Severn House

This first world edition published 2015
in Great Britain and the USA by
SEVERN HOUSE PUBLISHERS LTD of
19 Cedar Road, Sutton, Surrey, England, SM2 5DA.
Trade paperback edition first published 2015
in Great Britain and the USA by
SEVERN HOUSE PUBLISHERS LTD.

Copyright © 2015 by Caro Ramsay.

All rights reserved.
The moral right of the author has been asserted.

British Library Cataloguing in Publication Data

Ramsay, Caro author.
  The tears of angels. – (An Anderson & Costello mystery)
  1. Anderson, Colin (Fictitious character)–Fiction.
  2. Costello, Detective Sergeant (Fictitious character)–
  Fiction. 3. Police–Scotland–Glasgow–Fiction.
  4. Murder–Investigation–Scotland–Lomond, Loch–
  Fiction. 5. Detective and mystery stories.
  I. Title II. Series
  823.9'2-dc23

ISBN-13: 978-0-7278-8515-9 (cased)
ISBN-13: 978-1-84751-617-6 (trade paper)
ISBN-13: 978-1-78010-668-7 (e-book)

Except where actual historical events and characters are being
described for the storyline of this novel, all situations in this
publication are fictitious and any resemblance to living persons
is purely coincidental.

All Severn House titles are printed on acid-free paper.

Severn House Publishers support the Forest Stewardship Council™ [FSC™],
the leading international forest certification organisation. All our titles that
are printed on FSC certified paper carry the FSC logo.

Typeset by Palimpsest Book Production Ltd.,
Falkirk, Stirlingshire, Scotland.
Printed and bound in Great Britain by
TJ International, Padstow, Cornwall.

Acknowledgements

Writing any kind of book is a team effort to get to the best end result. So I'd like to thank all of the Ramsay Team, especially my agent Jane Gregory and her staff.

Special thanks to Alan for the coffee and the proofreading, to my long-suffering staff who have to put up with me never being where I should be and the Michty Me JWG for their advice over the years.

For *The Tears of Angels* I'd like to thank Michael Anthony Laphan for giving his name so generously for me to use and abuse in the telling of this tale, in aid of Clic Sargent, the UK's leading charity to help fight cancer in children and young people.

Thank you all,

Caro

Prologue

Looking across the loch the old man thought back to summers past. Golden memories of tartan rugs and sticky fingered picnics, of skinned knees and savage midges. A day spent hauling haversacks on to trams, running for trains, pulling on his mum's hand, desperate to get to the farm.

Now, eighty years later, in the glow of the mid-summer moon, he could still make out the old farmhouse and the glimmer of a bonfire with its plume of milky smoke. It seemed closer now, but as a child the dark water between had seemed to stretch to eternity, untroubled and unbroken.

At the water's edge he tried to catch the waves with his toes, shuffling back as the leading wave chased him. This was a game he used to play with his dad. If a wave caught you by the ankle, it stole your soul.

But his dad lied. Waves were not the only stealer of souls.

Bert grew up to learn that his dad's lies knew no bounds: eggshells gave you warts, ice cream gave you kidney stones and Saskatoon was just up the road from Govan. And the BIG lie. The lie that *Mum would follow*. Oh yes, his dad had been in fine form as he hauled him up the gangplank of the steamer, ignoring the scratches of the battered leather case on his son's knees, ignoring the screams escaping from his throat, and then his dad's quiet, forceful reply: *It'll be fine*.

Bert had never seen his mother again.

The moment of regret was broken by the assault of a wassailing vengeful demon: somebody on the far shore having a go on the bagpipes. The noise arranged itself into the 'Skye Boat Song' as somebody made a silhouette, dancing languidly across the flames of the bonfire.

Happy people.

Happy times.

Celebrating the summer solstice.

A quick look at his watch told him he had twenty-five minutes until they needed to leave for the airport. The Ben was now black on black; rain was on the way. According to local folklore, this was an omen that the loch was ready to give up its dead. It was also an omen for a sighting of the fabled white deer, drifting like wraiths in the water.

Bert lifted his phone, carefully switched it to video mode and scanned the islands, catching the bright yellow of the bonfire's flames burning like a dying star in the night sky. The bagpipe died then let rip with a blast, followed by a burst of drunken laughter. The dancers moved like marionettes under the moon. North of the bay Bert saw a boat moving towards them.

Then the whole loch hushed to stillness. Calm. Eerie.

Bert felt very alone. Very old. A shiver that might have been born of a chill turned to a quiver of exhilaration as he saw palmed prongs proud of the surface.

Then another. And another. The wakes intertwined and danced in the water. He could see noses and ears as a stag and two does glided out to the dark shadow of the island.

This was the stuff of his dreams. He kept them in frame as they reached the shore and a small female climbed out from the waves, followed by a bigger female and then the stag. They stood as statues on the shore, white against the sand. Then there was a flicker in the undergrowth, one last glimpse of their ghostly forms and they were gone.

He scanned across the bay, just in case, but he didn't see the deer again. Instead he saw the man in the boat, one arm held high, waving.

Bert waved back and started to walk up the beach to the hotel, heavy hearted. He wouldn't be back – he was too old. Then he stopped, seeing himself as that little boy, on the opposite bank, looking out over the water. He remembered how he had been the only calm one, totally at peace as everybody started searching, his mum crying and his dad frantic. Then the hysteria when they found the body.

He heard the hotel clock strike midnight.

The moon slipped behind a rogue cloud. He turned off the phone and pulled up his collar against the chill; the first few spits of rain pecked at his cheek.

Bert walked unsteadily back up to the hotel before his memories had a chance to follow.

Monday, 16 June

He was lying on his back, snuggled into a blanket of short grass on the hillside as if in deep sleep. His head was twisted slightly towards the rising sun, showing the ripped and broken skin and the rivulets of dried blood that had coursed from his nostrils to follow the contour of his upper lip before dropping on to the grass below.

Higher on the slope the horses were taking their time to settle after their restless night. They were calmer now, their peace betrayed by a nervous ripple of a silken summer coat and a flick of the tail at an absent fly.

The large bay and the small grey cob stood head to tail, grooming each other for solace. A rope collar hung round each of their necks. The free end of the rope dragged in the mud as the mare turned, ears pricking at the familiar sound of the kitchen door opening. She started to move, sensing company and breakfast.

Maddy noticed something was awry the minute she closed the kitchen door. Horses were nervy. They could take fright at a crisp packet if the mood took them. God knows how they ever survived in the wild; soft was the word for them, like a bunch of big kids. She stopped at the corner of the yard to look down the field; there *was* something different about them this morning. Becky, the big bay mare, usually needed a bit of edible encouragement to be caught but she was up at the fence, swaying on her front legs. Tommy, the wee grey cob, was keeping well back out the way. He pulled at the grass nervously. That was his *I'm Being Brave* act.

Maddy strode across the yard, two head collars over her arm, clicking her tongue to call Tommy. His ears pricked; he shook his mane so it bristled like a badly stuffed mattress. But he stood still, his head low like he was sickening for something. Maddy laid the head collars on the fence and climbed over, worried now. Tommy regarded her with his big plummy eyes but still made no attempt to move. She jogged across the field, her wellies sucking against the skin of her bare calves. Concern filled her heart when she saw the strange rope round his neck. It was a single loop pulled tight but the free end was caught under his rear offside leg. The silly sod couldn't even work out that all he needed to do to release himself was to lift his hoof up. God, he was beyond stupid sometimes. She ran her hand down his rump, asking him to lift his leg. Once his head was free he swung round and nipped her on the backside. Not much wrong with him, then.

She checked his flank, looking for signs of injury. There was nothing but a small red scab near his tail. Maddy started to pull in the rope, winding it round her hand like she did when she was helping her mum wind wool. The rope caught, she tugged. It stuck fast, she tugged harder. It freed and the bloodied hand bounced through the air towards her, waving.

DCI Colin Anderson stared into the rear-view mirror of the Golf, flicking his fingers through his hair. He'd had a haircut, some kind of magical haircut that had turned his blond hair grey. There was no getting away from it: he was forty-three and starting to look it – especially at this time in the morning. He looked at the dashboard clock and cursed, twenty past seven. His stomach noisily reminded him of a promise of a cuppa and a bacon roll.

Before he got the call.

Getting out the car, he cast a look at the sky. Brilliant blue. But the forecast said it would break today. He was reminding himself to check the weather on the net when he noticed the fat uniformed cop pacing behind the hedge of the maisonette, playing 'now you see me, now you don't' every time he passed the gate.

Control had said number sixty-eight, as if the smell of burnt wood drifting in the air didn't make it obvious. It was the maisonette at the top of the cul de sac, the one with the pink climbing tea roses on the front wall. Anderson guessed the garden would be tended by the downstairs neighbour, the deceased herself being ninety-two years of age. The neatness of the garden was a good sign; this was a caring neighbourhood. Everybody's front room looked on to everybody's garden; everybody's nose would be in everybody else's business. This was curtain-twitching country.

The fat cop strutting the garden jumped with fright when Anderson appeared from behind the hedge. Another uniform came out the neighbouring ground-floor flat, diagonally opposite that of the deceased, chin to his shoulder as he chatted down his radio. At the flat door he left a grey-haired woman in a blue nylon house-coat leaning against the rose trellis for support. From the distance, Anderson could see that although she was red-eyed and shaking, she still had the strength to glare across the square and stare down the eyes hidden behind the Venetian blinds.

'DCI Colin Anderson,' he introduced himself as the uniform approached. 'Who was that lady?'

'Neighbour,' he said.

The DCI sighed, and waited.

'Mrs Elizabeth Taylor. Yes, really. Elizabeth Taylor. She used to look in on Bella every day.'

'Bella?'

'Arabella Barr, the deceased.'

Anderson couldn't help but turn round at the tantalising smell as some sadistic bastard cooked bacon under an open window, adding a top note to the scent of charred wood. He felt his stomach rumble.

'The Fire Service are gone, the Prof is here. Old lady burned to death, highly suspicious.' He said it as if she was parked on a double yellow.

'And you are?'

'Hemphill. George. Sir. She was wrapped in her duvet, the duvet was set on fire then the front door was set alight.'

'From what side?'

'The inside. Initial inspection from Fire Investigation says that a lighted match was posted through the letterbox after the door was closed. An accelerant had already been splashed on the inside.'

'So they blocked her way out?'

'God knows why; she was housebound.'

'Bloody hell.' Anderson looked round. Such horror had no place amongst the pansies and the tea roses.

Hemphill continued, 'The neighbour, Elizabeth Taylor, saw the carers go in yesterday morning; she went in at five p.m. The late carers came in at seven to put Bella to bed. Then the neighbours across the road saw the van again, presuming it was another shift. The morning carers found her dead at half six this morning; both fires had put themselves out. Smoke alarm went off but no bugger heard it.'

'So the late-night carers set her on fire?' asked Anderson with mild sarcasm.

'She doesn't have carers that late. The professor is inside.'

'So did the neighbours see anything else?'

'Nope, and there doesn't appear to be anything missing or stolen.'

'OK, get a colleague to go with you door to door. Try and get a description of the bogus carers. Or their vehicle.'

Hemphill rolled his shoulders and smiled. 'It's been a long night, sir. I was hoping for a wee cuppa . . .'

'I'm sure Bella was too, but it looks as though we are all disappointed.'

The voice box for the door entry system on the outer doorpost looked well weathered, well used. The outer door had been left open, too warped to close properly. It revealed a deep red carpet covering a steep stairway, handrail on the left. There were greying tongue marks of flames rippling up from the blackened stain on the carpet, the stain at its widest under the letterbox. On the inside the same stain ran the full width of the door but only a few inches inwards, in an irregular shape. It did indeed look like the accelerant had been splashed around but the flames had gone out as soon as the vapour had burned off. The wall on the right side was similarly marked. The end plate of the stair lift had been charred and blistered but the seat was down and piled high with junk mail, topped by a menu for the Golden Diamond Chinese takeaway and two brown letters sandwiching a black envelope. Funeral notice, Anderson thought. How many of them have you seen when you reach ninety-two? His stomach tightened as he made his way upstairs, aware of the cloying smell of old smoke. He walked past the kitchen door to the bedroom, where O'Hare was leaning over a duvet, chiaroscuro in black and tea roses. The pathologist was touching nothing, just sniffing the air.

'You doing this by magic now?'

'It would be easier on your budget. Good morning, Colin. I hope I didn't interrupt your breakfast,' the pathologist said without looking up, leaving Anderson to talk to a mop of unruly grey hair.

He then stood to one side, letting the DCI have full view of the scene.

The small, wizened face of Arabella Barr was peeking out from the charred top of the duvet. Without the support of her teeth, the cheeks were sunken dark hollows, and by comparison her porcelain skin looked as though it was made of paper.

Scorched paper.

'Death by inhalation?'

'Not sure if that was technically what she died of, but she was definitely set on fire. White spirit, I reckon. She was a fit wee biddy for her age. Her only real complaint was a bad hip, so she couldn't manage the stairs and getting out of bed was an issue – hence the door entry system and the carers to get her up and put her down . . .'

'So she lay there helpless as they set fire to her . . . what kind of mind do these folk have?'

'I'll let Prof Batten answer that one. Bella had some continence issues so had a reinforced sheet underneath her, which happens to be fire retardant so the flames didn't have much to feed on.' He waved a pen around. 'She has third-degree burns around her abdomen and at that age she would lose a lot of fluid.' The two men stood in silence for a moment, listening to the ticking of the granddaughter clock in the hall. 'You are looking for a nasty wee bastard.'

Anderson looked closer. All he could really see was a bobble of grey hair, flattened at the back. The spidered strands of hair made her pink scalp look like marble. She looked too small to be human, too delicate. O'Hare lifted the remains of the duvet and filigree black wisps floated in the air like feathers.

Anderson felt a gasp escape from his throat. The nightdress was a patchwork of white lace and brown fringed holes through which he could see, and smell, blackened burned flesh, blisters rimmed in bright red, fading to baby pink.

A painful, slow death.

'Her "care alert" is over there. Can't say if she had time to try and reach it.' O'Hare sighed. 'She was ninety-two. Little old ladies who tend their tea roses deserve a better death than this, don't you think?'

Anderson nodded. 'Of course they do.'

'One of the neighbours told the fire investigation guy that she saw a council van three nights ago, driving around late at night.'

'Hemphill's doing a door to door. I'll leave you to it.' He crept into the living room, quietly respectful of an old lady's privacy. The light summer curtains had been opened, as had the hoppers on the window to let some air through. Free of the smell of the smoke, he could recognize the familiar accompaniments of old women: talcum powder, lavender water and mashed tea. A *People's Friend* lay open on top of a pile of newspapers on a side table with a hand-held magnifier and a pen lying together. A few horses had their names ringed in blue ink. She must have liked a flutter. A grab stick lay against the throw-covered armchair, and a plastic aid to turn the fire on and off was placed on the arm of the chair. Next to it was a small tapestry footstool, a pair of old tartan slippers sitting neatly beside it. The telephone had a loud volume feature and an attachment for the care alert.

Anderson laid his fingertip on the top of the Harvey's Bristol Cream bottle on the sideboard, disturbing the fine, silky soot. It was nearly empty. He thought he would have liked Bella.

He walked back out to the hall and stood beside the clock. A bowl of dusty potpourri stood on the small sideboard with a card tucked underneath which read: *Never complain about growing old, some folks don't get the option.* 'And I've never died a winter yet,' Anderson muttered out loud, quoting his own granny. The flat seemed incredibly clean, free of the usual clutter and gatherings of a long life. Bella had been tidy, throwing out what she did not need, no need to keep anything for a rainy day if every day had its fair amount of rain. Through the open door of the bedroom he could hear O'Hare's phone ringing, a millisecond before his own vibrated in his pocket.

'DCI Anderson? We have an incident.' The voice read out the postcode. 'Riverview Farm. Near Erskine. They will meet you on the road.'

He said thanks, hung up and stepped back into the bedroom, looking at the calendar. Pictures of roses, hints and tips for pruning and dead-heading. 'You said a neighbour had seen a strange van a few days ago?'

O'Hare looked at the date on his watch. 'Yip, she said Friday.'

'Friday the thirteenth.'

*   *   *

Elvie McCulloch had a whole two weeks off after her periods of surgical rotation and elective study for her medical degree had finished. Her dissertation had been submitted and she wasn't scheduled for any more clinic time for another week. Her road back to health had been long and painful. The difficult part was trying to cope with 'normal'.

Free time was an anathema to her so she was looking forward to spending the day at her other job at the agency. At half six she went for a slow fifteen-mile run, then after a shower and a smoothie for breakfast, she lay on the settee of her Woodlands flat watching the news. Some trouble over the new borders in the Crimea, some new horror in the Middle East and the usual gaggle of football managers talking crap. She dressed in baggy jeans and an old T-shirt, dirty trainers with broken laces and a stained, frayed, nicotine-scented hoodie she had borrowed from one of the retired cops she worked with. She had noticed the dark clouds gathering while she was out running so she slipped on her thin waterproof jacket. On her way to the office she practised her 'ned walk', rolling her shoulders, chin sticking out and hands deep in pockets. She had the crater skin; all she needed was a pit bull and a bottle of Buckie to complete the picture. As she crossed the grass up to Park Terrace, she noticed that strange Scottish summer phenomenon: the dawn had darkened the day.

Approaching the office she looked at the sign, as she always did. It was a bittersweet reminder of the past, friendships forged and good friends lost. *Parnell Fox; Private Investigations*. As her good friend Mary Parnell's husband Alex would be in the company of Her Majesty for a few years yet, Mary had taken over his security business and tried to use it for the greater good – mainly tracking down society's runaways and throwaways. Mary was on a cruise in the Med with her parents and her son Charlie, leaving Elvie to oversee their team of six investigators.

By the time she had opened up the shutters and turned the alarm off, the clock on the wall was twitching round to eight thirty. The office was quiet, the answering machine blinking away. The meeting table looked like the aftermath of a tea party for delinquent chimpanzees; four glasses, all dirty, nestling in the remnants of a takeaway. The air was scented with stale beer and chicken tikka, sweaty feet and God knows what else.

Typical of retired cops back from surveillance.

She opened the window, letting in the rumble of distant traffic with the fresh air. Then she put the chairs back where they belonged and started picking up screwed-up peanut packets, crisp packets and one empty can of dog food from the floor. The place still stank like the monkey house, so she opened the window a bit further and wandered into the back office to put the milk in the fridge and switch the kettle on.

Five minutes later she was sitting at a computer screen sipping a black coffee, reading through emails. A firm of car mechanics had paid them for tracing a vintage MG that had been nicked and renumbered. Not much money in that but the boys had enjoyed it. A small firm of decorators had paid up after they had proved beyond doubt that the two juniors were moonlighting and undercutting their boss, for cash. Another boss, his employee attending Zumba classes while off on the sick . . . not much wrong with that, thought Elvie, until she read the employee was supposed to be off work with a broken ankle. She herself had traced the mother of an adopted child, so he could thank her and reassure her that he had lived a happy life. It had been footwork, computer searches and educated guesses.

Her current case was more typical, a drug addict who had left home and now the family wanted him back: Iain Matthews – or Tattoo Boy, as Elvie called him.

She opened another email, recognizing the address and immediately remembering the case. An American had been trying to trace an old girlfriend. Fox Parnell had found the girlfriend's daughter Alexis, and she had informed them that the American had fathered a son but both kids had lost touch with their mother. The last comment on file, dated a year ago, was *Happy Families.*

Elvie wasn't surprised when she read the new email. Families, especially long-lost half connected ones, were toxic. Elvie saw the image of the clean cut handsome man in his late fifties, his black hair sprouting wings of grey. She guessed Italian ethnicity somewhere and read on.

GDiM@aol.com: My son is now living with Alexis. You have the address. Can you drive up and make sure all is well? He might be working away, but it's not like him not to be in touch. But please be very discreet. I'm concerned.

'No jokes about him keeping away from Costello's body. His chat-up lines are all about his beloved databases and his operational parameters.'

O'Hare moaned slightly as his back cracked with the effort of lifting his case over the fence. 'Why does Walker have to turn up everywhere these days? His presence makes it all more . . . political.'

'I would say messy.'

They both waved to their colleagues before starting the stepping stone game on the aluminium plates that lay on the grass in a wide arc. The plates marked the 'corridor of ingress', as Archie Walker, their new senior fiscal, would call it. Under that Barbour would be a very expensive suit. He kept his hair trendy short, which was faintly ridiculous on a man of his age. The sight of his number four caused Anderson to raise his hand, gauging his own.

Walker was taking advantage of chaotic Police Scotland to make his own mark. The mark he produced in his underlings being of the brown and skid variety. He might be a bit of an arse but he had a reputation as a man who got the job done, and wanted a good team around him.

He also had a reputation of having a wee liking for DI Costello, which had become apparent at the Christmas party. Walker had been very drunk, Anderson mildly so and Costello stone-cold sober as usual. Anderson had no intention of forgetting about Walker and Costello. All knowledge is power, as Bacon said. The thought made Anderson's stomach rumble.

O'Hare slid on a plate and his foot landed sideways in the grass. Anderson grabbed him by the elbow.

'I am getting too old for this,' the pathologist said.

'We all are,' agreed Anderson.

By the time he reached the crowd, O'Hare was muttering about a pulled hamstring.

'Looks like Costello is getting the benefit of the evidential database verbal experience again,' said O'Hare, standing for a minute to look at the two horses at the top of the field. He then turned his attention to the dark shadow on the grass which was mostly obscured by the legs and bodies of the assembled company. The forensic team and the crime scene manager were standing around in plastic lilac suits murmuring quietly and looking at the sky. The scene was strobed by the constant flicker of camera flash, soundtracked by the whirr of a video camera.

'Here she comes.'

There was no expression in Costello's grey eyes when she looked up and immediately hurried towards them along the plates, leaving the fiscal mid-sentence. 'Thank fuck you two are here,' she said, her voice clipped with desperation.

'Nice to be popular,' said O'Hare.

'Don't let it go to your head; Ebola would be more welcome than Walker,' said Costello curtly. She turned her face away as if she suspected the group might start lip-reading. 'Walker wants you to lead on this one, Colin, and you have to liaise with him directly.'

'He is not my boss.'

'No, DCI Anderson, he is not. But ACC Mitchum is, and it comes from him.'

Anderson twisted on the plates, but the body was still hidden by a sea of folk doing bugger all. 'OK, so what do we have?'

'You need to see it for yourself.' The words caught in her throat.

And Anderson became aware how quiet they were, how tense. Something had shocked the seasoned police officers and crime scene investigators.

Costello retreated to allow them access. The small milling crowd parted in front of them, eyes diverted, hands in pockets. No wisecracks, no patter.

Anderson took one step forward to see the young man in an anorak lying on his back, poised in the grass, his arms like a slave in an Egyptian wall painting; one sleeve up, one sleeve down, both bent at the elbows. His brown eyes were open, still staring up at the sky. He had a few days' growth on his chin. Young, but old enough to have a family. Walker was now kneeling, white faced, pointing in disbelief at the dark, bloodied staining around the sleeves. And the lack of hands.

Anderson was momentarily confused until Costello nodded at the plastic sheet that lay on the grass about four feet from the body. On it, like a makeshift art installation, were placed two coils of rope and two dismembered arms. The dark, crimson ends caught the light of the camera, curls of ligament and fronds of tendons and nerves, ripped and disrupted.

Anderson shuddered. 'Jesus.' He knelt down beside the fiscal, easy to do as his legs were ready to give way.

Walker explained, 'It looks like he was laid down, the rope tied round his forearms, then the rope looped round the horses' necks. They got the horses to gallop in opposite directions. Pulled his arms right out his sockets.'

'Total avulsion injury,' said O'Hare, with some admiration.

Anderson felt vaguely sick.

O'Hare hitched up the plastic trousers of his suit, ready to kneel down to join them. 'What did they use to make the horses bolt?'

'Maddy, the lassie who owns them, says the wee grey one has a small burn on its rear end, maybe a cigarette burn. But we are waiting for the vet on that one.'

Anderson stood up to get some fresh air. The body had voided both bladder and bowels and the smell of urine and excrement made a heady mix with the scent of damp grass and the silty taint of the river. He saw Costello looking closely at the arms lying on their separate plastic sheets, mottled purple and streaked with blood like they had been drizzled with raspberry coulis. She bent over, oblivious to his observation, and peered specifically at the third finger on the left hand. Then she turned to look up at him, grey eyes searching out his own left hand, his own wedding ring. Their eyes met and she had the good grace to look away.

'Sorry?' Anderson said, realizing Walker had been talking to him.

'It is a confusing crime scene. The forensic boys think the deceased walked from a car parked in that passing place, there.' He pointed back to the line of parked vehicles where two pieces of police tape fluttered in the breeze. 'There are drop marks at the fence at that point, then footmarks to where the body was deposited. Footmarks, not shoeprints, like they had shoe covers on. So, there are two sets of prints coming in, and only one going out. Plus some drag marks in but none out. So that makes three on entry and one on exit. And we only have one dead body, so we are missing a pair of feet somewhere. Like I said, confusing.'

'Satanic? Medieval? Gothic?' O'Hare muttered, as he acknowledged the questions going through his head.

'And what do you think of these?' Costello asked him, pointing to the forearms and the mottled skin puckered by the intricately tied rope. The flesh underneath was purple with a pattern of black that might be necrosis or dried blood. Or both. 'Expertly done?'

O'Hare shrugged. 'Somebody who sails? A climber? A nylon rope?' The pathologist glanced up at the horses and made the connections. 'So they got him into the field, tied his arms on to the horses then . . .' He shook his head. 'He was unconscious, surely? Dragged; probably backwards.' He pointed out that the victim's short dark hair was spiky with dirt and upended on the back of his head.

'He is a fit young man. Even if they had a gun to his head, he would have struggled – anything would be preferable to this,' said Anderson, looking into the battered, bruised and bloodied face of the young man. 'Somebody punched him, more than once.' Anderson heard Walker's phone ring and saw him lift it from his pocket and reject the call. His eyes met Costello's again; this time she looked away. That would have been his wife, then.

Anderson thought the dead man looked peaceful, at rest. He must have been unconscious when all this was going on – surely anybody with any sense of the pain and horror to come would have terror etched into every muscle in their face. He put his hand out, palm up, feeling the drizzle turn to rain.

'Right, let's get on with it.' O'Hare bent over the empty sleeves, each cuff a tunnel of blood. Costello crouched down in front of him and O'Hare handed her a sealed bag of nitrile gloves. 'Stick them on, will you? My back's giving me gyp.' The pathologist leaned forward uncomfortably and looked over at the plastic sheet. 'Can you bag the hands up, then the rest of the arms?' Then he said to Anderson, 'Well, he has the hands of a manual worker. Somebody who has a job in this part of the world can't be too hard to trace. I was going to suggest that the facial disfigurement was to conceal his identity.'

'No, that was sheer brutality, personal brutality,' said Walker as he approached, smiling. He was in charm mode. 'In the back pocket of his jeans we found a wallet, a driver's licence with photo ID, passport. We're fixed.'

O'Hare raised an eyebrow. 'Handy.' He looked over to the farm, then back at the body.

Anderson followed his chain of thought. 'And nobody heard anything?'

'Absolutely nothing,' said Walker, getting very close to Costello and receiving a glare to back off.

'I imagine getting your arms pulled out is a tad painful, so the fact that nobody heard anything lends weight to the theory that he was unconscious.' O'Hare shone his powerful torch on the battered face. It immediately looked older, more thirties than late twenties. 'No damage round the mouth, so not gagged; the blood there is not smeared. But he was bleeding from the damaged tissues, so alive when it happened, not alive shortly after it happened.' O'Hare carefully lifted the eyelids with his thumb, first one then the other. 'Pupils still a bit dilated.' He made no further comment and pulled a tape recorder from his pocket, ignoring Walker who was trying to kneel beside him to get a better look. Costello and O'Hare moved towards each other, closing the gap.

'You've got the pictures of these cuffs and the trails of blood into the mud?' O'Hare asked the photographer.

A nod. 'You can move him.'

The camera flashed a few times, O'Hare doing his own running commentary. The rate of flashing increased as Costello dipped her head forward, twisting as if she was looking under the dead man's chin. Then she slowly placed her gloved fingertip between his teeth, trying to prise open the mouth.

'Use a spatula for that,' warned O'Hare, shuffling the digital recorder before handing her a wooden strip. He adjusted the torch beam so she could see better.

'There is something in there, something black.'

'If that is a butterfly, I am out of here,' muttered Walker.

'Well, it's not Hannibal Lecter. No *Silence of the Lambs*. Did you see the sequel? Shut up Ewes?' quipped Costello as she took the ruler off a smirking O'Hare and placed it against the lips of the deceased, letting the photographer get close, his camera constantly flashing and whirring.

A corner of black paper came into view, then a fold. Costello swore and took an evidence bag from her pocket then gently prised the black, wet cardboard out of the mouth. The fold caught on the top teeth, and O'Hare reached forward to prise the mouth wider with a sterile spatula so she could pull it free. A black envelope. She dropped it straight into the evidence bag where it sprang open

slightly. 'Nice that they thought to leave us a message.' She stood
up, letting O'Hare start to record body temperature.

'What is it?' asked Walker, pointing at the black envelope.

'I need to open it first. I bet I can do that without touching it;
it's closed but not sealed.'

'No DNA on the glue then.'

Costello shook the envelope down to the corner of its plastic
cover and proceeded to bend it and wriggle it until the flap was
opened, her purple gloved fingers squeezing and manipulating.
She then waggled the envelope from side to side, and a black card
slid out to rest in the opposite corner of the plastic bag. 'Years of
steaming other folk's mail open,' she explained to Walker casually.
The card was black on one side, patterned with a white, magical
unicorn, winged and magnificent. She flipped the bag over. The
other side was a beautiful print of a court jester, the words *The
Fool* in gold lettering underneath.

'A tarot card?'

'Was that put in his mouth?' Walker asked the stupid question.

'Probably. The Fool – does that mean something?' asked
Anderson.

'Maybe O'Hare is right and this is satanic?' Costello caught
the involuntarily grimace on Walker's face. 'Something sacrificial?
We might find three virgins burned at the stake up here
somewhere.'

Walker pulled a sarcastic face. 'Oh Costello, don't be daft.
Where would you find three virgins in Erskine?'

Helena McAlpine sat on a bench on the main drag of the Botanic
Gardens, taking a breather before going back to the studio.

She wanted the company of strangers, of these strollers in the
park who moved slowly and aimlessly, burdened only by the change
in the weather. The noises of the gardens were muffled; heels on
the concrete, cars on the road, chitter chat of passers-by, rumbling
of buggy wheels on the path. She looked up, seeking a breath of
fresh air but finding none; there was no air to breathe. Leaden
clouds sat low over the city. It looked like thunder.

She would sit here and welcome the rain. She was warm but
still pulled her jacket round her for comfort, nestling herself into
the hard wood of the bench. Thinking.

O'Hare said, 'Interesting, that very medieval method of death. The Romans used to do a similar thing with tree trunks. They bent the trunks, tied the victim to them and when they cut the rope the trees would spring back and pull the poor bugger apart.'

'Thanks for that story. I will sleep easier in my bed tonight knowing that barbarianism is alive and well. The big question is where has Warren McAvoy been between the death of those boys and now?'

'Be careful, Anderson, I have no doubt that this case has the scent of shite about it. Nobody else will touch it. If you solve it, you will end up making the top brass look stupid. You'll make Bernie Webster look stupid and he's a popular guy. If you don't solve it, *you* will be made to look stupid, and it will be your name that they'll remember.'

Anderson stopped walking and turned back for a final look at the farm. 'I know I am dancing on eggshells, believe me. I hope Walker isn't looking for a fall guy.'

'Don't expect Police Scotland to rush to catch you.' At his car, O'Hare started to pull his wellies off, leaning on the boot and swearing about the pain in his hip.

'It'd be nice to know if he was drugged when he went into that field.'

O'Hare shot him his dour *doing my job now, are you* look. 'I'll let you know as soon as I can. But so you know, I didn't do any of the posts on the kids. Robbie or Callum.'

'Or Grace,' added Anderson automatically. 'Two boys last year, the wee lassie was the year before. Could you review them? Subtly?'

'Review the work of my own colleagues? We're really spreading the shit around.'

'So play the benefit of hindsight card. Talking of cards . . .' He turned to the passenger side of the car, reached over and pulled a black envelope from under the windscreen wiper. He passed it to O'Hare. 'Looks familiar. Black envelope.'

O'Hare stopped putting his bags in the boot of the car. Anderson handed him another pair of gloves from his pocket, 'It wasn't there when you parked.'

O'Hare looked round, his eyes scanning the fields around them as Anderson looked at the Avensis with its boot on the concrete of the road, the bonnet tucked into the hedgerow, the open fields beyond stretching down to the river. There was nobody there.

'How can that be meant for me? Who knows my car? Only had it a month.'

'Somebody who knows you. Somebody who knew you would be here. The people who did that?' Anderson looked up to the hill, up to the dead body. 'A cop would know that was your car.'

O'Hare pulled on the gloves and turned the black envelope over to find the flap was not stuck, just folded closed. It was a white tarot card this time, the same unicorn. He turned it over. An ornate picture of a man on a throne with sword and scales.

Justice.

Bernie Webster put the phone down slowly, sighed and scratched his belly.

Warren McAvoy had turned up dead in a field.

His arms had been pulled out.

Webster knew that was twelve months of his career gone for nothing. The team had always known McAvoy would turn up sooner or later – that was sod's law and sods like McAvoy always came to light in the end, rotting in a hole, stinking like the evil vermin they were.

He looked out the window into the main office of Alexandria Station. Three of the original murder team were still here, the team that had spent months trying to locate a suspected double, or even triple child killer. No lead left unfollowed. No stone left unturned. They had worked their arses off to trace him. Had he taken his eye off the ball? No, but he had been thinking of steering the case in a new direction.

McAvoy had vanished into thin air. Now he had reappeared. But how had he got off that godforsaken island – Inchgarten or whatever the hell it was called? But it didn't matter how. The fact was he had.

Webster thought back to the endless hours of surveillance of McAvoy's stupid sister going to the chippie, the DSS and the hairdresser. Even interviewing McAvoy's mother when they could find what doorway she was sleeping in. They had interviewed every mad publicity-seeking fuckwit.

He glanced at the date.

the old caravans and the stables so any noise would not reach the house where the family slept. Being summer, the horses were out overnight and accessible. Maximum time in and out? Twenty minutes, maybe less.

Anderson could picture the horses munching, the snip and grate of their teeth on the grass. Then the interruption, heads up, ears pricked, the incentive of a Polo mint maybe, and two horses move towards the killer with their slow, measured stride. Why did McAvoy think he was there? He knew he was a wanted man; he had been living under the radar for a year. So who would he trust?

Then there was the problem of the footmarks. The deceased had been dragged at some point. Yet the two sets of footmarks on the ground suggested he had walked. Three people entered the field, one left. One for the lab boys or a Channel Four illusionist.

He tried hard to imagine what came next. The killer whispering in the horses' ears as they nuzzled at his jacket, maybe. What had passed through McAvoy's mind at that precise minute, that split second when he realized what was going to happen?

Then the loop slipped over the head, pulling the ears through, letting the rope rest over strong, sloping shoulders. The tying of the free ends of the ropes to the forearms, knots now identified as 'blood knots' wound round the elbow and back down again. That had been practised and thought through. A sailor? A climber? The knots would take time and would need a compliant victim.

So when was the punch that knocked him out?

Then he must have laid McAvoy on the ground, arms out. Standing the horses back to back, getting the cigarette out ready. The vet had said the burns on the horses' buttocks were close to the tail, causing the horses to bolt forward with maximum power, maximum damage. That fitted with the face looking skyward. The body did not appear to have jerked to one side first. How does one person control two horses that are facing in opposite directions? Two people, not one? But then there was the single set of footmarks leaving the field.

Anderson felt a headache coming on.

The contrast was almost poetic: the scents of the night, the horses, the warm weather, and a peaceful summer pasture above a gently flowing river, to the horror of the dismembered body.

The solstice was on Saturday. The anniversary.

Nice touch, that. The rat had been flushed out and executed by way of celebration. DCI Colin Anderson had thought the manner of the execution was rather impressive. And the tarot card. The Fool. Fitting. Never mind, they had saved the country a fortune in trial costs and a long stay at Her Majesty's Pleasure.

Colin Anderson, now who was he? The name didn't mean much to Webster, so he presumed Anderson was neither a drinker nor a shagger. Webster allowed himself a little smile. If any shit was going to stick it would not be to him, he'd bloody make sure of that.

He looked at the clock – just gone noon. His fingers played over the buttons on the phone, thinking about Anderson's exact words. A body with McAvoy's ID had been found. The body was clean and well nourished. Clean and well nourished? Webster replayed the tone in his mind, searching for any nuance. Anderson was telling him that McAvoy had been looked after by somebody.

There had indeed been a stone somewhere that had not been turned over.

There would be a review, an enquiry.

Well, they could go take a running fuck. Webster would bet the contents of his secret mobile that any review would conclude that McAvoy had been hidden by the witchy weirdoes up at the holiday camp. Daisy, the one with the big tits. Anderson could content himself with doing them for perverting the course of justice; as McAvoy had died before being charged with anything, he was not technically a criminal.

In the outer office, one of the admin girls bent over to speak to DC Dorwood. Nice arse, bit on the hippy side but he was getting into that as he got older. His fingertips caressed the buttons on the phone but in his mind he was caressing the back of that skirt, the curve of her bum cheeks, the zip on that skirt, weird skirt, like pony skin. Kinda kinky . . . Was this the one that Woody from Traffic was shagging, or was that the blonde one? He'd need to ask.

He tried to drag his mind back to the McAvoy situation. The case had been scaled down at Webster's request last December when he reported that the most likely outcome was that McAvoy had committed suicide. Sammy Winterston had suggested, over a very nice pasta and two bottles of red wine, that it might have been helpful if he had killed himself before he murdered Callum McCardle and Robbie Dewar, but you couldn't have it all your own way, could you?

The admin girl stood up and laughed, sticking her ample chest into Dorwood's face, lucky bugger. Better tits than Sammy, but nowhere near as good as that redhead he'd been chatting up in the Horseshoe Bar . . . What the hell was her name, now?

It would come to him when he was not thinking about it. His hand left the phone and danced across the computer keyboard, all keys tapped with his middle finger, a habit left over from the days when he was a forty-a-day man.

Colin Anderson. Worked out of Partick for a while, made DCI and then . . . well, the site had not yet updated itself with Anderson's current remit. But he was based at Partickhill, west sector under Govan command. Bernie was north sector, which included Balloch and Loch Lomond. Anderson had been called to the McAvoy murder scene purely for geographical reasons, not because they were intending to commission a review of his work from another part of the force.

No need to get paranoid.

But every cloud had a silver lining. He picked up the phone and called Lyn, his third wife, telling her that he would be late home and why. She didn't question it. He thought about phoning Sammy Winterston, but she had been an integral part of his team and she would want to talk shop. She would be concerned for his future career, rather touchingly, before having any concern for her own. She'd want to empathise. Webster had something more horizontal planned to take his mind off it. He decided to phone the wee redhead he'd met in the Horseshoe Bar. She had been well up for it, if only he could recall her name . . . Dawn, Donna, Dione, Darlene . . .

He took out his blue mobile stored in a locked drawer at work where his wife would never find it, containing as it did all the contact details for his ladies, and his marks out of ten. The redhead answered on the third ring – turned out her name was Destiny, so he was close enough. She had a husky voice, could make a career on 0898s. He gave her a bit of chat – talk of a film but he'd heard

it was crap, talk of a play but he was too late in getting g tickets for them – sounding like he cared, then he mentione late supper and an early night at the Holiday Inn. He said he wo swing by the Horseshoe Bar and pick her up at eight. She to him a filthy joke about a nun in the bath and a candle. He w still smiling when he ended the call.

Before he put his blue mobile away he scrolled down, findin a number that only he had – the one person he needed to see befor his date with Destiny. He smirked at the joke, but when the phone was answered his voice was as grave as a mortician's.

'Hi, I've got some news for you.'

They were in the big incident room at Partickhill. The furniture had been rearranged to form a large central table where a tray of water jugs and flasks sat with a motley collection of cups and glasses. There were eight chairs in all, facing the front. The projector hung from the ceiling and the scarred whiteboard had been covered by the viewing screen.

A small woman with dyed red hair that Anderson had never seen before came in, ignored him and put a plate of shortbread fingers next to the coffee.

'Thank you,' he said.

She didn't look his way, just muttered 'Aye,' as she walked out the door.

There was no sense of who was in charge; it might be him, for all he knew. So he sat on the far side in the middle, the most egalitarian spot. He glanced at his watch, six forty-five. He was fifteen minutes early. There was no evidence or case notes lying around although he had seen the list of documents and articles requested. It had been comprehensive. Right from the fatal acciden enquiry into the death of Grace Wilson to school reports of Callun and Robbie, who had both been killed one year later. Berni Webster had done a good job. Anderson had asked him to com in at six forty-five, to settle things – one to one.

But he wasn't here.

So Anderson went through his own scribbled notes from th morning and tried to make sense of them. The location? The fa had been an excellent choice – the killer knew the area and kn it well. The smallholding sat on the far side of the drive, beyo

The killer must have hated him a lot.

He hoped the parents had good alibis.

He shuddered at the thought of the shoulder joints giving way. What did the killer do then? Watch the horses gallop off then place the folded card in McAvoy's mouth? Did the killer look at his victim, lying like a hieroglyph, the empty anorak sleeves and their comet tail of blood tapering into the grass?

The headache started pulsing. McAvoy must have been drugged. That was another thing that didn't make sense. Why do something so painful to someone who couldn't feel a thing? Why not dump him in the bloody river?

It was nearly seven o'clock. Anderson was trying hard not to dwell on what McAvoy went through in those final minutes of awareness. He needed to concentrate on the job in hand. He was walking a tightrope, investigating a murder that should never have happened if Bernie Webster's previous investigation had been thorough. He thought about sending Helena a text saying that he might pop over when he got away from here. He fancied a wee glass of something chilled and white to cheer him after this bloody, long and awful day. But he only got as far as taking his phone from his pocket when the peace was shattered.

The door banged noisily against its retainer arm, a mass of buff files dropped on to the table, two plastic cases of computer discs slid off the top. 'You teacher's pet?'

Anderson returned his phone to his pocket. 'Hi, DI Costello.'

'I found him in the corridor, gave him some stuff to carry. He's been at Bella's all day.' Costello swung her bag from her shoulder, businesslike, and slid the dark jacket of her suit from her shoulders. Then she rolled up the sleeves of her light blue blouse. She looked like an efficient, slightly cross secretary. DS Vik Mulholland was standing at the door, face hidden by evidence files. He stayed there, petulance in every sinew.

'Come in, Vik. She won't bite you. At least not in working hours.' Anderson got up and took the top box from him. 'How did you get on at Bella's?'

Vik slid into the seat beside Anderson. Costello looked at Anderson, one eyebrow raised – Mulholland was a front row, hands up first type of man. 'Hemphill the Lardy Boy said you have a victim with no arms. Is that true?'

'He has all his limbs but not all attached,' said Anderson, rubbing his temples. 'How have you left it at Knightswood?'

'I've sealed the house, the body's been removed. The fire investigation guys are happy. I had a good look round with the wee wittering neighbour, confirmed that nothing has been taken. I'm seeing Bella's daughter tomorrow. Hemphill is trying to collate the visitors to the square. Virgin Media have had their vans in the area; a black-haired woman has been walking her dog – small black dog – round the square recently; a grey Volvo estate did a U-turn there yesterday; and a council van with Bella's carers. Except Bella's carers were private, not council.' Vik waved his pen in the air.

'Nobody else has been in touch to take the case?' asked Anderson.

'No.'

'OK, get Wyngate to help Hemphill in the logistics. That constable has the IQ of a dried apricot. Concentrate on the van. Did you say a wee black dog? Get that checked out; the dog walkers will know it if it's local. Cusack reported a black dog at Riverview as well.'

Mulholland slumped in the seat, but scribbled down a few notes. 'I'm shattered.'

'Me too. I'm sure Costello will get us a lovely cup of coffee if we ask her nicely,' said Anderson, winding up his DI.

'Well, let me consider that.' Costello started to separate the files into three different piles, causing a landslide of shortbread fingers as she slammed them about. 'No. And you can both . . .' She stopped at the sound of the door opening behind her. Walker and DC Wyngate walked in, followed by ACC Mitchum. Behind them was a tall, slim, dark-haired woman, well dressed in a tailored skirt suit, a single silver chain at her neck, a lone charm hanging from the chain at her wrist. She looked very uncomfortable. The fiscal already had his gold pen in one hand, mobile phone in the other. ACC Mitchum was resplendent in his pristine uniform and shiny shoes. He strode to the front of the room, ignoring those already in it. Anderson shuffled forward in his chair. The woman hung about the door until Mitchum removed his glasses and pointed to the end of the room with the leg.

Costello was reminded of a documentary she had seen about the Nuremberg trials.

The woman in the suit nodded nervously at the Partickhill squad. The slight tic of her left hand adjusting her jacket collar gave her away. Costello noticed a slight smudge of subtle eye make-up, a faint redness round the nose. Either she had hay fever or she'd had a wee greet in the loos. That would be from the rollicking she'd just had, or the fear of the one she was about to get. She had the word scapegoat written all over her.

Bernie swirled the water round his mouth, spat out the remaining toothpaste and wiped his lips with the back of his hand. He smiled to himself in the loo mirror; a bit greyer, losing a bit of hair on top, gaining a few extra pounds in the middle, but he could still pull. Maybe not the babe magnet he used to be, but hey ho. He looked at his watch; he still had time to do what he needed to do and make the meeting with Mitchum and Walker. He'd arrive once the fighting was over. Anderson could wait. Sammy was a good girl, but she was only a DI and they had their place. As cannon fodder.

Yip, it would be better for him to get on with stuff here, leave her to the lions, then he could swan in and save her later. And she would be grateful. After all, he was the main man and they couldn't really proceed very far without him.

Ten minutes past seven he was in Glasgow city centre negotiating the one-way system to West Nile Street. They had agreed to meet in Patisserie Valerie. He could get a panini there before going to the station at Partickhill. He'd give that thirty minutes then he'd be out on the piss at the Horseshoe with Destiny. Once he got to the pub, he would explain apologetically that he had been offered a bite to eat at the meeting and it would have been rude to refuse. It would save him from buying her a meal, and there would be no receipt for Lyn to find and spark off the usual argument. Her needle was getting well stuck in that groove. She wanted a family. He had enough of them from his previous two wives. Lyn had money, though. And she kept the house nice and tidy; too nice to be disturbed by more kids.

He turned the Insignia into the lane next to the Patisserie, bumping the rear wheel on the high kerb. He edged the car past a white council van, two motorbikes and a pile of bulging refuse sacks before placing the police permit on the dashboard. He got

out with difficulty as the car was jammed in tight against the wall,
up behind a dumpster that was in bad need of a visit from the
midden motor. There was nobody about. He pulled the collar of
his jacket up round his neck to protect him from the summer rain
and the smell of the dumpster. The hot weather was playing havoc
with . . .

He hit the ground. His first thought was that he had tripped.
He didn't have time for a second.

'Is Bernie short for Bernadette then?' Costello muttered across to
Anderson. The DCI pulled his forefinger across his lips, telling
her to button it.

Wyngate fired up a laptop and started fiddling clumsily with
leads and remotes with all the expertise of a second-rate geography
teacher.

ACC Mitchum swept the leg of his glasses around the room,
doing a mental head count and choosing his target. 'DC Wyngate?
Get everything set up. I want to talk through this, once and only
once. Why is Webster not here?'

'I did tell him, sir,' said the dark-haired female.

'So where is he?'

'Don't know, sir.'

Mitchum flicked a look at his watch, then the clock. 'Well, you
all know me. If you don't know each other . . .' He pointed, the
leg of his glasses trick again. 'Walker from the fiscal's office. DI
Costello, Partickhill.' He indicated towards the dark-haired woman.
'DI Samantha Winterston, Alexandria, from the original case.'
Mitchum's voice hinted at some disdainful disappointment. 'This
is DS Vik Mulholland. DC Wyngate will collate the documentation. DCI Webster will no doubt join us, when the mood takes
him. And this is DCI Colin Anderson, who will be in charge of
this disaster after today.'

Anderson looked as though he had been presented with a huge
MOT bill. He was about to say something, but Mitchum kept
talking. 'Both Bernie Webster and Sammy Winterston will answer
to you. Directly.' An awkward smile passed from Anderson to
Winterston and was gratefully returned. 'Wyngate has pulled
together the visual material. Winterston will talk us through it.
Nothing that we say leaves this room. This case is one monumental

cock-up that makes me bloody ashamed to wear the friggin' uniform.' He put the specs back on his nose and rammed them up to the bridge. 'Jesus knows how the hell we're going to get out of this. The media are already all over it; Karen Jones is on my phone constantly. So we, and by we, I mean Police Scotland – no hiding behind divisions here – need to stay focussed. Right . . .' Mitchum directed his tirade in Winterston's direction. She looked steadfastly at the file in front of her. 'Basically we are here to talk about McAvoy and the total fuck-ups of the Grace Wilson investigation in 2012, and then the Dewar/McCardle investigation in 2013. Three dead children.'

Winterston flinched.

'So, DI Winterston, get started.'

'Yes, as deputy investigating officer, maybe you'd like to start. As your senior officer hasn't bothered to turn up yet,' snapped Walker, one-upmanship from a master of the art.

'Do you mind if I stand up?' asked Winterston, quietly assertive.

'Yeah, it will make you an easier target,' whispered Costello as she moved her seat back to let her new colleague out.

Sammy Winterston stood up and smoothed her skirt behind her. Costello looked down to notice her heels. They were too high, too expensive and too clean.

Winterston picked up the remote control in her hand and Wyngate showed her what button to press. She seemed in full possession of herself now. 'I think it might be best to start with a sense of place. On the east coast of Loch Lomond, three miles to the north of Rowardennan, is a small bay called Inchgarten Bay. Named after the island.' The laptop showed a few images: the loch, the islands, the small beach, the holiday village sign, the view from the beach, eight barrel-shaped lodges sitting neatly on the rise on the right-hand side. So far it could have been a tourist board presentation.

'Looks like a hobbit village.'

'It does. But in reality? Septic tanks and power cuts, no Sky, no mobile signal when it rains. It's basic.' Winterston paused. 'Before the death of Grace Wilson in 2012, it was a thriving but small holiday camp, most of it repeat business. Three families paid a retainer so they could use their lodges whenever they wanted.

The other lodges were rented out normally. All the incidents took place at the time of the solstice. At the solstice these three families liked the place to themselves.' She paused as a mutter of recollection flickered round the room.

'The Dewars, the McCardles and the Wilsons. The place is owned by Anthony Michael Laphan and his sister, Daisy Cerridwen Laphan. It was all inherited. Tony is a farmer who does not farm; he has a medical degree but doesn't use it. He does a bit of pottery. Daisy looks after the place, a woman of the earth if there is such a thing. Local rumour says she's a witch.'

'Complete pish,' said Mitchum angrily.

'It has a bearing on how the media reacted,' Winterston told Anderson directly. The screen now showed a photograph of a young girl, about four years old, dark curls. Thick glasses sat askew on her snub nose, hiding big brown eyes. The ruffles of her blouse framed her chin, with a red ribbon tied round her neck. The picture was familiar to them all. 'Grace Amelie Wilson died in what we thought was a terrible accident at Inchgarten Lodge Park, around midnight, at the summer solstice two years ago.'

For the second time that day, Costello looked at the clock calendar on the wall and calculated – they were five days away from the solstice now.

'Grace died after impaling herself on a metal stake.' The picture changed to the wee girl naked, the dark rosette of the wound near her collar bone stark against the pallor of her skin. 'It was all over the news at the time, very tragic. She was on holiday with Mum and Dad. They put her to bed at her usual time, but she must have got up later. Maybe to spy on the adults at their bonfire. Wee Grace was discovered missing from her bed when they went back to the lodge at two in the morning. Half an hour later they found her, dead. Her wee anorak over her PJs, her slippers on. She was at the Roonbay, down here, having fallen off the Rocking Stone.' The image changed again, back to a sunny, sandy beach with one large, dark stone. 'There are a few rocking stones around, balanced in a strange way so they—'

'Rock?' offered Anderson.

'Sit on it and you get pregnant, seemingly.'

'Can think of better ways,' muttered Costello, scribbling something down.

'It's about three feet high, three long, two wide and sits right where the water is deep. The Roonbay is the smaller bay south of Inchgarten Bay but really only separated from it by a strip of shrubs and the Rocking Stone. Grace seemed to have slipped from the Rocking Stone on to . . .' Winterston put the remote control down and starting talking with her hands. 'If you imagine one of those cradle things they rest canoes on. Well, it was one of them with the rubberized arms removed so only the sharp uprights were left. That was what she fell on to.'

'Four years old?' confirmed Anderson.

'Yes, old enough to cruise, as they say,' replied Winterston. 'That investigation ended with a verdict of accidental death by the fiscal's office.' She looked at Walker; she was not taking the blame for all of it.

He stared back at her. 'Accidental death with a degree of parental negligence.'

'Or a nice piece of misdirection.' Costello was looking at a photograph and gave it a minute's consideration before turning it over and lifting it up, showing it to the others. A white face and brown hair spread out over the coarse sand. The obscene star-shaped wound.

'The boys admitted that they had spied on their parents' party from there so she tried it as well. There was no huge murder theory about it. It was a tragic accident.'

'And since Madeleine McCann, the papers jump on anybody leaving their kids sleeping alone. The press didn't miss that one; the Wilsons left the country.'

'And McAvoy had an alibi, as you say. If he was working with kids, had he been through any disclosure at all?' asked Anderson.

'He hardly exists in paperwork, never mind disclosure. He's a weird hippy. His mum is the real deal, A-class, meths-drinking vagrant and he inherited the inability to settle down or remain indoors. He was quoted as saying that living in four walls would kill him. But during the routine investigation, we came across Warren McAvoy because he was around Inchgarten Bay at the time.' The image on the screen flicked again, and both Anderson and Costello leaned forward, examining the image, a fresh-faced young man, brown haired, brown eyed. Mentally they both super-imposed it on the bloodied face of the man in the field. 'He was traced as a matter of procedure but never formally interviewed.

He had a watertight alibi. He was very much on the periphery of things anyway; all he did was hang around the camp site helping. He was in a restaurant in Balloch with his sister Alexis, known as Lexy, on the night Grace died. He was twenty miles from the scene. But it was not thought to be a crime. The PM report on Grace was conclusive as to cause of death. Grace's parents moved away to the States. They came back for the inquest, stayed at the Lodge Park, funnily enough, but their daughter's death was put down to a very tragic accident.'

'Why do I feel a "but" coming on?' ventured Anderson.

Walker raised his pen, stopping Winterston before she restarted. 'Just to be clear, the fiscal's office did act. The owners got their knuckles rapped for not keeping the beach at Roonbay tidy. The three boys admitted they had taken the canoe down there and left the cradle by the stone, but the Laphans did not move it back. The parents confessed they had left Grace in the lodge alone—'

'And a mention of witchcraft in the tabloids, I recall—'

'It was all nonsense, DCI Anderson,' said Winterston.

'Colin,' he corrected, and was rewarded with a shy smile. Relief crossed her face.

'Nonsense as far as we could make out. The solstice was an annual private party for them, that's all. But the Rocking Stone has Druid significance, as they all have, and the place is atmospheric but—'

'Nobody goes round sacrificing haggis. But what about tarot cards?' asked Costello.

'What about tarot cards?' asked Winterston, her eyes lighting up.

'The body had one in its mouth, the Fool. O'Hare had one under the windscreen wiper of his car, Justice. Constable Cusack says he had the cars going past in convoy. Somebody could have leaned out the window . . . or come out the undergrowth of the hedgerow and placed it there. Three people walked past with dogs, Cusack is trying to trace them. No doubt the dogs will be walked same time tomorrow morning.'

Winterston started to flick the pages over in the file in front of her. She fumbled with the clip; a loose leaf slid from the small pile and drifted to the floor.

Costello picked it up and Mitchum was heard to mutter, 'Oh for God's sake.'

Winterston continued. 'McAvoy comes into the frame exactly a year later, on the Saturday the twenty-second, the longest day of 2013. He attacked the three boys while they were out on the island. Only one of them – Jimmy Dewar – escaped and lived to tell the tale.

'McAvoy had been living around there in his vagrant style, man of the woods, Bear Grylls type. He was good at outdoor stuff. He didn't have a job, never has had. I think the boys, and maybe their stressed-out dads, admired him, envied him his freedom. The solstice barbecue was going ahead as usual, and this time two boys, Callum McCardle and Robbie Dewar, died out on the island. They were both ten.' The image on the screen went blank for a minute, then two pictures came up, side by side. Again, everybody in the room recognised the faces immediately. 'Both boys had sustained head injuries, blows to the temporal region with a stone. The details are in the reports for everybody to read. No accident this time. They were on the island with the older Dewar boy, James. He was the one who escaped, taking the only boat. He witnessed McAvoy killing his own brother, Robbie.' Jimmy's photograph flashed on the screen, brown hair, freckles, a wide smile. He looked like the smart kid in any American film of the last twenty years. 'McAvoy had taken the three of them out to the island that night by a canoe, the Dreamcatcher. The same one whose cradle had killed Gracie. It was nearly midnight when Jimmy made his way back, hysterical and bearing the physical signs of his escape from McAvoy.' She pressed the remote and the picture changed to Jimmy, red-eyed, two lacerations on his forehead, blood streaming down his face. 'That was taken by his dad's iPhone at the time. McAvoy was stuck on an island with no boat. The current in the narrows is too strong to swim across. Nobody saw him get back to the shore. McAvoy vanished into thin air.'

Elvie stepped out of the shower and waited for the steam to clear. She raised her damp hands to her nose and inhaled deeply. She could still smell the 'street': rotten rubbish and urine. She had spent the day tramping around the areas of Glasgow where the homeless hung out. She had been propositioned five times, mostly by men who thought she was a bloke, which was an easy mistake to make with her masculine build, short, spiky black hair, toned muscles and the deep acne scars that pitted her cheeks. Stick her in a hoodie and she was one of the universally unaccepted.

She carried with her a photograph of Tattoo Boy, the seventeen-year-old heroin addict called Iain John Matthews who had run away from home three years ago. His mum was now dying of cancer; she wanted him found.

So far the Salvation Army had given her some details; the ink tattoo of his mum's name Hilda on the knuckles of his left hand made him easy to identify.

At times, Elvie was glad that she didn't understand people.

She hadn't found him yet but she would. She had missed him by two days when he had been sleeping outside Central Station, but the police had moved him on. Most likely he had gone down to the banks of the Clyde, probably the south side.

She sniffed under her fingernails and then set about them with TCP and Hibiscrub, just to make sure.

Afterwards she sat on her sofa with her laptop, the BBC news on low, half listening as she Googled Warren McAvoy. Some cop in a shiny uniform was saying there would be no comment until the body was formally identified. Her search didn't tell her anything that she didn't already know. He was wanted in connection with the deaths of three children. He was the shadowman who disappeared into thin air. Even wee Charlie, her friend's five-year-old son, knew that if he didn't do as he was told, Warren McAvoy would come to get him.

So the police of the whole country had been looking for him for a year when, according to his long-lost father, Warren had been living with his sister Alexis only twenty miles from where he was last seen?

That sounded nonsense to her logical mind. So Alexis must be lying.

It was the Parnell Fox agency who had tried to trace Patricia McAvoy for Geno DiMarco but only succeeded in finding her daughter Alexis. It was Alexis who had told Geno he had fathered a son but omitted the part that the son was a suspected double, maybe triple child killer.

Which was understandable.

The air in the meeting room grew stale, matching their attitude. 'And because your team could not find McAvoy, Winterston, somebody else did and took their own revenge. Which is a bloody embarrassment to us.' Mitchum seemed to take it as a personal affront. 'And it makes it very difficult to move the case forward. Interviewing parents of dead children is never easy, especially when we have to ask them where they were in the small hours of this morning. The public will want an enquiry into the errors in the original case that allowed McAvoy to walk free, not an investigation into who killed the bastard. They will want to nominate the killer for a knighthood.'

Walker nodded, his hands expansive. 'So do we all agree that Grace's death might not be accidental? That's been the belief of my office since the murders of the two boys.' He looked questioningly at Anderson.

'But you still have McAvoy's alibi for that night, the night Grace died,' the DCI replied.

'And it wasn't just his sister that alibied him; the waiters, the other diners agreed. We considered it unbreakable,' said Winterston.

'OK,' Anderson made a note. 'It was Dr Jo Darcy who did the original post-mortems on the boys. She's on mat. leave so I have asked O'Hare for a review. I hate jargon, but we are forced to go down the transparency line here.' Anderson ignored Costello's sarcastic face.

Walker nodded. 'Indeed. Any questions so far?'

Costello pulled out Winterston's seat for her, indicating she should sit. 'Was there anything you thought was not covered?'

Winterston shook her head. 'McAvoy disappeared into thin air that night. All those eyewitnesses on the beach? Nobody saw anything.' Her hand slapped on the desk, punctuating the words.

'Nobody?' asked Anderson slowly, seeing her problem.

'Not a thing. Seven adults, a dog, a clear night with good vision, barely dark. Although McAvoy could swim, the local met office said the solstice tends to bring a strong current in the narrows. The locals say it's not swimmable. Despite the evening being clear and sunny, by the time we got there, the rain was biblical. A lot of evidence was washed away.'

'Well, *he* wasn't washed away, was he? He obviously did get off the island if he resurfaced in a field near Erskine with no arms exactly a year later.' Mitchum was unimpressed.

'Nobody has seen him since. His sister Lexy maintains she has not set eyes on him and we have no evidence to contradict that.

He has no paper trail, he does not pay tax, he does not earn, and he doesn't have a doctor, no dentist . . .' She shrugged her frustration.

Mitchum opened his mouth again but Anderson got in first. 'What does your instinct say now? Are these related crimes? Grace? The boys? Warren?'

'Yes,' she said quietly.

'OK,' said Costello. 'So we need to break that first alibi.'

'You can't. The evening that Grace died, was killed, McAvoy was miles away having a meal at a restaurant with his sister Lexy.' Winterston was adamant.

'We will check it again.' Anderson was now flicking through a file. 'So from now on, we refer to Grace as the first murder. Adam Wilson is an engineer; Grace's mum . . .' He flicked over a few pages.

'Wendy. Housewife. She enjoyed the company of the other mums at the village over the holidays. The mums and kids stayed the entire summer holiday, the dads joining them as they could. The women relaxed, read books, went into Balloch, had coffee, visited the hairdresser's. The men climbed the Ben or went hillwalking with McAvoy acting as guide. They made fires and tents and stuff. McAvoy took the boys on adventures.'

'He liked being alone with the youngsters,' said Walker to Anderson meaningfully.

'So the men ran around and did stupid stuff in the woods, like a bunch of wee boys?' asked Costello.

'That's about it. They all liked McAvoy; he was odd but likeable.'

'Killers often are,' agreed Costello. 'But he has never been brought to trial.'

'No, but the general public think he's as guilty as hell.' Sammy grimaced in frustration. 'To us, he has remained a person of extreme interest.'

'So what happened last year?' asked Anderson.

'Well, on the night the boys died, the parents all had a fair bit to drink except Ruth McCardle. She was stone-cold sober, keeping a lookout for Callum. He was out on the island. He never came back; he died on the island from horrific head wounds.' Sammy wriggled in her seat slightly.

Costello looked directly at Mitchum for the first time. 'But, to play devil's advocate, if the alibi holds, then he was not involved in the first case, so should we be looking at him, and only him, for the second? Maybe he's a victim, not a suspect. Was somebody else on the island?'

'No. And Jimmy's testimony has never wavered,' Mitchum pointed out. 'He witnessed his brother and friend being killed by McAvoy smashing their heads in with a rock.'

'OK, but might there be no connection between the deaths of Grace Wilson and the deaths of the two boys a year later?' Costello argued. 'Maybe Grace was simply an accident. Only Robbie and Callum were murdered.'

'Too much of a coincidence,' said Mitchum. 'In the eyes of the public.'

'Three kids killed within a day of the solstice. Then McAvoy found dead this morning, killed in such a medieval manner.' It was the first time Wyngate had spoken; his eyes were fixed on the screen, on the smiling face of the boy. 'And Jimmy – how old was he?'

'Twelve. Even though he was injured, he got to the Dreamcatcher first and got enough water between him and the shore to be safe. It was a hugely traumatic experience. He has struggled with PTSD ever since. He has had to change school. The Dewars have had to move house.

'So Jimmy got away, barely, and raised the alarm. Sometime between then and the local cops going out – a space of an hour – McAvoy must have got off the island. By the time we got there the rain was horrific.' Winterston looked as though she was about to say something else but changed her mind.

'Theory?' asked Anderson.

Winterston said, 'I might have said, the rain was summoned. Have you ever been to Inchgarten Lodge Park?'

'No, but we are planning to go now.'

'You seen *Deliverance*? Might be worth it.'

Mitchum had left; Wyngate had sat down. They all started eating the shortbread.

'Bernie nearly gave himself a heart attack trying to find McAvoy,' said Sammy, texting. 'He'll be cross he's missing this.'

'Be assured, we are on the same team here, Sammy,' said Costello, nibbling a shortbread triangle, hand cupped underneath to catch the crumbs.

'Heads will roll, though,' said Mulholland, examining his fingernails.

'He's not answering his phone. He's not at the station. Lyn hasn't heard from him either.' Sammy shrugged her shoulders as if to say, *you know how it goes.*

'Did you ever meet Warren McAvoy?' asked Costello. 'What did you think? Without the benefit of hindsight.'

The others looked at Sammy, interested in her answer. 'I've only set eyes on him once. He's an insignificant wee ned.' Sammy shrugged. 'But the Laphans liked him. If anyone was hiding him, it would be them. They both thought Warren was innocent.' She stopped abruptly.

'And?' urged Costello.

'They are weird; something's going on up there.' She looked away.

'Like what? Witchcraft? Devil worship? Quilt making?' Costello suggested.

'I'm deadly serious. There was something I couldn't put my finger on. Tony is deep; his sister Daisy is mystical. Warren was weird. Bernie thought that we were getting nothing out of them and had toyed with the idea of going undercover.' She looked at Walker. 'But that was vetoed.'

'And what happened to McAvoy last night was not spontaneous. So if we are thinking that they were harbouring McAvoy and somebody found out, who moves beautifully into the frame?' Walker was thinking out loud.

'The parents?' suggested Costello quietly.

Walker nodded. 'And you realize how gently we are going to have to progress from here. The police did not do their job so they had to do it for them.'

Sammy put her hand up, palm up. 'Look, I know these people. Ruth has been shattered by the death of her son. Her life has fallen apart, she's lost her marriage, her home, her income. Her ex, Fergus, survived cancer but is drinking himself to death over Callum.' She broke off to explain further, 'The dads were in business together, Dewar McCardle. Then Fergus started drinking and

Eoin bought Fergus out to give Ruth some money and stop Fergus running the business into the ground.'

'What kind of business was it?' asked Anderson.

'Computer supplies, printing, that kind of thing. The latest reports say that Fergus is now in a drying out clinic. Ruth's medicated up to her eyes and wittering on about God. Eoin has just escaped bankruptcy. Isobel has gone back to teaching full time to keep money coming in. At the time of the murders they were both four-bedroomed detached with a four by four type of family, but . . . Well, things are different now. Ruth is in a housing association block in Mosspark.'

'My old stomping ground,' said Costello. 'But we get what you're saying; they've gone from Waitrose to Lidl.'

'But I can't see any of them doing anything barbaric to anybody.'

'Losing a child can change a person. How about Grace's parents?'

'Abroad. California, I think. There's a contact address in the file. But remember, Grace's death was considered an accident at the time.' She ran her fingers through her dark, glossy hair, the wishing well charm on her bracelet tinkling. 'Or was there a crime and we missed it?'

'And McAvoy has his alibi,' Costello murmured.

'I see your problem. It goes in circles,' Anderson said. 'But we need to break that circle. What was the report from this morning's scene?'

Mulholland didn't respond until Anderson poked him in the ribs. 'Here's the initial one.'

'Let's see it then.'

He opened a file with a map of the farm and the surrounding fields, already dotted with crosses and stickers. 'Scene of crime think the car was parked there on the grassy verge. The killer, who had four feet and wore shoe covers, walked along the tarmac, only leaving it to climb the gate. O'Hare has confirmed that McAvoy's body temp puts his death at three in the morning, roughly. The farmer was out at midnight and saw nothing out of the ordinary.'

'Uniform says nobody has been reported hanging around,' added Walker. 'But people do drive up and down that lane to get to the motorway. As well as dog walkers.'

'Four feet?' asked Sammy, confused.

'Well, it looks like two people jumped the fence from the landing pattern; impact marks suggest they are within average range of weight and height but one lighter than the other. And both McAvoy's hair and shoes show he was dragged at one point. But still only one set of footmarks came out.'

'So the killer walks in with a drugged McAvoy who is walking under his own steam at first, then dragged. Then he loses consciousness and they do the rope bit and attach the horses. Does that fit?' asked Sammy.

'It fits.' Anderson smiled at her.

'Only if the killer was capable of controlling two horses,' said Costello. 'That suggests two people, but there was only one set of footsteps out, so for now we'll say the other sprouted wings and flew out – leave that to the SOCOs. What else, Vik?'

Mulholland flicked the two pages back and forth. 'Tox screen will be ages. There are traces of hessian sacking on the fence. We could try and trace that but don't hold your breath.' He pushed the file away.

Costello glanced at Anderson. Mulholland was going through the motions, but only just. So it was Costello who continued. 'The vet confirmed cigarette burn marks on the back end of the two horses that had been in the field. And O'Hare has a friend who has a friend who confirmed the knot is used by sailors and climbers, blood knot. The rope was a common nylon one, easily available on the net and brand new, so no forensics on that. Wyngate here is trying to trace that and the tarot cards.'

'Waste of time,' muttered Mulholland.

Sammy ignored him, 'What do you think the card might mean? Is O'Hare next?'

'He has no connection with the case – the cases – at all, but he is taking precautions. How many tarot cards are there anyway?' Anderson asked.

'Twenty-two Major ones, I think,' Wyngate said. 'So it looks like we might be busy.'

Vik Mulholland's dinner had been waiting in the oven: steak with peppercorn sauce, sweet potato and broccoli. His mum had prepared it for him and left a beer in the fridge, and a note saying that she had gone to a concert and not to wait up. Like she was the child and he was the parent. He scooped the dinner into a poly bag, stuck it in the bin under a Waitrose carrier bag and poured the beer down the sink. He watched as it swirled and bubbled down the plughole, where it met a blockage and stalled, gurgling away to itself. Like his career, he thought. Quietly going nowhere.

He scribbled 'Ta' under her note and went off to have a cold shower. It made him feel alive, one of the few things that did. He lay naked on his bed in his mum's spare room for a while, at peace in the darkness, listening to the sound of the traffic outside. He phoned Sonja's mobile, got her voicemail, so he left a message asking her to give him a call when she got in. He wondered what the others were doing, right in the thick of this McAvoy case. He would be sidelined with old Bella and her tea roses. Yip, his career was going nowhere. His life was going nowhere. At his age he hadn't thought he would be back living with his mother. Not his decision. Not his choice. It was the credit crunch. His penthouse had to be sold before they repossessed it and the gut-crunching figure of the negative equity. Sonja was now running up debt on his credit card. He wondered where she might be at this time of night. Probably at a night club doing some promotional work.

At eleven p.m. he phoned her again and left another voicemail, *phone me back whenever you can.* He was going to add, *no matter how late* but thought that might sound a bit desperate. After that he slid into his cold bed and drifted off into a light and fitful sleep where he dreamed he was out at a nightclub, dancing with Sonja. Her arms were lovingly folded round his neck, her face nuzzling into the side of his neck. He could feel her warm vodka breath on his skin, wafting under his collar. She held on to him, tightly, drunkenly, then the grip changed and alarm bells were going off. He tried to pull away from her and he realized it was not Sonja he was dancing with, it was Bella. She was laughing; her flames started licking his body. He heard the ringing of the fire engine and he felt relief that they were on their way, then fear that they were never getting any closer. Then he realized it was his phone.

He reached for it in the darkness and swiped to accept the call.

'Hi, Sonja,' he said, opening his eyes, waiting for them to adjust to the pitch darkness.

'Sorry to disappoint you,' said the voice, 'not Sonja. Costello. Can you make Partickhill Station tomorrow, eight a.m.? Before you go off to see Bella's daughter?'

After Costello had rung off, he lay back on the pillow, checking his phone for any messages that he had missed; there weren't any. He had a nastily cheery thought of the trouble there would be if Sammy Winterston and Costello clashed. She hated it when there was another woman on the team, especially the same rank, and most especially if the newcomer got on with Anderson.

Mulholland gave it forty-eight hours.

Tuesday, 17 June

DCI Colin Anderson sat at the breakfast table, absent-mindedly fiddling with Nesbit's ears.

His daughter Claire held up a piece of toast. 'This looks like Jesus.'

'Eat it anyway,' said Brenda, filling the teapot from the kettle.

'It looks so like him.'

'It's a piece of toast,' said Peter, trying to read a text message under the table. Without looking, Colin reached over and took the phone off him.

Brenda held the lid of the teapot as she filled her husband's cup. She glanced over her daughter's shoulder at the toast.

'Look – eyes, hair, beard, mouth.' Claire peered at it through dark-rimmed eyes and three coats of mascara as her forefinger moved deftly over the features. 'He's a bit cross-eyed, I admit, but it is Jesus just the same.'

Colin was about to ask why she painted her fingernails black but decided this was not the time or the place.

'Well, you are the artist,' Brenda answered diplomatically. 'You can either eat it or exhibit it. Either way you are going to school.' She sat down, pulling the jacket of her business suit round her, feeling her heels click on the tiled floor. It still felt good, unreal somehow.

'I'll photograph it, then eat it.' Claire's phone came out, a few swipes, a dry click. Then she smoothed the marmalade into all the corners of the bread, like paint from a palette knife.

Brenda sipped her tea listening to her children chatter. Somebody was a knob for wearing Converse trainers, and somebody else was a knob for not wearing them. Somebody had an Xbox something and somebody didn't.

'Somebody else,' Peter said carefully, 'had mean and horrible parents who refused to buy him an iPad and he therefore was technically a deprived kid and could turn to a life of crime.'

Colin ignored him.

Brenda gave him one of her looks. He was getting so like his dad, blue eyes, dark blond hair. He was small for a thirteen-year-old, still to grow into his features.

'He had been doing modern history; they like to turn out socialists . . .' said Peter, smiling through his fringe. 'And it's a well-known fact that socialists need iPads.'

'A socialist would think more about fighting the evil of the corporations and use a pencil,' muttered Colin, slipping Nesbit the crust of his toast.

'You could lower yourself to use the laptop,' offered Brenda.

'You are the worst parents in the world,' moaned Peter.

Brenda raised her eyes and nodded at the clock.

Her husband looked at his watch. 'Christ!'

'Told you so,' said Claire, pointing to the half munched toast.

'I'll be leaving in three minutes. Those that want a lift may join me.'

Peter rammed his toast into his mouth; Claire climbed off the chair with the elegant gangliness of a young giraffe. Brenda stood up to fill the dishwasher. She looked at the *Daily Record*: a familiar picture of Warren McAvoy took up the whole front page. On the worktop was the pile of mail: the gas bill, a black envelope addressed to Colin and an offer to buy really expensive wine at a merely expensive price.

'Christ, they didn't mess about.' Anderson turned away from the picture.

'Well, if you get held up, I'll pick Claire up,' said Brenda, flicking some invisible crumbs from her skirt on to the floor for Nesbit so she couldn't see her husband's face.

'But she'll be at Helena's,' he said warily.

'Well, I'll pick her up from there, then. And remember I'm going out on Saturday night. Don't want to, but I feel I have to. Work's night out.'

'Nice of them to invite you.' Colin patted her shoulder, an extra squeeze, before walking out the kitchen to call on the kids.

Brenda heard the front door opening and closing, then opening again as somebody came back for something forgotten. Then it banged shut. Then the noise of the car engine, then quiet. She was doing an audit at a company on the south side today so she had another twenty minutes. She leaned against the dishwasher and looked over the mess on the table, the full washing basket, the calendar on the wall pockmarked with stickers for dental appointments and school project deadlines.

Family life.

Going back to work had not been easy but it had given her a sense of purpose, and a sense of perspective. OK, so her husband was in love with another woman. Men had done worse. Brenda was biding her time. Colin might have moved out temporarily, but now he was back. And he had never moved in with Helena. Over the last two years there had been a subtle shift in that power balance. She was the one with everything; she had everything Helena McAlpine wanted. She had the husband and the family. Helena could have wrecked the Anderson family, but never had. And Brenda was now trying to . . . Well, she had no idea what she was trying to do – keep an even keel? Helena had always taken a huge interest in Claire; they could spend hours talking about things that Brenda's accounting brain had no concept of. Helena was helping Claire put her portfolio together with a view to going to Glasgow Art School. Brenda didn't like it, but she had learned to accept it. The main thing was that Claire should never feel pressure to make choices. She could afford to be magnanimous. She had everything, including her health. She stopped feeling quite so smug. There were some things money couldn't buy.

Elvie McCulloch opened up the computer and stared at the headlines on the BBC webpage. A picture of Warren McAvoy filled the screen. Murdered in a field, less than twelve miles away. Exact details were being withheld by the police until further investigations had been carried out. She looked closer at a smaller picture of the crime scene, trying to distinguish the distant figures in the photographs. White van, a queue of cars around a field, a group of people standing, a tent being erected. There was a blonde head that might have been DI Costello and a taller one, darker blond, that might have been DCI Anderson.

The dead body was believed to be Warren McAvoy.

Geno DiMarco had been right to be concerned about his newly found son.

She leaned back, tapping her forefinger against her lips, thinking. Last night she had found Alexis McAvoy's address in the file, the

half-sister of the suspected triple child killer whose face stared back
at her from the computer screen.

She looked at the picture clipped to the file on Geno DiMarco
and studied the background. Over his shoulder there was an oak
panelled surround and she could make out the lower parts of framed
pictures on the wall: one of the sea, the other showing a cuff of a
military uniform, the third a hand holding a bouquet. Her mind
filled in the blanks: seascape oil painting, military portrait, wedding
picture. There was another single framed something sitting on his
desk, but angled away so all she could see was the back of it.

She had spent the small hours of the morning Googling Geno.
It all made sense when she found out that Geno had lost his wife
to leukaemia. Then he had set about looking for his long-lost girlfriend. Elvie could see the implied insult in that, like only checking
the spare once you get a puncture.

She would do what she had been asked, but first she would get
the story from the half-sister, Alexis, known as Lexy. She had been
the contact between McAvoy and Geno, so why was she being quiet
now? Because she had lost her brother and was grieving? Lexy was
facing the same choice as Elvie, to tell Geno or not to tell Geno.
It looked like she had made the same decision.

Bernie woke up with the mother of all hangovers. A jumbo jet of
wailing banshees was trying to take off in his head. His mouth felt
like gravel, he had diamonds sewn to the back of his eyelids. Every
bone in his body hurt.

And it was dark.

It wasn't cold but he felt cold.

He was lying on concrete. Solid cold concrete. He tried to get
up but couldn't move one leg away from the other. He thought he
might have had a stroke. His right leg wouldn't leave his left, no
matter how much he pulled it. He stared at it stupidly. Then noticed
the inside part of his trouser leg, rucked up by something – the tie
that bound his ankles.

This was bloody daft.

He pulled himself on to his backside, aware that his hands were
not similarly bound but they were not exactly free either. They were
fixed to something round his waist. And that was connected to his
ankle tie by a long chain. He was shackled.

Shackled and stuck in a corner of somewhere with a concrete floor.

Somebody was having a laugh.

He could hear birdsong – well, inner city birdsong – pigeons and crows. But no footfall, no chatter, no ringtone of a mobile. Some industrial site somewhere? His watch was gone; he had no idea how many hours had passed. He was hungry but not hugely so. Not much time had passed, surely. He did feel dopey, though.

What the fuck was going on?

Somebody was playing out a joke that had gone way too far. Or were they?

Lyn would not be expecting him. She might question it if he didn't phone home the next morning after pulling an all-nighter but it wouldn't give her cause for alarm. And Destiny would think he had changed his mind.

Then he realized that he had no real clear memory of what had happened. Or when. He could recall driving away from the office, but where was he going?

This was more than a joke, more than mugging. This was somebody he had really pissed off taking their revenge. God, that could be a long list. He had been heading up a major incident team for the last two years, but for eight years before that, he had worked closely with the organized crime unit. And ruffled a few feathers.

He shuffled against the wall and tried to sit up, tried to make himself comfy. He saw a litre bottle of water, with the top on it. A large straw had been pushed through a bored hole in the plastic top. He could reach it, if he dipped his head. He manoeuvred his legs so he could catch the top of the straw with his tongue, curling it until he caught it with his lips. As he drank he noticed the weird metallic taste in his mouth. Was that because the water was stale or because it was drugged? He was too thirsty to care. He drank long to quench his thirst, before resting back against the wall.

Then he tried to think about who might have put him here and what to say to get out of it. No need to panic yet.

So he thought.

The flat in McInnes Street in Balloch was one of four in a block, three of the gardens well tended. The fourth was a jungle. Anderson could guess which one was Alexis – Lexy to her drinking pals – McAvoy's.

It was ten past ten but the young woman who opened the door was still wiping sleep from her face. After a glance at their warrant cards, she shuffled back down the short corridor. A rolling tattoo that said something about death and roses floated from the bottom of her hairline and narrowed down the back of her neck to slide under her zebra-print onesie. Lexy looked older than her thirty-three years, maybe because she was still half asleep. She had three piercings along one eyebrow and a small bloodied mark on the side of her nose where another had been removed. She stopped outside a freshly painted white door and smiled, friendly enough as she flicked a hairsprayed pelmet of fringe – black then blonde then black again – from her face. Only a slight tremor in her fingers hinted at the nervousness underneath. Anderson knew she had been on both sides of the law. A previous history of reset – receiving stolen goods and selling them on round the pubs – but nothing much and nothing recent. She didn't believe in paid employment.

'You have found him, then?'

They could have been returning a lost dog.

Anderson sat down on the Ikea settee as Lexy closed the cover on a brand-new iPad Air, and moved it on to the coffee table, next to a copy of the *Sun*. McAvoy was the front page news. Costello gave it a good look as she shifted a pile of celebrity magazines on to the arm of the seat and sat down. On the window ledge the remains of a cigarette burned in an ashtray, smoke still swirling.

'Yes, not in the best of circumstances, Lexy.'

'So somebody got to him? Poor sod.'

'In a very nasty way.'

Lexy sat down next to Anderson, knees folded underneath her, stripy feet under a cushion.

'He was found in a field, out near Erskine.'

'Across the water?' Lexy shrugged.

'Yes. You were not close to your brother?'

Lexy pouted a little, looking for the trap. 'Not seen him for ages, have I? Nobody has.'

'We will need you to come down to identify the body.'

'Fine. How do I get there? Do I get expenses?'

'We'll send a car for you, don't worry. When was the last time you heard from him?'

'Ages ago, must be nearly two years.' She rubbed her upper arm, comforting herself. Not comfortable with that particular untruth anyway. 'Hardly seen him since that night at the restaurant.'

'The night Grace Wilson was killed?'

'Yeah, so he didn't kill her. And he didn't kill those boys neither. No matter what that wee shit said. So you'd better find who did for him.' She got up to get the cigarette then sat back down, ignoring them both for a moment, giving herself time. She shook her head, the blonde and black pelmet fringe jiggling back and forth.

'Do you have any idea where your brother has been?' asked Anderson.

'Nope.'

'No idea at all?'

'Ask those weirdoes up at the lodges.' She turned her head. 'What's your name again?'

'Colin Anderson.'

'Well, Colin Anderson.' She bit her lip. 'I've not seen him for nearly two years and I keep getting hassle. So stop it.'

'Can I have a glass of water?' asked Costello, wafting imaginary smoke from the front of her face.

'Whatever.'

'Is the kitchen through here?'

'Aye.'

Costello slipped across the small hall, opened a few kitchen cupboards. Empty. Her nose sensed recently smoked cannabis. She found a small glass and took her time cleaning it under the tap. The kettle was full, two cups sat in front of it. Two cups.

There was a cork board on the wall, stuff stuck to it higgledy-piggledy. An invite to a thirtieth birthday party, a coupon for forty pence off her next jar of Nescafé. An appointment card for somebody called Shinaid at Curl Up And Dye. A well-thumbed takeaway menu from some gourmet palace called Sammy McSingh's. There were items marked, enough for two: mixed pakora, pathia and dansak, both lamb with side orders of boiled rice and chips. She sipped the water, it was warmish. She hadn't let the tap run long enough. There was a strip of photo booth pictures, Lexy and another woman with similar piercings, her chin sitting on top of Lexy's head, pulling faces. She swivelled it on its tack and looked at the other photographs underneath. Costello ran her fingertip over the board looking for any other wee snapshots, then her nail hit the corner of a tarot card. The Devil.

Despite the water, her mouth went dry. She put the glass down and pulled gloves from her pocket, then gently unpinned the card from the board and slid it into an evidence bag.

She slipped back into the hall. Lexy was jabbering on about her human rights, every sentence starting with 'See me'. Anderson wasn't talking at all. Costello looked into the bedroom, a tribute to B&Q design, all new, even the carpet. Money had been spent in here recently. On the bedside table was a framed photograph, taken at a funfair somewhere, a pier in the background, grey on grey at the point of the horizon. Blackpool maybe? Lexy had her arms round a smiling young man. His face was covered partly by a swathe of windblown dark hair. As a moment of emotion caught for eternity, it was a great picture. Bugger all use to identify the bloke, though. Was it her brother, Warren? Same smile? Same teeth? She lifted the frame and tilted it to the light; the glass was smeared over the man's face. Why would Lexy kiss this photograph?

'Have you received anything strange in the post recently?' she asked Lexy as she walked back into the living room, dangling the bag with the tarot card in front of Anderson, who then looked at Lexy. 'Like this?'

'Aye, I thought it was somebody from the bingo having a laugh.' But her face searched Costello's looking for reassurance and found none. 'Why, what is it?'

Lexy looked from one to the other, frowning.

'Do people generally know that you are Warren McAvoy's sister?'

'Half-sister, yeah. But we hardly knew each other.'

'You look quite close in this picture you have in your bedroom. Sorry, I couldn't help notice it as I walked past,' she lied as she held out the photo frame.

Lexy looked past Costello, out of the window, thinking about something she didn't want to think about. 'And?'

'You look close, that's all.'

'Aye.' She shrugged. 'He's my brother, family and all that.'

'Can we borrow that picture?'

'No!'

'You'll get it back.'

'It's the last pic of me and my brother; I'd rather it stayed here.' Lexy turned towards Anderson.

'But you can't object to me copying it?'

Lexy nodded reluctantly as Costello got out her mobile. 'So is that you finished?'

'Well, we will take the card from you if you can sign that wee label there. You'll get it back.'

'Don't want it back. I know nothing about it.'

'If it is known that you are Warren's sister, it might be better to take care, until we get this sorted out. Don't talk to the press, keep your door closed, don't answer the phone unless you recognize the number display. Here's my card. Put it somewhere safe and don't lose it.'

She tucked it in the pocket of her onesie.

'Don't open your door, don't let anybody in. Put the number of the local station in your phone. They know who you are; they'll get somebody here quickly if you need them.'

Lexy suddenly looked very young, her eyes wide as she stared at them through her fringe. She drew her knees up to her chin. 'Why?'

Costello sat down on the chair, thinking about the young man in the field, lifeless eyes staring at the sky, the tarot card lying in the plastic sleeve. 'Maybe you need to hear it all, Lexy.'

Amy Lee pulled open the can of soda and slugged back a good mouthful. Grandpappy didn't like her drinking it, but he was a grumpy old git so what did he know? She needed a good grade for this project but he wasn't making it easy for her. He had been snappy and more useless than usual when she had asked him about his background. Not the Canada bit of his background but his 'ethnicity', as the teacher called it. Calgary had two hundred ethnicities and the most common one was Scots. That was when she knew what her project would be on. A twenty-minute presentation entitled, 'So this is what I am'. As she had moved house nine times in her fourteen years, she had no real roots. She knew what she was. Lonely.

Britney was going to do hers on 'the cellist'. It was suitably highbrow for the school favourite at Revelstoke, BC. She was all music and classics and putting her artistic soul into stuff, practice and the loneliness of the long distance cellist. Amy Lee had told her to write that. She smirked and took another mouthful of soda, feeling rather superior. Britney wasn't learning any piece of music that Amy Lee couldn't hum while standing on one leg.

No, Amy Lee was taking the project more literally – this is who I am – this is my DNA. Her 'dad' was from Vancouver and an arse, so there was no way she was going down that road. But from what Grandpappy said there could be a few candidates for her 'dad', and Amy Lee thought the guy from Vancouver was way too stupid. End of. Then Mom had walked out and forgotten to come back. Then Grandpappy had moved them from Vancouver to Thompson, Manitoba then Ramsay, then Banff, then Saskatoon then Revelstoke, BC. Amy Lee didn't know if her mom knew where she lived nowadays. She had tried to write to her, but Grandpappy said there was no point.

So she had grandparents as parents and she was lucky. The oldies had gone back home to Scotland for his birthday last year, leaving her to stay with Britney. He'd taken his new phone, so he had a huge chunk of photos she could use if she could find it.

What was it with calling it back home anyway? Silly old goat hadn't lived there for eighty years and still called it home. Maybe that's why he found it difficult to be at home anywhere else.

So far she had found out that Grandpappy was born a 'Colquhoun'; Amy Lee was Amy Lee Cohoon, which made her life a whole bunch easier. The Colquhouns had a kilt and owned bits of Scotland including some islands and a piece of water, and had fought beside the king. Or against the king. Or something.

She made a note to find out. She didn't think Grandpappy was going to help. Immigrants could be sensitive, her teacher had said. She put a note about that too: people could be sensitive about where they came from. She made another note in her wee spidery writing, *sensitive about why they had to leave.*

Gran, who was Grandpappy's third wife, was a French Canadian, which some Canadians liked to call themselves no matter how many generations of Canadian were in there before the French bit. Mom told her once that 'Vancouver Dad' was Scottish on his mom's side too and that's why he drank so much. So that made Amy Lee fifty percent Scottish, twenty-five percent French and twenty-five percent Canadian – and that last bit was a whole bunch of mongrels.

She was going to do her project, look into the family background

'Plates too dirty, but the van was clean. It was a Citroën Berlingo.'

'You are a star. Can you give us the name of the American?'

'I can. But won't.'

Costello opened her mouth but a raised hand from Anderson shut her up. 'We respect your professionalism, Elvie. Lexy is not doing a formal ID until tomorrow; it might be better to leave it until then. Maybe let her break the news to her dad, stepdad, whoever.'

There was the hum of traffic from the loudspeaker as Elvie processed this. 'OK.' She cut the call.

'Elvie's great, isn't she? Just information, no shite at all. As she said, it's all black and white to her. Why are we leaving the ID until after Lexy has seen the body?'

'Getting our ducks in a row. Christ, listen to me. Ducks in a row? I've been spending too much time with Archie Walker.'

Professor Mick Batten, behavioural analyst, chose his usual seat in the corner of the café and ordered a black coffee. He removed his hat and placed it carefully on top of his notes, tucked in the angle of the seat. It was a smart coffee house, typical of the type that been springing up all over Glasgow. It was one of the many changes in the city over the few years he had lived here; the rise in begging on street corners, cash for gold shops becoming as common as bookies.

Batten sipped his coffee, enjoying the rush in his arteries. It was his only sin now he was trying to keep away from the hard stuff. Alcohol was too easy to make friends with in Glasgow; it was so much of the social culture – difficult to avoid, so easily accepted. His commissions of work as an analyst were rare now – everybody and his dog had taken courses in profiling these days – so he was doing yet another study on alcoholism for the Scottish Government. It would show how things would continue to improve if alcohol was made more difficult to buy. It was a no-brainer.

But the criminal work was his passion. He was honoured that Mitchum had requested his secondment to the McAvoy case, a poisoned chalice but a welcome one.

He looked at the front page of the *Daily Record*. The sidebar said, *The Death Of The Shadow Man*. The McAvoy case had them rattled.

He studied the face of the dark-haired young man, Warren

of Grandpappy and find out if he was related to Mel Gibson or William Wallace or whoever.

She typed out: *This is what I am.*

Grandma had said that Grandpappy had been called Robert Colquhoun when he was born, and that Amy Lee should leave it there. So Amy Lee wasn't going to tell them what she was doing until it was done. She had logged on to a few websites and put out a few requests for help. Amy Lee had always known the name of the boat: the *Caledonia*. Grandpappy had an old postcard of the majestic-looking steam ship on his bedside table. There was a circle round one of the portholes. She had asked about it once. On the net, she had found that it sailed out of Greenock. That was a place to start.

She needed a bit of help, a few wee enquiries about how and where to find out where Robert Colquhoun had been born. The Colquhouns hung about a place called Loch Lomond. She could pick up the trail from there. One reply had come back from a company 'Parnell Fox Investigations' that traced missing people in Scotland. She had no money, of course, but all she needed was for them to tell her how to go about it. She Googled them and found a murder case around the same Scottish loch in 2013. She took that as an omen. Scotland was tiny. How many bits of water could there be? She scrolled down the names, saw one called McCulloch.

Elvie McCulloch? That sounded kinda trendy and kinda Scottish, so Amy Lee opened her email and started typing, quietly. It was two o'clock in the morning; she was scared she might wake Grandpappy up.

Anderson walked out to the Golf, dodging the reporters with a hard 'no comment'. Costello walked with her head down, seeing Karen Jones out the corner of her eye. The journalist had her habitual cigarette hanging out the corner of her mouth, sucking on it like it was her life blood, dressed in denim from top to toe, skinny jeans. She jumped up when she saw Costello and came bristling over.

'So what can you tell us?'

'You should know better, Karen.'

'We will be asking Lexy for her story. My editor's given me an open cheque for this one. You might want to get your side in first. Lexy'll put the boot in.'

Costello had to sidestep to get round her. 'Any well-respected journalist would wait for the press conference.'

Jones ignored the slur. 'So where has McAvoy been for the last year? Who's been hiding him? Was this an act of vigilantes? Do you . . .'

It was on the tip of Costello's tongue to tell her where to go but instead she smiled and accidentally bumped into her so that Jones was forced to step backwards into the gutter. Where she belonged. 'Oh, sorry,' Costello said, now free to open the passenger door.

Anderson drove out, watching the group of journalists swarming up the path to the front door of Lexy's flat.

Costello phoned the local station and asked them to get round to Lexy's to disperse the media and make sure that they didn't get to Lexy, and pretend to be doing it for her benefit. Then she cut the call.

'She won't thank you for that if they're going to wag pound signs in her face. *My life with my child killer brother.*'

'The child killer brother that I hardly know but I have his picture beside my bed? Is anything that comes out her mouth true?'

'No.'

'They don't sound alike, brother and sister. Well, half-brother and sister.'

'They're both involved in criminality, as Archie Walker would say.'

'Criminals aren't the problem. It's the crime,' Costello mimicked Walker perfectly.

'Did he say that?'

'Might have been the other way round, I wasn't listening,' she said pulling the tarot card in its plastic sleeve out from under her jacket. She was examining it, thinking about her dinner, when her mobile rang. She glanced at the caller display. 'Blast from the past,' she said to Anderson, accepting the call. 'Elvie? What can I do you for?'

'Do you want to put me on speakerphone?'

'Why would I do that?'

'Because I want Anderson to hear this.'

Costello looked round, while turning on the loudspeaker on her phone. 'Why? Where are you?'

'Behind you.'

Costello said to Anderson, 'She's in the car behind us.'

'Yes,' said Anderson. 'I heard. Why?'

'What are you doing, Miss McCulloch? Not following us arou looking for business, are you?'

'I was here before you.' Simple statement of fact.

'So how did you know where Lexy lived? And why were y there?'

'It's my job.'

'No, your job is a student of medicine; you should be cutting dead bodies and healing the sick.' Costello looked at Anders Elvie McCulloch, sister of the murdered Sophie McCulloch. All t time that Sophie was missing, Anderson's major investigation tea had been sympathetic but unable to commit to looking for h officially. Sophie was a grown woman; she could disappear if s wanted to. Tragically, they had all been wrong.

'Mary set up a missing persons' agency,' said Elvie with h characteristic bluntness.

'We had heard that rumour,' said Costello.

'Two years ago the agency tried to trace a Patricia McAvoy f an American man. Turns out he's Warren McAvoy's father. He had heard from him for a few days. He's worried.'

'And now you know why. So McAvoy has a father?'

'Yes. But we only found Alexis. She told him she lived with brother.'

'That's crap!' Costello shook her head, thinking of Lexy's f Two cups beside the kettle, but only one bed. 'She struggles w the truth. Elvie, did they make contact by internet by any chan Lexy has a new iPad, expensive.'

'By Skype. Can I talk to Lexy now?'

'We'd rather you didn't,' said Costello carefully.

'A journalist called Karen Jones knows about horses and cards. It didn't mention any of those details in the paper.'

'Christ!' cursed Anderson. 'How do you know that?'

'I stood behind her and listened. Said it was a "he" who told Do you have someone watching the house?'

'No.'

'Well, somebody is. Just watching. White van, mucky nu plates. It drove off when your car pulled up.'

Anderson and Costello exchanged glances. 'Can you give number?'

McAvoy. The 'most wanted'. He pondered what was there in his background. The vagrant son of a vagrant mother and an unknown father. A child killer who was untraceable. Clever enough to get away and kill again. Intriguing.

He sipped his espresso and withdrew further into the back corner of Costa Coffee, waiting for the two o'clock low level train. He needed to get an idea of the man. He liked that name, shadow man. First obvious thing, he had been living somewhere and someone had sheltered him. Secondly, before the murders there would have been escalation, assaults on children before. McAvoy seemed to have come from nowhere. And disappeared again.

He turned his back into the corner, opening up the ring-bound file of photographs that had been hidden by his hat, all stamped and dated by Gordon Wyngate on the orders of Mitchum. In the front he had a few press clippings, a few printouts of stuff he had found on the internet.

It was intriguing that almost everything known was in the public domain. Everything up to when the two boys were killed. Then nothing; McAvoy had indeed slipped back into the shadows. He was always on the sidelines, talked about, glimpsed in passing, anecdotal evidence of him being here and there, but nobody admitted to actually talking to him. He was Lord Lucan for the new millennium.

And the couple at Inchgarten Lodge Park spoke words, but said little. It was the obvious place for Warren to be; everybody needed a stone to hide under.

The media reaction was predictable. First was shock at the horrific death of a pretty wee four-year-old, accidents do happen. Then shock turned to accusations of parental neglect. Given it had happened on the longest day of the year, there had been a few murmurings about witchcraft at the time. Then a year later, exactly, another two children died . . . Shock, horror, murder, suspicion.

The press had linked the death of Grace with the deaths of Robbie and Callum, although the police had not. Overnight McAvoy was a triple child killer because of the testimony of the surviving boy. All without trial or verdict. The quiet holiday camp at Inchgarten had come under intense scrutiny, correctly so. Even with his stranger's clarity, Batten was not sure they were wrong. Flowers had been laid at the Rocking Stone where the girl had died. Wendy Wilson's tears over the tragic accident were front page news, worsened by the fact that Grace was a much waited for miracle baby, conceived after years of failed IVF. Then a year later the boys were killed, the tears of Ruth and Isobel followed.

The investigation had stalled. The grief passed and the tide began to turn. What were the parents doing drunk? What was going on in this community tucked away from the world? Why were so few people invited to stay in this so-called holiday park? Four weeks after the double murder, the parents were satanists and the deaths were some kind of ritual that had gone wrong.

Batten looked for the name of the writer of that particularly vitriolic piece: Karen Jones. That was familiar.

He flipped over the page to look into the bright blue eyes of James Dewar, the surviving boy. His story never changed, probably because it was true. But a boy with distraught parents would automatically remember what his parents wanted him to, that was the nature of traumatised children. Two interviewing psychologists had walked away, uncertain. One had mentioned foreshadowing, where the truth can be unwittingly and universally rewritten in a few frantic moments. Batten had seen it many times. First witness statement: *I saw him pull something from his pocket.* After the witness realizes the victim was stabbed, the statement becomes *I saw him pull a knife from his pocket.* And he would believe it. It would be Batten's turn now to interview the boy, one year on. He would reinforce the validity of his version or break it.

But first he needed to get on that island and get a feel for the place. Which was a problem. He hated boats.

He took a sip of his espresso, turning back to McAvoy's face. The shadow man. A worn, weary face for one so young, but the big brown eyes were languid and peaceful.

Batten opened up a small map, scaled on to A4 paper, the open forest, the loch, the island, the places McAvoy loved to roam free when at the loch. Even when in Glasgow, he lived within a quarter square mile. Either one place or the other, held in by boundaries only he could see. Something to make him feel secure.

The city because that's where he and his mum had been together, sleeping rough. From the age of thirteen, he had survived foster parents and occasional home visits when Patricia was sober. Alexis had got a council flat when she was sixteen. When Warren turned sixteen, he disappeared from the system. He had taken to the country, to the lochside and his own idea of survival. He was a child of a single parent whose heart had been broken when her workplace closed and drink became her solace. Warren had given up on school, but was bright and independent. Did he envy other kids who had all that he had never had? Had he envied Grace and Callum and Robbie with their close-knit families? It would all be in the background reports.

He closed the file and drained his coffee. He needed to get into Inchgarten Lodge Park; he needed to shine a light into the shadows.

DI Sammy Winterston pulled a few faces at herself in the mirror then ran the small red foam bud of 'Raspberry Sorbet' round her lips. She fluffed up her short hair and dug about in her handbag for her breath freshener.

She was going back in time to a case she had failed to solve. She had met her lover on that case. Not the sort of thing either of them would want to come out now.

DCI Anderson seemed OK. She felt she could guide him past parts of the investigation she might not want examined too closely. She would simply offer to revisit those aspects herself, confident that nobody was going to look over her shoulder. So why did she feel so uneasy?

She checked her phone. Nothing. And what the fuck was Bernie playing at?

This afternoon she was interviewing the Dewars, with DS Vik Mulholland, the capable but ill-tempered hottie. She had almost lived with Eoin and Isobel Dewar through the worst nightmare any parent could have. All made a thousand times worse by what they had gone through to have Robbie. It was heart-breaking and now she was about to bring it all back up again.

Wrecking ball time.

One last look in the mirror, a last fix of the hair, and she went to find Mulholland, wherever he was sulking.

Anderson walked into the incident room and slammed the door shut behind him. He had a good look round to see who was there, decided it was safe and then let rip. 'Who the fuck has been leaking this stuff to the press? I mean, what kind of low-life little shitbag is risking their pension by selling this . . . *The Death of the Shadow Man, police incompetence.* Crap. Crap . . .' he waved a copy of the *Daily Record* in the air, '. . . and anybody who—'

'Oh, be quiet,' said Costello, walking in behind him. 'It's nobody in this room, so there's no point even asking that question.'

Mulholland added, without looking up, 'And to really make your day, sir, you have a press conference later on. I think the blabber has been blabbing even more. The blogosphere is alive with stories about witchcraft and sacrifice and a young man "screaming in terror as his arms were pulled out of their sockets". Direct quote.'

'Whit?' The anger turned Anderson's eyes the cold blue of a polar ice cap. The assembled company experienced a similar change in the atmosphere. 'And how did they know that?'

Mulholland shrugged nonchalantly. 'No idea. Some sad git has an internet take on *Where's Wally*, called "Where's Warren". They have a caption of DCI Bernie Webster's face looking down a toilet.'

'What is the matter with these people?' said Anderson, as Costello leaned over Mulholland's shoulder for a better look.

'They've caught a likeness of him, though, round the eyes and—'

'So,' Anderson interrupted, 'the meeting with Marion Barr? Bella's daughter. How did that go?'

'How did you expect it to go? It wasn't a bank holiday trip to Millport for a pokey hat.' Mulholland did not look up from the cartoon; the sarcasm had been laid on with a trowel.

'Vik? You have just interviewed the daughter of a woman who was set on fire. Are you so desensitised? So tell me, how did it go?' Anderson leaned over and closed the DS's laptop. Mulholland nearly got his fingers out in time.

'Oh for God's sake, O'Hare is getting back to me. Then I'll prepare a report for the fiscal. The neighbours are adamant they saw a van with council lettering. The council didn't send it. Nobody got the number but they noticed two carers. What more do you want me to say or do?'

'Dig deeper.'

'Dig deeper, into what?'

'Ask Hemphill to do another house-to-house until they get every-body in, then review.'

'I've told you. I've been through the house with Miss Barr and

Bella's neighbour; nothing had been taken,' said Vik in response to Anderson's unasked question.

The door opened and Sammy Winterston came in, a waft of Coco Chanel following her.

'You ready, Mulholland, are you up to speed?'

He capped his pen. 'As I will ever be – got fuck all else interesting to do.'

'I'll lead, you second,' said Sammy, hoping she didn't sound too keen to control the interview.

'You are my senior, so it is as you wish . . .' said Mulholland, getting up from his seat.

'Good luck and be kind,' said Anderson. Then, as Sammy closed the door behind her, 'When did he get so useless?'

'I blame his mother,' muttered Costello.

Isobel and Eoin Dewar were in the informal interview room at Partickhill. They sat in silence, side by side on the edge of the settee. He had his head down, twiddling his thumbs and staring at the carpet, dressed in a well-fitted lightweight suit with the tie loosened off. He was well-muscled, fair hair cut in a number two. He looked caged in the small room, his heel tapping constantly on the carpet tiles. Isobel had arrived straight from the school. She sat pulling her beige jacket tightly around her as if she were cold, her arms crossed, palms clasping and unclasping her shoulders. Her face was pale, too pinched to be pretty. Her blonde hair needed a good shampoo. She was so colourless she blended with the magnolia paint of the wall behind her beautifully. Isobel was ten years older than her husband, but looked about ten years older than that.

They were united in the fact they both wanted to be anywhere but here.

When Sammy had phoned them requesting a meeting, Isobel had flatly refused to let the police come to the house. *Fed up with it all* was how she had put it, her voice both strong and quivering. After a pause, she had added, 'We'll come to you, where? How long will it take?' She didn't have to ask what it was about. It was all over the news.

Their son, Robbie, had been killed the year before, a month before his eleventh birthday.

Since then almost everything in their life had been about Robbie. Or because of Robbie.

Eoin looked ready to go through it all again. He was a handsome man, capable but crushed. He got up as Sammy entered the room, opening his arms, hugging her.

'I'm so sorry this is all coming up again.' Sammy leaned over and placed her hands on Isobel's shoulders. 'This is DS Vik Mulholland.' Sammy introduced him, there was a flurry of handshakes over which Sammy explained that he was not on the original case, and a new team was investigating McAvoy's death. She was liaising.

They both nodded. 'Bernie's not involved in this, then?' asked Eoin.

'He will be, he's trying to free himself up,' lied Sammy, ignoring Mulholland's puzzled glance.

'So our question is where has McAvoy been all this time?' Eoin asked.

'I wish I knew. More than anything in the world I wish I knew.'

'So what about you, DS Mulholland, where do you come into this?' asked Isobel.

'Just new eyes, that's all.' He rose to get the coffee.

'I suppose you are sorry for my loss?' she snapped.

'Isobel!' said Eoin, placing his hand on her knee in warning. She pulled away.

Mulholland put a cup of coffee in front of Isobel, then a milk jug and a small bowl of sugar envelopes beside it. All very normal, all very mundane for a conversation that would bring back memories of her staring at her ten-year-old son in the mortuary.

Mulholland sat down, a weariness on his shoulders. 'I don't think anyone can know what it is like to lose your child. So I don't pretend I do.'

Isobel nodded, tendrils from the blonde hair piled on top of her head waving around. She must have been an attractive woman until the grief ate away at her. 'Thank you for your honesty. Stay childless, then you will never know this grief.'

Mulholland stared into her deep blue eyes, pools of torment, and felt guilty.

Eoin cleared his throat. 'You know Saturday is the anniversary of . . .'

Isobel looked at the ceiling and swallowed hard as Eoin picked up a package of sugar and started grinding the granules between thumb and forefinger, waiting for an answer to his unasked question. A tear rolled down Isobel's lined cheek. She thumbed it away.

'The date might be of significance for somebody,' said Mulholland.

'It's significant for the killer,' said Sammy. 'But we don't want you to—'

'Where were you on Sunday night, through to Monday morning?' asked Mulholland.

'In bed, asleep, together. No witnesses,' Isobel retorted.

'She went to bed early. I was working the next day, had to be up at seven.'

Isobel started to cry, then blew her nose hard. 'Sorry. But I relive it every day, every single day. Then I saw the bloody papers this morning. The press were camped outside the school; they won't stop phoning Eoin's work. Thank God we moved house. But I am not going through all that again.'

Eoin placed his right hand over hers; the left kept working away at the sugar.

'How is Jimmy?' asked Sammy.

'He's still having counselling, still having nightmares, problems at the new school. He's left Glasgow High; he's now at the local state school. Sammy, we want Jimmy to know as little as possible about this. We want the new house to be free of these bad memories. I want to remember Robbie as he was. God knows, we waited so long to have our boys, our lovely boys.' Eoin squeezed his wife's hands. 'We all know that bastard McAvoy killed Robbie. Jimmy was so lucky to escape.' Isobel looked at the ceiling again, chin trembling, more tears streaking her cheek. Eoin nodded, a tired, weary nod, like the emotion was repressing him. Sammy looked at the clock. The room fell quiet.

Anderson heard three bolts being slid back behind the door before it opened. It was caught on a chain; a bearded face looked through the narrow gap.

'Police,' said Anderson, holding up his warrant card, Costello following suit. 'We were looking for Ruth McCardle.' He let his tone drift into a question.

'Hello.' The door opened. 'She's through here.' The man paused after he closed it behind them. 'I'm the Reverend John Gibson.' He shook hands with both the detectives while keeping his voice low. 'Ruth heard the news yesterday.'

'So she knows.'

'Indeed. Mr Webster phoned her, didn't want her seeing it on the news first. She had a bad night . . .' He rubbed at his ginger beard. 'I wouldn't put your warrant cards away if I was you, she'll want to inspect them. Through here . . .'

He walked them through a small hall full of half unpacked boxes, tennis racquets, a jumble of old trophies, crushed duvets and vacuum packed, unrecognizable items squashed beyond recognition, before opening the door into a small living room. The sofa was covered in a rumpled duvet, it looked still warm. The bright sunshine was blacked out by grey curtains closed tight over the windows. Two big green plants stood on the window ledge, the only real sign of life in the room. A thin, grey-haired woman sat on a chair near the fire. She seemed to be wearing black pyjamas and a dirty dressing gown, easily looking ten years older than the press conference twelve months before. She bore little resemblance to the pretty woman with the raven hair in the photograph on the mantelpiece.

'The police to see you, Ruth. Do you want me to stay?' asked Gibson.

Ruth gave them a half-hearted smile and leaned forward as they presented their cards. She studied their photographs, then their faces, before folding them over and handing them back to Costello. For a moment, their hands touched. Costello got the impression of rough, cold reptilian skin.

'May we have a seat?' asked Anderson, taking the duvet from the far end of the sofa, and sitting down, showing Costello that she was to lead.

'Of course, forgetting my manners.'

'Do you want me to stay or can I put the kettle on . . .' asked the minister again, brushing something from the leg of his trousers.

'Don't go . . .' The words were out of Ruth's mouth like a bullet. 'Please.'

'I'd love a cuppa,' said Costello, settling into the sofa nearest Ruth. 'Sorry, did we wake you up?' She shuffled forward, concerned but not overpowering. She felt the seat warm through her trousers, and presumed that the minister had been sitting here as well. No doubt saying the same words.

'I've not slept, sorry for the mess.' She swept her hand over the coffee table, the small, bony fingers roughened and red. There was a half-drunk cup of cold coffee, old enough to have developed a layer of scum on the top. The piece of toast on the side plate was half eaten. Three boxes of medication were stacked against the cup but too far away for Costello to read the label properly. A glass of water was beside them.

Anderson studied the mantelpiece. Pride of place was a school picture of her son Callum, wide smile and squinty tie, who had died aged ten, killed by person or persons unknown. Probably Warren McAvoy. And he wondered how anybody lived with that. Or did they just exist? Then he saw the Bible, well thumbed, sitting on the arm of Ruth's chair. Ruth and the minister had been reading it before they arrived.

'Sorry, I'm not much used to having visitors these days. Is this about McAvoy? You found him dead?'

'We found a body we believe to be him,' said Costello carefully as the minister ghosted into the room carrying a tray of cups.

'Tea? Coffee?' he asked, looking at them in turn, at Ruth in particular. 'You must eat something.'

'Coffee, my colleague will have tea,' said Anderson as Ruth shrugged.

'So what can I do for you?' Ruth asked as the minister left the room.

'We wanted to talk to you, Ruth, to introduce ourselves. We can go away and come back at some other time if you prefer.'

Ruth shook her head.

'The investigation into McAvoy's death will be by us; we are all new faces to you.'

'I don't understand. Why are you investigating the death of that piece of crap?'

'Ruth!' Gibson had come back in. As he poured the tea, he said conversationally, 'I think they might need to know who killed Warren McAvoy and—'

'I want to know who killed him too,' said Ruth, 'so I can shake him by the hand.'

'A very human response but not a very humane one,' he said, calmly. 'Beloved, never avenge yourselves, but leave it to the wrath of God, for it is written, "Vengeance is mine, I will repay, says the Lord." That's what the Bible says. You know that.'

'It also says an eye for an eye, tooth for tooth, hand for hand, foot for foot, burn for burn, wound for wound, stripe for stripe, and on it goes.'

It sounded like a common exchange between them.

'Ruth, Warren should have been brought before the courts, so the whole story came out. That would be justice for Callum and Robbie, not this. This is revenge. Now do you want a cup of tea or not?'

Ruth's face remained almost expressionless, just a faint flicker of something. Her eyes half closed, a slight tightening of her mouth. Costello had seen that look many times before; when a relative identified a loved one in the morgue. It was a lack of anger, an acceptance of pain, an acceptance that life would no longer be the way it was before. A life of whys beginning.

'Ruth!' The minister's voice was sharp but Ruth reacted, reaching out to take the proffered cup of tea. The thin, bony fingers of her right hand curled round the handle.

'We need to know where McAvoy has been for the last year, since the night—'

'Since the night he murdered my son?'

'Yes,' said Costello bluntly. 'I know this is distressing, but can you run us through what happened that night?'

'I've told you a hundred times.'

'You haven't spoken to these two before, though. New faces, Ruth, so it might help if you go through it,' said the minister, earning a grateful smile from Anderson. 'Somebody helped McAvoy escape justice. You want them caught.'

Ruth looked into the fire and shivered, reliving some terrible memory.

For a few moments nobody said anything; the gentle click of teacups on saucers was the only sound. The minister waited; Anderson and Costello followed suit.

'Fergus never liked flying, so we holidayed here.' Ruth shrugged at the fire.

'Ruth's husband. He has battled with alcohol. At the moment the alcohol is winning,' Gibson said helpfully.

'He's a drunken bastard,' said Ruth.

'Do you have any idea where we might find him?' asked Costello.

She shrugged. 'Hospital? Drying out clinic? Cemetery. I don't really care.'

Gibson said, 'He sometimes attends addiction counselling, Robertson Centre, in the city centre. But not recently,' he added to Anderson.

'You never told me that,' Ruth said scornfully.

'A shepherd has many sheep, Ruth,' Gibson reproached her.

'So, Ruth. You spent the whole summer at Inchgarten Lodge Park, didn't you? Always in the same lodge?'

'Bute, the lodge with the best view of the . . . island.' She closed her eyes wearily, then continued. 'We had some lovely times. I used to do my tapestry, play with the boys.' Her eyes drifted towards the photograph of her and Callum on the TV, the boy holding a tennis racquet. Ruth looked incredibly young, incredibly happy in a Nike T-shirt, headband, some strapping on her left wrist. 'Eoin and Isobel were there as well, every year. Jimmy, Robbie and Callum. The three amigos.' Her eyes floated up to another picture, this time a framed pencil drawing of Callum. It was also sitting on the mantelpiece, waiting for a hook. The artist had caught the boy in a sombre mood, a sad smile and big brown eyes.

'We'll get that put up on the wall for you, Ruth, it's a good likeness,' said the minister.

'It is.' Ruth smiled at the picture, her eyes welling up. 'It only arrived on Saturday. It's lovely. Reminds me that last summer I had a son, a husband, a job, a nice house, and now I have nothing. Except drugs.'

'And your faith. Maybe this McAvoy situation will bring you some closure,' said Gibson. Then added, 'Nothing can hurt you more, can it? Not after all that . . .'

Her hand left the cup and rested on the Bible. 'Yeah. Have you spoken to Isobel and Eoin?'

'They are at the station now.'

'Isobel has held it all together, hasn't she? No idea how.'

'Do you still see them?'

She shook her head. 'Too many memories. Eoin gave me this film, though.' She picked up her mobile phone. 'I look at it every day. You'll have a copy, on the file,' she added with some bitterness.

She handed it to Gibson who handed it to Anderson. He watched the short piece of film, listening hard to make out what was being said. The boys in shorts and wet T-shirts, all scratched arms and bruised thighs, pushing a canoe off a stony beach into the water. A man, thin and dark-haired, walked into view. Right into the water, bare feet, soaking his trousers. A deeper voice spoke over the gurgle of the boys' chit-chat. The thin man got them to line up and slipped a crew saver over each of their heads, making them adjust the straps. The voice who held the camera was asking if there was one for him. 'Over there,' was the answer. One boy, Jimmy, said it was 'gay'. The thin man in the frame turned to the camera; there was a full face shot of him saying, 'Nothing gay about drowning. You go in there you don't come out.' Anderson couldn't make out what was said next. The thin man patted Callum on his head, a slow pat on the cheek, and turned to the left. The filming stopped.

The frame where McAvoy turned to the camera was the one they had used in the publicity shot. McAvoy. Costello was cricking her neck to look.

'Eoin and Fergus had been friends since university, then business partners. The boys were pals, but not really Isobel and I. She's a typical teacher, bossy, bit older than the rest of us. Could be a right royal pain in the arse.'

'And Grace?' Anderson was still holding the phone.

'Yes. If you had caught McAvoy when he murdered her then my boy would still be alive.' She nodded at that little shadow of pain. 'I have noticed the date and I'm quite happy that McAvoy is dead. But I can't help you. Can I have my phone back?'

'Ruth,' the minister spoke, a compassionate rebuke.

'Were the boys close?'

'Very. The three amigos, like I said. Every summer, Christmas, Easter. All the school holidays . . .' she choked on her words.

'Just the two families?' asked Anderson gently.

'When the incident happened, yes.' She drifted off, looking at the fire. 'Happy days.'

'You were a bit of a champion, back in the day? The trophies in the hall?' asked Anderson.

Ruth smiled rather shyly. 'In my day.'

'Did the boys play tennis?'

'At Inchgarten, yes. They played all sorts. Eoin had his own boat at that time, taught them how to sail. Tony let them hang around the farm. I spent a fortune on computer games at Christmas and Callum preferred jumping on bales of hay. What can you do?' She bit her lip. 'McAvoy never said much to us but he chatted away to the kids. He hung around with the boys, hillwalking, climbing, lighting campfires. They would get a sing-song going and we'd pass the whisky round and they'd toast bread in the flames. There was always a big pot of soup on the fire and we'd sit there all night. It never got dark . . . it never seemed to get dark at all,' she narrowed her eyes, recalling, 'in those days.'

'Sounds like a *Boy's Own* adventure. What happened that night?'

'Well, they were messing about in the canoe. We watched them until they got to the island. We saw them on the shore. Then we had something to eat and Tony gave us a tune on the pipes. "The Skye Boat Song", can't hear it now without greetin'. They had a dram, I stayed sober. Then about midnight we saw Jimmy coming back in the canoe, paddling on his own, like a ghost on the water, shouting. You know the rest . . .'

'In the end, Robbie and Callum were found dead. No sign of McAvoy.'

She sighed, letting her thoughts flow. 'Tony called the police, then went out in the wee motorboat, the Scoob. Jimmy was curled up in a blanket in Isobel's arms. I kept asking where Callum was. I kept thinking he would turn up, behind a tree or safe somewhere. McAvoy vanished into thin air.' Her head dropped, her eyes closed, tears and snot streaming down her face, dripping off her chin. 'Sorry.'

'You should get some rest.'

They stood up. Costello placed her cup back on the tray and squeezed behind the coffee table. As she passed the window, she nudged the curtain open a little; it was blazing sunshine outside. 'Can I ask you one more thing, Ruth?' She felt the leaves of the plants, catching her thumb in the damp earth. 'I know you will have turned this over in your mind many times, but did you ever, ever see any sign that McAvoy was capable of murder?'

'Would I have let Callum anywhere near him if I had?

*   *   *

By five o'clock, Elvie was back at the office. She was still thinking about what she was going to say to Geno and when. She needed time to think those things through, rehearse the various options in her head. She wasn't good at people.

And Costello had told her to wait.

She filled out a time sheet and expense claim for her trip out to Balloch. She read a few emails: Avril at the Missing Person unit – Police Scotland had another report of the Tattoo Boy Iain Matthews moving to the south side, around Kinning Park, so Elvie might want to change her search pattern.

Elvie thanked her and asked her to pass on anything else she heard, before opening her personal email. There was one from her mum, asking when she was coming round for dinner. She typed back that she was snowed under with work, but that she would go out and see them soon. That was what you were meant to say. The 'Buddhist lie', somebody had called it. Elvie had learned the hard way that lying was easier. The next email was her tutor saying that her essay was excellent, and the feedback from the surgery rotation was good. How did she feel she was coping? Elvie knew that was another lie, a precursor, a cushion for something else further down the email. She scrolled through: nice things about her – academically. Oh yes, here it was. *Would she like to come in for advice re some complaints about her interpersonal skills?* Same old, same old. She tried to be so careful, tried to be empathetic, but to her anything beyond 'you are ill, do this and you will feel better', was a real problem.

She left that email unanswered and opened the Fox Parnell email account.

One unopened email from somebody called amyl@satnet.com; the subject line was Help with Project.

Can u help me? I'm 14 and doing a project 4 school. About my grandpappy, genealogy and all that. He left Scotland from a place called Greenock in a boat called the Caledonia. Can you tell me how I can find out more? How old he was when he left? He won't tell me . . . He's v old now and v grumpy, he ended up in Saskatoon, but has been all over . . . Is it really cool in Scotland? Grandpappy loves it. Look forward to hearing from you. Amy Lee. PS cool name by the way. Do you have sideys like Elvis?

Had the girl never heard of Google? But Elvie thought about it.

She had to improve her interpersonal skills – she would have to learn to care even if it was on email – so she emailed back.
Do you want me to have a wee sniff around for you?
There it was, not really committing herself to anything. How to end it? Maybe a personal response to what the girl had said would do the trick . . .
No sideys.
There was a picture attached to the sender's name. A more Canadian girl she couldn't imagine in her own very unimaginative mind: a green American football top, shaggy brown hair, huge smile, perfect teeth. But the sporting top was something she could relate to.
You play football?
Elvie
She sat back and was about to log off when the email arrived. Geno.
Just been on internet. Is it true? Is Warren dead?
Knowing the limits of her empathy, she logged off anyway.

'Were there any ritualistic aspects to the killing? WERE there any ritualistic aspects to the killing . . .?' Anderson slammed a drawer in the filing cabinet closed with the palm of his hand. The bang made Wyngate jump.
'So did you tell them that there was a ritualistic aspect to the killing?' asked Costello dryly, her pen following a line of text on the computer screen. 'They pulled his arms out, how much more ritualistic can you get?'
'But how did they know to pose the question?'
'And you said, *I have no comment at this time.*'
'Yes. But they knew. Who the hell is tipping off the press?' Anderson slumped forward, his head in his hands.
'No idea, but Elvie said it was a "he".' Costello slipped Grace Wilson's fatal incident report under his nose and turned to Mulholland. 'What did you think of the Dewars?'
'The Dewars are way too close to Sammy to be productive. It was a counselling session, not an interview. They are suspects. She never asked them for their whereabouts and she—'
'Is that Isobel?' She pointed to a picture on his desk.
'Yes, taken last year.'

'She older than Eoin?'

'Ten years. Why?'

'She looks terrible, but then . . .' the door opened.

'Behavioural analyst, he's been waiting downstairs,' said PC Gillan, hovering at the threshold. 'Thought I'd bring him up.'

Anderson wasn't listening. He still had his head in his hands with his eyes staring into his palms, so he missed Costello's slow, sly smile as she nodded to the tall figure who took his hat off, wafting the scent of patchouli round the office. He smoothed his bald head as if he believed he still had hair there.

'Is that what you are now?' she said to the figure at the door. 'A behavioural analyst?'

'So I am told, only because it comes in a different column in the budget.'

'Do you want to analyse him?' She pointed at Anderson, making swirling patterns with her forefinger at her temple, indicating some mental deficiency.

'How are you doing, me old mucker?' Professor Michael Batten thumped the DCI on the back.

'Well I never . . .'

'Mitchum is desperately trying to avert a media disaster, that's all. I saw the press conference. That did not help. Got a feeling you were ambushed there, Colin.'

Wyngate placed a coffee in front of Batten, who sat down and adjusted the leather thong round his neck, eyeing up the report the DCI was supposed to be reading.

Costello looked at the silver eagle fastening at the top of his breastbone and the hat. 'Are you having some kind of midlife crisis?' she asked. She popped the top of a can of Diet Coke.

'Aren't we all?' he answered. He fingered the photograph of Grace, caressing the bridge of her nose. He didn't look at the post-mortem photograph, the dead were no good to him. 'You getting anywhere with this?' He continued without waiting for an answer, 'The big issue is, so few people actually knew McAvoy and anybody who does has a vested interest or prejudiced opinion. Who is DI Sammy Winterston?' He screwed his eyes up as he looked round. 'Should I know her?'

'She's our link to the two cases and she was on the original investigating team into Grace's . . . fatality,' Costello said.

'And they found there was no crime, fallen off a Rocking Stone? How eerily sacrificial can you get?'

'Don't you start, the fiscal said there was no crime,' said Costello defensively.

Batten slid his jacket off his shoulders, getting ready for a long session. 'The folk up at Inchgarten Lodge Park knew McAvoy before all this so you should go up there and interview them again from scratch, look behind what they say. He didn't go from nice guy to child murder in a year – there will be a path, a progression. There always is. Were there any signs of cruelty or bullying? And I think we should look round the geography of the place. That will be in the budget – geographical profiling. I don't know the loch and I don't do water.'

'That'll be bloody useful,' said Costello. 'As in lace parachute.'

'Oh, I will go, but I'll stick to terra firma. I get sick on the Birkenhead ferry. Anything at Riverview?'

'Bugger all. The forensic boys are already being told to pull out. Budget, Mitchum says, but really, who cares who killed McAvoy?' explained Anderson.

'And the geography of the farm?'

'People know it: dog walkers, golfers, the yummy mummy jogging brigade.' He folded his arms. 'But the killing of Warren McAvoy was a well-planned operation.'

'Maybe they had a year to prepare for it.' Batten walked over to the board: McAvoy at one end, the three children at the other. Small pictures of the six parents.

'They?'

'Something about it suggests a team effort. Maybe all the parents getting together?'

'Is that a joke?'

'Where is Fergus McCardle?' asked Batten.

'Nobody knows.'

'Exactly my point,' Batten shrugged his shoulders. 'I don't think you'll get much out of them. If they – any of them – are behind this then they are way ahead of our game plan, ahead by months. We need to go to where the whole thing started. Back to where Grace died, where McAvoy was last seen one year later. The horror at Riverview has its genesis back at the solstice in 2012.'

Anderson made a quick decision. 'I agree. But I have an appointment at the mortuary. Mulholland, come with me. Costello, can
you and Batten review everything we have and organize a trip to
the island for Mick?'

'Dry land for me.' He snorted. 'I want somebody else to risk
getting wet.'

Costello smiled slyly and picked up her mobile, 'I might know
just the lady.'

Anderson had intended Mulholland to drive him to the mortuary
but his sergeant seemed rather distracted, so he decided it might
be safer to drive himself.

'You got any ideas?' Anderson asked as the car was swallowed
by the cool air of the Clyde Tunnel.

'About what?'

'The case, Vik. A suspected child killer has been found with his
arms pulled out. We are about to introduce a woman to the dead
body of her brother. And you seem to be applying the same concen-
tration as if you were filling out a parking ticket.'

There was no response.

'What do we pay you for, Vik, exactly? You need to snap out
of this.'

Mulholland made a small growling noise, but kept looking out
the window. The car became suddenly bright as it emerged from
the tunnel.

'Seriously, I can't have any passengers on this one. We are under
intense scrutiny here. Look at all the media camped outside the
station. You need to focus more. It's no good telling me that Sammy
didn't push the Dewars; you didn't either. The husband's alibi is
the wife, for God's sake! You don't know them; she does. She was
being good cop but you sat back and looked at your fingernails.
So if you don't buck up your ideas or sort out what's wrong then
you are off the case.'

'It's personal.'

'Personal gets left at the door.' Anderson stopped at the lights
on Drumoyne Road. It was the long way round but he wanted to
give Mulholland the chance to talk. 'I know that you had to sell
your flat and that you owe a shitload of money, but you have
a good job. You have a roof over your head until you save up for

a new deposit. Some would say you are sitting pretty, your mum making you big dinners every night . . .' Anderson left the sentence hanging.

'How did you know that Brenda was the one?'

'What one?'

'THE one. How did you know that she was the one you wanted to spend the rest of your life with? But then, even if you thought that then, you don't think it now. Otherwise you wouldn't be messing about with . . .'

Anderson rammed the car into gear, although the lights were still at red. 'I'd think very carefully before you finish that sentence.'

'You are one of the most level-headed people I know and even you have a double life, so what is the point of it all?'

'You and Mick should get together, swap your midlife crises and back copies of *GQ*.'

But Mulholland was dead serious. 'It's all shit.'

'Are we talking about Sonja?'

'I think so.'

'If it wasn't money it would be a woman; it usually is.'

'Two women. Sonja and my mother. My mother is very keen for Sonja and me to get together and produce lots of babies. Mum's now talking about moving out to give us the flat.'

'Lucky boy.'

'I was hoping that my penurious state would buy me some time.'

'Not such a lucky boy, then. If you have to think about buying time then something's wrong. Might be the right girl but wrong time. Have you spoken to Sonja about it?'

'I never get to speak to Sonja. Every time she comes to the flat Mum's there. When Sonja goes out I seem to be at work. I see more of Costello than I do of my girlfriend.'

'That would depress anybody.' The atmosphere lightened a little as Anderson pulled away from the lights. 'You can't live the life your mum wants you to live, not at your age.'

'My mother is Russian,' Mulholland said blankly, as if Soviet misery was an inherited condition. 'Maybe I should rent a flat. But that will eat into the deposit and I'll never be free of her. If I don't get away I'll end up looking after her as she gets dementia and starts to dribble. I'll be the bachelor who stays at home, putting his mum's teeth in a jar.'

A brief image of Bella's slippers crossed Anderson's mind. 'You're too fond of designer suits to think about getting them covered in baby sick. There are some things you have to give up, you know. Beige carpets, a full night's sleep, nice clothes, your mental health. Everything comes round to this small person that screams at the top of its voice for no reason whatsoever. I think Brenda and I never spoke to each properly for about five years; it was all nappies and being tired. What do you and Sonja have in common, exactly?'

Mulholland make a soft humming noise. 'We like nice clothes, we spend money.'

Anderson snorted.

'What about your situation?' asked Mulholland, half interested, half making a point.

Anderson indicated to turn right, waiting for the traffic to clear. 'It's weird but very calm. All that stuff about women wanting to talk everything through is bollocks. It's a conversational no-go area. Costello has a theory that both women love Claire so they don't want her to ever feel conflicted. Wisdom of Solomon. There might be something in that.' He swung the car into a reserved space at the new mortuary. 'We need to soft-pedal. Lexy lies as easily as she breathes. It will be interesting to see if she recognizes what's left of her brother. The brother she's not set eyes on for years although he lives in the same flat, seemingly.'

'Wish I had a flat like that; I'd never have to look at my mother.'

Costello hung up the phone on O'Hare and looked at the notes scrawled in front of her. It was half past six; she could ignore his request for some video footage and go home. Or stay and watch the shit fly.

She stayed. O'Hare was not a happy man. If he was right, there would be quite a few unhappy men around. She searched for the video files on the computer and found Batten was already viewing the film of Warren McAvoy on the beach with the children. She recognized it as the same footage Ruth had on her phone. PN332/WMCA 101. She sent the link to O'Hare at the mortuary. Then she sat and watched it again herself.

O'Hare's initial report was that the deceased seemed to have enough painkillers and tranquillisers in him to stun a hyperactive elephant. Why beat someone's face to a pulp when they could feel no pain? Extreme, personal anger towards the victim, or to make him unrecognisable. She paused the screen on a face-on picture, very close to the image used for the manhunt. McAvoy. His left hand was in view, held out at an angle like he was asking the children to be quiet for a minute. She tried to gauge the look in his eyes: annoyance? A quick flash of anger caught forever on film. There was no glint of gold or silver on his finger but she thought the man lying on the ground might have worn a ring at some time. The man on the screen had slightly discoloured teeth; the man on O'Hare's table had squinty but reasonably white teeth. McAvoy was so skinny he could dodge raindrops; a year on he was slim but well-muscled.

She tapped the desk in front of her, staring into McAvoy's face. New teeth? Married? New haircut, brand-new haircut. Most people slipped out of society to disappear. McAvoy had done the opposite. He had slipped in.

And somebody had helped him.

A rich American father walking on to the scene like some personal bank? How far had this American bloke looked into his son's background?

Costello couldn't see Lexy going out of her way to mention that Warren, her potential cash cow, was a suspected child killer. She got up and drew a red line under the word *suspected* on the board. Warren had never been convicted; they must not get carried away by the rhetoric.

'Hi Alexis, thank you for coming along.' Anderson nodded at the young po-faced family liaison officer while Lexy flicked the hair-sprayed pelmet of zebra fringe from her face. The fringe seemed more prominent than it had been yesterday. She was dressed in studded jeans and a skimpy pink T-shirt that rode up over her tanned midriff. She looked relaxed enough but that slight tremor in her fingers was still there. Anderson wondered if it was a tell of grief. Or of deceit.

'So what do I have to do?' asked Lexy, still fiddling with her hair.

'I'm Amanda,' the liaison officer introduced herself, 'and I'm sure we agree that Lexy doesn't *have* to do anything.' Amanda smiled at Anderson. She looked about twelve, wholesome and humourless. Anderson wanted to smack her in the face repeatedly while explaining the rules about life in the big world, where young children die at the hands of evil men and they shouldn't get away with it.

'We would like you to tell us if you recognize the face we are about to show you,' he said gently, addressing Lexy directly.

Amanda opened her mouth to soft-foot Lexy again but Anderson got in first. 'We would like you to stand here and look at that window. When you are ready the curtain will open. You tell us if you recognize the person behind the curtain. And tell us their name if you do. That's all. If you feel you can't go through with it, at any time, say so.'

'At any time, Lexy, say no.' Amanda again.

'No, I'm fine.' Lexy shrugged, her hair bounced. 'Go ahead. It's just that I haven't seen him for . . . well, carry on.' A brief swipe of fingers through that fringe.

That'll be deceit rather than grief, then, thought Anderson, his mind recalling the bedside photo. 'OK. You are aware he died a violent death, he has injuries. So be prepared.'

Mulholland turned his back as he always did at this moment. Anderson braced himself. He felt Amanda do the same. You could never predict the reaction. A gentle nod, a small utterance, hysterics, collapse. Sometimes, just sometimes, absolutely nothing. He had Lexy down as a functional nodder and studied her face intently as the curtain slid back. There was nothing but a slight recoil, her eyes opened wide. An imperceptible shake of the head, as if not understanding. It was a common enough reaction – difficult to know what it meant to be dead. They were not coming back. Gone forever.

Lexy glanced at Anderson. He tried to read her expression but it was gone before it could register. She looked back towards the window, to the face staring up. The dark brown hair framing a scarred and swollen face, fractured nose, lips cracked. She walked one pace forward and placed her hand on the glass. Her mouth open, a small sliver of drool spilling from her bottom lip, her eyes welled up. The mouth hung open a little further.

'Oh my God,' she whispered. 'My God. My God. My God.'

'Lexy? Do you recognize that man?' Anderson asked softly.

She said nothing; the shock had rendered her speechless. Her eyes darted from Amanda, to Anderson then back to the face behind the glass.

'Is that your brother, Warren?'

She opened her eyes wide and quickly nodded, her fringe bouncing. Her voice when it came was clean and clear. 'That's my brother.' She turned back, one last look, one last slow breath, her lips moving as if asking herself a question. The tears fell freely now.

'Thanks, Lexy, I know that wasn't easy. We'll be in touch. Thank you for your time.' Anderson nodded to Amanda to take her away.

They waited until the swing doors had closed.

'She got a fright, poor girl. Elvie McCulloch said they had reunited recently. Maybe she didn't want to say so; it must be tough to have a child killer for a brother.' Vik sniffed. 'So what now?'

'Let her stew, I think. Maybe seeing him dead on a slab might change her mind and she'll tell us where he has been for the last year. Where did they get that fucking Amanda from? An advert in the *People's Friend*?' He looked at his watch. It was nearly seven. Then he heard the inner door opening. O'Hare popped his head out and checked the room to ensure they were alone.

'Can I have a word? Now.' O'Hare was curt, not like him.

Mulholland and Anderson exchanged looks as they followed him through the door and down a corridor with that aroma of vinegar and bleach that was unmistakably mortuary.

The professor opened one door after another, the air equaliser hissing every so often and each room getting more clinical. Then he opened another door into an office and sat down behind the desk. Before Anderson and Mulholland had taken a seat, he threw two photographs at them.

'What am I looking at? A photo of a tooth? And a finger?' asked Anderson.

'And a haircut.' He handed over another two photographs.

'Yip, Warren McAvoy,' agreed Anderson.

'Slim, male, in his late twenties. Five feet nine, dark-haired, brown eyed and no distinguishing marks that we know about. His arms are on the table with him but they are not attached to him. Costello suspected he normally wore a wedding ring. But he was not wearing one when he died. It's a habit of single women to check the indentations on the third finger, left hand of men. Seemingly.'

'OK. He must have got married, then. Something we should chase up – it gives him somewhere to hide,' suggested Mulholland. 'That explains the ring. The expensive haircut is explained by the fact we know he has come into money.'

O'Hare regarded the two detectives, a look of vague amusement flicking over his grey, lined face. 'And he must have shelled out for a very expensive veneer on his right upper canine. And good dental hygiene, which is clever for someone who doesn't have a dentist. The veneer you can buy if, as you say, you have come into a bit of money. But dental hygiene? You can neither buy nor back-date. This is a guy who has always looked after his teeth. Always.'

Anderson felt his heart begin to sink.

'Look, why are we even talking about this? His sister has identified him,' protested Mulholland.

O'Hare seemed in a better mood now. Smiling his quiet, superior smile, he placed a sheet of paper in front of Anderson, pointing with his pen at the familiar genetic bar code pattern. 'DNA profile of deceased person here, DNA profile of Alexis McAvoy there. They are no relation at all.'

'But they had the same mother, different fathers?' asked Anderson.

'Oh, I am sure Warren McAvoy and Alexis McAvoy have the same mother and different fathers. But that is bugger all to do with that poor sod lying out there. He is not Warren McAvoy.'

The evening was pleasant and warm as Anderson walked up to the station from the car park, listening to the rumble of the traffic, thinking it would be nice to go home and lie in silence on top of his bed with the window open and enjoy the warm evening air while contemplating the end of his career.

As he turned the corner he was stopped by an outstretched forearm.

'Hi, Costello, have you taken up hanging around on street corners now?'

'I'd get paid more.'

'Don't bank on it. Have you heard?'

'Everybody has heard. You don't want to go in there right now.

The monkey chiefs are in, screaming and pulling their hair out. They want to know what you're going to tell the press.'

'Nothing. If McAvoy has killed somebody and dressed the scene to make it look like he himself was murdered then I might be happier to let him continue to think that.'

'It would seem a tad unsophisticated. He'd know we get to the DNA quickly.'

'McAvoy is not sophisticated. He chose somebody the right height, weight, build, and slipped in the ID; that was close enough. God, I think it even fooled Lexy for a minute when the curtain pulled back – then she realised. And she was scared. So we have left her to stew.'

They stood leaning against the wall, faces to the sunshine, listening to the traffic like two naughty kids sent out of class.

'It's your case, Colin, don't let them bully you. Christ, get walking. Karen Jones has appeared at the corner for a smoke. I get the feeling somebody is keeping her up to speed, whether you like it or not.'

Anderson took her by the elbow and walked round the building, through the lane where the cars were parked. 'You think it's somebody from the original investigation? Sammy?'

'I don't want to. But Bernie's team had a good working relationship with the press; they needed the media behind them to find McAvoy.'

'But they didn't, did they? And now we have to think that McAvoy is still out there. And that is a scary thought.'

'Sammy made a good point. Inchgarten Lodge Park is basically two people – two people who might be harbouring a killer. Bernie felt he made no headway with them, but you agreed with Batten when he said we need to look round there, back where it all started. McAvoy got off that island somehow.'

Anderson looked at the sky again, puffy clouds drifting on a soft blue backdrop. The image of Bella's wizened little face floated in front of him. A good wee woman who had lived a good life. 'I'm worried about Mulholland. On one hand he's going out with somebody who looks like Angelina Jolie's prettier sister and—'

'Bottom line? He lives at home and his mum irons his pants for him,' Costello cut in.

'How do you know his mum irons his pants? Did he actually tell you that?'

'No, she did.'

'Who, Sonja?'

'No, his mum. But yeah, Vik is about as useful as a cat flap in an elephant house.'

'Indeed.'

'So we can do without him around, eh?'

'Yeah.'

'Good,' said Costello and walked away, leaving Anderson to worry what he had agreed to.

'Not McAvoy!' Sammy's face was ugly with anger. 'How did we get that wrong? But it was front page news that McAvoy was dead! Oh my God!'

Her anxiety seemed genuine, Anderson noted. Either she was not the leak or she was a very good actress. His jury was still out.

Walker sat on one of the desks in the incident room, glasses off, finger and thumb rubbing at his eyes and swearing gently, which had been his default position since he had finished ranting. Mulholland was leaning back on his seat, staring at the ceiling. One by one they lifted the receivers off each desk phone; the ringing echoed down the corridors. Through the open windows they could hear car doors slam and engines rev.

They were being hunted.

Costello stood at the board, unpinning McAvoy's photograph and moving it to the centre. From victim to person of extreme interest.

'Can I say something?' Wyngate raised his hand like a swotty schoolboy.

'If you feel you have to,' said Anderson, slumped over Costello's desk.

'Well, I've checked to make sure. Our press release never said that the body was McAvoy. The wording is clear. The body had the ID of, we went no further—'

'But somebody told the press that it was him,' said Costello.

'Nobody from our team,' muttered Mulholland, his gaze leaving the strip light and falling on Sammy.

'Well, I never said anything,' protested Sammy, her face flushing red, hand on her chest, protesting innocence.

'What Vik meant was that the press would know your team better than ours, with regard to this case. Bernie must have courted them at the time, for the manhunt for McAvoy. He might have said something,' argued Costello, standing up and approaching her, arms folded.

'If he has, then he's around somewhere, so why has he not been in touch?' said Sammy weakly.

'It was said at Riverview that there might be a cop behind all this,' Anderson commented as Costello took a step closer. 'Bernie disappeared right after I phoned him.'

Sammy looked from him to the fiscal, burst into tears and fled from the room, knocking the spider plant from the top of the filing cabinet. Wyngate caught it before it hit the ground.

Costello said, 'I think Sammy and Bernie might have been close.'

'Close?' Walker raised an eyebrow.

'Married man, single lady type close,' said Costello pointedly.

'And how close was he to retiring? Months? And this was the big case that he never solved?' Mulholland let the accusation lie.

'Look, his wife hasn't heard from him since yesterday early afternoon. His phone hasn't been used. His colleagues are phoning the hospitals. Something has either happened to him or . . .' Costello didn't want to be the first to voice it.

'His wife thinks he has run off with some slapper. Wouldn't be the first time,' said Walker. 'I had a brief word with her earlier, but she *is* worried. Either McAvoy has got hold of him or Bernie got hold of "Mr Field", our armless friend here, thinking he was getting hold of McAvoy. DCI Anderson? Get Bernie up on the wall. One way or the other we need to find him.' He got up from the desk, tapping the folder on his thigh. 'And that is an instruction from the fiscal's office. You can continue with the party line that we are looking at McAvoy as a missing person. But we are actually looking for him as a person of interest.'

'OK.' Anderson nodded slowly. 'So if that poor sod is not McAvoy, then who the hell is he? He's not on any database.'

'But if he had McAvoy's ID, then McAvoy must have put it there; there must be a connection between them,' reasoned Costello.

Batten came through the door after a gentle knock, holding a plastic envelope. 'I've heard. So I thought I'd deliver some more bad news. This was delivered to this station.' He placed the black envelope on the table in front of Costello.

The room fell silent.

'It's addressed to you.'

She looked at it then looked away, as if by not seeing it, it would disappear.

'Open it, it won't harm you. And I wouldn't worry about destroying any forensics; he's too clever for that.'

'I'm not bloody well opening it,' said Costello.

'You bloody well are.'

'No, you do it.'

'Fine, it doesn't bother me,' said Batten. 'Never had you down as a mamby pamby girlie type.' He opened the black envelope carefully, as if he was opening yet another council tax demand for money he did not owe. 'You have the Sun.'

'The Sun? What does that mean? Do I have to get my tits out?'

'Do you have the card pulled from McAvoy's mouth – I mean the man who is not McAvoy?'

'Mr Field. It's on the board, as is the one from O'Hare, sealed.'

Batten took Costello's card over to the whiteboard and stood looking at all the information. 'OK, I'm going to sit here and take all this in. Don't mind me.' He pulled a chair out and sat looking at the board, immediately drifting into a world of his own.

'Whoever is sending these knows exactly who is working on the case,' said Anderson. 'Which reinforces the cop idea.'

It was Mulholland who spoke first. 'What about Lexy? She might be the connection between McAvoy and the victim. Maybe she was expecting to see her brother but saw somebody else, somebody she knew and cared for. Victim was a pal of Lexy's, McAvoy takes him out, gets him drunk, drugged, whatever. Then takes him for a walk in the field for some reason and pulls his arms off.'

'Why? Why would he do that?'

'Why would anybody?'

Costello held her head in her hands. 'We only have her word for it that the man in that photograph was McAvoy. Following Vik's logic, Mr Field could be the man in that bedside photograph, somebody she did have feelings for. There's no record of her having any long-term man in her life; Bernie's surveillance team would have clocked that. It was dole office, tattoo parlour and hairdresser. And I bet Mr Field was married. That might be why Lexy didn't want to say who he was and why the relationship was covert.'

'So if we accept that the shock on Lexy's face was not because it *was* her brother, but because it was *not* . . .' Anderson tapped the photograph of the deceased and scribbled Mr Field underneath with a marker. 'It might well be McAvoy has learned some new tricks. He might have played his cards very well, pardon the pun. His ID was on the body, remember. So where is he now?'

'Well,' said Costello, 'the only place he thought of as home was Inchgarten Lodge Park, so I have booked the Eigg Lodge at the campsite for a triathlete in training and their coach.'

'No way!' said Wyngate.

'Not any of us couch potatoes. Elvie McCulloch.' Costello smiled at Vik.

'Thank God!'

'And you, Vik, are her coach. All that fresh air will be good for you. So now you can go home and pack. All shell suits and stop-watches. Lots of steroids and stuff.'

'Wait,' said Batten, 'that could be dangerous.'

'Which is why we are using Elvie,' said Costello.

'But she's an ordinary member of the public; you can't expose her to that kind of thing.'

'She can go but I'm bloody not,' said Mulholland. 'No way.'

'Every way, Vik,' Anderson stepped in. 'It will be good for you, as she said: fresh air, thinking things over, real undercover stuff – couldn't be better.'

'No.'

'I don't like ordering folk about but I will, Vik,' said Anderson, folding his arms.

'But—'

'But nothing, it will be good for you. That's an order.'

'And here are Wyngate's notes on Daisy and Tony Laphan,' added Costello. 'And a dog called Mr Peppercorn, who barks at all things.'

'But did not bark the night of Grace's murder,' said Walker automatically. 'Or the night the boys were killed. OK, they were far away on the island, but if Grace was murdered, and that is what we are thinking now, then it makes sense that the dog was familiar with the murderer. An old adage but a true one.'

'OK, so all we need to do is go through the dog's contact list,' said Mulholland.

'Probably got less dogs in it than your address book,' sniped Costello.

'Makes more fucking sense than me in a tracksuit.'

'Do you the world of good, you miserable git.'

'Enough, you two,' Anderson interrupted. 'Meeting first thing tomorrow. And keep me updated about Bernie – I'll get a trace on his car.'

Batten asked lightly, 'I'd like to ask who put that line under the word *suspected*.'

'I did,' said Costello, 'to keep in mind that he's innocent until we can prove something. McAvoy has never been convicted of any crime.'

Batten got up and tapped the file lying in front of Costello. 'This whole manhunt is based on media bias and one witness statement – that of a twelve-year-old boy. Now in what other circumstances would you put so much store on one uncorroborated statement? I've no doubt he was questioned vigorously and he passed muster, so to speak. But now we have two similarly built men, one of them carrying false ID. The key to this is Jimmy. Nobody else.' He placed his fingertip on the file on Costello's desk.

'You'll have to get past his dad first,' said Costello, standing up to Batten.

He looked her straight in the eyes. 'And maybe the reason McAvoy has never been convicted of any crime is because the bastard hasn't been caught yet.'

The living room of the Dewars' house was not at all what Costello had expected: none of Isobel's sophisticated, restrained good taste. Everything in here was ill fitting and nothing matched. The brown carpet was a little worn, covered with two blue rugs. The sofa was too big for the room, as was the coffee table. The yellow and navy cushions matched the sofa but were at odds with the carpet. The curtains were bunched at the hem. Then she remembered they had recently moved.

It had taken a lot of persuasion to get permission to come out to the house; only the threat of bringing Jimmy into the station actually got them through the front door. They found him sitting in an armchair dressed in a Liverpool football top and shorts, a tall, lanky boy, eating chips with his feet up on the coffee table.

He grumbled a typical teenage 'hello' as Isobel clunked him on the side of the thigh. Eoin ushered him from the room as his wife waved a folded newspaper about to disperse the smell of vinegar, muttering apologies.

'Makes me hungry,' Batten smiled as he settled himself on the sofa.

Costello sat sideways on the easy chair next to the fire. It had a cashmere throw over it, and there was a fine watercolour original of a loch in winter over the fireplace. That was more Isobel Dewar.

Costello leaned forward. 'There is no easy way to say this. The body found at Riverview Farm was not Warren McAvoy.'

Isobel pointed a bony finger in Costello's face.

Costello waited until the penny dropped.

'What do you mean, it wasn't his body? You said—'

'It had McAvoy's identification. But it wasn't him.'

Isobel took a deep breath. 'OK, wishful thinking.' She rubbed her upper arm and slowly closed her eyes. She seemed genuinely shocked.

It was Eoin who spoke next. 'Jesus Christ.' He lifted his hands and ran them over his hair. 'No, how can that be . . .?'

Costello did not answer directly. 'I need to ask you a strange question: have you ever seen anything like this before?' She opened the file and took out the tarot card, the Fool.

Isobel hardly glanced at it. 'No,' she snapped and turned her head away, but Eoin's face betrayed something, a flash of recognition, before he managed to look away.

'Mr Dewar?'

He didn't miss the formality of his surname; she was over with nice. She was a Detective Inspector now. Eoin gave her a tight little nod.

His wife stared at him. 'What?' she sniffed. 'I've never seen that before.'

'Mr Dewar. It's important.'

'We got two. Can't recall them. Priestess? And a Ben Hur-type picture. Not that picture, but the same design, black and gold. Where did you get that one?'

Costello ignored him, glancing down her list of tarot cards. 'The other would be the Chariot?'

'Maybe.' He flicked his finger at the black envelope, not looking at the card. 'What is this about?'

'How did you get them? In the post?'

'Yes, a couple of weeks ago . . .'

'Sent here?'

He nodded.

'Eoin?' Isobel interrupted.

Costello silenced her with a raised hand. 'Do you still have the cards?'

He shook his head. 'It meant nothing to me. I stuck them in the bin.'

Now Costello turned to Isobel. 'Mrs Dewar. You don't seem the type, but have you ever consulted a tarot card reader or a psychic about Robbie?'

'Of course not.' Hard blue eyes met Costello's again. 'My son speaks to me every day. He is still alive, in my heart, in my head . . .' The tears began to stream in earnest now. 'So I don't need to speak to any fu— anybody like that. What has this got to do with us or Robbie?'

'Or Warren McAvoy? Unless you think that he sent them?' Eoin swore quietly under his breath.

'We aren't sure. Isobel, it might be better if you went to stay with a friend or your mother. Whoever sent you the cards knows where you live.'

Batten coughed gently. 'I think there might be other ears listening,' he pointed at the door. Eoin threw his eyes at the ceiling.

'Would you mind if I keep him occupied?' asked Batten. 'Just a word, Liverpool fan to Everton fan.'

Isobel was about to say no, but Eoin nodded. 'Go ahead. Please don't upset him.'

'Of course,' said Batten with his clinical smile, his object achieved.

Costello waited until he had left the room and heard Batten's voice saying, *OK, young man, what are you up to?* and Jimmy's young teenage voice replying that *nobody ever told him nuffin* followed by *You got anybody yet?*

'That might not be for your ears, and my granny always said folk who listen at doors never hear good about themselves. Now explain to me this Liverpool thing . . .' Their voices faded. They were walking along the hall going somewhere out of earshot.

'I don't want Jimmy upset. I'm not having that.' Isobel reached out, holding her hand out for Eoin. Costello could not help but notice the casual curl of his fingers into hers. 'It takes him ages to get to sleep at night as it is.'

'He has fairly grown, hasn't he?'

'Can't keep up, he goes through the fridge like a plague of locusts. At least he's normal in some ways.'

'He was close to his brother, wasn't he?' Costello let her eyes drift up to some photographs on the dresser. 'Is that the boys together? And your dog? A black . . . what is he?'

'Cockapoo. Casper. We think the neighbours poisoned him – one of the reasons we moved. Jimmy was heartbroken.'

Costello pulled out her notebook but didn't write anything down. 'How is he now? With the new house and new school?'

Isobel shuffled in her seat a little. Her head turned towards the door of the living room, anxious to know what was going on the other side. 'He has been better at the new school. He had been very disruptive, fighting, being bullied and being a bully, if the truth be told. He has no friends. It's very difficult. People know who he is.'

'We think it prudent to be extra vigilant with everybody who has a connection to the case. We have no reason to believe that Jimmy is at risk, but he is the only witness to McAvoy's crime and we now have to consider the possibility that McAvoy is still alive.'

'And now it's the anniversary,' Eoin said, eyes in the middle distance, then focussed on Costello. 'You think that bastard is going to come back and try again? Try for Jimmy?' He put his hand out to Isobel; she flinched at his touch.

'Not really, but his safety is our first priority. It might help if Mick speaks to Jimmy one-to-one. He could try to find out why McAvoy attacked Robbie and Callum at that moment. It might have some bearing on what McAvoy feels about Jimmy. They seemed close on the films I've seen.' Costello held her breath. It was complete rubbish, of course, but they seemed to believe it.

'What about Ruth – she got one of these?' Eoin pointed at the tarot card.

'She is being interviewed as we speak.'

'Robbie was killed by that bastard, ten years old and battered to death. Why did we let them go out?'

'Because they were young boys and they wanted to go to the island?' suggested Costello quietly.

Eoin curled his fingers back into Isobel's as his wife went quiet, staring out across the room.

She rubbed her forearm, pulling up her blouse to check a deep magenta bruise. Tears rolled down both cheeks. 'Jimmy liked the Dreamcatcher; it would have been his idea to go out, an adventure to go out that late. It was barely dark. We thought it was safe.'

Costello noticed the shift in her mood, as obvious as the bruises. 'Was McAvoy good with boats?'

Eoin shook his head, 'Not particularly.' But his eyes lay on Costello quizzically.

Isobel sat up straight. 'I'll take Jimmy to my mum's.'

Costello glanced at the clock; the longer Batten had with Jimmy the better. 'There's no need to panic. Here's my card; phone if you need anything, day or night.' It was Eoin who reached out and took it.

Costello opened the folder again. 'Can I show you this picture? Do you know who this is?' She handed over the picture of Mr Field.

'Is that him?' asked Eoin but not before Costello noted that familiar flash of recognition.

'Yes. You know him?'

Eoin's eyes narrowed. 'Not easy to recognize him, his face is a mess. I can't place him but . . .' He let out a long, slow breath.

'But?' prompted Costello.

'It rings a bell. Sorry, I'm trying to think . . .'

'Do you think he looks like McAvoy?' asked Costello.

'In passing only,' said Eoin. 'Isobel, look. Who is this guy? I've seen him around.'

Isobel shook her head.

Eoin handed the photograph back. 'Sorry, I can't recall.'

Costello heard movement out in the hall. 'It might come back when you're not thinking about it. Give me a call if it does.' She stood up.

'Did McAvoy do that to him, what it said in the paper?' asked Isobel.

'Somebody did.'

Brenda looked at the clock; it was getting on for eight. She had been late getting home from work and was thinking about making some salad for tea. There had been no communication from Colin or Claire. Peter would be round at his pal Graham's, playing computer games, no doubt. Graham's mum would send him packing when she'd had enough. Colin could be back in five minutes or at five in the morning, she was used to that. But where was Claire? Still at Helena's? She checked the answering service on the house phone, then looked into Claire's bedroom in case she had fallen asleep. She was just checking her mobile for any voicemails when it rang.

'Hello, Mum?' Her daughter's voice was clipped, panicky almost.

'Yip, where are you, Claire?'

Her daughter's voice got higher, shrill. 'Mum, I'm at Helena's house.'

Brenda checked the kitchen clock again. 'I gathered that. I think your dad was going to collect you but he might be held up, so if you can—'

'Yes, Mum, it's just that . . .' Claire couldn't speak for sobbing.

'What is it, love?'

'It's Helena.' Her sobbing went quiet. 'Can you come over? I don't think she's very well. She's being sick, she's in bed but . . . well, I . . .' and she started to cry in earnest.

Claire was already at the front door when Brenda pulled up outside the house in the terrace. Her heart was thumping. She wanted to be anywhere but here, yet at the same time some morbid self-torture of walking into Colin's lover's house, this most desired address, meant she couldn't stop herself. She had texted Colin and told him she would update him. So far there had been no reply.

'Oh Mum,' said Claire, 'I didn't know what to do.'

'It's OK, love. Where is she?'

Brenda walked into the hall, taking in the parquet floor, the Turkish rugs, the art and the porcelain. Beautiful, fragile, but still a home. Claire was still dressed in her school uniform and had taken her shoes off, running about another woman's house in her socks. She wondered if Colin did that. How 'at home' were they here? Claire never took her mucky shoes off in her own house; what did that say about them?

'She felt sick at work so I came back with her. Then she was really sick. I had to open the bathroom door to get her out and I had to help her to bed.'

'You did the right thing. Is she here? What has she had to eat?' Brenda continued to climb up the stairs, looking at the beauty of the light from the oriole window playing on the patina of the floor. The smell of freesias and oil paint was now tinged with the bitter smell of vomit.

'Tuna sandwich; she only ate a wee bit. I ate the rest.' Claire opened a big white door, knocking on it gently first. The room was a symphony of brown and cream; the curtains were closed against the evening sun, bathing the room in sepia. Helena lay still on her back, on top of a white duvet, a white duvet that covered a huge double bed. Brenda tried to push the thought of Colin and Helena rolling around on it from her mind.

Helena's eyes opened slightly as Brenda entered the room. Her brown jumper had slid off her bony shoulders; her grey trousers sagged between her jutting hip bones. Just for a moment, both women held their breath. Brenda saw the yellow sheen on the pale skin, the thin, lifeless hair.

Helena's fingers crawled across the top of the duvet, reaching out.

The old woman trudged up the wooden stairs, counting. The factory had been derelict for many years, but from the minute the gates closed it became a haven for the homeless. She always wound her way back as if drawn by some invisible flame.

In the eighties she had worked here, when the production line was a hotbed of chatter and gossip. It had been her life to pull out the misshapes: the broken caramel wafers, those only half covered in chocolate, sometimes two stuck together, or one somebody up the line had already taken a bite out of.

She had gained a lot of weight, of course, and that had prompted the diabetes and the loss of three of her toes. And now the fourth wasn't smelling too good.

She counted the stairs, pulling herself up on the handrail as she dragged her bags behind her. Nine, ten, eleven. Stair fourteen was missing. She had put her foot through it once before and been stuck for a day. Two days? Three days? Until one of the graffiti boys from the Plantation part of the city had come in to work on the Green Devil and had heard her calls for help. He'd been scared shitless and done a runner, thinking she was a banshee. But when he'd reached home and thought about it, he had called the police. That had been a month in hospital – it was when they had amputated her toes.

But she was OK now. She had her wee den on the third floor, a huge area with twin lines of pillars and the Green Devil taking up the full height of the far wall. It had given her nightmares at first, with its blood-red eyes and shards of teeth, and she had been scared of the Plantation boys with their loud music and tattoos. But two years ago they had finished their artwork and left. She was alone with the howling, screaming wind, the dancing ghosts of a loyal workforce and the Devil.

She kept to the far corner where most of the windows were well boarded up. It was warm tonight, but in the winter, rain and snow drifted in and the bitter cold winds chased her down. Many times she had been woken by frozen rain stinging her face. But on a windless, gentle summer night like this, the factory was quiet. None of the clattering and screaming that usually echoed round the walls and inside her head.

She settled down, putting her Morrisons bags in a pile and kicking open the old duvet that she had pulled out of a skip in the West End; she'd had to fight for that. Then she put her hood back up, and got settled in. Two cans of Special Brew and a polystyrene tray of bits of burger and fries that she had scavenged from the bins outside McDonalds at St Enoch's. She always found a load of gherkins in that bin. She cooried into the duvet, reliving conversations with Aggie and Janet – the girls on the line – with their white hats and constant chatter. Wilma from the office's new up-do, the shift manager's latest squeeze, the new girl with the hips and the stilettos and the Marilyn Monroe huskiness. It was all she had in her life and it was all she needed; she had been happy. Then redundancy came and everybody moved on. She was left behind, her past and her present were the same thing, her life had stalled. She had worked at the factory since she was fifteen, left when she had the kids, then came back. She didn't know anything else.

Or anyone else.

Didn't even know her own children now. She wasn't sure what happened there – a drift apart.

She was still trying to remember them when she fell into her usual drunken stupor. She never heard them come in. The first kick in the temple woke her up; the second kick got her in the ribs. But she had not lived on the streets for all these years without some sense of survival, so she rolled, pulling the duvet tight up round her neck, curling herself up, making herself as small as possible. They would get bored and go away.

She thought she smelled petrol and heard splashes. In the dark she saw the bright, single flame, hanging in the air like a flower held by an angel. Then the brilliant light came rushing towards her and she knew it was God welcoming her to heaven. It was all going to be OK.

Anderson held the phone out from his ear. '. . . So you made the identity without waiting until the DNA was through. You did not ask them to confirm the DNA before you went ahead? Is it not procedure to . . .' He checked the number recognition: Karen Jones. '. . . Another monumental cock-up . . .'

'How did you get this number?' he asked politely.

'Do you deny that? Did you tell his sister that Warren was dead?'

'So it was Lexy who gave you this number?' He doodled Lexy's head with its sticky out fringe and stuck a hatchet through it.

'Are you trying to stop the bereaved from talking to the press, DCI Anderson?'

'Well, if it wasn't Warren then Lexy is not the bereaved, you stupid cow,' he muttered, hopefully loud enough for her to hear as he slammed the phone down. So, now the press knew that the body was not Warren McAvoy. He and Walker had been on damage limitation for hours.

He looked at his watch and the number of unread emails in his inbox. Somebody was sending him lots of links to the Where's Warren Facebook page; the police were now dressed as Wallys in red and black stripes. He checked his text messages instead. Brenda was at Helena's house; a doctor from NHS 24 had come out and given Helena an injection. Brenda said Claire was sitting in the lounge watching TV, all was OK for now.

Another one timed at twenty to midnight said Helena was feeling better and had sent them home.

Colin immediately started dialling, then stopped. He should go straight out. Helena was ten minutes away at most. But if she was sleeping what good would that do?

But he could nip round there and make sure she was OK, then he could concentrate on his job. Looking in his jacket pocket for his mobile, his fingers found Helena's house key, on its own key ring. It burned in his palm.

He pulled his mobile out, pressed her number. Straight to voicemail.

He'd go home, calling in at Helena's on his way past. He slipped his jacket on, picked up his car keys and saw the fatal incident report on Grace Amelie Wilson. Clipped to the front cover was her photograph, a small round face framed with unruly brown curls. Underneath that were his early notes on Bella, ignored, at the bottom of the pile.

Somebody was writing a symphony for his heart strings.

He opened his office door when a voice from the vacant incident room made him jump.

'Hi, Colin.'

He saw Batten wave his hand from above Costello's monitor. 'Have you been here all evening?'

'Well, alone with James Dewar. He has a nice computer set-up, that boy, better than mine. Call of Duty . . .'

'I don't like Peter playing that,' said Colin, sitting down, glad of the distraction.

'Boys will be boys, Colin. Jimmy plays it with his dad.' He pulled a face, eyes still on the keyboard. 'Jimmy is an interesting kid. He still needs to talk through his ordeal, he's not over it.'

'Doubt if he ever will be.'

'But as a family they remain engaged with the Inchgarten, probably because of Robbie. His dad researches a lot of local history, and Jimmy's homework for English, My Favourite Place essay? Still Inchgarten Bay, after all that has happened.' Batten was thoughtful.

'It's where he last saw his brother, that's understandable.'

'And you have seen this? The video of the boys?'

Anderson felt guilty at the relief he felt for an excuse to stay there. If he was caught up here at work, he couldn't go up the road and check on Helena. Equally, he couldn't go home and face Brenda's polite concern.

And the undertones that carried.

Anderson decided to toss a mental coin. If it was the same video as the one on Ruth's phone, he could go. 'Is it the one from Ruth's phone? PN332?'

'No, this is Production number 410.' Batten reeled it off without looking as Anderson slipped his jacket off again. 'This is more Warren than Callum. I'm watching the interplay.' His eyes were fixed on the screen, elbows on the desk, chin resting on his hands, his focus unwavering. As Anderson leaned closer he dropped his right hand to cradle the mouse, a click, a pause then another click. Then the hand went back to the chin, another few minutes transfixed to the screen.

This piece of film was new to Anderson. The monitor was full of images of Inchgarten Lodge Park, a canoe on the water and the two Dewar boys, Robbie and Jimmy, wading in the shallows, pointing at the Dreamcatcher and talking to whoever was holding the camera.

'This is from Eoin Dewar's mobile before they set sail.'

'The day they were killed?'

'No, this is two weeks before.'

'Is there no sound?' Anderson put his hand out to click in the volume, but was halted by Batten's strong grip.

'I've turned it off. Better to watch, don't get distracted by the words. Look at the body language, the faces. Interpret what you see. Eoin is telling the boys how to stop the canoe floating away, Isobel is paddling, hugging Robbie. It all says happy families so far. Well, happy families then; now the Dewars don't only sleep in separate beds, they sleep in separate rooms.'

Anderson looked at him in astonishment.

'I can snoop too, you know. But the family dynamic works well here, they are happy together. The Dewar boys seem confident. I take it the McCardle boy couldn't swim?'

'I have no idea.' Anderson pulled his seat closer as the film cut.

'Five minutes later, that's Callum McCardle. Thin wee thing, three stone when sloppy wet. Obviously the focus is on the Dewars as their dad is filming. Typical, the Dewar boys are paying no attention to what Dad is saying, everybody's getting very wet. Here the view swings round as the canoe floats away; we catch a better view of the McCardle boy, and that there . . . is Warren McAvoy. The shadow man.'

Batten pressed pause.

Anderson leaned in closer. 'Flesh and blood, eh? The man himself.'

'Not "Mr Field".'

'Not the man in Lexy's photograph, not the man in the field . . .'

In silence they studied the thin, dark-haired, pale-skinned man in his ill-fitting khaki trousers rolled up to the knee, getting very wet. He was bent over the wee lad who was standing knee deep in the water. The boy held on to the man's arm, his grip tightening every time a wave slapped against his puny knee. Warren was adjusting the boy's crew saver, making sure it was right. Then he stood up, obviously asking the boy to twist it from side to side, making sure it fitted. He held his arm out, steadying the boy as he let go. The boy had a nervous grin on his face, half laughing as a wave tickled the bottom of his shorts.

Warren ruffled the boy's hair, patted his cheek and walked towards the camera. His head left the top of the frame. Callum stayed in focus, laughing, gripping the braces of the crew saver with one hand, saying something to the other boys.

'Look at that,' said Batten.

'At what?'

'Look at Callum's arm, stretched out. He doesn't want Warren to walk away and Warren does not want to walk away. Callum is not comfortable. Look at the way Warren comforts him, doing Fergus's job as a Dad. This is all very interesting.'

Anderson watched as Warren turned his shoulders, maybe answering Callum. The answer was a shy thumbs up from the boy, a smile. A smile of complete trust.

'This is difficult to watch,' he checked the date. 'Two weeks later he battered that wee lad's head to pulp.'

Batten touched the mouse and rewound the film a little. 'But Callum trusts him.' He waved a hand at the screen. 'I need to get to Inchgarten. How are the arrangements coming along to get me there?'

'Costello has already set the ball rolling.'

'Mm-hmm?' His eyes didn't move as he clicked again to rewind the film.

'And Mitchum is giving us four bodies for a tail on Eoin Dewar. Eight would be better but the budget is tight. The wife is going back to her mother's.'

'You should look at this footage, you know.'

'Can it wait until tomorrow? I have a bit of an emergency at home.'

'No, you don't, or you wouldn't be hanging around here.'

Wednesday, 18 June

The sun was kissing the horizon when O'Hare pulled the Avensis on to the patch of waste ground, rocking over potholes and the kerbstones of old roads that went nowhere. The motorway thundered overhead.

Costello had been pleased to be pulled from her bed, she hadn't been sleeping anyway. The shit was hitting the fan big time. The news on Radio Clyde was bad enough, stating that the body had been wrongly identified. God knows what the early editions were going to say. She had been thinking about Eoin since the meeting the previous night. He was the alpha male. He had lost a child, his house, his business. She couldn't condone what he might have done to Mr Field, but she understood it.

Wyngate was trying to find a connection between Eoin and Riverview. They needed something concrete in this case of shifting sands.

Despite the heat there was a small fire burning in a grate, four men huddled round it, and two more were amusing the two uniformed officers standing guard at the entrance to the old factory. From the security of the car, it all seemed very good-natured. One young gentleman in tracksuit bottoms and a very dirty vest was offering a constable a drink from his can with his badly tattooed left hand. The officer was refusing with good humour.

'Is this where they hang out now?' Costello asked. 'The homeless?'

'The "domiciliary challenged"? This is one of their des reses. They need, they deserve to be taken off the street and cared for. No point in chasing them until they end up on my table, body fat too low to survive the winter, lungs eaten by TB and liver destroyed by parasites. We are a third world country, Costello.' O'Hare opened the automatic boot lock. 'But they will spend the summer down here, the winter up there under the motorway, warm but full of carbon monoxide. The younger ones sleep on the iron beams above the concourse at Glasgow Central.'

Costello turned to face him, grimacing in disbelief. 'I thought that was an urban myth.'

'Well, I have the proof. They end up on my table when they turn over in their sleep and hit the concrete below, not nice. Really puts the commuters off their Costa muffins.'

O'Hare killed the engine, and they both sat for a minute watching the scene in the headlights. The young man in the dirty vest was treating the two cops to a display of nifty Astaire-style footwork while holding his precious can of lager steady.

'Shouldn't happen in a civilized country, should it?' said Costello. 'Look at them, so young.'

'Young indeed. All sorts now, you know. Some of them are well educated. Some ended up here by bad luck, some because of mental health issues. Some of them have no home to go to because home means systematic abuse of all kinds. Violence like you wouldn't believe.' Then O'Hare remembered who he was talking to. 'Of course you would believe it. Sorry.'

Costello was leaning forward in her seat, watching Dirty Vest Travolta throw a few shapes. She noticed the cops had their hands on their radios, the tall one keeping an eye out back and front, fearing an ambush, wary that Dirty Vest was merely causing a diversion. Those two had been down here before. Dirty Vest finished with a traditional *Saturday Night Fever* step sequence. 'I was thinking that we seem to be doing this all the wrong way round. Chasing the victims rather than chasing the perps. Poor sods.'

'They are the visible nuisance, though, Costello, that's why the money goes into making them disappear. It's got better PR value than solving the problem with better housing, better social care . . . Oh, don't get me started.'

'I think *he* wants us to get started.' She nodded to the uniformed constable who was walking towards the car while talking down his radio. He looked as if his chin was tucked into his left armpit.

'He'll be calling up our reg in a mo. Come on, better put him out his misery.'

'Who the hell does he think we might be? Tourists wishing to watch the natives?'

'Damn sight more entertaining than those bloody pandas.' O'Hare nodded at Dirty Vest, who was now grinding his face into the ground, in a Buckfast-fuelled breakdance. He heard one of the cops tell him to get up before he caught something.

'You here for Dotty?' asked the approaching constable, an older man whose years had not mellowed him.

'If that is the name of the deceased, then yes,' said O'Hare.

'Murphy,' he introduced himself. 'She's up there,' he said. 'Can't leave her alone, not with those hyenas circling.' He looked over to the four figures still huddling together, thin fingers wavering over the fire. Dirty Vest was now trying a Cossack variation on his theme. His friend pointed at him like a magician's assistant, bouncing slightly to the beat of silent music. Costello could hear the occasional burst of expletives and the punctuation of laughter, a shared joke. A small wiry brown dog pattered over the waste ground towards them with a crumpled chip poke in its mouth, crossing on the diagonal as if it was practising dressage. It lifted its head, looked straight at the car, at Costello, then O'Hare, dismissed them and went on his way.

'Up here. I've left two colleagues with her. That lot would have nicked her back teeth if she'd died with her mouth open.'

Elvie was scrolling the internet, checking reports about McAvoy, when a chat box opened.

Great to hear from you, are you online right now . . . wow this is sooooo amazing.

Hi Amy Lee, it's seven in the morning here.

It's the middle of the night here. Fab! ZZZZZZZ

Amy Lee, have you thought about this?

Yip. It's like a school project thing and Grandpappy is Scottish so I thought that would be really cool to see like where he came from and all that.

Have you ever been here?

Way no! I've been all over here though. Vancouver, Manitoba, Ramsay, Banff, Saskatoon and Revelstoke. That's all the places I've been to school. I learned to rap it. Not that any of them managed to teach me anything. Awesome ;) U ever been here.

To Canada. No.

GP goes back home a lot – every yr that ends with a three and every year that ends with an eight, so that's like . . . mmmmm . . .

Once every five years, does it take him that long to save up ☺

You know my GP, he's soooo mean!

Most Scotsmen are.

He got himself a really froody Samsung for the eighty-fifth birthday, I showed him how to use the camera on it so I have some pictures of places from that. He doesn't know I looked. It looks nice, like Banff.

Maybe that's because Banff is named after Banff. OK, so what would you like to know?

I have a few dollars left over. Can you tell me what I'll get for my thirty dollars, Canadian dollars? I don't know what that is in your money.

No worries, just tell me what you would like to know. What's GP's name?

He's Bert Cohoon but was born with different spelling. Do they own bits? Bits near Loch Lomond. That's where he goes on his holidays.

I'm going there myself tomorrow.

You going looking for clues? Hurrah. That's awesome.

Not really, but if I find any I'll let you know.

Haaaaaaa.:) Right on Elvis!

So when is his birthday?

Next Friday, 20 June 1934, like antique. He's crumbly.

So he has long birthday?

???? ☹

It's the solstice.

Murphy led the way. 'It was not an easy crime scene to secure, and we weren't sure it was a crime scene until later. Murder is murder in the eyes of God and the law. A homeless alcoholic setting themselves on fire with cheap alcohol and a dropped cigarette is not unheard of, but I've never heard of a homeless person shooting themselves with an arrow then setting themselves on fire.'

'An arrow?' repeated O'Hare.

'Arrow?' repeated Costello, to make sure.

'Yip,' he stopped and turned to face them. 'This is a hangout for all sorts: drugs, homeless, spray painters. They have their wee community, mostly they keep out of the way of the traffic, but I am not having them used as target practice and filmed for YouTube.'

'Lead on,' said O'Hare.

'Nobody from major investigation has been out yet, so I thought I'd call you, Jack. It doesn't fit right with me.'

'Oh, I thought this was a legit call,' said Costello, stopping in her tracks, then recalling that she wasn't getting any decent sleep anyway.

'It is now that you know about it,' said O'Hare, putting a hand on her shoulder and pushing her on.

'Watch yourself. There are some difficult stairs and rotten boards. Try to stick to the path that we've secured. She's up on the third floor.'

'I see what you mean about not being able to secure the crime scene,' said Costello. 'So what happened here?'

'Well, we got a phone call from a mobile, a boy from one of the spray-painting gangs that hang around here, from Plantation. He uses this place a lot, knew her as Dotty. He was pretty shaken up when they saw the flames and realised she was underneath. He knew it was her wee den.'

'Did he see anything? Anybody?'

'Thought he heard footsteps, more than one person. Maybe a white van driving away. That gang love their art, as they call it, bloody weird. God knows what they take to inspire that.' He turned to go up on to the next floor and pointed to the wall painting of dagger-toothed ghosts, red eyed and sharp clawed, tearing through a wood of . . . limbs, Costello realized as she got closer. The paint flaking off the walls cast shadows on the floor of what was once a busy biscuit factory, Gray and Dunn. The home of the caramel wafer. It was a sad and pathetic place now. It seemed deader than the mortuary.

Murphy put his hand out, pointing. 'Watch your feet there, biohazards, as they say.'

'Pile of vomit, as we say in the CID.'

'Ex-stomach contents,' added O'Hare.

'Pavement Pizza.' Murphy chuckled. 'But to answer your question, they didn't see anybody specifically. One of them presumed it was a couple of folk from the soup kitchen. They did hear noises but everything in here echoes.'

O'Hare muttered to Costello, 'Two of them? Old lady set on fire? Seeing a pattern here?'

Murphy caught it but didn't ask further. 'She's up here in the far corner. It's cool up here – with the height of the building, the wind has a good flow through.' Murphy had done the job for a long time, telling the pathologist what he might need to know. 'And life was pronounced extinct by the police surgeon at two a.m. this morning. She was dead as soon as the arrow hit her – nobody survives that. It smells as though an accelerant was used, just a smell that shouldn't be there. Paraffin? Might be wrong.' He shrugged.

Both O'Hare and Costello walked past two officers who were looking out of a fractured window pane on to the street below. There was a pile of boxes like a shanty town dwelling with a few plastic bags piled up on top. The concrete near them became blacker and the acrid smell of smoke was still heavy in the air.

There was a bundle of blackened mass that could have been a melted black bin bag. Closer, the form became clearer: a dead human being. An overcooked carcass skewered by an arrow.

Costello stood back, diverting her eyes. She started to feel angry. 'Is this all there is? No arc lights, no scenes of crime?'

'Well, look at the crime scene. It was well contaminated and not easy to keep secure. And let face it, she's—'

'What? Not worth it?'

Murphy smiled. 'I was going to say that she's not going to be easy to trace. Anybody she hangs about with is rarely coherent . . .' He looked away from the anger of Costello's stare. 'It would be too much investment for not enough return. Sign of the times.'

Costello walked into the next room through a large concrete archway, leaving O'Hare to open his case and persuade Dotty to give up what secrets she was hiding. She looked along the length of the room at the central pillars with peeling paint. Little filigree fingers, waving and pointing, wafting this way and that in an invisible draught that she couldn't even feel. She closed her eyes. This place gave her the creeps.

She wondered how Dotty got here, what path in her life brought her to this end. She walked round through a hole in the wall through to the room next door. Some old filing cabinets were still here with signs of more recent life: a rolled up fleece, a few old cans of Irn Bru, a few bottles, a wrapped up brown paper like a chip supper. And the dragon painted on the far wall. The art was the product of a dark childhood.

She jumped at a noise again, a rattle of claws. The image of the dagger-toothed demons eating their way through a forest of flesh crossed her mind. Something was up here with her, something of flesh and blood. She looked back and shivered when she realized how far she had walked from Dotty and the others. She backed up, feeling more secure with her gloved hands against the wall, but also a little stupid, four grown men within shouting distance. Couldn't stop an arrow, though, could they?

It would be a rat. But the noise was loud, in tempo, not like the scurry of a rat. Too quick for a person. It was pitter pattering its way towards her, like the draught making its way up the stairs, winding left and right. She bit her tongue, this was ridiculous. She watched the top of the stairs, staring at eye-level, when something lower caught her line of vision. The wee dog . . . trotting round like it owned the place. It ignored her, following a well-worn circuit up to the gap in the wall, hopped over and began to sniff at the pile of plastic carrier bags lying beside the victim.

'Get that bloody thing out of here,' said O'Hare.

'Watch out, they bite. Probably feral.' Murphy extended his baton and started making shooing noises. The dog ignored him, pulling at the Morrisons bags, shaking at one as if shaking a rat, ripping it open and selecting some tasty morsel before trotting away with it, back the way it came.

'Costello?'

'Yeah?' She stepped over the disrupted plastic bags to stand beside the pathologist.

'See this?' He indicated something long and thin with his gloved forefinger. 'An arrow right enough.'

'So she was hunted?' Costello looked round. 'She was cornered up here.'

'This burning is intense. So I think the arrow came from a bow and it went deep. The arrowhead is missing; it will be in the body tissue somewhere. And this is more charred than the rest of it, so the arrow was alight when it was fired, if you'll pardon the pun.'

'Murphy, did you get the addresses of the boys who were here, the graffiti lot?'

He passed the buck smoothly. 'The Plantation boys, everybody knows who they are, fancy themselves as Banksy.'

O'Hare was still stroking the arrow, his purple gloves pulling on the rough edges of it. 'It's rustic, homemade, has the aroma of pine.

It's not an easy thing to do, fire an arrow. You have to be very strong.'

'As she lay there like a sitting duck.'

O'Hare turned to what was left of the body. 'But Murphy, I think she *is* going to be easy to ID. One tooth and lacking in toes? I don't think they've been burned off, so that means amputated. And that means heart disease or diabetes, but there will be a medical trail. She will not be nameless for long.'

'I thought she was called Dotty?' said Costello.

'Only because it rhymed with Potty,' Murphy told her.

'Fair enough.'

She turned round, thinking about two old ladies, both set on fire. But it looked like a different accelerant had been used this time. The killer liked to leave a message. She prodded one of the plastic bags with her toe. Two polystyrene burger boxes from McDonald's toppled out; a pristine black card fell on top of them. She vaguely heard O'Hare say something to her as she reached down and picked it up.

'Costello!' O'Hare's voice was sharp, but she opened the black envelope anyway. She turned the card up to show her two companions.

Temperance.

Costello was sitting beside the radiator wishing it was on as Sammy had opened all the windows and the draught felt arctic compared to the warmth of the day. She was attempting the Where's Warren puzzle in the morning paper. This time a Cumberbatch Sherlock was looking deep in Loch Ness. The newspaper felt it was doing a public service by reproducing the cartoon in full to show the internet was not taking the case seriously.

She wiped the palm of her hand down her trousers. No matter how many times she washed her face and hands, she could still smell burned flesh. Sammy had given her a squirt of her Coco Chanel; it was almost worse than the smell of stale urine. She had also given her a tub of moisturiser, for the 'more mature' skin. Costello had tried not to be offended.

The smart money was on Dotty being Warren's mother. The tarot card was now up on the wall. Temperance: the card for letting go of past guilt. It would be funny if it wasn't so sick.

Wyngate banged through the door, carrying a box that smelled delicious. 'Brekkie!'

'There was another death last night, Gordon. Tuck in before you get started.'

He turned round and looked at the wall; the diagram was getting more complicated and more crowded. Two victims of fire, one dismembered. And the original three children. Warren's face still centre stage. Lexy and Eoin's photographs were starred, both under surveillance but for different reasons. And a snapshot of the boys from a film at Inchgarten, Warren McAvoy in the background, a crude bow lying in the foreground beside an empty quiver. The words 'Restricted Information' over it in black handwriting.

'So what's it been like working here?' Wyngate asked Sammy as she delicately unwrapped two slices of toast – dry toast, Costello noticed – from a small brown bag and placed them in front of her before holding her cup out for Wyngate to fill.

'Thanks,' she said, flashing him a beaming smile. 'Everybody here has been so nice.'

'They can be if the wind is in the right direction,' muttered Costello.

'I never realized you were *that* Costello.'

Costello felt her heart jump, the scar on her forehead jagged in remembrance.

'Sorry, didn't mean to bring it up.'

'Can't choose your family,' said Costello, looking into the break-fast delivery for her own fried egg roll, with extra buttered toast.

'I don't have any family myself. So is there nothing going on between you and that fiscal?'

'Not while there is breath in my body,' said Costello casually, unwrapping a bag with COST written on it to reveal her fried egg, runny yolk in a buttered roll. Without being asked, Wyngate poured her a cup of tea. 'Walker's wife phones him every five minutes and he runs like a puppy. All that stuff in here is bravado. His wife is never at any functions or the Law Society Dinner. He always attends alone.'

'Bernie is a bit like that. Nobody ever sees the wee woman. He doesn't want her to talk to somebody she shouldn't.' Her eyes glazed over.

'We've still not heard from Bernie, you know,' said Costello, stopping in mid-chew. 'He's not turned up in any hospitals. Or mortuaries. That's getting on for forty-eight hours.'

Sammy shook her head. 'I called his house last night. Lyn is in pieces. It's as if he's disappeared off the face of the earth.'

Wyngate said, 'We've got alerts out looking for the car. The Dewars' house and workplace have been checked. There was a casual call to Ruth McCardle. I think Batten's going to check out Inchgarten.'

'You don't think that he's run away to Spain with some fancy tart, knowing that this case was coming back to bite him?' Costello backhanded some yolk from her chin. 'His timing is rank rotten.'

There was a slight pause before Sammy answered, 'Lyn said he's taken no clothes, and his passport is still there. He left his office exactly the way it should be.'

'So it crossed your mind as well?'

'The more I think of it, the more I think that he got a tarot card and has been taken by that bastard McAvoy. The timing is, as you said, rank rotten.' She choked slightly.

Costello stopped chewing again. 'You really think we're looking for a body?'

'Well, I'm worried.' Sammy wiped a tear from her eye. Costello recalled the redness round her eyes the day they had met.

'Maybe you should . . .'

The door opened. Anderson came in, carrying two plastic envelopes. 'Glad you two are here. Look at these.'

'Not more?' asked Costello with her mouth full.

'One for me at my house. One for you, Sammy, sent here to the station.'

'Oh my God!'

'Do you want to open yours? I got the Emperor, black envelope but the card was white. Oh, and Ruth McCardle has been on the phone complaining about the press coverage.' He sat down in an empty chair beside them. 'Any more coffee in the pot? I've had about two hours' sleep.'

'Ditto,' said Costello to nobody.

'The Emperor means . . . rational sensible thought,' said Sammy as Wyngate obliged with the coffee flask.

'She's been swotting up this stuff,' said Costello, nodding at Sammy as she opened her card.

'The lovers.' The word choked in Sammy's throat.

'Really?' said Costello, her small teeth ripping apart a bit of toast.

Sammy looked at her then looked away, hands trembling.

'Enough,' said Anderson. 'We will put the "Happy Families" to one side until Batten the mind-reader turns up. So, new orders. Nobody is to be solo – stay in pairs at all times. I'm a bit worried about Elvie up at Inchgarten. If McAvoy is behind all this, that is where he'll be. We might be better going in mob-handed.'

'So he can hide for another year? We need softly softly.'

'I don't think that is such a good call, Costello.'

'Then you don't know Elvie like I do. And she was going up there anyway, remember? She's employed by the agency acting on instructions from Warren's dad. At least she has Vik reining her in. You should be more worried about Bernie.'

'We are doing what we can,' Anderson said slowly, poking his tongue round his mouth as if he had toothache. He looked at his watch. 'Walker and I have a meeting at nine to soothe the angry breast of the press. Then I am going to see Ruth. Batten will be on his way out to Inchgarten by taxi. Costello, can you go out with Vik, spend a couple of hours checking it out, get some bearings?'

'Can he not go by himself?'

'What have I just said? Two. Together. I want you to give the place a once-over, let me know what it's like. God knows when I'm going to get out there myself. Walker wants me here, and only here. The surveillance on Lexy and Eoin is proving useless.'

'So if we're not thinking of Warren as serial killer of the decade, but thinking of the killing of pseudo-Warren as an act of revenge, then my money is on Eoin. He's fit, strong, and he can handle a boat. I bet that means he can tie blood knots . . .'

'Anybody tracked down Fergus yet?' Anderson asked.

'Last time I saw him he was in pieces,' said Sammy, 'as you would expect. I've never seen misery like that in another human being before and I never want to see it again. He had cancer a few years back and started drinking as soon as he got the all-clear. He'd cleaned himself up but then hit the bottle again when Callum died.'

Anderson raised an eyebrow.

'Bernie was digging into their,' she licked her fingers, 'medical histories. Of all the parents. And Fergus nearly lost them the

business. The house has gone. You've seen the state of penury
that Ruth lives in. I remember them at the press conference, Fergus
looking away into the far distance. He was lost already.' She
pursed her lips.

'Or was that because he was already planning his own justice?
I could understand that,' said Costello.

Anderson sipped his coffee. 'We have alerts out for him as well.
Addicts can't stay away from their fix; he can't stay hidden. I'm
just thinking about that thing that Ruth said: it was Eoin and Fergus
who were the real friends.'

'In case they are still "real friends", you mean?'

'What did they do at uni?' asked Costello.

'Who?'

'Eoin and Fergus. They met at university. Ruth said so.'

Sammy shrugged her shoulders. 'I can't recall.'

'Gordon, can you check that? And how was Eoin at the press
conference? Can you remember?' Costello was looking at the photograph of Eoin on the wall, the strong, handsome alpha male.

'Eoin? Full of resolve, eyes narrow, throat tight, concentrating.
Coiled spring type. Always reaching out for Isobel, like she needs
to be held. Needy.'

'They were doing that hand thing yesterday. The company is still
running but scaled down, is that right?'

'I think so.'

Costello nodded and scribbled something down in her book.

'You know that issue with the footmarks,' Sammy pointed to the
board, 'four feet in, two feet out. Do you think one of them rode
out of the field on a horse, to confuse us? I'm just thinking about
there being two of them seen walking towards a white van at Dotty's.'

'And two carers seen at Bella's,' said Anderson. 'She *is* linked
to all this somehow,' he added before the others had a chance to
question it. 'Hemphill is trying to find the link, but she has no
connection with the boys or Inchgarten. Is Dotty's DNA back?'

'No.'

'Bella's neighbour said, "two carers, the old one and a young-
ster"', Anderson continued. 'What gave her that impression? A big
one and a wee one. Eoin is tall and strong. Fergus is a weedy wee
thing.'

'So are we not thinking about McAvoy any more?' Costello

asked. 'He was number one suspect before breakfast. Or do we think he has an accomplice? What has changed?'

'It could be two hell-bent on revenge,' Anderson said. 'Or Warren on some mission which only makes sense in his head. Killing the families he never had? Either way we're getting bloody nowhere.'

'We can't make any sense of it until we know if Mr Field was killed because they thought he was McAvoy. Or did McAvoy kill him and place the ID to put us off the scent?' said Costello.

'I'd be happier talking about what we do know,' snapped Anderson.

'McAvoy doesn't make friends. Daisy is too unfit. Tony is a weed,' said Sammy.

'I need to wind this up, press conference calls,' said Anderson, getting up and taking his coffee with him. 'We are releasing no information about the arrow. And before anybody tells me, I learned at school that Robert the Bruce got his bows from the wood of Inchclonaig, which is near Inchgarten. Somebody else might know that as well.'

'I did,' said Walker, who was standing at the door. He flicked his wrist at Anderson, warning him to watch his time.

'You would.'

Anderson spoke quietly to Costello. 'I want you to search Bernie's office. Bring back anything you think might be relevant. I'll take Sammy out to Ruth's. By the end of the day I want to know where Fergus is. It's a common feature in this case, folk floating about in the ether.'

'Nowadays we depend so much upon the electronic footfall,' Costello said. 'We are kind of lost without it. Makes me think that some part of that is deliberate.'

'Just one more thought,' said Anderson in her ear. 'When you search the desk, don't lose sight of the possibility that Bernie might be involved, however unpleasant the thought.'

He got up and left, leaving Costello sitting looking at Bernie's face on the whiteboard. A cop pushed too far by a case he couldn't prove?

'Anybody interested in the fact that Fergus McCardle was never at any university of any kind?' said Wyngate into the air. Nobody was, so he got up, went to the board and drew a grey arcing line from Fergus to Eoin like the jet stream from an aeroplane, destination unknown.

*   *   *

The sun was blinding, the car was hot. Elvie turned off Elvis and his suspicious mind on the CD player. She was getting restless. She needed to get out and have a run and a stretch. Less than an hour out of Glasgow city centre, she was now in the middle of nowhere. She was supposed to leave the Polo in a field, surrounded on three sides by some very ancient trees. There was no sign of any human life. She had driven past the small sign for Inchgarten Lodge Park twice, and carried on past it until she ran out of road. Her fourteen-point turn to avoid the ditches was impressive, but she had eventually found the field. She picked up her rucksack from the back seat of the car, making sure her hybrid laptop was inside, along with her phone, swimming costume and all her running stuff. Then she went round to the boot and picked up a box and a bag from Waitrose, full of food and goodies packed by her mother. She had also brought her own duvet, pillows and towels. Just in case. But they could stay in the car for now.

She set off across the field, the bronze-tipped grass showing signs of a long, hot summer and more verdant growth from the recent rainfall. She followed a path that led into a small gathering of trees, then across a wooden bridge, where the path turned, probably down to the lochside. She could hear a dog barking in the distance.

Elvie could recall the map perfectly; this path would come out at the Roonbay or the Round Bay as it appeared on the older maps. So called because it was small in diameter – almost a lagoon. That was where Grace had died in 2012, near the Rocking Stone. Elvie looked around her as she walked. The hills were green and splendid, not too steep, good for hill training. The bitter cold water would be great for swimming. She was supposed to have a bike but she didn't intend going too far away from here.

She owed it to Geno to find out what had become of Warren, good or bad. She also owed it to Costello, who was letting her put a foot inside the investigation, although she knew there would be a greater advantage for Police Scotland than there would be for Geno DiMarco. And she had to suffer Vik Mulholland, Mr Cheekbones, looking over her shoulder, keeping an eye out in case she overstepped her mark and ruined any future prosecution.

Warren McAvoy had not been killed in that field. So, he was still alive. Out there somewhere. Or here, somewhere.

She walked along the path that skirted the bay, small bushes growing in a fringe round the sand and the huge stone right at the water's edge. This was where Grace had fallen; the wee girl had snuck out of the lodge and gone down to Roonbay to spy on her parents and their party at the bonfire.

Midsummer's Day.

The summer solstice. Midnight.

Robert Cohoon's birthday. The unrelated fact flashed through her mind.

The barking of the dog was louder now. She went round the bigger bushes to a copse of small trees and saw Inchgarten Bay beyond, larger and with a more subtle curve than Roonbay. The island sitting out there in the water. It looked close and peaceful but looks were deceiving. It was a long way, a very long way in cold water. The lodge park and the bay were carved out of a recession in the land. The natural curve of the loch would easily encompass the island, and there was a strong current through the channel between the bay and the island. You'd need strong arms to row that on a windy day when the current would be at its most powerful. And Jimmy did that. Testament to the adrenaline surge from terror.

She stood for a moment taking in the view, dropping the bag and the box to the ground. The trees, the loch, the island, the sand. The crescent moon cut out for the remains of a bonfire, a small wall build round it with old rocks and bricks bordered by four huge old trunks of trees, arranged like bench seats, one to each side. At the far side was a single storey, stone brick building, the wide door closed. Some kind of old boathouse, but the lack of grass at the door showed it was in constant use. Behind it was a hedge, with the roof slates of an older building just visible. Near the boathouse there was an old pontoon with a small dinghy tied up against it, nodding and nudging in the water. On the other side was a larger wooden motorboat in need of a good lick of paint. Up on the shore, lying at a kilter, was the kayak which she recognized as the Dreamcatcher, bright psychedelic eyes painted on the front. She looked back to Roonbay, to the Rocking Stone right at the water's edge, where the loch was inky black. From the strong sucking sound of the waves against the stone, she reckoned there was a deep rock shelf under the surface. It had looked so benign from the other side. The place was dangerous.

The farmhouse sat slightly higher on the hill, a pretty stone building, not quite roses round the door but not far from it. She could see the road going up the back of the hill, the road to nowhere.

She turned at the sound of barking, suddenly close. A huge dog, the colour of salt and pepper, came running down the grass to greet her, with its hackles up and tail wagging, mixed signals just in case. Elvie stood her ground, letting the dog take his time.

'Hoi!' The voice echoed like a foghorn down the hill and on to the water, from the high lodge. 'Mr Peppercorn! Don't you dare!' A maze of bright yellow and blue appeared through the hedges. 'You OK with dogs, hen? Up you come. It's Elf Eh McCulloch, is it?'

'Elvie,' said Elvie quietly, picking up her stuff.

'I'm Daisy. How are you doing, hen?'

'Fine, thank you.'

The figure appeared in full, swathed in a long, strappy dress. Fuzzy headed, her hair a mop of brown. A good four stone over-weight, but proportioned in the way that so charmed the old Masters; her beauty and curves deserved to be caught in oil. She had the widest smile and bluest eyes of any woman Elvie had ever seen.

Daisy Laphan, the sister of the owner. 'Oh, up you come!' The welcome in her voice was genuine. She held her arms out as if to envelop Elvie in an embrace, but wrestled the box from her instead, then the Waitrose bag, saying how nice it was and she was so slim and so strong and didn't really need a hand with the bags at all with her being so fit an' aw.

Elvie slid into step behind her, letting Daisy talk, looking at the two rows of lodges, four in each row, staggered so that the ones behind had a view of the loch between the ones in front. Lovely wood, but not well maintained. It was the sort of thing that would have her mother's boyfriend out with a paintbrush in a flash.

The 'Eigg' was the second last one in the front row, angled slightly to look more up the loch than out to the island. At the bottom of the few steps up to the front door, the woman dropped the bags. 'No come far then?'

'No.'

'In you come,' she thundered up the stairs, booted the door open with her heel, 'let me take that bag from you, till you get in. You've got enough to feed the five thousand here. I do all the food if you want. Good stuff, all fresh, loads of fish. My, my, you are one skinny b . . . you are. Jesus, where do you put it all? I suppose it's all that running about and all that stuff you do. I'm nipping out to get my hair done now, so you make yourself at home and make sure your wee pal gets here safe and sound. Glorious weather, innit?' She stood in front of Elvie, hands on hips, and nodded.

'Yes,' said Elvie simply, not really knowing if any of that had been a question.

Anderson recognized the noise of locks being pulled back. Ruth's head appeared round the door, eyes sleepy, bed hair. 'I'm having a real bad morning.'

'Ruth, we need to talk. It's DCI Anderson. I've Sammy with me.'

'Hi, Sammy, what are we talking about? I've seen the news.'

'We need to talk about McAvoy. Can we come in?'

'The door's open, isn't it?' and they followed Ruth into the darkness within. She was wrapped in her grey dressing gown, sitting in front of the TV. 'What about him?' She took her place under the duvet on the chair by the fire; the room smelled of body odour and toast. 'Sorry, the place is a mess. I've only been awake for half an hour.' She rubbed her face with her hands, a little shake of the head. 'I'll need to put the kettle on . . .'

'I'll stick it on for you,' said Sammy.

'You might need to wash some cups.'

Sammy left to go into the little kitchen, leaving the door open.

It was Anderson's turn to sit down. 'So how are you feeling?'

'Like shit. Some days are awful, others are worse.'

'I'm sure this is not helping.'

There was the flicker of a wry smile. She made herself comfortable in her seat and pulled the duvet tighter round her, sitting like a small, vulnerable maggot. 'So what are you going to say? You don't know where he is, do you? He's slipped away again, the shadow man.' She shivered slightly. Her grey eyes looked somewhere beyond the window.

It seemed worse than any ranting or raving, as if Ruth had come to expect no better.

'So you know that the person we found is not McAvoy.'

Ruth looked at him, then out the window again. 'But you said it was him? Or did I misunderstand?' She shook her head. 'Not that it bloody matters.'

'It was somebody with McAvoy's ID. Somebody went out of their way to make us think that the body was McAvoy.'

'McAvoy himself?'

'We tried to keep it quiet but somebody told the press.'

Ruth thought about this for a moment. 'You wanted to let him think that he had succeeded in fooling you.' She nodded slightly. 'Yeah, I can see him do that. He's clever. You haven't found him yet, have you?'

Anderson ignored the jibe. 'The other theory is that somebody was impersonating McAvoy a bit too well, and somebody killed him, thinking that they were killing McAvoy but killing an innocent man in error.'

Ruth screwed up her eyes slightly. 'And why would an innocent man be going about pretending to be Warren McAvoy, for the sake of the good Lord?'

Anderson thought about Lexy and the new laptop. 'We have some ideas about that.'

She waited for him to expand but he didn't. 'In either case, the man who killed my beautiful boy is still out there?'

'We think so.'

'At least you're honest.'

Sammy came in carrying three cups. 'Ruth, do you have any ideas?' She put milk and one sugar into Ruth's cup and stirred it before handing it over.

'About what? About somebody who might want McAvoy dead? Yeah, a few, like the phone book. McAvoy himself is a dangerous, evil man who took the piss out of us for years. Never forget that.'

Anderson thought of the shadow-faced man on the video, the way the dirty fingers had ruffled the boy's hair, the thumb drawn down the boy's cheek. 'I would have trusted him with my son, the little I know of him.'

Ruth's face seemed to light up. 'Well, you're a fool. What age is your son?'

'Peter? A little older than Callum.' He sipped at his tea, too strong for him, way too strong.

'Than Callum would have been,' Ruth corrected. 'Just a boy, you have?'

'I have a daughter too.'

'A very talented daughter, by all accounts,' said Sammy, smiling over the top of her cup. 'Wants to be an artist.'

'Tough game,' Ruth smiled. 'Fergus was interested in art. The Glasgow Boys.'

Sammy continued, 'Claire works at a gallery in Glasgow on Saturdays, but she's hopeful of getting into art school, Costello was telling me. Helena McAlpine's.'

'You might know her as Helena Farrell,' said Anderson.

'Even I've heard of her.' Ruth's face fell. 'Good. Nice that they do something they want, not something they feel they have to.'

'And what about Callum?' asked Anderson. 'What was he like?'

'Quiet, academic. A little nervous, maybe. Cautious. He was a boy who would spend his life looking before leaping. A nice boy – deserved more, you know. He deserved a life.'

Anderson tried to change tack. 'And you? What kind of kid were you, Ruth?'

She seemed surprised by the question. 'Never academic; I was sporty.'

'How are you keeping now? Do you get out at all?'

'Not really. The neighbour's dog came in through the back door yesterday. I was exhausted walking it back round the corner. Can't get used to having neighbours. Found it difficult to be on my own until I started going to church.' She placed her cup down on the coffee table and seemed to fold back into herself. 'I found some comfort there.'

'And how did you meet Fergus?'

'I ran my car into the back of his, strange but true,' Ruth answered smoothly.

'And Eoin and Fergus met at university?' Anderson asked, noticing the delay before Ruth answered, searching for a lie.

'Yes. Fergus got kicked out but they stayed friends. So you think McAvoy killed this person? He might be around here somewhere, watching us.'

'Do you want protection, Ruth? The Dewars are moving, just in case.'

A small smile played on Ruth's lips. 'I have enough. I don't go out. I can't. I don't open my door. Somebody runs me to church and brings me back. If McAvoy comes near me it will be him who needs protection.'

'You must go out sometimes, shopping.'

'The neighbour goes and gets for me. I'm sure some folk think she lives here, she's in and out that much.' She looked directly at Anderson, then her eye drifted off again. She shivered.

'One strange question, Ruth, have you received anything weird through the post?'

'Like what?' she asked, but her voice quavered a little.

'Like a tarot card on its own?'

She nodded, slowly. 'Thought it was a sick joke. In a black envelope. Death card. I thought it was from those that said I was a witch and all that crap that started flying around.'

'The death card doesn't mean . . .' Sammy started but was stopped by a glare from Anderson.

'So what is that about?'

'We don't know. Do you still have it?'

'Threw it in the fire; they're not Christian.' She looked into the fire for a long time. 'What keeps going round in my head is that Callum saw Robbie get murdered. He was running for his life. He knew he was going to die and I know, deep in my heart, that he was calling out to me. But he died alone. How can I sleep at night, knowing that? Knowing I was sitting round that fire, eating and enjoying myself.' She sniffed. 'That is what I can't live with. Can you imagine what that feels like? Knowing your son died alone, in the darkness?'

'No, Ruth, I can't,' said Anderson.

'Would you mind doing something for me?'

'Yes, of course.'

Ruth's hand went over her mouth. 'It's that I've always wanted to do something to mark the spot, put something there, flowers, but I've never made it back. I don't want him to think that we've ignored him. I do pray, of course I do. But he was a child, he needs to know. Something I could leave there for him, things I have kept . . . A wee cross, his bear maybe. And the anniversary is coming up. I want to do it then. On Saturday.'

In the end they had taken Vik's old Audi – not an old, old Audi, just not a brand-new one. His love of new cars had gone the way of his love of posh flats, victim of the credit crunch. He was sullen and silent most of the drive to Loch Lomond. *Spend half an hour checking it out, getting some bearings* was what Anderson had said. Costello had translated that as *Get that sulking git out from under my feet.*

Costello had tried opening up with a few of the usual conversational gambits about the case, some sarcastic comments about the weather – *the nights are fair drawing in* – and then she asked, 'Why are you so friggin' miserable all the bleeding time?'

'Look who I work with.'

'And are those jeans the best you could do, undercover?'

'So what do athletic coaches dress like?' He held down the front of his green Hollister T-shirt.

'Not in designer jeans.'

'They are the scruffiest things I have.'

Costello looked at the immaculate, unstained Armani jeans, the Converse shoes and wondered, not for the first time, what kind of world Vik lived in.

'I've brought my designer gym bag,' he grumped, then continued to ignore her, rolling his eyes like a petulant teenager asked for the nineteenth time if he was wearing clean pants in case there was an accident. Only when she asked him to take the road to the west side of Loch Lomond did he speak.

'Why up this way?'

'To get a better perspective from the opposite bank,' she replied, fighting with the folds of a recalcitrant map.

'I could do with a better perspective right now,' he muttered before turning up the radio, warnings of traffic jams on the lochside road.

Costello thought he didn't suit being a moody git. His handsome face, with those Johnny Depp cheekbones, suited being mean, smouldering and arrogant. She'd always thought of him as two dimensional, and witnessing him sad and reflective gave a depth to his character that she didn't want to think existed. He usually had the same depth of personality as a fried egg. She turned slightly to look at his perfect profile as he drove, elbow resting on the open window, the blue water of the loch beyond shimmering under a bright blue sky. He could have been a Hollywood pin-up on his holidays.

She asked him to pull in at the car park at Luss and offered to buy him a coffee at the takeaway stall that was well hidden behind the tourist buses. He declined with a dismissive wave of his hand.

She told him to get himself down to the pier where there was a plaque that would tell them which island was which, and that would give them a good sense of the geography of the opposite coast. Rowardennan, Milarrochy Bay, Inchgarten Bay.

Most of all she wanted to get him on his own out on the pier to talk to him, or closer to the water so that she could chuck him in. Maybe even stand on his head until he confessed what was bugging him.

Mulholland watched her go and sighed with relief. A wee woman in jeans, a fleece and hillwalking boots that had never gone further than the local garden centre. Her blonde hair scraped back into a ponytail so small it was ridiculous.

He wished he liked her more. He wished he liked her full stop.

He wished they had a better relationship, like a brother and sister. Then he remembered that Costello's own brother had tried to kill her. It was an effect she had on people.

Dot's killing had not turned up on YouTube for public titillation. Prof O'Hare was struck by the thought that if he was relieved about that, then society was doomed. He finished off the email to Anderson, telling him the preliminary results of the latest tox screen. The victim at Riverview had been a habitual smoker of cannabis, and on the night he died he had a large cocktail of benzodiazepines and something with the chemical spike of amitriptyline. They wouldn't know until the full toxicology tests came back, but that could take weeks. He pre-empted Anderson's question as he typed. 'Depending on the time of ingestion, the victim would have been drowsy and increasingly compliant. Sleepy, maybe to the extent that he lay down of his own free will. Conjecture on my part, but the findings are within the realms of reasonable speculation. He either ingested the drugs himself via overdose of prescription meds or somebody drugged him.'

O'Hare stood up and rubbed the muscle at the back of his thigh. He was sure he had ripped a hamstring while at the crime scene at Riverview. He settled back down in front of his computer with a cup of coffee. He had the DVDs of all three crime scenes and the post-mortem reports of Robert Allan Dewar and Callum Hyslop McCardle, both aged ten. He also had the photograph file of the post-mortem of four-year-old Grace Amelie Wilson. The medical histories of all three children had been delivered and were on his desk somewhere. He spent a couple of minutes shuffling things about, until he had the documentation of each child in different piles for direct comparison. Then he turned on his computer.

His colleague Jo had carried out the posts. They seemed straightforward; both boys had severe impact injuries to the cranium. In both cases the temporal bone had fractured, a free piece impacting the brain. Robbie had suffered more damage than Callum because McAvoy, the killer – the *suspected* killer, O'Hare reminded himself – had had more time. The forensic team had not found any evidence that pointed to McAvoy as the killer. And no evidence that he was not.

All the injuries supported the statement of the one eye witness, Jimmy, the sole survivor.

The blows had been inflicted with a blunt instrument, probably a rock picked up off the beach. He clicked the pictures on, head wound after head wound, lacerations, bald and cold, obscene in their nakedness once the hair was shaved away to leave the splits in the skull open; sable scars on nacreous flesh. Both boys had died by the same hand, probably killed by the same stone.

He looked at the pattern of the bone fragments, imagining McAvoy hitting the children. McAvoy was five feet nine inches tall. Robbie was four feet six, Callum a little shorter.

He then viewed the file on Grace – it had been deemed an accident. There was no evidence to the contrary. He clicked through the images on the DVD as he read; it all fitted a fall from the stone on to the canoe cradle.

He opened the files on the boys, reading his way through them, noticing the dates, looking for any rhythm, any pattern. He sat back then decided to go through the whole lot again.

Vik Mulholland leaned on the rails at the top of the pier, feeling the gentle breeze in his hair and watching the hypnotising darts of silver flash as the sun caught the water. It was a beautiful day. He felt like crying. He dare not turn round, scared that Costello would come back and catch a glimpse of the moisture in his eyes.

All these happy people eating ice cream and drinking coffee pissed him off.

Involuntarily, he felt his hands tighten on the rail, like his brain knew that some evil emotion was gearing up to tell him to jump. It was getting harder to ignore the cold feeling that seeped through him. In truth, it frightened him, that darkness. He had no idea why it was there or how to silence it. Everywhere he went a dark shadow followed; everywhere he went that little voice got louder. One day that shadow would swallow him up. It would consume him and the person he used to be.

He looked down into the water, still, deep, dark. In the past he had never understood why people jumped off bridges or in front of trains, but he was getting the idea now. Oblivion. And that frightened him too. Sonja had got home about three in the morning. He had feigned sleep until he heard her breathing settle into gentle snoring beside him.

A shadow fell over him. For a minute he thought the shadow of his depression was looming large and real, but it was Costello with her usual bad sense of timing. Her boots had been light on the wooden planks, as light as creeping Jesus. She had her sunglasses on. She had bought him an Orangina. Either she was in a good mood or she wanted something.

'You thinking of jumping then?' she said hopefully.

So she wanted something.

'You looked at the thingy? You figured out where we are yet?' She thrust the cold can into his hand then she leaned her back on the rail. He was glad she couldn't look him in the eyes, or maybe she was under those glasses. She pulled the ring on a can of Diet 7Up.

He tried to unwind the fingers of his other hand from the rail; his knuckles had gone white. He had an irresistible urge to allow himself to slide under the rail away from her, into the water, never to be seen again.

'If you're going to be sulky and silent, can you do it in your spare time, please? This is taxpayer's money you're wasting, so friggin' do some work and tell me which one of these islands is Inchgarten.' She waited for him to answer, still looking out over the water. 'And then think about these hotels. It was a Saturday, summer, weddings, guests out for a smoke – they would look across the water, people do. I've not seen any of that in the case notes; I'm wondering how thorough Bernie was with this. We might need guest lists, home addresses. Start plotting who was where when.'

'I don't know where I am.' His words were breathed out on to the wind.

'Physically or metaphorically?' She gulped down a mouthful of 7Up then belched quietly. 'That's better.' A cob swan appeared from under the pier; the pen came out a few seconds later, each hopeful of a crumb. The swans quickly decided the couple on the pier were not worth bothering about and glided elegantly away to the beach, where some American tourists were eating burgers.

'In every way,' he muttered. The words this time floated over the top of his can of Orangina. He was happy for them not to be heard, or to be heard but ignored. Then he could say that he was right and nobody cared. The words were all the substance he had, something that floated on air and disappeared, something without form.

'So how is it going with Sonja?' Costello asked.

She didn't seem to be making fun of him, but with Costello it was difficult to tell.

'Fine. She's great.' He trotted out the platitudes, the expected responses, while what he really wanted to say was, she makes me miserable. She makes me feel old. Then Costello would ask why and he had no answer for that. Then she would interrogate him. He had seen the biggest hardmen fall under her interrogation. Slipping into the water and drowning quietly was looking an attractive proposition.

'She doesn't make you happy, though, does she?' Costello took another noisy slurp.

'What makes you say that?' he snapped.

'Because you are a miserable git when you should be swanning around complaining that you don't get much sleep these days due to excess shagging.'

'You were tired this morning. Was that due to Walker the stalker?'

'That will never happen. It was O'Hare, in fact.' She looked back out to the water.

He stayed quiet, looking down at the rippling carpet, blue on blue. Thinking that the roots of his shadow were down there and getting ready for him.

Costello walked along to the plaque which was supposed to be brass, supposed to be mounted on a wooden plinth. At the moment it was covered in rancid ice cream or something even more disgusting. She tried to keep her imagination from working too hard on that one. It certainly stank. Bits of whatever had got caught in the engraved wording; at least it made it easier to read. She started with 'you are here'. Her eyes flicked up and down over the water, ignoring her own little niggle about the waves that slapped the stanchions of the pontoon. She didn't like it. It make her think of dark, foggy nights, drowning under the ice. She bit her lip to stop the thoughts; she had things to do here, a job of work. She needed to get her brain in gear.

She found Inchgarten, the bay with a small diagram of the Lomondstone – the Rocking Stone, she presumed. It was a drumlin of an island. From this viewpoint it looked like a wedge of cheese. She lifted her binoculars to her eyes. It lay to the north on the opposite side of the loch before it narrowed; from here it looked close to the far shore, but the map indicated that the shore receded at that point. The slow, sandy curve of Inchgarten Bay where the holiday lodges were, where the children had been enjoying their summer holidays . . .

Looking at the map, it was fairly obvious civilization stopped at Rowardennan. The lochside road became a single track and swung away from the water side to skirt the Ben, then went nowhere. The Google street view showed a gate, a no-entry sign on the path that swung away to the left and led to Inchgarten Bay as a single track road. Any walker descending the Ben from that side would meet the road and walk along back to Rowardennan and its coffee shops. And public loos.

Nobody ever went as far as Inchgarten Bay. Costello had heard of it before but would have been hard pushed to find it on a map. *Up around there somewhere . . .*

But Robbie and Callum had died there, wee Grace had died the year before. McAvoy had slipped into his own shadow. She realized why Anderson had wanted them to come down and have a wee reconnoitre.

Something niggled at her. From the sound of it, McAvoy had been well liked and . . . And? Unsophisticated? Was that the word? Yet that scene at Riverbank showed a high degree of planning. She was sure Anderson had been struck by the same thought. Something in the service was very rotten, as Shakespeare might say.

She wondered if the murders had been bad for business. Or perhaps good for business? You never knew with people. They had to knock Fred West's house down before it became a tourist attraction.

There was nothing much to see on the island, even less on the far shore. Just a wee sandy strip, a big rock and trees. She could make out a gap – probably the path that went up to the lodges themselves, a few outbuildings and a house that might be a working farm. A building closer to the water that might be a boat shed then more rocks, more trees and the rise of the Ben. Then it was sheep as far as the eye could see.

Vik joined her, managing to be silent and annoying at the same time. Then he spoke.

'You've met Sonja, Costello, when we had that meal at Tony Macaroni's. Did you like her?'

'Can't say if I liked her. But I didn't trust her. Never trust a woman who doesn't steal your chips.'

O'Hare got fed up and figured he would be quicker driving round to Partickhill and telling them in person. Ten minutes later he met Batten in the main office and asked where Anderson was.

'In his office, he's going out again in five minutes,' said Batten, not able to take his eyes off the pathologist's briefcase.

'Well, this will take four.' He knocked on Anderson's door and opened it without waiting for a response.

'Yes, I know that,' Anderson was saying down the phone. 'I'm afraid I'll have to go; I need to give some attention to some new information.' He put the phone down. 'Which your constant phone calls preclude me from doing.' He looked at his colleagues. 'Professors. I am honoured. Please tell me you have something I can use, either of you.'

O'Hare opened his briefcase and started to explain. In ten minutes Anderson's desk was a chaotic pile of drawings, photographs, files and printouts.

Anderson sat quietly absorbing it all. 'OK,' he said, rubbing at his eyes with the palms of his hands. 'Wyngate has come up trumps by threatening vets with all sorts to release details about their patients. Dead patients. And the Dewars spread their business around when it came to vets. Either they are very unlucky, or their pets are subject to harm and they don't want anybody noticing a pattern.'

'As I would have expected,' said Mick. 'Eoin Dewar?' The

psychologist was already flicking through emails and printouts. 'Cassie, Jerry, Tom, all dogs. Petra, Bubby, both cats. No pet ever reaches old age. Causes of death are both uncommon and unpleasant. The kitten in a car engine, then turning the ignition key.' He pointed at O'Hare. 'And you say all three boys were subject to some kind of abuse while at Inchgarten.'

'Physical abuse, yes. No sign of sexual interference, thank God. They have injuries that may have been sustained by doing their outdoor activities – as the hospital accepted. The Dewar boys go to hospital, Robbie more than Jimmy throughout the year, but Callum doesn't, so it's in the Dewar house. Kids learn what they see. Jimmy is a bully – he might have learned that at the hands of his dad. The bullied go on to bully if they can find a weaker victim.'

'And that points at Eoin. Eoin the big man.'

'And it is never severe stuff, more anxious parent than broken limbs, but when you put it together . . . Burns from the bonfire, banged heads from falling off logs . . .'

'But why would they not say?'

'Why does any victim keep quiet? Fear. Speak out and lose your dad? Some choice.' Anderson was scornful. 'Scared of Eoin, scared of McAvoy. Where they in it together? What the hell was going on up at that campsite?'

Elvie dumped her bags behind the door and watched the undulating figure of Daisy Laphan make its way down the path. If she herself was short on female hormones, Daisy had them to excess. She was lovely, all shining skin and soft, light hair; Daisy looked like she had a halo of springtime round her. If these murders needed a fit and lithe person, then Daisy wasn't in the frame.

She turned to look at the lodge itself. Wooden floors, Swedish style chairs and sofa, a tiny area for a kitchen, but as Daisy said, all the food was served at the Boathouse. The windows had been opened; the only smell was perfume of bleach and furniture polish. It was very clean.

Elvie looked out the window to the loch. The lodge had its own decking in front of the big French window. The voile curtain had been pulled back and halfway down the path she could see something that looked like a whirlpool or a Jacuzzi, protected from the elements by a faded blue plastic cover, which had caught a thick arc of dead leaves. Last year's leaves.

She thought about what it reminded her of. It looked like a town from those old Westerns where everyone had deserted. Daisy was the last woman standing. It was eerie. Elvie could hear Sophie saying, 'Inchgarten Lodge Park welcomes the Grim Reaper.'

She smiled to herself. Sophie was always with her; not even the Grim Reaper had separated her from her sister. Opening her bag, she took out her swimming costume. The weather was very hot but the water in the loch would be one degree above freezing. So she was going to go for a swim. With a wee walkabout first.

Instead of heading down the steps to the path that led to the shore, she cut right across the fronts of the other lodges, looking for signs of life, signs that Warren might be being kept here somewhere. But it all looked rather broken down and dilapidated, cobwebs on the windows, the curtains twisted, the wood needing to be revarnished or restained, peeling paintwork. She passed the front of the Boathouse; the top half of its stable door was open, covered by mesh to keep the flies out. The big table was set for a meal, chairs pulled round, the Welsh dresser covered in odd plates and dishes. Elvie sneaked a look round then scissored over the lower part of the door. Beyond the dining part of the Boathouse was a decent kitchen, not quite professional but set up for more people than Elvie had ever catered for. She stood, looking round and listening to the hum of the fridge freezer and the deeper hum of a generator behind that. It was cool in here.

She walked further back into the Boathouse, which was warmer – because the door was open? She looked out on a huge, well-kept vegetable patch, a few beehives, a small greenhouse and an abandoned wheelbarrow.

She came out the way she went in, and walked down to the shore, passing the house where the boats were kept – which was not called the boathouse. She struggled with that fact but accepted it. As she neared the midden she spotted a man on the hilltop watching her, through binoculars. She waved at him. He waved back so she walked on. The path was worn and seemed public. When it turned sharply right, she ducked into the hedge on the left, to a private place, out of sight of any overseers. Elvie crawled on her knees to get through the dense growth. She judged she must be between the midden and the side wall of the boat shed, parallel with the bay. She stood up again, her back to the hedge. The grass was thick underfoot and smelled as though it was fermenting. Nobody came this way very often. There was the wall of a small outbuilding to her left, a huge apple tree in front of her. Was this the back garden of the farmhouse? It must be here somewhere, hidden away from the holidaymakers. The apple tree was huge, old and gnarled. A wooden seat circled its trunk and round the seat was an abundance of daisies, buttercups, goatweed and dandelions.

Quiet, secluded, private. Could have been miles from anywhere. Hidden. The image of Edward Woodward burning to death in *The Wicker Man* flashed through her mind; Sophie had loved that film.

Keeping close to the hedge, she edged her way to the window at the back of the outbuilding. The black paint of the window frame was fractured and flaked, the glass grimy and covered in cobwebs. A moth-eaten curtain hung off its rail and a white fungus was slowly forming a lace pattern across the bottom of the pane. She leaned into the window, looking through her cupped hand. A dark room, a fireplace, a . . . she struggled to make it out . . . an unmade, huge Victorian bed? And on the top of the high mantelpiece there was a lot of picture frames. Each one held a face, much too far away for her to make out anything but the most basic of details. Little faces.

Little faces of little children.

She carried on with her walkabout; if he asked she would say she was nosey. Before reaching it she noticed the patch of flat land – used for tennis or football or something – through the gap in the large trees that lined the loch side of the path. She noticed three holes in the ground, big enough to break an ankle over. The grass was worn, in a linear strip up to one particular tree. She walked up it and felt the bark, pecked with irregular holes, some grown over, some more recent. Too big for darts. Too random for them to be evidence of something being nailed on. Archery?

The door of the boat shed was lying open, not only open but off its hinges. Inside was a smell of dampness, a huge stack of water sports equipment: canoes, paddles and oars piled up against the wall. On the far side a large fridge and a mouldy pool table. The right wall was a jumble of wellies. She heard the dog bark – somebody was coming. And the stink here was awful. She turned back to the water's edge, ready to slip out of her leggings and

T-shirt and into the cool loch. After that smell she was looking forward to it.

By noon Professor Batten and Mr Peppercorn were sitting together at the lochside like Belle and Sebastian. The dog had been easily bribed with some KitKat. Batten adjusted his hat and continued to watch the figure on the beach – Inchgarten Bay, he presumed. Her hair was wet and she was dressed in leggings and a T-shirt. She was stretching with the grace of a ballet dancer and the strength of an elephant. She was strong, there was no doubt about that, but no amount of strength could stop an arrow through the heart. Wyngate had texted him an update as he got out the taxi. The DNA confirmed that Dotty was Patricia McAvoy, mother of Warren and Alexis McAvoy.

A sick mind was at work here. Sick but clever.

He got up and strolled round the bay towards Elvie, Mr Peppercorn trotting back and forth between them, waving his plumy tail. Elvie was standing on one leg, pulling her other foot up behind her, and he took off his Crocodile Dundee hat.

'Professor Batten?' she asked without changing her posture.

'Indeed, you must be Elvie.'

'Yes.'

'Did they buy your story?' He placed his briefcase down and slipped off his jacket, folding it over the top of the case. Batten was now dressed in jeans and a long-sleeved T-shirt. Then he put his hat back on his head; he could feel his scalp prickle with sunburn.

'Yes. Does that matter?'

'Probably not. This place is deserted,' said Batten conversationally.

'It is now.' They were standing on the shore, looking out towards the island. 'What do you want me to do?'

'I want you to go and explore the island.'

Elvie looked back at the psychologist in his jeans, his briefcase at his feet. 'OK.'

'So row out to Snooky Bay, then follow my instructions.'

'Why? The place has been searched many times.'

'You can only find something if you know that you are looking for it.'

'What am I looking for?'

'No idea.'

'That is not logical.'

'I want you to run through the events of that evening, forgive the pun.'

She didn't flicker.

'Three of the four people involved have never given testimony. The one that did was a terrified child.'

Elvie bounced on her toes a few times. 'OK.'

He pointed out over the water. 'There are over sixty islands out there. They have wallabies, graveyards, churches and white deer, follies, all kinds of things, but they do appear and disappear as the water rises and falls. It had been dry for days before the boys were killed. And as the witchcraft theorists relate, the heavens opened the minute Jimmy got back to the mainland, like they had conjured up the downpour to get rid of the evidence. The run-off from the land into the Faloch, the Fruin and the Endrick rivers meant that the water level rose considerably. And it drizzled on and off for the following week. Who knows what they missed because it was under water?'

Elvie started to walk down the shore. 'And they have missed it for a whole year?'

He noted that strange quality, asking a straight question without a hint of criticism. 'Maybe. It depends where they were looking.'

She looked at him. 'Why do you wear that hat?'

Elvie paddled out to the island on the Dreamcatcher, paddling it one to the right, two to the left to keep on course for the island. Once clear of the protection of the bay, the wind picked up. The sun was hot but the wind-chill made her eyes water. Once she reached the obvious landing ground, the sandy patch on the south edge of the island locally called Snooky Bay, she pulled the canoe up on the middle of the sandy beach and walked through the narrow path in the long grass to the two big rocks. And looked around. She was sheltered from the wind here. The sun warmed the skin at the back of her neck. She could hear some noisy insects buzzing away over her head and flipped them away with an open palm. Across the water she could see Batten, sitting on the Rocking Stone where he had a clear view of the island, his face in the shadow of the big hat.

She switched the phone on, attached the earpiece then clipped her phone to her waistband. 'Can you hear me OK?'

'Yes, OK. The weather's lovely here, how about you?'

'The same.' Deadpan.

'Elvie, I want you to imagine you—'

'Not good at that.'

'Well, go exploring; where would you run?'

'OK. Going to my right takes me along the beach. In front of me is the start of the cliff. To the left is a kind of wall thing that runs from the rock face into the water.'

'Can you get over that? It's an old folly, Elvie. From the photos I've seen it's supposed to look like an old castle.'

'It looks like a wall. Of a castle.' She made her way over to it, climbing through thorns and bushes, and patted the old stones of it with her hand. 'It's too high to climb over. Hang on. There's a convenient boulder to stand on. The wall has a tall, narrow aperture in it, like they had for firing arrows through.'

Batten barked down the phone. 'An archer's hole?'

'If you say so. Do you want me to get over it? It's the only way forward from here. There's no other reason to hang about on the bay.'

'If you can get over the wall, then go.'

'It's bloody high.'

'I was told you were fit.'

Elvie sprang off the stone and got a hold on the floor of the arrow slit, then scrambled up and over the top, dropping down on the other side. Even for her it took a fair bit of effort.

'This side is much lower than the other; the ground is wet and marshy. It's quite a drop. I can see a vague path . . .'

'OK, so follow it. Talk to me as you go, what you're seeing?' Batten knew she should start describing the Jungle, part of the island that was largely overgrown and inhospitable.

'The path goes through the woods up to Snooky Hill, small trees overhead. Steep rock to my right, like a cliff. The water is right on my left, it looks deep. Ahhh, I can't go straight ahead, the rock is jutting out here.'

'Left?'

'Immediate left is a narrow path with a drop about a foot, right at the water.'

'Go that way then.' He heard a rustle and an impact.

'OK, I am now battering back bushes and stuff, getting scratched to blazes.'

'Keep going; can you see anything of the campsite?'

'No, I'm right on the other side of the island with Snooky Hill in between, and about four feet below is a maze of bushes and ferns and bracken, all kinds. My feet are wet.'

'So you might be below the water table. Where do you fancy going now?'

'North-west.'

'Why, is it less dense there?'

'The path goes that way. There's no way the boys could have come this way – they would have been covered in scratches.'

'They *were* covered in scratches – that's why they called it the jungle. Keep going.'

'This is getting overgrown and nasty.'

'It's the only way to the north side.'

'Shit!'

'What?'

'That hit me in the face, nearly took my eye out.'

'Oh, I thought something important had happened.'

Elvie cursed over the phone and battered some branches out of her way in anger. Then she saw something lying in the mud, muddy brown and half rotten but folded, the material making peaks in the undergrowth. She picked it up between her thumb and forefinger and shook it out. 'I've found a top. Might have been green once.'

'Means nothing, but I'm beginning to like you, hen.' Batten began to text back to Wyngate at the incident room – a single question, and one line of text. He could hear Elvie breathe heavily out on the island. 'And?'

'And it is overgrown above ground but if I look down, the ground is clearer, as if there has been a narrow pathway at one time. I'm not looking for a body, am I?'

'No, the dogs would have found it last summer.'

'Good.'

'Unless it was washed away and washed back up again. The currents here are famous for that. Keep going. You're a wee kid on an adventure.'

'No, I am not.'

'Keep going, or are you getting tired?'

'No.' She pushed her way forward. The foliage got thicker, the ground was slippier. The rocks had been wet until very recently.

Batten's phone beeped. 'Light green T-shirt. Army colour.' He was congratulating himself that his hunch might be right when he heard a gasp and the sound of something falling, like a sack of potatoes hitting the ground. Then some extreme swearing.

'Well, I'm much lower now. I've fallen about six feet. Don't think I've broken anything.'

'You OK?'

'Yeah. It's slimy here. Looks like it could get covered by water most of the time.'

'Keep going.' Batten had to keep the excitement from his voice.

He heard her footfall cease, her breathing went quiet. 'Prof? There's something here, a pair of doors. Half-submerged, two doors hidden behind loads of greenery.'

'Can you see the far shore?'

'Too overgrown.'

'Can you open the doors?'

'Not without getting very wet.'

'So get wet then.'

She slipped her feet in, soaking her trainers and her leggings to above her knee. She reached forward and tried to yank the doors open. The wood was damp and rotten, covered with green moss. 'The hinges are rusty, one of them has been pulled off. It's twisted.'

'Can you still be seen by somebody high on the hill?'

'No. I've a canopy of leaves over me. This stinks of damp wood and animal shite, and it's all rank rotten. I'm standing in brown mulch.'

'Is there a roof?'

'There are some bits of decayed wood, covered in green moss, good camouflage.'

'Can you get in?'

'You want me to go in there? Bloody hell . . .' Elvie knelt down into the stinky brown water; a cloud of insects flew out. She waited for them to fly away and then leaned forward, sticking her head into the heavy warm air. 'It's a hut half built in the water. I can see the loch out the other side, it sits about six inches above the surface of the water. The rest is solid, well solidish. I can see bracken and trees round there.'

'But open water beyond.'

'Must be, I'm very close to the waterline where I'm standing. Can't see much – it's very dark.'

'Is it big enough to hold a boat?'

'Barely. Oh, wait . . .'

'What?'

'On the far corner there's some yellow casing. It's all faded, mottled and brown round the edges. Emergency yellow, though. It might be a canister for a life raft. The small ones, the ones that blow up? It's empty.'

Batten dropped the phone to his knee and looked over the water. 'Empty. So now we know.'

Batten waited patiently, enjoying the sun and the solitude, the slap and chatter of the waves on the rock. He heard the phone buzz.

'Hi, I've taken the photos.'

'Great, could I ask one more thing? Just to prove a point. Swim through the boathouse, come out the other side and find out what's your quickest way back to land. Take the Bluetooth off. I'll be keeping an eye out for you; as soon as I see you from this vantage point, you can swim back to the island.'

'Why?'

'It's interesting.'

'OK.' She battered her way through the waterside of the door, pushing hard with her arms. Then she was plunged out to the cold waters of the loch, deep, dark water underneath her. One hard push and she was out of her depth and into the sunshine. She listened, sensing the way the water was moving, getting her bearings. She needed to go north, north-east to get past the northern tip of the island.

She swam strongly, noticing the change in the current; not so easy to swim out from the shelter of the island. But after about ten minutes she had cleared the north end of the island and turned to look at the shore, saw Batten and raised her arm to wave at him.

He didn't seem to be paying any attention so she trod water for a while, waiting.

Then he turned and saw a distant, elegant arm moving to and fro like a lone flower being blown in the wind. She was fit, strong, a good swimmer and dressed appropriately. How strong a swimmer was McAvoy? How did he fare in the power of the solstice current, the strength of the wind? In water that killed most people within a few minutes of immersion.

He watched the arm, back and forth, back and forth, raised his own in response and she was gone, under the water.

Waving or drowning?

Anderson got the nod that Lexy McAvoy was now in one of the interview rooms. He cursed and looked at his watch. He had to have an important transatlantic conversation first.

The big man sitting in his house somewhere in Connecticut looked right back at him. Anderson had no idea what he was thinking. He was a good-looking American in the De Niro mould. Ridiculously square jawed, ruggedly handsome in his late fifties with black hair sprouting wings of grey, a third generation Italian American. He could see Warren in him, though, diluted but there all the same. He was the shadow of his dad.

Geno DiMarco leaned forward and cleared his throat. Anderson was treated to a hundred-watt smile. With perfect teeth.

No wonder Patricia McAvoy had succumbed to his charms. In the greyness of the biscuit factory where she had worked, Geno would have been a lively spark.

'I'm sorry I have so little news for you.'

'Yip, I'm following it in your press. First my boy was dead but now he isn't?' His fingertips tapped out a beat on the leather top of his desk.

'Somebody went out of their way to make us think that he was dead.' Anderson let the question hang.

Over the Skype, Geno's head disappeared for a moment. Then returned. He looked worried. 'I don't know my boy, Mr Anderson. You think he's killed some kids? That's a hard one to take.'

'He's never been convicted of any crime,' Anderson said. 'But I have some bad news for you. We found Patricia. She was dead, murdered.'

'Little Patty? Jesus.' He covered his eyes with his hands, liver spotted and wrinkled, much older than his face. 'You know, I'd been looking for Patty for a while. Then the agency found Lexy. And

Lexy found Warren, or so I thought. I've not heard from Lexy . . . she OK?'

'She's OK, we know where she is. Is she like her mother?'

The American shook his head. 'Not at all. Patty was a hoot, a real fun girl.'

'So why did you want to find your son now, after all this time? Thirty years? It's a long time to decide to come back into his life.'

The man across the Atlantic leaned forward. 'I never knew about him, it was Patty I was looking for. I lost my wife.'

'I'm sorry. Did you have any children?'

He shook his head.

Anderson was not going to be swayed away from the difficult question. 'Mr DiMarco, have you ever met Warren? In the flesh, I mean?'

'Nope,' he shook his head. 'Facebook, Skype. But I have sent over money every month, well, to Lexy for Warren. He was Skyping me every second day for the last, oh . . . eighteen months or so . . .'

'Every month? Eighteen months,' Anderson repeated, wondering how much money had changed hands. What was this worth to Lexy?

'Mr DiMarco, can you tell me who you think this is?' Anderson held up a photo of the body from Riverview Farm, Mr Field.

'That's Warren. Well, that is Warren on Skype.' DiMarco nodded.

'He's not your son, I'm sorry.'

'Sorry for what? Lexy scamming me for money? She played me; I kinda admire that. But I had my money's worth, though – I got to talk about Patty. My Patty, Patty McAvoy.' He puffed his chest up a little. Then crumpled. His eyes darted down to the picture frame on the desk. 'This was my wife, Daria.'

'I'm sorry,' Anderson repeated.

DiMarco smiled to himself. Anderson got the impression that he was lonely.

'I want you to find Warren. And find the guy who murdered his mother.'

'And if they are one and the same?'

He shrugged. 'You have to do what needs to be done.'

Anderson thanked him and closed the Skype connection. He sat looking at the face in the photograph, the face who was not Warren.

'So how was he?' asked Sammy, appearing at his shoulder, close enough he could smell her perfume.

'Fine, he seems a nice bloke, vulnerable. Perfect victim for a scam.' He walked over to the board and picked up the marker pen, standing thinking, his pen tapping on his chin.

She turned to watch him, like he was a teacher giving a private lesson.

'So,' he tapped the picture of the burned body, 'this is Warren McAvoy's mother, but this,' he tapped the picture of the body from Riverview Farm, Mr Field. 'This is not Warren. The DNA tells us that. This is the man in the scam. Where the hell does Bella come into all this?'

'If she does at all. You think Lexy took the poor sod for a fortune?'

'He was ripe for the taking. We'll deal with Lexy later. So,' he looked back at the board, 'we have gone full circle. We are right back to the night of the summer solstice. That was the last time anybody saw McAvoy alive, and since then he has been . . .'

'The shadow man.'

Elvie had said goodbye to Batten and had a shower up at the lodge. Then she set up the laptop in the small, cool bedroom on the dressing table. The machine beeped immediately: Gaynor Matthews, the Tattoo Boy's sister, was asking for an update. She thought her mum was holding on, just waiting for her son to walk in the door. Elvie knew that cancer took its own destructive course. It didn't wait for any errant family members to put in an appearance. But she also knew she couldn't say that.

Amy Lee's chat box started to blink as soon as Elvie logged on. She didn't seem to want an update, just a chat. Her brown hair and wide smile flashed at the bottom of the screen. Elvie typed, mindful that she needed to work on her communication.

Sorry, Amy Lee, I've been busy, I'm up at the loch. She thought of a link, something that might make electronic small talk. *Loch Lomond is the home of the Colquhouns. Or Cohoon, as you lot like to drop the unused vowels.*

Hiya! AL here, how u doing. I've gotta be quick. Yip, Grandpappy, like really old dude, did spell his name different. What a nerdy nerd. So you on the loch then, you getting your feet wet ☺ Is it as awesome as it looks? Grandpappy doesn't know but I took his phone and looked at all the photos and the videos. A few of the loch. One's dead dark. But it would have been dark as it was night-time, midnight ☺*. It was all a bit scary . . . what is it doing today?*

Today it is sunny and sparkly. When was Grandpappy last here?

Last year, for his b'day so we don't have to buy him cake ☺ *He should be reducing as he has a bad knee. And a bad attitude. You have a Grandpappy?*

What kind of question was that? No I don't, you are very lucky. But I've found something out for you. Just a quick Google search of the embarkation records. On 30 September 1934, two Colquhouns sailed, father and son. The age is right; both of them gave their hometown as Glasgow. That was on the Caledonia, a steam ship, sailed out of Greenock.

Oh, would that be right? Grandpappy says he wasn't from Glasgow but a place called Govan with big fields and cows and mountains and stuff, you know that place? The Colquhouns had a castle there. Back in the day . . .

Yip, I know it. I think we might be talking about the same person though. Can you tell me, does your Grandpappy sometimes tell porkies?

???

Lies, fibs.

All the time! ☺

Lexy was sitting in the interview room, drinking a mug of coffee and twitching for a cigarette.

Sammy Winterston sat opposite her; Anderson wanted her to lead on this one.

'I remember you,' said Lexy, a sly look on her pasty face, 'Oh yeah, I remember you from last year, you and Bernie the Bonker.'

'His name is DCI Webster,' Sammy bristled.

'Aye, whatever.'

'We have a problem, Lexy. I'll cut the crap. We know that the body is not that of your brother. End of.'

She shrugged.

'So can you tell us who that young man in the morgue is, please?'

Lexy folded her arms. 'I thought he was my brother.'

'No, you identified him as your brother, when you knew it was not. Why?'

There was a flicker . . . 'I didnae say that, you did.'

'No, Lexy, you said it, not us.'

'I thought it wis, I really thought it wis.'

Sammy said quietly, her voice softer, 'You got really upset when you saw that face, and when you realized who it actually was. That was somebody you cared for.'

Lexy shook her head, the fringe bounced. 'I thought it was Warren. I told you, I haven't seen him for ages.'

'According to Geno DiMarco, you saw him last week. He can't have changed that much.'

That got a reaction. The imaginary cigarette flicked up but her lips only found her fingertips. So she rearranged her fringe instead. The minutes ticked by. 'OK, I was keeping that quiet. I was making a few bob. My brother and I were making a few bob, so what? But I thought it was Warren, you had said it was Warren. I couldn't see his face proper, so I didnae want to look. So I presumed it was him.'

'So the man on the table, the dead man, is the man who Skyped?' asked Sammy.

'Aye. My brother.'

It was Anderson who spoke this time. 'No, it isn't, Lexy, and if you sign a statement to that effect, when the DNA says otherwise, you will be in deep shite.' He took a deep breath. 'You've never done time, have you, Lexy? You won't like it.'

Lexy became a little more wary. And then the hand came up to flutter with the fringe again, the little tell of deceit.

'Right, so you still are telling us that the man lying dead in the morgue is your brother and he was the man who claimed to be your brother when Skyping Geno DiMarco. Or scamming Geno DiMarco. Just so I am sure, Lexy.'

'He gave us money. It was the right thing to do; he was his son.'

'No, he wasn't, Lexy.' Anderson made his voice sound tired and irritated; it wasn't hard.

But Lexy was defiant. 'Yes, I hadn't seen my brother for ages. I thought that man was him, in fact I still do. And I'm not saying anything more or signing anything until I see a solicitor.' And she folded her arms over her chest. It was the end of the interview. As far as she was concerned.

Sammy stood up to go. Anderson followed her, then paused and walked back to the table. He leaned right over Lexy. 'I'm getting fucking pissed off with this. I don't give a shit about you or your brother, but we have another body in the morgue – your mother. Don't worry, we won't ask you to identify that body seeing you're crap at it. And you haven't seen her for a while. She died a horrible, slow, painful death. And here's the weird thing, she had a tarot card too. Like yours. So think on. We'll get a car to take you home. And when you get home you can have a long think about any strange incidents over the last few days, anybody walking up your garden path that shouldn't have. Any little knocks on the door, pizza you never ordered. They only need to get lucky once. Once. But you take care now. A lot of care.'

He shoved the folder at her, a buff folder that contained one photograph of a mutilated body lying in a field.

And he left the room.

'That was cruel,' said Sammy.

'Well, I'm getting fucking nowhere being nice.'

Costello presumed this was the right place. A flat field up a narrow winding lane, and lots of trees. The only car she had seen for six miles was a taxi and she had nearly driven into that, much to Vik's horror. Single track road and all that. But Costello could see the Polo parked in the only bit of shade in the entire field. She looked round, they could have been anywhere. Costello knew Vik hated trees, and countryside and all that shite. She was going to enjoy this. She got out the car, Vik pulling his backpack from the rear seat as Costello lifted her shoulder bag. 'So your protégée is already here,' Costello looked round. 'Yip, there's a sign.'

'Bloody hell, they don't make it obvious, do they?'

'Bernie says quite clearly in his notes that they do no publicity. God knows how folk find out about it. Or how they make money. Probably wife swapping or witches' city breaks. Or Tupperware. That can be the work of the devil.' They walked slowly along a grassy path that darkened as the sunlight became dappled by the branches overhead. The path was well worn. It brought them to a wooden footbridge rising high over a small stream. Mulholland looked at the bank of the burn; the water was running lower than normal at the moment. He leaned on the handrail looking down into the water, enjoying the sun on his back, the quiet buzz of insects underneath him.

'Is there any news on Bernie yet?' he asked. 'I mean, is this dangerous?'

'Nope, he has vanished into thin air. And of course this is dangerous. You don't think he found something about this place and they turned him into a frog? That is definitely Elvie's Polo; I recognize that wee sticker of Elvis on the back. She'll look after you. But don't take her on over a hundred metres, your ego will never recover.'

'I do have my own lodge, don't I?' he said, pulling himself away from the bridge, their footfall hollow on the wood.

'Not exactly,' and with that Costello swung her bag over her shoulders and walked away.

They heard a dog barking in the distance.

'So the dog would have barked in the night,' said Mulholland to himself.

He watched her go. Hating her and her existence. Now he had to stay at this bloody Lodge Park. Nobody was going to buy their shitty story. All that was happening was the holiday camp was short of money and they were taking advantage of having another two guests. Waste of time. Waste of money.

But he had forty-eight hours at the loch, in the sunshine. Life could be worse. He would be away from the rest of them, away from Costello, away from Sonja. Elvie McCulloch was a wordless mutant.

Yes, it could be worse.

He left the bridge and started to walk down the path, into the deep cover of the trees, sounds of wildlife everywhere. He stuck his iPod and Gogo Street in his ear so he didn't have to listen. Elvie would be out most of the time; Costello had said that and it rang true. She would be running and swimming; Vik could please himself.

He planned to sit down with a paperback thriller and stopwatch and scrutinize all the comings and goings. Of the owners; Tony and Daisy Laphan, and anybody else who was hanging about. They had given him a good video camera; it was maybe not such a mad idea after all.

He sighed as he followed the narrow path towards the water, feeling the warmth of the sun relaxing his shoulders. Suddenly he was right at the water's edge with the loch glistening in front of him, crystal clear. It twinkled in the sunshine, triangles of shimmering light dancing across the water. He stood for a good few minutes listening to Gogo Street singing about the uncrossable mile, it was fitting. He was going to walk away but the weight of his rucksack held him back slightly, like a hand resting on his shoulder. Then he saw Costello standing slightly higher, on the grassy part of the beach. So he sat down on a large jutting rock and waited.

Costello ran the binoculars over the water again. Some idiot was swimming, a strong swimmer who was obviously insane. And obviously Elvie. That water would be freezing one inch below the surface. There had been another drowning that morning, a man dipping into a reservoir to cool down. Costello watched the slow, effortless stroke, the regular breathing. Elvie was a fair distance away, but clearly visible.

She stopped suddenly, a flash of flesh in the water as she flicked over. Costello watched carefully, thinking Elvie might have cramp and get into trouble. But Elvie bobbed up again a few feet further on, swimming back the way she came. Just lengths in the water. Costello continued to watch, mesmerised by the elbows turning over with a perfect rhythm. Then the elbows stopped, a black-haired head popped up, a glance at a watch on the wrist then a casual breast-stroke to the shore, where she walked out of the water, strong legs climbing the rocks on to the sandy shore.

Costello continued to watch as Elvie bent down to pick up a towel and began drying her hair. She looked from the lithe, muscular figure of Elvie to Mulholland in his designer Wayfarers, Hollister T-shirt and Armani jeans. How much would it cost to bug the single lodge she had booked for them both?

She jumped at a tap on her shoulder, the scent of patchouli oil in the air.

'She puts on a good show, doesn't she?'

'Makes me tired watching her. Have you had a fruitful time, Mick?'

The psychologist's face was grave. 'We need to get back to the station, now. If you look over my left shoulder, do you see somebody?'

'No.'

Mick shuffled round a wee bit. 'Now? Small guy, faded blue T-shirt, sitting on the hill up there, binoculars.'

'Oh yeah, I see. Is he that Tony bloke?'

'Maybe, we need to get going.'

'Yeah, come on. I'm driving Vik's car so we might not survive.'

'You can always—'

His voice was cut off by a scream coming from the water. They both stood still, watching Elvie get up and run.

Bernie woke up, still in his cold, dark place. The concrete walls seemed to be closing in on him. He got the impression that it was daylight somewhere, just a warmth about the air. It made the stench of his shit and urine much worse. He would have been sick, but he had nothing to be sick with. His water bottle was empty, mouth and eyes were dry. His tongue felt like an old slipper. His mum used to say that.

Strange how she floated into his thoughts, hadn't seen her for a few months, a year . . . was it more than a year? Lyn went to see her every week . . . but couldn't recall the last time he . . .

He closed his eyes against the dense darkness. It clawed at his eyelids, at his skin. He had no idea where he was, and that was what bothered him. He had been involved in murder investigations for over twenty-five years. How often had he walked witnesses through the experience? Teased little details from them that they didn't realize they knew? He now tried it on himself. He came up with bugger all. He had driven into the lane, got out the car and some mugger hiding behind the dumpster had hit him over the back of the head. They had stolen his jacket, his wallet. He was lying in a gutter cushioned by dumpster overspill . . . and that was as far as he had got. So why was he not still there? Why was he here in some kind of garage with concrete walls, concrete floor, and no windows? He was held with chains that fastened his wrists in front of him, a connecting chain to his ankles. Once his eyes had got used to the darkness, and had regained focus from the concussion, he found he could make out a few shapes.

He had been drugged. Maybe they had put something in the water. As time had passed, the water had run dry and his mind had cleared.

He tried to concentrate. He could hear traffic outside, which sometimes got louder as a single car came close then passed, moving slowly as if going to park. He heard a few bangs and scrapes, in close succession, then back to the traffic. It did strike him that they had not taped his mouth, which they would have if there was anybody about to hear him scream.

'Will he be all right?' asked Costello as Vik lay on the ground, very pale and very shivery.

'I think he has broken his fibula,' said Elvie.

'I don't think he's very good with pain. How did he manage to fall over nothing?' Costello was stifling a laugh.

Batten pulled her to one side. 'Well, he wouldn't be the first one to fall off the Rocking Stone, would he?'

'No, not at all.' Her voice suddenly serious.

'I think I need to tell you something,' said Batten, watching Vik wince. 'If that chap we saw was Anthony Laphan, then he used to be a doctor – older, greyer, but definitely him. He passed me as he went up the hill.'

Costello nodded. 'Sorry, means nothing.'

'Get Wyngate on to it. He killed a child. Not intentionally, medically, but how many child killers do you get round a bonfire at Loch Lomond? You need to look into that.'

Costello spoke briskly to Wyngate on her mobile as her eyes drifted past Batten, but the man had disappeared. 'And how old was the child?'

'Four or five.'

'Christ.' Costello repeated that to Wyngate, hearing his fingers clatter on the keyboard, and added, with Batten's prompting, the information about the pale green vest that Elvie had brought from the island. 'Great, bye,' and she cut the call. 'Same age as Grace. And he still can't find Fergus McCardle at any university, even on enrolling day.' She was quiet for a few moments. There was the singing of the birds, and the slap of the waves.

'You are sure that's him?'

'Positive. We'd better get Vik to hospital.

Costello walked behind them as Elvie and Mick got the stricken Mulholland to his feet and half carried, half frog-marched him back to the car. The ten-minute walk took over half an hour. If Mick was right, Tony Laphan had not flagged up in the original investigation. Why?

Once in the clearing, Vik was deposited in the back seat of the car as Costello's phone went. 'Hi, Col?' She sat on the bonnet of the car and listened.

'I'll be brief. Thea Delany. Killed by an overdose of antibiotic administered by an overworked junior doctor called Anthony Laphan. It was big news at the time, late nineties. Medical mismanagement. Thea's senior consultant suggested putting the drug in spinally, which Tony did. Without reducing the volume. Thea died a few hours later. It was all very sad, but the prof in question was quoted as saying Tony hadn't checked what he said, while saying off the record that the kid was going to die anyway. So he became the villain of the piece as the overworked junior quietly had a nervous breakdown. He was an exemplary young doctor. Career ruined. The case changed the way notes are recorded, the way case discussions and the decisions made are finalized. But a very promising career was in tatters and a child died. The senior consultant was a bit too keen to get to the golf club rather than hang around and supervise his juniors. Wyngate has dug up a lot of stuff, which Bernie either missed or dismissed. Extra sad as Thea was a much treasured child, the result of years and thousands of pounds of fertility treatment. Thea's parents bore no ill will to Laphan; they even took up his offer of a holiday at the campsite. What the hell is that terrible noise?'

'Nothing really, it's only Vik. We're heading to the hospital, the Vale. Don't worry, he fell off the Rocking Stone and broke his leg. Made of chocolate.'

'What?'

'Yup. He fell off the same stone that Grace did.'

She heard Anderson move round at the other end of the phone.

'How long do you think you're going to be there?'

'Well, Dr Crippen and Florence here say that's he's fractured his fibby something; it will need a plaster but no op. A couple of hours should do it. I have Mick with me; he has a theory about how Warren got off the island. And Elvie found a bit of clothing. It's good stuff. What do you want me to do? Chase up Tony?'

Anderson was silent for a moment. 'Not yet. I presume Vik will want to go home now?'

'No, I think he wants to get back to Inchgarten. His mum lives four flights up, remember. The lodge here is on the flat.' She started to whisper. 'I think Vik would be better being involved. It could really work in our favour. And Mick wants Wyngate to source the original interview material of Eoin and Jimmy Dewar.'

'Anything else he wants? Jam on it? My arse in a pie?'

'You should be glad that your team are so dedicated, working with broken limbs and while being bitten alive by midges.'

'So while Vik is in the Vale, you go to the local nick. I am going to email them with the photo of Mr Field. Take it round as many of the hairdressers in Balloch as you can. Try and get a name. Bernie's surveillance team never clocked Lexy and Mr Field together, so that, and the wedding band, suggest a covert relationship. If they were avoiding being seen in the area, that might suggest the wife lives nearby and they didn't want to risk running into her.'

'You'd know, being the expert on having affairs,' muttered Costello.

'Young guy, trendy haircut, done in the last week, O'Hare reckons.'

'And this is Lexy's friend? Mr Field?'

'I think so, and we have found Bernie's car in Asda car park, Govan.' Anderson paused. 'And no sign of Bernie. No signs of violence either. Just be careful, you're on Bernie's patch now, don't antagonise people. What is that awful noise?'

'Vik screaming again. Nothing to do with his leg, he's screaming 'cause I'm sitting on the bonnet of his car.'

Anderson looked at the wall. There was now a manhunt out for DCI Bernard Wilson Webster, supervised by uniform at Partick. Bernie's handsome, sweaty face was on the board now. Suspect? Victim? It was difficult to know. His wife and his colleagues had no knowledge of him receiving a tarot card, but it was hardly the kind of thing that would crop up in casual conversation.

He was now wondering what column Warren McAvoy belonged in.

He wiped a space clean with the cloth and wrote 'Michael Anthony Laphan AKA Tony' above it. He reached over and found the CD he was looking for – the pictures of the search of the island on Sunday, 23rd June 2013, the day after the boys went missing. He had scanned through these before, but he looked again. Photographs of a crime scene that were not any scene in particular. He clicked on and on. Mostly around the sites where the bodies of the two boys had lain a few hours before. Anderson noted Sammy and Bernie standing on the periphery, standing very close. Another with them laughing. It couldn't be all doom and gloom at a crime scene, but laughter like that in front of the crime scene photographer was not best practice – not when the press were after your balls. He clicked on . . . Sammy and Bernie, Bernie and Sammy. Eyes locked, some looking at the crime scene, some laughing with each other. Bernie dressed in a light suit, shirt and tie with his trousers tucked into wellies. Sammy with some kind of hillwalking boots on, a dark suit, plain jacket and a pale green collarless top underneath. He clicked on through the day, following the path of the photographer on Snooky Bay where Callum died. Then on the Scoob round the folly, more photographs from the site of Robbie's death on the other side. The photographs were timed at three p.m.; the bay at Inchgarten was in the distance. The photographer had taken a few shots to get the distance and the lie of the land, the Narrows – and the beach. Another of Sammy and Bernie, his hand on her elbow. Not walking on uneven ground. Not moving at a pace. He switched to a piece of video, a panning shot showing the island closest to the bay. And the rocks. The edge had caught Bernie and Sammy high on the grassy dunes, his hand still on her elbow. Both standing still. Anderson thought how many times he had touched Costello's elbow and in what circumstances. To guide her. To warn her. To shut her up when she was heading towards Karen Jones. He had grabbed O'Hare by the elbow at the Boden Boo when he had stumbled.

Sammy turned to look at the camera. Something was different about her – hair pulled by twigs, flushed, her jacket buttoned right up. Right up. On a hot summer day? He closed in, then flicked back to the pictures at the start of the day. He printed out both and asked Sammy to come in to see him. Sometimes he hated his job.

'Hi, sit down.'

She sat smiling, legs crossed, slowly, she was a little nervous. Anderson didn't say anything. Sometimes it was better not to. You learned more that way. He put both the pictures in front of her. She looked from one to the other, a bright ball of embarrassment blooming in each cheek as Anderson used the tip of his pen to point to the vest top, then the lack of it.

'Oh,' was the only word through her lips.

'Oh, indeed. I have a problem, Sammy. DI Costello is coming back here with a top she describes as a light green vest top. When Warren was last seen he was wearing a green coloured T-shirt from an army surplus shop. Two things that can be described in a similar way but are quite different. What am I going to say to the forensics lab when it comes back with your name as a DNA match? Or can you spare me the expense?'

'It's mine.' She didn't expand further, just kept her eyes on the photograph. 'We were searching the island, over on the far side. I took my jacket off and tied it round my waist, and then my top got ripped, right down the front.'

'And you left it at the crime scene?'

'I took it off; it was covered in all sorts of bugs. Then put my jacket back on. I'm not sure where I was when I noticed I had dropped my top. It was disgusting that day, really hot. The rain had been torrential, it was a quagmire.' She shrugged, looking at him but not right in the eye. She fiddled with her bracelet, making that bloody Tinkerbell noise.

He tapped the desk with his pen. 'For your own safety, I don't want you leaving this station. Can you look out the interviews that feature Eoin Dewar? All of them. In order. And the file on Michael Laphan and the Delany family. You'll find the connection easily enough.' He added, 'Batten is a busy man.'

'Of course,' she said lightly, but it didn't seem news to her.

'And tell me, have Eoin, Isobel or Ruth phoned in to see how we are progressing?'

'No,' she answered. 'There's no word on Bernie yet, is there?'

'No more word, just the car, sorry. You'll be the first to know when there is.'

The internal phone rang, allowing Sammy to get to her feet and leave.

'Hi, it's Bobby on the front desk. The lovely Lexy McAvoy has come back in – she doesn't want to go home.'

'Good, stick her in the interview room.' He put the phone down. It was nice when a plan came together. He fancied another wee chat with Lexy. Without Sammy being present.

After dragging a bald man round various hairdressers with names like Hair Rods, Gold E Locks and the Dome Domain, Costello eventually struck lucky in a monochrome salon called Curl Up And Dye where Pharrell Williams was being happy. None of the staff were.

Costello recognized the name of the salon and asked for the badly spelled Shinaid. She turned out to be a teenager, blonde, her hair stripped of all colour, and she nodded at the picture of the man with Lexy – her image having been removed – stating that 'he was one of ours'.

An older woman, with blue talons for nails, immediately stopped her blow-drying and came over. 'Who wants to know?'

Costello flashed her warrant card. 'We want to know if you cut this man's hair; it would have been last week sometime,' she said, recalling O'Hare's words about a very recent haircut.

'I'm not sure that we can tell you that information.'

'Oh, I assure you that you can. And will. He's dead and all confidentiality died with him.' She slid another photograph over the top of the one that had been part of Lexy's, showing the battered, dead face of Mr Field. She tilted it so only the older woman saw it, then slid the 'Lexy' picture back over it.

'Oh my God. Eddie, Eddie Taylor. I cut his hair myself.'

'Address?'

The blue talons tapped at the keyboard. 'The address is 128 McInnes Street.'

'That's Lexy McAvoy's address.'

The woman nodded. 'Yeah, they live together. She's in here a lot, her fringe needs a lot of maintenance.' She smiled, being helpful now as everybody in the shop was listening, straining to hear over the noise of hairdryers and Pharrell Williams.

'Did he seem local?'

'Yeah, he's a wee chatterbox. He spoke to anybody.'

Costello caught the inflection. 'Anybody?'

'Even the weirdoes, you know, them on the hill.' She had lowered her voice. 'All that business about her brother.'

'From Inchgarten? Tony and errr . . .'

'Daisy. Yeah,' Blue Talons tutted and rolled her eyes. 'You know what they're like?'

Costello smiled knowingly. 'Weirdoes, but nice with it.' She folded the photo away but made no signs of leaving.

Blue Talons lowered her voice. 'Well, you know the rumours?'

'I've heard all sorts,' smiled Costello, encouragingly.

'You go there if you're having trouble, you know . . .'

Costello nodded, having no idea where this was going.

'I mean, it's only rumours, but I heard they dance round the fire, naked in the moonlight, and drink some witches' brew. They do something with a horny goat. Christ knows if it's true but it works. Wee Freya and . . .' She stopped laughing. 'Then there was the business with the kids . . .'

'Terrible. But thanks.'

Back out on the street, Costello ignored Batten, who was perusing the price list of the Hippy Chippy as she phoned Wyngate and asked him to do a missing person search for an Edward Taylor. There was already a shortlist of possibles on the computer, and it flashed up a match straight away. Edward Taylor lived less than two miles away. Wyngate offered to text her the postcode. 'Reported missing by his mother.'

'Should be interesting, then. Let Anderson know that we are on it, but are having some chips first. And can you do me a favour: find out what Tony Laphan's dissertation was about? Did he have any interest in anything particular as a student?'

'Why?'

'Because I say so. And any wee girl called Freya, anything at all on the fringes of the case.' She cut the call.

After a hurried tea and a roll on chips, Costello parked Vik's Audi outside a modern four in a block in Bride Street, Alexandria. She nudged it into the space too far, forgetting about the spoiler, and heard the grating of metal on concrete.

'Oops,' said Batten.

'What happened to my mum?'

'She was murdered,' Anderson said brutally. 'We have your DNA on the database so there is no doubt she is your mother.'

Lexy flicked her fringe as if she was brushing Anderson's answer away. It looked less ridiculous now.

'She wasn't that one who was set on fire, was she? Read about that on Facebook.' Lexy seemed unmoved. 'Can I have a cup of coffee? I don't think I can go home. Now.'

Anderson opened the door and asked somebody to put the kettle on, then leaned against the wall, arms folded, and listened to her. She spoke like she was talking about the weather.

'I haven't seen Mum for a couple of years and it was fairly rubbish for the twenty years before that, so I'll pass on the mourning, thanks.' She rubbed at her nose with the palm of her hand, the cartilage making a clicking noise. 'Once she lost her job, she lost the plot. Warren and I were all over the place, foster homes, two children's homes. It was crap. Mum couldn't cope with anything. Us. Life, whatever. She was a gypsy, being indoors killed her. Where was she?'

'Here in Glasgow, in the old storage place. The Gray Dunn building?'

Lexy smiled at Anderson. 'The old biscuit factory? That was where she worked.' She fired her forefinger at him, pausing as the door opened and two mugs of coffee were handed in with a plate of ginger nuts.

'They set fire to her, Lexy.'

Lexy sighed, tapping the teaspoon against the side of the mug more than was necessary. Anderson thought she looked very young all of a sudden. And vulnerable. 'Easy target, so go figure.'

'And Warren, where would he be?'

It was back, that little half smile, that tremor. She turned and looked at Anderson. 'Why's it all got to be about him?'

'I was asking if you knew where he was so that we could tell him about his mother.'

'He might have killed her. Did you think of that?'

'Do you think he did?'

'No idea. Mum's had a long affair with the bottle. But that's how she was, she liked to drink . . . out there she could drink, out there she had to.' Lexy looked up, listening to the sounds of the city. 'Anything, Basso, Tarps, raw alcohol. Foot flat on the self-destruct pedal. It wasn't going to happen to me so I left them both to it.'

'Hard to live with,' agreed Anderson.

'Well, she left so we didn't have to live with it. I had already moved out.'

'Then Geno came along.'

'Yeah, Geno.' But Lexy's mind was elsewhere. She picked up a biscuit and bit at it. 'I hate soft ginger nuts, don't you?'

'I dunk mine.' Anderson watched her carefully. 'We know Warren got off the island.'

She looked up. Her voice was wavering as she said, 'I didn't know that.'

'So he is out and about. Three children have died. Your mother has died. The man in the field, tortured, killed.' He picked up his coffee, instant but a good instant. He leaned against the wall again.

She nibbled at the ginger nut but didn't seem able to swallow it. He let her panic.

The front door was opened by a young woman in a fluffy dressing gown, with damp hair and chubby tear-stained cheeks. She had a line of white dribble down her left shoulder. Baby vomit. She looked from one to the other curiously, then something clicked. Her eyes closed, her head fell forward.

'Mrs Taylor?' said Costello, reaching out an arm in case she fell.

An older woman appeared, dark haired with old-fashioned glasses at the end of her nose. She grasped the younger one by the shoulders and guided her back inside.

'Yes,' the older woman said, 'we are both Mrs Taylor. Have you found Eddie?'

Costello heard Batten take a step down behind her. 'Can we come in for a moment? Might be better.'

The young woman turned and buried her face in the older woman's shoulder. Mrs Taylor senior looked Costello straight in the eye; she gestured with her head that they should go through but she was not happy about it.

One minute later, they knew that life would not be the same again. Alison had lost her husband, Wilma had lost her son. Alison had collapsed on to the settee in hysterics, across her mother-in-law's knees. Wilma was calmly stroking her daughter-in-law's hair, beyond tears.

'How old is the baby?' asked Batten.

'Nine months, a boy. Teddy, after his dad.'

'Just the one child?'

'Yes, not been married two years yet.' Wilma continued to pat Alison's head. 'So how did you find him?' The question was directed at Costello.

She looked at Alison, wondering if she was listening. 'We can't reveal exact details, but a man of his description has been found fatally wounded in a field . . .' Her voice tapered off, suddenly aware of the tiny living room, clean, ironing done, clothes piled up on the back of an easy chair. A baby chair took up most of the available floor space.

Wilma watched her. 'Alison hasn't slept a night since Teddy was born. It's been even worse since Eddie failed to come home.'

'Do you think she's up to answering a few questions?'

Wilma shook her head.

'So, Wilma, do you recall Eddie meeting anybody new or if he was worried about something?'

'Not that I am aware of. But I don't know if he would have told me anyway. I'm his mum, after all.'

At that point the baby started howling from upstairs, bringing Alison back from wherever grief and exhaustion had taken her. Wilma went to get the baby, Costello and Batten were left looking at the heaving mess on the settee.

'Was he with somebody else?' Alison asked, eyes rimmed red, the skin at the corner of her mouth cracked and angry; she looked like a broken puppet. 'I think he was shagging around.'

'We don't know that.'

'You never think that it's going to happen to you. He went to work, left a message he'd be late. He was going to see his gran. I don't think I remember the last time I saw him, the last words he said to me.' She dissolved into a pool of sweat and tears and snot.

The volume of howling increased as Wilma came down the stairs holding the ball of bright pink bawling flesh, which she handed to Batten. Silence descended. 'I'm putting the kettle on.'

Alison spoke, her voice suddenly clear and steady. 'It was on Facebook. Eddie wasn't the guy found at the farm, was he?'

'We are still making a few enquiries. Can you tell me Eddie's granny's name?'

'Betty? Elizabeth Taylor,' said Wilma as she came through from the kitchen. The screaming resumed with operatic proportions as she prised the baby out of Batten's hands.

Costello made their goodbyes. The noise made any decent conversation impossible. She closed the door behind her, only partially cutting off the baby's screaming.

'Jesus!'

'There's a whole PhD going on in there. I have damaged my eardrums.'

'Tough. I'm going to text Anderson and make his day.'

*   *   *

'OK, Lexy.' He put the photograph from her own flat down in front of her. Lexy looked around, arms folded, her eyes wary. 'Cut the crap now. We know that this is not Warren. So who is he? Whoever killed your mother, killed this man, and might have Bernie Webster.'

'Saves him from Sammy, I suppose,' but her humour fell flat.

Anderson made a mental note but let it go. 'If he dies and you could have stopped it, I will make your life a living hell.'

Lexy drained the mug and placed it on the table, none too gently. 'It's Eddie; he's my kind of boyfriend. Kind of.'

'Yes, we know; Costello has been round to tell his wife that their wee baby is going to grow up without a father.'

Lexy bit the corner of her lip.

'We are getting a warrant to search your flat right now. We'd make less mess if you told us what we might find.'

She ticked the items off on her grubby fingers. 'Eddie's wedding ring, his driver's licence in the bedside cabinet. All Warren's ID was fake, bought it for twenty quid. It was kind of proof for Geno. But he never asked for it.' Her eyes welled up. 'Kept thinking that Eddie might come back, until I saw him lying in the morgue.'

'When was the last time you saw him?'

'Saturday night. We went out for a curry, down to Sammy McSingh's.'

Anderson kept his voice light. 'That's where you were the night Grace died?'

Lexy was biting her lip again.

Anderson waited and waited.

'Yeah, the food is good, get bevvied, cheap taxi back.'

'Have you seen your brother at all in the last twelve months?'

'No.'

Anderson dropped his head into his hands; he suddenly felt very tired, very hot. 'So, to clarify. You were with Eddie the night Grace was killed. Not Warren?'

Again she went quiet, then said, 'Yes.' Her eyes fell to the photograph of her lover lying in the grass, eyes open, staring at the sky. 'Sorry.'

'One more question. Did anybody come to see you or try to speak to you after the news about Warren broke?'

'Like who?'

'Anyone.'

'I dunno. That Karen came up to the front door; a few others knocked and went away.' She rubbed at her eyes with the palms of her hands. 'Oh, and somebody walked up the path then changed their mind.'

'What do you mean?'

'They went away.'

'They?'

'Two of them, came out a white van. I thought they were from the council so I didn't answer. I owe my council tax. They walked right round the house.'

'Would you recognize them?'

'I only saw them from above – I was upstairs. Two men, dark hair, that's all. Why?'

By half past six, Vik was hobbling back down to the water's edge where he had fallen: the Rocking Stone at the Roonbay. It took him ten minutes of limping to get there, his thigh muscles aching as he held his bad ankle up. He wasn't sure if the crutches were helping him or hindering him.

Then he sat on the stone, making sure his weight didn't move it before clumsily dropping the crutches beside him where they clattered against the stones like giant chop sticks. He stuck his bad leg out. He would worry about getting back up again when the time came.

He pulled his fleece off; the sun was dying but it was still warm and he was sweating. Or maybe that was the pain.

He looked across the water, so brightly silvered it hurt his eyes. He should have brought his shades with him. He tried to stand up then sank back down again, the throbbing pain in his ankle winding itself up to warp factor ten.

He cursed quietly under his breath, his eyes returning to the water and to the little island lying seemingly close enough to touch. All he had to do was reach out.

Getting his bearing, recalling the photographs on the board. He was sitting on the rock where Grace had fallen to her death. He twisted, looking behind him to the right, to Inchgarten Bay and the bonfire, looking at the lie of the land. He turned back to his left, towards the path that led through the woods to the car park. Behind him were the lodges. The bay curved into a few trees on an outcrop, growing bushes and brush, then the bigger sweep at Inchgarten Bay. Grace was only four. Could she have crawled out of her bed, through the door of the lodge then skirted down to the water? Was she climbing the rock, watching the adults having their fun, their bonfire and eating burnt sausages? She would have wanted to see all that, like a kid staying up for their first Hogmanay. Chasing a magic that was always elusive.

He found it difficult to believe it was an accident. Somebody must have enticed her down here, helped her on to the rock. Then what? Pushed her so she fell on a spike? That was rubbish.

He let the pain in his leg subside. It was not ideal here but it was better than being locked in the office with Costello and her unsubtle probing into his private life. She had said the budget hadn't allowed her to book them a lodge each. She was a bloody liar but then Elvie was surprisingly nice, a good listener, not fussy like his mum. She had that cool kindness that good doctors should cultivate. She had examined the strapping, set him up on the settee with the remote control and a pile of cushions. She had gone out and not returned.

He checked his mobile, one bar of signal. Still no message from Sonja. She was probably getting ready to go out somewhere. He stuck it back in his pocket. And sighed, content. Aware that the depression that had been sitting hard on his shoulders was burning off in the late summer sun. Talking to Elvie had awoken something in him, talking man to 'man', about a job without the constraints of Police Scotland. No politics, nobody watching their back, just a free flow of ideas – the way they did in the pub, in the old days. Passion for the job, passion to catch the bastard who had killed three kids. They were both after Warren McAvoy. Elvie had told him Batten's theory about how he had got off the island. How had the original search team missed that?

'Hi,' a figure blotted out the sun, a shadow fell over him.

'So how is the invalid feeling now? I heard what happened. I'm Tony.' A small, thin man extended a hand down to Vik, a firm handshake. Mr Peppercorn was standing beside him, wagging his tail, ears perked up like Vik might be of use as a toilet.

'You OK with the dog?'

'Is he yours?'

'When he wants to be.' He moved round to sit on the stone next to Vik, who shuffled along a little, leaving only inches between him and the dark, deep water. The gentle breeze lifted his fringe to reveal a receding hairline. He was older than he appeared, late forties maybe. Vik could smell garlic and curry powder. 'How is your mobility?'

'Rubbish, I keep tripping over the crutches,' he said, thinking about his own vulnerability.

'Might be better using just the one, easier to get used to. Spiral fracture?'

Vik nodded.

'Painful but not nasty.' He looked out over the water, eyes creased at the corner, looking for something or thinking about something. 'Why are you here? Another cop. I can tell by the haircut.'

'I am. Elvie isn't. She's a friend of Warren's family.'

'He doesn't have any family. We don't count that waster of a sister or her arse of a boyfriend. Why all this cloak and dagger stuff? Do you not trust us or something?'

'Just trying to get to the bottom of it.' He found himself adding, 'Nobody was supposed to notice I was a cop.'

'No skin off my nose, you can crawl about on your bum pretending to be Beyoncé if you want. Daisy and I don't care.' He grimaced as if suffering some physical pain. 'What Bernie and his girlie struggled with was the concept that we all want this resolved. We really do. I knew Warren well, had known him for years. Lovely young man. Odd but lovely. A quiet man, drifted about, in the shadows.'

'His mother has been killed.' Mulholland looked round, conscious of the fact he was on his own, and that he couldn't get away. Then he saw a movement from further up the beach. Elvie doing some stretches, but watching. He was touched. 'Do you know that the body we found was not Warren?'

'I gathered. Another cock-up. So where is he?'

'We don't know.' Vik watched Tony, but the other man's face was turned towards the evening sun. He thought he may as well get some information. 'Did Grace die here?'

'Right here.' Tony nodded without taking his eyes off the water. Mr Peppercorn jumped up on the stone and sat beside him. Tony placed an arm round the dog's neck, his fingers ruffling the thick speckled coat. The dog panted, his long tongue hanging out the side of his mouth like a slice of spam. 'That was a dreadful night. I told them not to remove the stake. But they did, Adam did. She haemorrhaged. It would have been fatal anyway, but you try anything in those circumstances. I remember the boy screaming, Wendy going to pieces, Adam's hands covered in blood. Warren had nothing to do with that; he wasn't even here that night.'

'How do you know?'

'He just wasn't here,' he said with a slight shrug of his shoulders.

He could have been in the shadows and you wouldn't have known, thought Mulholland, looking at the bushes behind him.

'The way Bernie was larking about was disrespectful to the memories of those boys, and Grace. The way they carried on.' Tony snorted. 'You should go back to square one, to what you know, not what you have been told or what Bernie thought. Otherwise you are going to end up the same blind alley he did. You need a new perspective.'

'Elvie McCulloch was sent here by Warren's dad. To find out the truth.'

'Warren's dad? Bloody hell,' Tony nodded at that. 'I'm pleased to hear that. She can tell his dad that Warren was a fine man. Totally without ego. I used to think that if I could capture that essence he had, that ability to see the world in the big picture, then I would earn a fortune. More like him and the world would be a better place.'

'He wouldn't have the words child killer chalked on his forehead.'

Tony shook his head. 'Warren could spend his days lying on the streets of Glasgow freezing, huddled in a doorway, and still feel empathy for the poor buggers in the rat race rushing for their train. He drifted in. He drifted out. No one owned him. There's a lot to be said for that.'

Mulholland didn't think it was prudent to point out that, charismatic though he might have been, Warren probably returned here the minute things got a bit tough on the streets. The manipulative nature of the serial killer. 'Hence why you didn't think too much when he went missing?'

'Ask Daisy how much she misses him. He worked his arse off, that lad, the place hasn't been the same without him. It's running down, it needed his energy. He was a man of very simple needs, he knew what was important in life. No, Warren didn't judge anybody, didn't judge me.' He looked off into the distance. 'This is a very beautiful place, but a very sad place. You know that Grace wasn't the first child to die here. There was wee Angela Colquhoun years before. The rumour is they never got to the bottom of that one either. Terrible how some places are cursed.'

Mulholland was making a mental note when Tony added, 'But that was a long time ago, when my granddad had the farm.'

They watched Elvie for a few minutes, standing at the water's edge, hands in pockets, looking out to the island. 'Which boy?' asked Vik. 'You said you remembered the boy screaming.'

'So what's happened to you?' Batten pointed at the dirty strapping round Jimmy Dewar's right wrist then shook hands with Eoin Dewar. He sat back on the reception chair in the informal interview room, opening a can of Irn Bru to look unofficial, friendly and safe. 'Though I'll warn you to speak up. I spent five minutes with a baby and I think it's deafened me.'

Jimmy gave a sardonic teenage smile and wriggled in his seat a little, pulling up the jeans that hung round his hips. He then folded the wires of his headphones round his fingers. 'Fell off my bike.'

'Again,' added his dad, shaking his head.

'I read your essay, quite liked it.' Batten ran his thumb round the top of the can. 'So was that true, your favourite place on the planet is still Inchgarten?' Batten directed the question somewhere between the father and the son. Jimmy had seemed to have grown even more as he slumped back on his chair, long legs at an awkward angle, scribbling on the fabric of the strapping, emphasising the weave. 'I would have gone for Rio or Acapulco. Anywhere with better weather.'

'No, I think he'd stick with Inchgarten. Lots of happy memories in a short life. If, well, if . . . I would be saying that as well, it was a boy's paradise. All that adventure right on our doorstep. That's why we went back year after year.'

It was relevant and pleasant, but Eoin was dominating the conversation. 'And do you miss it, Jimmy?' asked Batten.

A reluctant nod from the boy.

Eoin opened his mouth so Batten quickly asked, 'And how is the new school?'

'Kinda OK.'

'Miss your old pals?'

'Not really.'

'I think he misses his old teachers more. Mrs Grieg, you liked her, looked like Jessie J.' Eoin cuffed his son. It seemed friendly enough.

'Saw you giving it all that at parents' night,' Jimmy made a mouth with his fingers and thumbs.

'Well, don't tell your mother.' A conspiratorial smile.

'Was Mrs Grieg the one you did the essay for?'

'Yeah,' the boy smiled, brightening his face, an easy smile. 'I'm usually crap at English.'

'And when you were there on your holidays, what would you do?'

'Went sailing with Tony and Dad, and played pool.'

'If the table wasn't covered in mould. We ate a lot, Daisy's stuff.'

'Yeah, she doesn't do any exercise, but she's fun.' Jimmy rubbed his wrist.

'And the others?' probed Batten.

'Uncle Fergus sleeps all day,' he answered, a raised inflection almost forming a question.

'Come on, Jimmy, what was your favourite?'

'My favourite?'

The boy seemed to be struggling, not to recall but to forget.

'It's OK,' Eoin encouraged. 'You liked the Dreamcatcher?'

'Yeah, the big canoe. You're close to the water, we could go really far and it's so quiet. With the big paddles, I could go myself.'

'We didn't allow that,' Eoin told Batten.

'But we did it anyway,' retorted Jimmy.

Another conspiratorial smile.

'And Warren, at the start? What was he like?'

'Nice, seemed nice.' Jimmy's voice was suddenly clipped.

'Until, what happened on the island?' Out the corner of his eye Batten saw Eoin bristle, but kept his focus on the boy.

'Until then, yes.' Jimmy shifted his weight in his chair, uncomfortable with the memory.

'Can you talk me through it?'

He looked at his dad, who nodded.

Jimmy pursed his lips, then spoke. 'We took the boat up the shore. Warren pulled it high on the beach . . .'

'He hadn't done that before; he did that thinking that the boys wouldn't be able to get off the island without him,' Eoin added.

Batten nodded as if grateful for the interruption. 'So you pulled the boat up . . .'

'We climbed the folly wall, we were going right round through the jungle. We had passed the cliff at the north side, found the small bay there. It's very rocky. The three of us were there, then . . .' Jimmy stared at the floor, breathing quickly.

His dad placed his palm on the boy's shoulder. 'Just tell it as it happened.'

'I heard noises, then I saw . . . Robbie on the ground and Warren had this stone, hitting him.'

'Then?'

'He looked up and saw me, so I turned and ran. He chased me, all the way back, round the path. I heard somebody behind me and I thought it was him but it was Callum. I got him through the slit in the folly. I had to pull him hard. He fell when he landed. Warren came after us and . . .' The boy started to cry.

'So you and Callum got back through to Snooky Bay but Warren still came after you?'

Jimmy sniffed.

'And then?'

'Warren was faster, he got to Callum. I managed to get to the boat. He couldn't get away; I couldn't save him.' Jimmy looked at Batten, his eyes wide and tear-filled. He started howling; his dad put his arms round him, nestling his face deep in his son's hair.

The interview was over. Batten got up and held the door open for them, thinking about this tall, thin boy. The pets he had loved had gone. The brother he loved had gone. He nodded goodbye to Eoin as he walked past. Jimmy had a paper tissue at his nose, wiping away the snot. Batten looked closely at him, feeling another hand-kerchief being forced into his own hand. Jimmy's eyes never met his, they were staring at his dad's retreating back.

'Bye then,' he said as the desk sergeant took them through the next set of doors.

Once they were out of sight Batten looked at the hanky. Jimmy hadn't been scribbling on his strapping, he had been scribbling on the tissue. The message was short.

Never fallen off my bike.

At seven in the evening Vik hobbled across to the Boathouse in response to foghorn Daisy's clarion call that dinner was ready. When he got there, Daisy made sure he could sit comfortably on the bench seats, fussing over him, clucking away like a chicken and not letting him get a word in edgeways. He exchanged a few glances with Tony, who rolled his eyes in a 'Women!' kind of a way while flicking through a hillwalking magazine. Daisy jabbered on, even when she was in the kitchen. The voice never stopped. She still believed in their pretence of triathlete and trainer. Daisy told him that she had got Elvie a special breakfast for the morning so that not a drop of fat would pass her lips. But that he, Vik, needed to heal an injury so he needed good protein. He was glad when Elvie joined them, fresh from a shower, short black hair spiking. Vik had never seen such bad acne scars on a face. It didn't seem to bother her.

Elvie walked and talked the part of an athlete, whereas Vik knew his knowledge was limited to a Garmin and a tube of Ralgex.

The food was wonderful. They had dined on the sort of food that furred the arteries just looking at it: trout in butter and broccoli in garlic sauce, side order of sweet potato chips.

The trout was from the loch, beautifully cooked. The candles lit the table. The door was open, a mesh hanging over it to keep the midges out. The dessert was freshly made scones with fresh cream and ice cream with meringues. Afterwards, Tony told them stories of sculptures gone wrong, pots he should never have potted, things that went in the kiln decent and came out positively obscene. He was funny, entertaining and lively. Daisy only ever stopped talking because she was eating.

Elvie had finished all her chips and started on Vik's leftovers, her long, thin fingers sneaking out and nicking them off the side of his plate. She listened like she was listening to a foreign language and translating it. And by the time she had, the conversation had moved on and she had missed it. But when Tony mentioned again, the historic murder of a child on the lochside, her brown eyes had flicked up to meet Vik's. And he knew she was listening. He realized, with a pang of pity, that her life might be a rather lonely existence.

Apparently Angela Colquhoun had been killed, aged four, by her mother. Or so it was said. Tony's grandfather had known her. The mother had been sentenced to hang. It was startling to hear the details with the background of friendly chit-chat and chocolate meringue. Vik had to remind himself that he was supposed to be suspicious of these people. The weirdest person round the table was Elvie. But they completely accepted her as, he presumed, they had accepted Warren.

Then the whisky came out, clear whisky in a lemonade bottle. Elvie excused herself. Vik was starting to feel the pain in his leg and thought a wee snifter might help.

When he got back, eventually, Tony had walked him back and he couldn't recall who was using the crutches. He let himself in the lodge, clonking his way up to the decking and then trying to open the door the wrong way round.

He sank on to the sofa and waved goodbye. He checked his mobile, his voicemail, then lay back to think about Angela Colquhoun. The laptop was still lying open and sat on his blanket hibernating. He was thinking about the way Elvie had stolen his chips. And what Costello had said.

He was about to put the laptop on the floor and fall asleep on the settee when he realized she had left a document open. There was a message from Elvie at the top: *Will talk to you about this tomorrow.*

He maximized it and began reading Elvie's notes. The girl was a bright cookie, a medical student, so it was no surprise to him that her notes were succinct and precise.

Angela Colquhoun had been strangled, at the Rocking Stone, on 21 June, 1934, which was a Thursday and the summer solstice. She was four years old. Her mother pleaded guilty and was nearly hanged. Elvie included a few links to various famous true crime websites that detailed the case. The body had been moved. There had been a delay in alerting the police. Why did a family from Govan go up to the lochside? Devil worshippers?

Then typed in her own font, *Interesting, don't you think?*

Costello was feeling guilty, but only just. She was parked in the McDonald's near the Southern General Hospital thinking things through. It had not been an easy evening. She had dropped Batten off at Balloch train station then driven out to the small cop shop in Alexandria where Bernie Webster headed up the CID. It was a small white single storey building, more farm worker's cottage than a centre of law and order.

Anderson had phoned her and told her not to submit the vest for forensic examination but to bring it back to Partickhill. Did any police officers know about it, or just Batten and Elvie? Vik knew. Anderson explained his predicament, hearing Costello rummage around the evidence bag. 'It's a female's top, size twelve. I know Warren was a skinny wee guy but it's too small for him.'

'Well, it's Sammy's. It got torn during the search and she took it off. Then lost it.'

'It is torn indeed,' Costello had said, her voice full of disbelief.

She had then driven to Alexandria, starting to wonder about the lack of depth of the initial investigation. Wyngate, not the most observant of police officers to start with, had already come to that conclusion himself. There were only very slim files on the parents and the Inchgarten locals, but Warren had been pursued vigorously. But there was nothing to suggest that Bernie's team had tried to break Warren's alibi for the night of Grace's murder. Anderson had checked back the receipt from the original investigation. At Sammy McSingh's, Lexy and her vegetarian brother had eaten lamb? That should have been picked up. The bigger question was why did Warren go along with that? He had a whole year to correct the facts of his whereabouts on the night Grace was killed. But he had not.

So where was he? Killing Grace was the obvious answer. His sister fortuitously handed him an alibi to keep the secret of her affair with Eddie.

Costello had tried to keep her face pleasant as she walked into Alexandria station to see the original team she now spent her working day criticising. And they knew it. She got lots of questions about Sammy, lots of concern about Bernie. They both seemed popular with their workmates but Costello herself was met with icy smiles. She wondered how she would feel if the boot was on the other foot and Colin was missing and another detective came on her patch to help out. She would have welcomed them. She would have given all assistance, not the polite little nods she was getting now from the two officers who accompanied her. A beardie and a non-beardie with funny teeth, they looked like Benny and Bjorn from Abba. Did they have something to hide or was it her own paranoia? Maybe Bernie and his team had a nice little scam going on here and they did not want her digging about.

But it wasn't about Bernie. It was about Robbie and Callum and Grace.

Bernie's own office was opened for her by 'Benny'. The desk was well ordered, much tidier than Colin's ever was. A picture of a woman in her mid-thirties, the long-suffering wife, probably, sat beside the phone. There wasn't much else on the top, just routine detritus of office life: calendar, coffee mug, computer. Costello had permission to burst the locks, with a hammer if needed. She made sure she was crouched low between the desk and the wall as she tackled the drawers. Benny and Bjorn stayed chatting at the door of the office. They talked mundanities to each other while watching her every move, talking about the case, about Bernie, about Grace. Then someone asked whether the Partickhill team thought they were doing any better?

She had a quick search, answering the questions in friendly monosyllables as she found a toothbrush, a few batteries, some pens, some cassettes for a voice recorder, then she discovered a blue mobile phone under a desk diary. She slipped that in her jacket pocket, keeping her hand low so they did not see.

'You found something?' asked Benny, walking over.

'Just his diary.' Costello pulled it out. 'Do you know if he still used this or did he keep his diary on a cloud?'

'His work would be on the cloud. Don't know about a diary. He kept a change of clothes over there.' Bjorn pointed to a spare chair, pulled out from the wall.

If they wanted her to walk over there, she wouldn't. She stood up and flicked over a few pages in the diary. At the front there was a request for the school records of the parents – Eoin Dewar, Fergus McCardle, Isobel Swanson and Ruth Hyslop. School records? Struck out as if he had received them, then a note to himself to request medical records. Fat chance of getting them. On Monday the 16th he had made a note of an appointment to see Anderson at night, before the rest of them. She flicked to the front, a list of names and codes, passwords, thinking they would be safe locked in his drawer. She pulled out her own phone and photographed it, all the time fending off questions disguised as casual chit-chat, but when they saw her with her phone the questions became a little more direct.

'Should you being doing that?'

'Well, I don't want to take it with me, otherwise you wouldn't have a copy. There might be something in there that you need.' She passed the diary over to them, getting a look of stone.

The other drawers contained a few thin buff-coloured files, some of which they had been looking for. She couldn't be sure but the codes were familiar. The file on Ruth was thicker than the others; a quick flick through showed handwritten notes ripped out of non-issue notepads. She bundled them up together; they were all relevant to the ongoing investigation.

'I don't know if you should be taking them. You should put in an official request. They are Bernie's personal files.'

'If they're personal then going through the usual channels will not help. And as they are on police property . . .'

'Apply for them in the proper way.'

'Oh, I thought we already had. But to clarify, Bernie is missing, this might have something to do with his disappearance and you want me to go back to Partickhill and speak nicely to a fiscal then come back with a bit of paper? I'll have no trouble with that as Archie Walker has just about moved in.'

'So, you won't mind doing it then.'

'If you insist.'

'We do.' Was there a hint of a threat?

At that moment another DCI appeared. 'We have been coopera-tive, DI Costello. It's late.' He took the files from her, 'I'm sure you would be better going home now.'

'Perhaps,' she smiled at him on the way out. 'But I'm going straight to talk to the fiscal. I've counted the pages, so no tearing anything out.' She joked in perfect seriousness as she said her goodbyes, feeling as welcome as a wasp at a picnic, and got back into her car.

With the mobile in her pocket.

She drove to McDonald's and bought a tea and doughnut in the drive-through. She pulled out the phone and played with a few buttons. It belonged to somebody called PC McGarry and it wanted a code.

McGarry? The name meant nothing to her. She got out her own

mobile and opened up the image of the diary. Munching on her doughnut, she pulled the screen large to read any code next to PC McGarry. Nothing.

She then Googled PC McGarry and chuckled. *Trumpton*. He was the beat bobby in *Trumpton*. PC McGarry 452. She tried four five two to unlock the phone. It asked for another digit, the white space flashing at her. She tapped 0.

The screen lit up.

She scrolled the contents, her mouth going dry as she saw the names. K. Jones? Karen Jones? Talk about being in bed with the press. She flicked through the text history, sexual and explicit. There were eight others she did not recognize. She couldn't help herself – she had to look at the photographs. They were even worse. She looked at them all, recognizing Inchgarten Lodge Park. In some Sammy was there but not on police work – well, not the kind of work she was paid for. And Karen Jones was hardly wearing anything. She saw a compromising photograph of the young female fiscal Costello had got friendly with on a violence against women course. Then she shut the phone.

It was amazing Bernie had any energy left to do any bloody work.

Anderson was still at his desk avoiding going home. He had been busy and was now sitting with the blinds closed, thinking.

Eddie Taylor had a granny. Called Elizabeth Taylor. The granny's neighbour had died. Her name was Bella, she had been set on fire. Her murder did not match that of her neighbour's grandson, but it bore similarities to Dotty's murder.

It looked like they had killed the wrong woman. So there would be proof back at the maisonette in Knightswood where Bella lived. Anderson had walked through the house, still full of that smell of stale, stinging smoke. The curtain twitchers had done their job – Mrs Taylor the neighbour had come knocking. She was very correct and proper, a thin, grey-haired lady in blue trousers and a blue blouse, blue cardigan. Even her hair had a blue tinge in the light. Her eyes were red, she was fiddling with a handkerchief she had stuffed up her sleeve. She mentioned a tragedy in her own family. Anderson had nodded that it was a difficult time for all. She had regarded Anderson with intelligent blue eyes and asked what he wanted. She knew where the tarot card was straightaway. She had picked the mail up from the top of the trolley, sifting through them and placing each letter down as if waiting for Anderson to say snap. She stopped at the black envelope, the one he had thought was a funeral card. No address, put through the door by hand. It had been opened. The judgement card lay inside, Anderson was now turning it over in his fingers. Mrs Taylor had thought it was lovely, the picture of the unicorn.

Why would Warren McAvoy go after his sister's boyfriend's grandmother? It made no sense. And as McAvoy couldn't drive, he would have needed a driver. That made another person evil enough to go along with him.

It was getting very late.

But on the good side, Helena was back on her feet, feeling woozy but much better, just a tummy bug. They had had a long chat on the phone earlier in the day. He checked his messages. The conference had not gone well, then Archie Walker had summoned him. Then the ACC had had a go as well.

There was still no sign of Bernie. Anderson was starting to feel sick in the stomach when he thought about what his colleague might be going through.

His door banged open and Costello walked in and switched the lights on, saying, 'Just the two of us, please' to Walker and Batten, who were still out in the investigation room. She closed the door and placed the blue phone down on his desk. 'We have a problem. More than one.'

Five minutes later Colin had his head on his desk. 'I thought it couldn't get any worse.'

'Well, it has.'

'I gave her a chance to say what was going on between her and Bernie. PC McGarry four-five-two.' He turned the mobile over in his palm. 'God, the village bobby in *Trumpton*. Bernie obviously watched the same TV programmes that I did as a kid.'

'Well, I think it's fair to say he has a playful nature. But he's in contact with Karen Jones, so that answers that question as to how the press were so well informed. And we need to find somebody called "Crecy". Plus there's a file in that office about Ruth that is not a duplicate of ours. They would have killed me rather than let me walk out of there with it. So much for one unified force.'

'Did you ask politely?'

'Indeed. I was lucky to get out before I was lynched. They want me to go through official channels.'

'So be nice to Walker.'

'Go to hell.' She leaned forward. 'But Bernie was after their medical records. Why, do you think? Mental health issue somewhere?'

'Doubt it. Somebody would have said something by now. Oh God, what is going on? Sammy's very close to Ruth, she knew what she takes in her tea, without asking. Milk two sugars.'

'I noticed.'

'And why were you sticking your fingers into the plants?' Anderson asked.

'Folk with well-watered plants remember to water them. It's a sign of being organized, of being aware. And the pencil drawing, recently ordered. Her mind is focussed. More focussed than Sammy Winterston's.'

'But what was going through Webster's mind – school records, medical records?'

'Of the parents, not the boys? I'll chase them down. See if I can find anything. Webster was a good cop so you never know what he might have spotted. Before all this stuff started with Eddie in the field, he was investigating the parents. So it must have been for the killing of Grace.'

'And he knew about Tony's record but dismissed it totally.'

'Or wasn't paying attention?'

Anderson's mobile pinged. 'Text, Brenda.' He read the text and grimaced. 'She wants me to go round to Helena's to check on her.'

Costello looked at her watch. 'Well, it is nearly midnight, Colin. So you should be, well, somewhere other than here. Must admit Brenda is doing well, after her personality transplant.'

Anderson ushered Costello out of his office before she started. A headphoned Batten had three maps rolled up beside him; he looked like a man with a mission. Wyngate was huddled over a computer monitor. Walker was by the wall, twitching, with his hands in his pockets. Sniffing after Costello, no doubt. His phone went and he slipped into the corridor before talking down his mobile – to his wife, probably.

Costello couldn't see Walker's wife asking him to go round and spend time with his girlfriend.

'What's Batten doing?' Anderson asked Wyngate.

'Watching the film of the first Dewar interview. Again,' said Wyngate. 'I'm still struggling, trying to place who was where on the night of the killings. Surely that is important.'

'Highly. You keep at it. Ask Walker if we can arrange a re-enactment for them, a reunion. Then we'll throw in a firecracker. See what comes up.'

'He'll never allow that.'

'Don't know until you ask.'

'I've already asked him to get a warrant for the medical records. I'm not pushing my luck. Why is Batten still looking at Dewar's stuff? Have you found something suspicious about Eoin?'

'Nope. And our surveillance hasn't picked up any suspicious behaviour.'

'That's all we need on this case – the confusion of somebody behaving normally.'

It was midnight when Anderson got out to Helena's house. When he arrived she was in the kitchen, moving around unsteadily. He could have knocked her over with a sneeze. Now she was on the settee, sleeping, wrapped in a blanket. An empty cup on the floor, a bottle of morphine sulphate. Her back must really be sore. He adjusted the cushion under her head and felt something: glossy paper. He pulled out a photograph of Claire. Colin lifted it up and placed it on the arm. She would see it when she woke up. He kissed her forehead and left, closing the door behind him.

Bernie was drifting in and out of consciousness, happy to be in another world where he was sitting on a beach with his first wife and the kids when they were young. Eating ice creams, the scent of Nivea sun lotion and listening to the waves race across the sand. Happy.

Then he would wake up tasting the salt of the sea, realizing he was tasting the salt of his own tears.

Thought he was looking out of a window but there was not even a gap of hopeful light in the ceiling. Hoes and a rake in the corner, oil stains on the floor. They started to come alive and dance. He could hear the *Sorcerers' Apprentice* from somewhere inside his head.

His mouth was dry and stinging for the want of water. His stomach had forgotten about food – it was all about fluids now. The pain refused to leave; it flitted around from joint to joint. Every time he shifted his weight it got worse somewhere else. There was a limit to pain, surely. He needed to pee again. It had not dried since last time, and he couldn't ignore the cloying mass between his buttocks. Or the repulsive smell.

He was a feeble little man, lying in a dark corner, peeing and shitting himself.

Thursday, 19 June

Batten was on the phone being charming as the team gathered. It was eight thirty a.m. A late start for them. Costello was ripping off the jagged edge of her fried egg, looking at the latest Find Warren cartoon online. This time they were up Ben Lomond, Warren being the pantomime villain right behind PC Plod. The joke was wearing thin. Archie Walker, the fiscal, walked in. He didn't say anything, but held up the front pages of the *Daily Record* and the *Sun* before sitting down.

'I need a coffee,' he said, 'a strong one. Where is Karen Jones getting this stuff?'

'No idea,' said Anderson. 'Initially, it was via Bernie. But he has been under the radar for a wee while, so either there's another leak or Bernie is working for the other side, so to speak. And Sammy Winterston won't be joining us this morning. She's under the weather.'

'Might be safer for her to be under lock and key,' Costello said to Walker.

'Moving on,' said Anderson, 'Batten is on to something.'

Walker said, 'I know when my attention has been diverted.'

But he listened in to one side of the phone call, hearing Batten say, 'Oh, dinosaurs, yip, well, on his computer, and that would be normal? Oh right, yeah.' Batten was nodding. 'Mammals . . . oh mammoths, sorry, yeah. Well, thank you. I certainly will, no problem . . .' There was a seductive flirtation in the psychologist's voice. He put the phone down. 'Robbie's class project at school, ancient man. Hunting with impaling pits, which echoes the way that Grace was killed.'

Anderson had been hoping for more and couldn't disguise his disappointment. 'So what?'

'So his dad helped wee Robbie with his homework. It's a link, a suggestion of an idea planted.'

'Right, so he had shown that to Warren and it sparked off something in his mind. What? To pull a canoe cradle over then push a wee lassie on to it?' Anderson held his head in his hands. 'Sorry. But she was four years old, pulled from her bed, half asleep. They could have led her anywhere, done anything.'

'Vik's report says that Warren wasn't there,' said Wyngate, scrolling through a log.

'Vik has been told that Warren was not seen there, it's not the same thing,' Anderson pointed out.

'My point is,' argued Batten, 'that idea had been implanted in Eoin's mind, that method of death. He's a trusted dad. Might be good to find out what sport he did, review the other methods of murder. The T-shirt was overlooked, there was time to—'

'What T-shirt?' Walker was confused.

It was Costello who answered. 'We found a green vest top on the island. Initially we thought it was Warren's but it was Sammy's. It got torn while she was searching the island with DCI Webster.'

'Really?' said Walker.

'And the surveillance team caught Eoin coming back last night; they hadn't noticed he had gone.' Anderson shook his head. 'So do we ask him where he went? If we do, it shows we're watching him.'

'Then we don't. What's the significance of the green top?' asked Walker.

'The same significance of Lexy's nickname for him: Bonking Bernie,' said Costello.

'Were you going to inform me of this, DCI Anderson?'

'Only found out myself last night. Look, there are more important things. As our local fiscal, can you get Bernie's personal files out of Alexandria, asap? He wasn't a bad cop; he might have been on to something.'

'And Mr Fiscal, Eoin is very protective over Jimmy. The boy might have been coached. It's all smoke and mirrors. We need to know where everybody was exactly that night. Exactly,' said Batten.

'The reconstruction?'

'And I need to re-examine the family dynamics.'

'So Warren killed the boys, and Eoin is on a revenge spree? And Eddie Taylor was killed by mistake.'

'Yes, maybe and no. Bella was killed because the killer thought she was Eddie's granny, so they knew he was Eddie.'

'So that leads us back to Warren. He killed the boys and went into hiding.'

'He could be bloody anywhere.'

Walker shook his head. 'No, hold on a moment. Why was this stuff on the island not found at the time?'

'It was underwater by the time the search team got there. Simple. People keep forgetting about the weather. It was pouring down by the time the bodies were discovered,' said Anderson.

'And the Inchgarten locals would have known that. OK. So does the Eoin revenge theory fit in with the tarot cards? Is that what you and Batten have been wittering about?'

'It's as if they're being left as calling cards. They might have no significance other than they are relevant to the person it is left with. And that is because they want us to know that they know them.'

'Somebody who knew Sammy and Bernie were at it like rabbits.'

'Everybody seems to have known that.' Wyngate blushed slightly.

'Somebody who knew O'Hare's car,' Anderson continued. 'Someone who knows where I live but not where Costello or Sammy live.'

'Anybody we have interviewed?' Costello asked. 'And are we thinking Fergus is Eoin's number two, if we are following his revenge theory?'

'Still not found him, have we?' said Walker.

Wyngate flicked over a few pages of a notebook. 'You have no idea of the nutters we have talked to to trace these cards, but the bottom line is they are easily purchased over the net. There have been some packs sold at a psychic fair in the Central Hotel late last year but the stallholders had no real recollection of who or when. But they paid cash. Of course.'

'Well, it's more about the psychology,' said Batten.

'Oh please, no!' groaned Walker.

'Ivory and ebony, the good and the bad,' Batten explained. 'The side of the angels and the side of the devil. Somebody wants us to get this sorted. O'Hare, Costello, Anderson all got white cards, so we are on the side of the angels. Eddie Taylor, the woman the killer thought was his grandmother, Patty McAvoy, and Lexy McAvoy all got black cards. So the killer knew that Eddie was Eddie and not Warren, as Colin says. Then they went for his granny. Anybody involved in the previous investigation is lumped in with them too, so they need to suffer. That will explain why Bernie might be in deep trouble now. And somebody is telling the killer what's going on; that Anderson is in charge, for instance?' Batten put his own tarot card on the table. It was white. 'I am on the side of the angels. Even so, we must be careful to warn our nearest and dearest that they might be on some lunatic's hit list. We are dealing with an unstable mind; any perceived slight could result in a change in game plan.' The rest looked unconvinced. 'Think about Bella – he killed the wrong one. Just because they saw Mrs Taylor go in and out of a house, letting herself into the house with a key. One little old lady looks like another when you set fire to them.'

'Can I say something?' asked Wyngate, gently, to remind them that he was there.

'Only if it's helpful,' said Anderson.

'Fergus Dewar and Eoin McCardle never went to university together. We didn't really get anywhere with the medical records with no warrant. But Costello had said something about Tony Laphan's interest when he was a medic student . . .'

'Forensics pathology?'

'And rocking stones.'

'Can I kill him now?'

Wyngate ignored them. 'Fertility. It's the link. Both Eoin and Fergus are members of HIM. Help for infertility for men. Same organisation, that's where they met.'

'What?' said Costello.

'So what? They had kids. They had treatment, they got over it,' argued Anderson.

'Well, maybe, but the couple that lost their child under Laphan's care? They had years of treatment to have Thea. Thea dies and the following year they go to Inchgarten on holiday and nine months later – they have another kid.'

Anderson looked at Walker, both confused. 'So it's how they met. It explains their friendship,' said Wyngate. 'And then they lost those children.'

The room was quiet for a moment. 'That is really rough,' said Anderson.

'And one more nugget? I've been trying to find a link between the McCardles, the Dewars and the farm. Nothing at all at first,' said Wyngate. 'Then I tried their company, Dewar McCardle. I asked them about the old signs they have at the farm. Back in 2008 Dewar McCardle subcontracted out their print work once they had designed it. Eoin went out to take photographs for the farm's planning application. And Riverview had horses at livery in those days.'

A hum of satisfaction thrummed round the room.

'So Eoin knew the site. All we need to know is that he had an archery badge when he was a boy scout. Or did he learn that too while studying ancient man with Robbie? Don't worry, I'm joking.' Anderson looked thoughtful. 'Maybe Bernie had made that connection and that's what he was looking for. Can we force Eoin's hand in some way? Archie, what about a re-enactment? Get everybody there, film it? Shake the bag, see what falls out, Hercule Poirot style. Ruth wants to go to mark the anniversary anyway.'

'Indeed. Vik has said his cover has been blown but they don't seem to care at Inchgarten,' said Costello.

'And it won't help if it was all Warren, will it? I mean, as far as he's concerned, nothing has changed. We started off thinking that nobody has seen him for a year and now, nobody has seen him for a year. Lexy is safe in her cell,' said Anderson. 'She's quite happy.'

'But we do know that Warren had a way of getting off the island, and that makes a huge difference,' Costello pointed out.

'Although nobody saw him do it, and they would have done as the life raft came round the top of the island. He wouldn't be able to steer it against the running current. Remember the biblical weather? He would have come into sight. That life raft could have disappeared at any time in the last twenty years. Tony says he didn't even know it was there,' argued Anderson.

'So he says. Now.' Costello was unconvinced.

'That side of the island was out of bounds for the boys, it's not easily accessible.' Anderson turned to Wyngate. 'Any news on the council van?'

'It wasn't from the council. And forensics say the tyre marks at Riverview are from the type used by many cars but it is worn, so if we get a suspect vehicle we can match it,' said Wyngate.

'Eoin. Printing company. Could copy and print out a council logo no bother,' suggested Costello.

'If your auntie was a man she'd be your uncle.' Anderson walked over to the board and started to summarize connections. 'Mick, do we agree all this is by two people? Fergus and Eoin? Or Warren and somebody as yet unknown? With a lack of any identifying evidence pointing us in another direction, Fergus and Eoin fit the profile. They are good friends, they are the wronged in a terrible crime and they have suffered loss, a loss so much more tragic if there had been fertility issues. So they blame the police as well as the person they think is the murderer. Warren got away, they have no closure. They have had time to plan this. We can confirm the dead man was Eddie Taylor because he was complicit in McAvoy's false alibi. And there is the motive: if McAvoy had stood trial for the murder of Grace then he wouldn't have been out to kill the two boys, would he?'

'But it wasn't thought murder at the time,' said Costello quietly.

'And we have already provided an alternative version. Somebody spurred on by seeing the death pits on the computer. A wee girl taken from her bed, drowsy and compliant at the promise of joining the adults,' said Anderson. 'She would trust Uncle Warren.'

Costello walked up to the board. 'So the revengeful dads? Eoin is still behaving like a squeaky clean person and using our resources while nobody can find Fergus.'

'And have you seen this?' Wyngate handed Anderson an A4 sheet of paper. 'Vik is looking at the other child murder on Roonbay. The one in 1934. I've checked the log and Sammy had picked it up but Bernie refused to take it further.'

Anderson read out the note, Costello peering over his shoulder. 'Angela Colquhoun, four years old, strangled to death. Right by the Rocking Stone.'

'Way too much of a coincidence,' said Costello.

'It's famous because the mother was nearly hanged. There was strong feeling that she should swing. It's history, but it is relevant somehow.'

'And look at that,' Costello pointed. 'The date. Angela was murdered at the solstice.'

The car bumped along the single track road, Anderson fretting about his suspension, cursing Archie Walker, wondering why he had ever been bored by those all-day meetings in air-conditioned rooms with nice biscuits and comfy seats. It was fair to say that his enthusiasm to visit Inchgarten Lodge Park had evaporated.

Costello was muttering about Sammy, 'I mean, did she give us any info without us knowing it first? You said she helped Lexy out. She hand-fed the Dewars.'

'She's a good cop. It was her case before ours. Maybe she was playing her cards close to her chest. It's natural enough. And she was obviously in love with Bernie and trying to protect him. I think the original team knew they took the easy way out. To them it was Warren cut and dried.'

'I'm not so sure Bernie thought that. Why was he going through the old files of the parents' school days, their medical files?' said Anderson.

'We need to wait until we see them.' The Golf hit a pothole and juddered to a halt. 'Shit!' Anderson stuck it in reverse until it was on level ground and then selected first. 'This is creepy, probably something about only virgins beyond this point. Enter only if you have three toes.'

'Three nipples, isn't it?' said Costello. 'It's all a bit abandon hope all ye who enter here.'

'Certainly need to abandon hope for any decent suspension. I presume that nobody ever uses this road.'

'It's the main way into Inchgarten Lodge Park, but a good way of keeping good Christian folk out,' she said cheerfully, noticing that Anderson was a little reluctant to stick his foot on the accelerator again. But he did.

Eventually the single track road opened on to a clearing where two cars were already parked: a small Polo and a red Fiesta.

There was a strange howling noise that made Costello jump as she got out the car. 'Jesus! You know that dog that guards the gates of hell?'

'It's just a dog.' Anderson turned, walking slowly off the wooden planks towards the large barking dog who raised its speckly hackles. 'Or maybe not . . .'

Costello hid behind him. 'You're good with dogs. Let it smell wee Nesbit and it will know you're friend not foe.' She pushed him forward.

The dog jumped slightly to the side and barked again; three deep woofs resonated through the forest. It turned its head and pricked its ears at some noise that they could not hear. Then it pranced towards them, sniffed round the bottom of Anderson's trousers and deduced that Nesbit was not an issue. After a quick sniff at Costello's boots, Mr Peppercorn raised his leg and peed on her trousers.

*   *   *

'That is weird, isn't it, makes you think the place might be haunted or cursed or something? What are the odds of four wee kids dying in such close proximity but so many years apart?'

'There's no coincidence.' Elvie was sitting on the floor, her long legs crossed. 'One would have planted a seed about the other. The location is the link. Obviously.'

'So the original team knew about wee Angela,' said Vik, thinking how relaxed he was, staring at the ceiling, talking crime to Elvie. His phone went, it was Sonja. He ignored it. 'But they decided there was no connection.'

'That's illogical.'

'Well, they had McAvoy for the boys. Grace was an accident. Cut and dried. I'm not so sure.'

Elvie turned her head as if listening for something. She looked at her watch, 'That will be your boss arriving? Mr Peppercorn is barking.'

They followed the dog along the winding dark path as the trees above closed over, blocking the sun. Until once again they were in brilliant light as the trees opened up and the golden sand of the beach came into view. They realized they must have been winding their way down to the water's edge since they parked the car. The beach was a perfect crescent of rocks and boulders carpeted by sand, one large rock standing proud. At the moment, somebody was sitting on it. The wooden lodges sat on the higher ground to the right of them, an older stone-built farmstead ahead. Far out in the bay was Inchgarten Island, looking much further than it did on the map. They both stood for a moment, sharing the same thought. Jimmy, a frightened wee boy, rowing to get back to shore in the dark as his parents partied here on the bay. His parents making too much noise to hear his screams. Did they all accept the first thing he said, was that the version which stuck? Who knew what he might have seen or imagined he saw?

'Do you know what Batten has in the back of his mind?'

'Don't know if *he* knows what's in the back of his mind.'

They walked closer to the rock to see a rather large lady perched on it. Her lemon flower-print frock was bright against the loch beyond and the dog was now sitting beside her. She was intent on her task, splashing something in the bucket in front of her then dumping it in the water.

'Aye?' she said without turning.

'Police.' They held out their warrant cards.

She turned at them and flashed them a mile-wide smile. 'You looking for Vik and Elvie?' She slipped off the stone and wiped bloodied fingers on the front of her dress. She'd been gutting fish. As she advanced towards them in her bare feet, her curves moved and undulated under the fine fabric. 'Daisy. How are you doing?'

'We are Vik's colleagues.' Anderson was trying to hide behind Costello now as she strode towards them, as subtle as a Viking galleon in full sail. And just as unstoppable.

She checked her hands were clean then shook hands with them. 'Vik's doing fine, bloody idiot. Here for two minutes and falling on his arse. What a dope.'

'Indeed,' said Costello in full agreement. 'Your dog peed on my leg.'

She laughed a huge belly laugh, bits of her anatomy wobbling and jiggling, the ankle-length dress barely containing her voluptuousness. 'Oh, Mr Peppercorn, he's a right one.'

'Miss Laphan?'

'Aye.'

'Do you know these people?' Costello held out her file of photographs.

Daisy looked closely. 'That's Lexy. Silly bitch. That's Lexy's man . . . Eddie somebody, he helped Tony with the tractor once. Both got stupid haircuts. He's married, though, I can sniff that a mile away.'

'So they have been here?'

'Oh aye. We know each other, see each other in town. See her at the hairdresser's, she's never out of there with that daft haircut.' She continued to walk up the beach then stopped suddenly, standing hands on hips, resolute. 'You after Warren too?'

Anderson thought she wasn't as happy as she looked, not half as daft either.

'After the truth. Is your brother around?'

'Tony. Aye.' She shrugged her shoulders, sending a wave of flesh down her body. 'Come on, we'll find him,' and Daisy walked away into the sun.

*   *   *

The jetty was rotten through. On it was a small man with thinning brown, waving hair. His checked shirt was open-necked and smelled of sweat and sheep.

'Tony,' he introduced himself. 'How are you doing? You not keen to come out to the island then, see where it happened?'

'Not exactly keen,' said Costello, feeling sick even at the thought of it.

Tony sat in the middle of the boat, kneeled down, picked up a paddle and secured it to the side. He then pulled the outboard motor on-board, securing it with a large bolt.

A dirty yellow canoe, the Dreamcatcher, was roped to the shallow end of the jetty. 'I'll pull that up to the shore. If you want to go over, we can take the Scoob.' He had turned as he spoke, narrowing his eyes slightly, like he was gauging the wind. A wind that Anderson was not aware of.

'You normally keep the boats here?' Anderson asked as he walked along the jetty towards the boat with the outboard motor, Costello lagging behind.

'No, we keep them up on the beach. The Dreamcatcher used to live up there, not much need for her now. The Scoob is normally round the bay, nearer the farm.'

Costello looked at the water with a snip of fear. 'So how much water is there exactly?'

'Biggest inland water area in the country by the surface. Seven hundred feet deep, the bottom is full of rocky shelves. Inchgarten is about a quarter of a mile away, but the current through the narrows is very strong.' He looked out to the island.

As Anderson stood out on the end of the jetty he was aware of the cooling wind and was glad he was wearing a fleece.

'The Inversnaid laird,' said Tony, following him. 'There is always wind on the water.'

'It's strong.'

'It funnels down the glen, you see. There have been a few scientists who've come out and poked and prodded with their machines and their instruments. Once the wind gets up and moves down the water, it produces a huge amount of energy, stirring up the really deep water.' He rolled his hands, one over the other to demonstrate. 'So, a huge volume of water, being stirred and moved. But on the surface you might only see a wee ripple and if you were sitting in

a small boat, you might feel it as a small surge and then a pull
back, but that is all. Debris on the floor of the loch can be swept
up in it – small wrecks, all kind of things. Things, bodies, caught
in the rock shelves can get dislodged. That's the real explanation,
but we tell the tourists that it is a Hand of the Gods, sweeping his
fingers through the water, stirring it up. Some folk used to think it
was the spirit of the kelpies and their dead, coming to the surface,
coming to life. But it is a geographical, meteorological event. Hot
air, cold air, all that kind of thing. Same effect that causes the Loch
Ness Monster, but don't tell the tourist board that.' He smiled. 'Loch
Ness is longer, deeper, the glen is narrower, so it's exaggerated.'

'So it washes up all kinds.'

'Oh God, aye. For every five bodies that go in, the loch will give
one back. Might have to wait years but it will give up the dead.
You can tell; the water gets pockmarked, nitrogen being released
from the vegetation lying at the bottom of the loch. It works loose,
comes up and the surface of the water bubbles like somebody has
flung a thousand small stones at it. Or as if the Gods above are
crying. It's the tears of angels. So when you see that, the dead will
follow. You can bet your life on it.'

'It's that warm draught, I felt it on my face. Bloody eerie feeling.'

'Yes, that will be it.'

'And it stirs up the dead?'

'It does indeed.' He nodded at them, emphasizing the point.
'The bodies tend to come up here. That lassie in Milarrochy Bay?
She went all the way round and came up a year later. And four
that went in drunk over at Luss? Over five years to get them back.
But it is a natural phenomenon.'

'And are there any other natural phenomena? People come here
and nine months later they have a baby?' Costello's voice was half
humorous.

Tony's eyes crimpled at the sides, he smiled. 'Look at the place;
it has romance in its soul.'

'And the Rocking Stone?'

'I was a doctor once; I had an interest in fertility. The Rocking
Stone has as much effect on fertility as sticking Maltesers in your
ears.'

'Or dancing naked at midnight with some horny goat?'

'Never tried that. But horny goatweed is a similar chemical

structure to Viagra. That'll be what you've heard about.' He laughed. 'And the Rocking Stone is a natural phenomenon; the rocking is driven by the height of the tide.'

'But it can't aid fertility, though, can it?' Costello let the question lie.

Tony nodded. 'I get the inference. It's relaxation, it's no stress, it's away from it all and good food. Away from the rat race, the chemicals, the pressure. Stop worrying about it. Let nature do her thing.'

'Even with the Delaneys?'

'I felt I owed them,' he said plainly. 'A break, a holiday.'

'Hi,' said a voice behind them. It was Elvie. 'You need to come up to the lodge.'

Tony stood back, letting the rope run through his hands. 'Saved at the last minute, eh?' From what? thought Costello.

Anderson looked at the laptop, studying the film of the island taken by Elvie's phone. It helped him get some perspective on the place without getting in a boat. He had heard Jimmy's version: an adventure on the way out, a terror-fuelled chase on the way back. What seemed idyllic from the shore was a dark, thorny mass with one path. It could be deadly to stray from it. And in the moonlight of the mid-summer night?

Costello's mind was more occupied watching Vik and Elvie. They seemed to be getting on very well. Vik even smiled twice.

Anderson was asking Elvie all kinds of questions. What had she seen? What had she felt? It was great interviewing somebody with no imagination. At a shout they turned to see Daisy standing at the top of the jetty. 'I've put the kettle on. Want to join us?'

'That would be nice,' said Costello loudly, helping Vik up.

'The food here is bloody fantastic. But there's a horrible smell in here. Like dog pee.'

Anderson walked off first, joining Daisy in the sun. 'We're thinking of doing a reconstruction on Saturday night, is that OK with you?'

'Like they have on the telly? Fine by me, son.'

'There will be a few vehicles about on the road. The routes of entrance and exit.'

'Only have two. One forty minutes longer than the other. But aye, if it helps Warren, you fill your boots, son.'

'Thanks,' said Anderson, walking towards the Boathouse. Either they had nothing to hide or what they were hiding was very well hidden.

She walked off, Mr Peppercorn trotting along behind her, his tongue hanging out in the heat. She looked back at Anderson with moist eyes which didn't suit her face. 'Cup of coffee makes everything better.'

They followed her, her floral yellow dress side-shifting and sliding over her hips as she walked. Anderson watched, a man who could never understand the attraction of skinny women. He got an elbow in the guts from Costello.

Outside the Boathouse Daisy stopped. 'There's a hose round there if you want to wash your leg down, hen, otherwise the drive home is going to be a wee bit rank.' She smiled as she spoke, 'It's too hot to be going about in a car stinking of pish.'

'Indeed,' agreed Anderson.

Vik managed the steps of the Boathouse without too much difficulty; Elvie slipped into the bench seat opposite him. They knew the place well already. The Boathouse had a huge table with two bench seats at either side, covered in cow hides. The door was open, as were both windows. Despite the heat of the day, a small fire was burning in the wrought-iron fireplace and two sheepskin rugs lay in front. Mr Peppercorn immediately folded up on top of one of them and went to sleep, snoring loudly right from the first breath.

'Take a pew,' said Daisy. Anderson hung around near the door of the kitchen, enjoying the smell of something baking. She looked him right in the face and said quietly, 'And you are in need of something restorative. You're being pulled in too many ways, son, too many women. But it will all sort itself out OK – these things do.' She disappeared through the small wooden archway. Anderson heard a switch going on, a fridge door being opened. She came back and handed him three mugs, homemade from the look of them, and a plate of gingerbread that smelled so delicious, Anderson felt his stomach squeeze. She nodded to the table. As he sat down, Daisy came back with a bowl of cut fruit, bananas in thick slices, melon in fine slices, apples halved across to see the star of Venus. She placed them in front of Anderson, who was sitting on the end of the bench seat, staring out the open door, down to the beach and the water beyond. He was looking at Inchgarten Island.

She handed him a jug of cold milk and a packet of sugar. 'We don't stand on ceremony here. Help yourself to the gingerbread.'

Anderson could feel his mouth water, he could see the moistness in the cake, and it was calling to him. Vik began to cut the cake into pieces . . . the aroma of sweet, fresh ginger was tempting.

'Help yourself, I'll leave you to it.'

The coffee and cake were delicious, both Elvie and Vik were tucking in.

'This is lovely.' Anderson realized he meant it. The peace was then ruined by Costello blundering in, adding the smell of wet denim and dog pee to the ginger.

Mr Peppercorn looked up, disregarded her and went back to sleep.

'So, Vik? Any thoughts on Warren McAvoy?'

Vik shrugged, licking the crumbs of gingerbread from his lips. 'They all say the same thing. He was a lovely boy. Life was precious to him. So that doesn't fit in at all with what we think.'

'Something is not right,' said Anderson, noticing the way Vik poured Elvie another glass of water, without being asked.

'No, it's not. But where the hell is he? Did he use that inflatable to get off the island?'

'We have no idea. Have you looked in the other lodges?'

'They seem empty,' said Elvie. 'I've been around all times of day and night, not seen anybody of his description.'

'They believe there was somebody else on Inchgarten that night,' said Mulholland.

'But there wasn't.' Costello sniffed her coffee and pushed it away.

'You don't know that,' said Elvie. 'Daisy has known McAvoy for more than ten years and never heard him raise his voice in anger. He did talk to trees and they answered back.'

'Interesting,' said Anderson, wondering if there was anything in the gingerbread. He was starting to feel very mellow indeed. He hastily took a slug of hot coffee. Elvie gave him a long, intelligent stare.

Costello poured herself some water, looking at the glass and pondering how well it had been cleaned. 'Do they have any idea where he might have been? He had been missing for almost a year . . .'

'No. But they think he has the ability to go anywhere,' said Vik. 'He could climb trees and walk across the top. Skylining, it's called,' he added. 'His party trick was to walk from here to the car park without touching the ground.'

'And he goes flying,' said Elvie, nibbling at an apple.

Anderson chuckled. 'So you think he's up a tree?'

'No,' Elvie looked quizzical. 'No, but he lived by different rules. You won't get anywhere looking for him in the places you'd look for normal folk.'

'So Warren wasn't normal?' asked Costello.

'That's one point everybody agrees on.'

'Why does she cut the apples that way?' asked Costello, noticing the fruit.

'It aids fertility,' said Elvie, and both Anderson and Vik burst out laughing.

They walked out into the sunshine and Anderson sniffed the air. 'There's a train station in Balloch, isn't there? I don't know if I can have you in the car stinking like that . . .'

'I'll spray perfume on it.'

'You need to spray napalm on it,' said Vik.

Elvie was looking deep into Anderson's eyes. 'Yes,' she said, 'but I think you should let Costello drive the car. You sit here, in the sun, get some air.' She turned to Costello. 'Can I show you something? Follow me. You two can keep Daisy here.' And she walked away.

'What was that about?' Vik asked.

'No idea, don't care,' said Anderson.

'What if she turns Costello into a frog?'

'She'll have my eternal gratitude.'

Anderson watched as Elvie took Costello to the water's edge. It could have been a conversation about the weather, or the island. There was just the slight turn of the head as Costello checked her bearings, something Elvie was telling her about, somewhere behind the Boathouse.

Sammy had walked into Partickhill Station telling the front desk that she felt a lot better and needed a chat. She wasn't quite well enough to return to work, she said. Her hands trembled slightly as she tapped in her access code on the keypad.

Denied.

Fighting back tears, she made her way back out on to the street, her embarrassment making her hurry. She bumped right into Costello.

'How are you, Sammy?'

'I wanted to clear the air a bit.'

Costello was surprisingly friendly. 'I was peed on by a dog.'

'Is that not lucky?'

'That's birds. Let's walk a bit; we can get a tea up here.'

'I have a confession to make,' Sammy said as they set off. 'I've been talking to Ruth. I think of her as a friend. Thinking back, I might have said too much at times. I'm sorry.'

'Tell us something we don't know,' Costello said but not unkindly. 'Have you been talking to Karen Jones?'

'No.'

'Do you know who Crecy is?'

'Who? No.'

'Would it surprise you to know Bernie had a secret phone?'

'Would it surprise me? No.'

'Crecy is on it. It's a pay as you go mobile. We phoned Crecy's number and it was answered, but nobody said anything. We'll find him, though. Or her. All texts to that number have been deleted. I know it's not you; I've just phoned it and your phone didn't ring.'

Sammy gave her a wry smile, then looked at the pavement. 'I don't know Crecy. Did Bernie have a lot of other women?'

'He did. Plenty of them. But you enjoyed it, he enjoyed it, so forget it. He's not worth sacrificing your career over.'

Sammy played with the charm bracelet, spinning it round, making its Tinkerbell jingle. 'I did love him, and it was more than that.'

'He promised you a load of shite,' Costello walked on.

Sammy wiped a tear from the corner of her eye. 'Then I saw Lyn, I mean, she's nice. I liked her. She has no idea what he's like.'

'I don't think Walker's wife has an idea what he is like either. But I'll sort him out in my own way. So tell me, what goes on at Inchgarten, in the hidden room behind the apple tree? The big weird bed?'

Sammy opened her mouth but nothing came out.

'It's all about fertility, isn't it?'

Sammy looked away, across the traffic. Tears again.

'I'm sorry. Bernie had the snip. He was going to leave Lyn. We should—'

'It's nothing to do with you, Sammy. It's about Grace and Robbie and—'

'No. No, Costello, you don't understand. They wouldn't tell us, but infertile couples go there and have kids. It works for them, Costello, it works.'

Costello saw the desperation in the other woman's face. 'What does? Sitting on a Rocking Stone at the solstice and eating an apple cut across the way?'

'I have no idea, it just does. I had to believe that.'

Costello nodded slowly, and gave her a hug. She watched her walk away in the shoes she had been wearing the first day they met. A tall, slim woman formally dressed in a red blouse and black trousers, hurrying like she was late for a train. She turned left into a side street and vanished from her sight. A white van drove past and indicated, a slow left turn.

Costello had already turned round, away from the sun, thinking if it wasn't Sammy talking to the media, then who was?

They had caught Eoin at his work, out of place behind a desk, like a man caged. He looked much more at home on the beach with the boat and the boys.

Anderson started by asking about Ruth.

If Eoin was surprised he didn't show it. 'Ruth? Well, she always had her own life, her own agenda. Always doing her sporty stuff, a steady hand and a keen eye. And a heart of stone, she could be a real bitch. Poor Fergus.'

'Not a good break-up with Fergus, then?'

'I think Fergus found the break-up of the business more painful, to be honest.'

'How did things change for him?'

'He didn't care by then.'

'What type of company employs yours?'

'Anybody who wants a logo, signage. We now subcontract out the computerised logo, for embroideries that go on sports shirts, that kind of thing. The more modest end of corporate branding.'

'Do you deliver?'

Eoin paused, surprised by the question. 'Mostly we post out. DHL.'

'And before the downsize?'

'We had a fleet of vans.'

'What type of vans?'

'White, VW Caddies. All gone now.'

'And they had the Dewar McCardle logo on?'

'Yes. Why?'

'Can you tell me if Fergus was drunk when the boys went missing?'

'Not drunk like the spectacular drunk he can get now, but yes, he'd had a few. I think we all had. Except Ruth, of course.'

'And you went over on the boat that night?'

He shook his head. 'Later, yes, but when I first saw Jimmy I tried to wade in, but Tony was getting the Scoob. You have no idea how that felt, to only see one kid on the boat.'

'But you didn't know then what had actually happened. They could have been lost, or had an argument,' said Costello, feigning boredom, pretending to have received a text message and fiddling with her phone. She dialled the Crecy number. She heard it try to connect.

Eoin shook his head again. 'Deep down inside I knew that bastard had killed my boy; I knew it as soon as we discovered they were missing . . . it was Grace all over again. I had this sixth sense something awful had happened. I was right.'

'And thinking of Grace, the method of death, impaling. Jimmy seems to . . .' Anderson was lost for words.

'He found the body. He does obsess about it. His last therapist said he was working his way through it. I'm not sure. But then, I don't have the right letters after my name, do I?'

A phone rang. Costello tried not to look at Anderson. 'You were so convinced something had happened to the other boys? At that moment . . .?'

Eoin apologised and lifted his desk phone, 'Yeah, I've got that, I'll call you back.'

Costello looked down; her mobile was still unanswered, still ringing out.

'How did I know? I knew because Warren McAvoy was there. He killed them and escaped right under your noses. We couldn't find him and one year later you are still looking for him, aren't you?'

So Eoin thought that Warren was still alive. Or did he know that? 'Did you know there was a previous death on the bay here?'

Eoin nodded slowly. 'It's a famous murder. A wee girl. Robbie learned about it at school.'

'Does the name Crecy mean anything to you?'

Eoin pretended to look nonplussed. But not quite quick enough. 'Apart from the battle? No.'

'Did the boys do that in school as well?'

'I'm not sure where you're going with this.'

'Can you tell me if Jimmy and Robbie are your natural children?'

Eoin leaned forward slightly, a slow sigh. 'Jimmy is, Robbie was not. I had issues. Frozen samples, et cetera. But we used that for Jimmy, but that is confidential. Jimmy does not know. And that has nothing to do with any of this apart from . . .'

'Yes?'

'It's how Fergus and I know each other – it's the reason the four of us are friends. Fergus had cancer, the chemo did for him. Callum was an artificially conceived child, so please leave it at that.'

'And why always Inchgarten?'

'Because we like the place.'

'How are you feeling now?' asked Anderson, sinking into Helena's big sofa. He wanted to sleep.

'It has stopped being agony. I think I must have pulled something when I was sick the other night.' Helena moved round on the settee, adjusting the hot water bottle at her back. 'Thanks, the heat really helps. How's the case going?'

'It isn't. There are so many little threads that will not pull together.'

'Shame that something so awful happened somewhere so beautiful.' She shifted her weight slightly. 'Maybe I'll come down with Claire once this is all over. Introduce her to the mood of the landscape and all that crap.'

'When this is all over,' he looked at her as she winced at the pain and readjusted the cushion for her. 'Helena, can you be wary of anything you get in the post, especially if it's in a black envelope?

I'm not totally convinced that there isn't a complete nut job behind all this.'

'Is that Mick's diagnosis? A complete nut job?' She was half asleep already.

'You need to listen to me, Helena. Any weird cards you get in the post, here or at the gallery. You must let me know as soon as it arrives. You listening?'

'Why would they send anything to me?'

'I don't think they will but I want you to promise.'

'I'll promise you anything as long as you shut up and let me have some sleep. It's these pills. Make me very drowsy.' Her eyelids flickered and closed.

'No chance that I can have some then? I could do with a sleep like that.'

'Can you turn off the phone charger? It buzzes too loud.'

Anderson couldn't hear a thing.

It was ten to midnight when Anderson's phone bleeped. He turned to Helena, who was still lying curled up on the settee with the hot water bottle at her back. He spoke quietly. 'How long has he been on the move for?'

'Just ten minutes; he's been heading south out of town on his own but he's slowing down now. We're in Easterhouse. We got wise to his wee trick – he keeps an old Citroën parked in the street behind his house. Looks like he's pulling in to park now, outside a block of really run-down flats in the shit end of nowhere, deepest Easterhouse. And he's getting out, looking around, taking stuff out the boot.' Anderson heard the driver say something, 'Yip, we're going to have to drive past. We can't hang round here without being noticed.'

'OK, you park up and keep an eye on the car. Let me know if he goes anywhere.'

Friday, 20 June

'Nothing has changed. A shadow crossed the window of the upper right flat then someone fiddled with the curtain. I think that's where they are. The two on the other side look empty,' said the cop sitting in the passenger seat of the surveillance car as Anderson leaned in the car window.

Anderson looked at the depressing, run-down flats. Easterhouse was a deprived area, the regeneration project hadn't got as far as this street. 'Why would a guy like Eoin Dewar come to a place like this?'

'You OK to go in there on your own?' asked the driver, leaning forward to look round the other cop.

'The doc here is coming with me. I don't think Eoin will start pulling my arms out because I ask him why he's here.'

Anderson and Batten walked up the garden path, pausing at the entrance door, which was hanging off its hinges. A couple of tyres lay on an old mattress in the corner of the overgrown garden. They couldn't see much beyond that in the darkness, in the lack of street light.

'Nice, innit?' said Batten.

They went up the stairs, trying to ignore the smell of urine. Behind the door of the upper right flat was the quiet rumble of somebody talking, a hum of a radio or something.

Anderson knocked at the door.

The inside of the flat fell silent.

Anderson knocked again. 'Mr Dewar, can we have a word?'

The door opened. Eoin stood behind it, a little sheepishly. He opened the door fully to reveal a badly decorated hall lit with a single bulb, and the door to the living room was open. Anderson was hit by the stench of body odour and some kind of alcohol? Industrial? Antibacterial?

'Sorry to bother you, can we come in?'

Eoin said something over his shoulder that Anderson did not catch; a weak voice flitted back from the living room.

'Why did you try to give us the slip?'

'Why are you having me followed?'

'You are a suspect in the murder of Edward Taylor. Can we come in?'

Eoin seemed to think about saying *who*, then said pleasantly, 'Of course. There's somebody in here you need to meet anyway.'

He walked across the worn lino of the hall into the front room. The first thing Anderson saw was the photograph of Callum McCardle sitting on the shelf above the fire, one photograph and not even a very good one at that. The Hermit card stacked on the other side, like it was a holiday postcard.

'Visitors, eh?' said the voice from the bed in the corner. An old figure was propped up against two pillows that sat against the wall. The bed was a single one, an old divan.

The man had no flesh on his bones, buttery parched skin drawn over his cheeks so tight it looked as though it might burst. A red rash scampered over his nose and into his cheeks, around his dull, yellowed eyes. A hand was withdrawn from the sheet and extended out to greet Anderson. He took it, shook it gently. It felt very fragile.

'DCI Anderson? You going to find out who killed my boy?'

'Fergus?'

There was no mistaking the pain in his eyes, or the pleading in his voice. Or was it guilt eating away at him? Anderson pushed the thought away. The man was a husk.

'Aye. I'm afraid the drink has got hold of me. Sorry.'

'Why are you here? Surely you should be . . .'

'Where?' The thin cracked lips pulled across gums interrupted by a few teeth. 'This is better than where the council put me, better than any home.'

'He means he can still drink here,' said Eoin, with a trace of bitterness. He picked a few cans up off the floor.

'He's worse than a wife.' A wee guilty smile.

'Does Ruth know you're here?'

'Oh, for fuck's sake. Don't go telling her – I want to die in peace.' His eyes flitted across to the clock on the small TV, as if death was a minute away.

Eoin pointed to the small settee. 'You two can have a seat there; I'm getting some stuff organized. And I didn't give you the slip; I'm just not insane enough to bring the Jag here.' He lifted up two carrier bags and took them into another room, the light went on. Anderson followed him, standing in the doorway watching the bread, the wet wipes, the water and the cans and cans of lager being arranged on the worn but clean worktop.

Batten sat down on the sofa, crossing his legs casually. 'How long have you been here for?'

Fergus shrugged, 'No idea. I was admitted. I dried out. Ask him.'

Eoin answered from the kitchen, 'He was in high dependency for four days, hospital for another eight weeks. Stopped the taxi on the way back here so that he could buy a bottle of vodka.'

Fergus screwed up his face. 'I had nowhere else to go.' He looked round like he couldn't remember how he got to this place.

'They gave him a hostel bed. But he couldn't stay off the juice. So he left and one day got hit by a car. He gave A&E the name of the company.'

'Only bloody thing I could remember.' He tapped the side of his head. He was barely recognizable as the dark-haired man at the press conference, the man who had stared into the middle distance looking for his son.

'And you have been looking after him ever since?'

'He's the only one who looks after me. Ruth wouldn't. She's nuts.' He looked at Eoin.

'Yip, and what you didn't lose you managed to throw away.' Eoin could hardly disguise his disgust. What was it Costello had said, *Alcoholics do not have relatives, just hostages.*

Batten moved forward, lifted up his jacket to sit down on the end of the narrow bed. 'You tried the programme?'

'I've tried them all.'

'You have an infection. I can smell it from here.'

'Imagine how bad it smells from where I am.'

'I've told him that, I've tried to keep him clean with the antibiotic wipes but . . .' said Eoin, fussing around.

'It's fine.'

'You can die from that, you know. Look at the mess of you.' Batten's hand rested on the narrow knee under the sweaty duvet. Fergus went into a coughing fit, body wracked, blood and mucus spilling slowly from the corner of his mouth.

Eoin handed him a small plastic container that had contained Häagen-Dazs ice cream in a previous life. The coughing went on and on, Fergus spat and wheezed. Until he fell back on to the bed, exhausted with the effort.

'If that chest infection doesn't kill you first . . .' Batten pulled out his phone.

'Eoin, you must have told somebody where he was, otherwise he wouldn't have got the card here, would he?'

'I didn't tell anyone.'

'You told Bernie,' said Fergus.

'Sorry. He's right, I did,' said Eoin. 'I'll leave you to it.' And he left with a small wave of the hand. He'd had enough.

'Can't blame him,' shrugged Fergus.

'Well, we're having a reconstruction of the events. Callum's death. Saturday night. I'm calling an ambulance now. Cut the crap until then. After that you can do what the fuck you like,' said Batten.

Fergus nodded as Anderson lifted his mobile to get the tail back on Eoin.

'Your machine has gone ping again.'

'It will be Amy Lee.'

'Does she never sleep? It's the middle of the night over there. I mean, she must get out her bed to email you.'

'I don't think Grandpappy approves so she's doing this when he's asleep.'

'So she's doing this behind his back? I find that odd.'

'Yes. Oh, she's attached a clip of film, seven minutes of it. I'll download it.'

'Taken at night from the other side of the water by a blind old codger. Good luck with that.'

'Thank you,' said Elvie, perfectly serious. She waited as it downloaded. Vik was lying back on the settee, falling asleep with his cast up on a cushion. She opened up the video file, turning the sound down. She noted the date. The film had been taken on the Saturday night, 22 June, 2013. Time stamped 23.51. It was just before midnight that Jimmy had come rowing back across the water.

The film was bumpy but surprisingly clear. She leaned forward, clipping her earphones into the laptop, and turned the sound up. Breathing. Then the quiet rush of water slapping against the stanchions of the jetty. The visual field moved. She heard the crunch of shingle, then the softer sound of coarse sand underfoot as the old man walked, the slight wheeze of his breath. Then there was a squeak that morphed into tuneful bagpipes from somewhere, the sound slightly distorted. A bright piercing, light in the film, a glow far across the water. The islands came into view. She leaned forward, seeing dots at the fire. The focus honed in, nobody doing very much. This was before Jimmy had returned. Then the film panned across the loch, shades of grey for a moment, then the water turned oily black with the islands in dark grey. She pressed pause. There was something in the water. Its yellow form stark against the black. It was an inflatable. There was some movement on it; she watched closely to try and make out what.

She noted the time. The film flicked back to some more islands, black water, and another little grey island. The fire was out of shot. She saw something ghostly climb out the water, followed by another, then another. Deer?

Then a scan back, the focus hunting around as if looking for more deer. The bonfire shot across the screen. The noise of the bagpipe again.

'Vik?'

'What?' he asked sleepily. The whisky round here really was very good quality, if totally illegal. Elvie didn't drink it, of course. He wondered if she had any fun.

'You need to come and see this.'

'Later.'

'Now.'

He hobbled over. And stood behind her looking at the screen. He watched it twice in silence, hearing his heart thump. A tickle crawled up his neck. 'Elvie? Do you realize what this is?' He leaned forward to ruffle her hair, letting go the crutch, and fell over . . .

The door opened. A light shone in his eyes, so bright he could not see a thing. Even with his lids closed he could feel the retinas burning. 'Shine it away,' he said, but it came closer. He sensed only one of them. The shackles tightened right up so he could hardly move – a tape over his mouth and a hood brought down over his head. He tried to say something but they were too quick.

And the cold hand of fear gripped him. He heard a squeal, realising that it was himself.

Deftly, he was pushed across the concrete floor. His captor was strong and seemed tall. He tried to plead, squeaking and squalling.

Then he felt cool fresh air and the ground underneath him was softer, grassy. Something at the side of his right knee, pressure on his left shoulder, and he was pushed over on to a hard surface. His shoulder stung as his body weight landed on a hard, cold, ridged surface. It was the panelled floor of a van of some kind. His mind went blank. They had kept him, watered him. Where were they taking him now? He knew he was still squealing as they closed the doors. Two doors. One over, then the other. Then the noise of the handle going down. He tried to work out where the door was in relation to his feet. He heard a voice, one he recognised, talking outside. Then the door opened, somebody got in the driver's seat. The floor bounced slightly with the extra weight.

Then he heard a muffled, 'OK.' A key twisted and the engine fired.

Bernie summoned his energy and as the van went round a corner, he slid slightly on the floor, into something warm and soft. He could smell it, it smelled human, reminded him of home. He could imagine contours, he could smell scent. Coco Chanel? There was someone else in here with him, someone he should know.

The van went uphill. He felt the pressure change on his shoulder and tried to wriggle towards the doors, the faint incline helping him. The warm lump beside him did not move, but he could sense it breathing. If he could get close and kick the doors with his feet, something might happen. Something they might survive.

They had something on the film. Elvie had watched it twice and gone to bed. Vik had replayed it over twenty times, seeing a little more each time. They needed to get it enhanced.

Vik had searched on Google but there were no mentions of men overboard that day and the news had been full of the boys' murder, so any boating incident on the loch that same day would have been reported. Unable to sleep, he started an internet search on Angela Colquhoun and became increasingly disturbed by what he was reading. He wished Elvie hadn't gone to bed. She should be here, lying on the floor, discussing theories.

He tried to reach for a pad and pencil that lay on the coffee table but it was too far away. And the sofa he was on was too comfortable.

So he started to copy and paste, making up his own little

narrative as he went along. It was sad but not controversial. Angela had been strangled on the banks of Loch Lomond at Inchgarten. Her body found at the bottom of the Rocking Stone. The mother had nearly hanged for the murder of her four-year-old daughter. This was in the mid-nineteen thirties and public opinion was starting to sway against capital punishment; there was some enlightenment as to why a mother might kill her daughter: illness, not evil.

It crossed his mind that 'Grandpappy' was a Colquhoun, if one spelled phonetically.

He read on, looking for a reason why Angela's mother had moved the body to the stone. It said, in an effort to conceal – Vik snorted at that. In an effort to conceal the crime, the body was placed in an exposed place. The place where Grace had been found all those years later.

Ina Colquhoun had stayed quiet and taken her punishment, damned by the fact that small, feminine hands had strangled the child. What had happened to the husband? Vik read on with his fingertip tracing the words. The couple had a six-year-old, Robert. Robert Colquhoun.

Grandpappy? Bert Cohoon. One and the same? A huge coincidence, surely? But if not, no wonder the old guy didn't want young Amy Lee poking about in his past.

He opened up Elvie's emails and read back the conversations with Amy Lee, his heart thumping. The old guy had been here on his birthday, the longest day. He had been here when the murders happened on the island. He starting phoning the three hotels on the opposite side of the loch, got lucky on the third one. Mr and Mrs Robert Cohoon had stayed there, left in the early hours of Sunday the twenty-third. They had asked for a late checkout. Old man with a bad knee.

Vik thanked him and ended the call.

He read back over the emails again. He was an old man mourning the loss of his wee sister eighty years before, returning to the scene of crime every five years. Some vigil to keep up.

He had no idea how long the van had been travelling for, more than ten minutes but less than an hour. It had stopped once, somebody else had got in and he felt the weight of the van tilt slightly. Nothing was said then the van set off again, turning sharply as if it was doing a U-turn. It was moving through the city now, stopping at lights, taking bends at right angles. Then it picked up speed, out on the open road. The warm body beside him rolled slightly; at one point he thought he heard it groan before it fell quiet again.

Occasionally they went round a bend, causing him to roll and his weight to shift from the back of his hip to the front. The arm he was lying on jabbed him painfully until the car straightened back up again. He worked his way to the doors, bending his knees slightly, and waited until the next curve, until he felt the car was slowing. He counted to ten and kicked with both feet; the door gave a little then held. He kicked again, trying to jackknife his body off the floor to gain more strength. The doors flew open this time. Bernie had no idea if he fell or if he rolled. He tucked his head in as he struck concrete and then tried to get on his feet, or roll away. Get away.

He lay for a minute breathing in the fresh air, enjoying the sense of freedom and a moment of exhilaration as he heard the van drive away. Then it stopped. The engine wasn't turned off; he heard footsteps coming towards him, one set. Then he felt a sharp pain as he was kicked in the head. Then he passed out.

He woke up with pain stinging his head and the taste of blood in his mouth. Now the van was moving very slowly. He heard no indicator. It bumped a fair way then settled on to steady ground, going up a hill, and then it stopped.

The doors opened and immediately slammed shut. He scraped his fingernails as much as he could against the lining of the boot, wriggling his fingers against the shackles. No matter what happened to him now there was something of him here. He would take something of this with him.

They were quick. They lifted his torso, pulling him out the tail doors of the van and letting him drop on to the ground head first. That scared him. Now he was squealing through his lips. Behind the tape he was gagging for breath. They didn't unshackle him, just forced him to walk a short way, grass and soft earth under his feet, then concrete. He heard, or sensed, something going on behind him, another set of feet, another person fighting for breath. He tried to call out, two against two, a fighting chance.

There was no answer.

Now he was cold, there was a chill in the wind. Cold night air fresh in his nostrils. He felt he was high up, a sense of space around him.

He felt something wrapped round his ankle; he tried to sidestep to kick it away but his legs were held together. The tape went tight then slack, but he heard it being ripped. He was being tied on to something. Somebody? He smelled the scent again, immediate memories of Inchgarten, on a long summer day on the island. He was about to recognize the smell when he pivoted backwards, something hard catching him on the thigh.

He heard a familiar hum, a rattle that got ever louder. Ever closer, ever closer.

And then he plunged into nothing.

Costello parked the Fiat behind O'Hare's Avensis. It was twenty-five minutes past three in the morning but the single track road that wound its way up on to the bridge looked like Sauchiehall Street the day the circus came to town. The approach to the bridge was a mass of vehicles: a fire appliance, an ambulance, three police patrol cars, the mortuary van, the scene of crime vehicle and two Scotrail engineering trucks. The small bridge itself was lit up like a seaside disco; flashing multi-coloured lights that prismed off mirrors and sparkled on fluorescent jackets.

Costello couldn't see a thing.

The track over the bridge only went to an old cemetery, but underneath the bridge ran the main west coast rail line. Down on the track, in the distant darkness, she could make out the yellow end of a Scotrail train. The last train to Glasgow Central was going nowhere. The track was closed.

She walked slowly towards two figures on the top of the bridge, carefully picking her way over cables and multicores. There was a bigger crowd underneath the bridge, a swarm of fluorescent jackets catching the arc lights. Torch beams were swinging left and right, picking out yellow and aluminium triangles. The bearers were advancing in a specific pattern. Somebody had organized an inch-by-inch ground search on a railway line under an isolated road bridge. There was forensic activity on the top of the bridge. She didn't need to be Jessica Fletcher to work out they had a jumper.

On top of the bridge, a lone figure sat on the wall in a green plastic suit, shoulders hunched. His face was turned away, his back to the activity below. As Costello approached she realized it was O'Hare. Then she noticed the black and pink bloodied pile lying on the plastic body bag. Then another, bits of torn bin liner, flashes of red fabric, a bit of a – human? – leg? A red, stumpy mess. She slowly walked forward, fascinated while trying not to look.

'So what happened here?' She sat beside O'Hare, then looked behind her over the wall to the train track below. Four SOCOs walking away in a perfect line. As she watched, one stopped. The line stopped. The first one bent down to place another yellow marker. He straightened up and the line set off again, making its slow progress. 'What are they looking for?'

O'Hare looked straight ahead, staring into the black night. 'Two bodies. Parts of two bodies.'

'Two?'

O'Hare stumbled over his words. 'Yeah, two. They had ropes round their ankles. Dangled from here, tied to a vehicle, probably. Dangled down there, in front of the train. Left hanging there for the train coming.'

'Jesus Christ!'

'We called you when we found the tarot card.'

Costello forced herself to look back at the bodies. Back at the one with the flashes of red fabric. The rope had cut into a slim ankle. There was one black shoe. Clean, high-heeled.

'Which one? Which tarot card?'

'The Hanging Man.'

Vik closed the phone. He had never heard Costello's voice so clipped, a sure sign she was upset. They had found Bernie and Sammy in the worst possible way. Eoin had slipped his surveillance. Again. It had all gone very wrong.

He couldn't sleep now. After Costello, Wyngate had called him; the underlying message was clear: be on your guard. Vik couldn't help his mind racing. Everything going on here, including the horror on the bridge, started with wee Angela all those years ago. The butterfly effect. Fully awake now, he spent a few minutes Googling her name, Grandpappy's name with both spellings and Vancouver. After ten minutes he caught sight of the name Amy Lee in the *Richmond News*, a five-year-old whose mother had gone missing. He scrolled past the picture of a smiling brunette holding a child in her arms. Judy Westland had gone out for the weekly shopping and not come back. Her estranged husband, James Westland, was not available for comment. Amy Lee was being looked after by her grandmother, Edie Cohoon. The date was 15 June, 2004.

For some reason the family had then moved east to Manitoba. He looked at Google maps. They had moved a thousand miles.

Then he Googled Amy Lee Westland, Robert Cohoon and Edie in Manitoba 2006. Nothing there, but Amy's name came up in the yearbook of St James Ravenscraig School a year later, somewhere called Thompson, Manitoba. And there was a picture of the children in that year in the *Thompson Citizen*. He flicked over a few editions of the paper. Another woman found murdered, strangled.

Then Amy Lee had moved to Ramsay in Calgary.

He lay down and stared at the wooden ceiling for a long time, thinking about Amy Lee emailing at midnight because she didn't want Grandpappy to know she was looking into his past.

He wondered what secrets Grandpappy had.

The incident room was empty, cold, even in the mid-summer sun. The team were being interviewed about what had gone wrong. Batten knew they had done nothing wrong; they had been outplayed. He had pointed out that Sammy's card was black – he had pointed it out but not pushed the point home. She shouldn't have been allowed to walk about on her own. But Sammy was an intelligent, experienced police officer. She trusted somebody – Bernie?

So Batten was back in his default position, hiding behind the computer monitor at Costello's desk watching Jimmy's interview while nursing a huge mug of black coffee. His eyes were tracking backwards and forwards. His hand nudged the mouse to stop, play, stop, play, rewind. He had headphones on and he appeared to be listening and watching intently.

He was looking at a room which could have been a dining room. The Dewars were sitting round a table with Eoin and Isobel on either side of a younger Jimmy.

A female voice said, 'Sometimes it's easier if you draw what happened.'

Jimmy nodded, chin sticking out, teeth biting down hard, twitching. All signs of inner turmoil. His mind was trying to remember things he would rather forget.

'Only if you want to, Jimmy,' Isobel said with a reassuring pat on the shoulder.

'Are you up for this? It would be really helpful. Here's a map of the island. It's not very good, I'm afraid.'

Jimmy smiled, looking at the piece of paper. He was handed a pencil, the film kept running. Jimmy smoothed out the paper on the table top and lifted the pencil.

'Just draw on it where the Dreamcatcher landed on Snooky Bay.'

He pointed the tip of his pencil on to the paper, looking up for reassurance.

'Yes, that's Snooky Bay, there's the folly wall . . . the narrows are down here, I've put them in blue to help.'

Jimmy leaned forward and drew something, with the tip of his tongue out.

When he finished, 'So then the four of you climbed the folly wall?'

He nodded.

'So draw that then.' He did.

'And where did you go afterwards?'

'We went,' he drew as he spoke, 'round the bottom of the cliff round here, round the path, Callum and I . . .'

'Yes, Callum and you. Did you stay back for some reason? Where had Robbie gone?'

'Robbie was round here with . . .'

'With Warren?'

Jimmy nodded. 'Yes.'

'Then you walked round the pathway following Robbie and . . .'

'He was hitting him.'

'But what did you see, Jimmy? I know it's difficult, but what did you actually see?'

Jimmy was still for a moment, the pencil poised over the paper. 'I was looking at the cliff, I heard noises. Robbie made a noise, crying. I saw Robbie on the ground and Warren had this stone, he was hitting him like this . . .' Jimmy raised his hand high in the air and brought it down violently.

The ferocity silenced them; the only noise on the video was the hum of the camera.

'Then?'

'He looked up and saw me.'

'And?'

'I ran . . . He chased me . . . But he . . .'

The pencil hesitated, then the tears started. The boy started to scream and howl. The paper was torn and the table was overturned as the boy fell to the floor, curling himself into a ball.

The screen went blank.

Batten pulled a polythene A3 size folder from Costello's desk. In it was the piece of paper that showed a rough outline of the island, and the narrows marked on one side, the loch on the other. A wavy outline of a small canoe parked against the curved line. Pencil point driven through. The rest of the paper had been crumpled, then carefully straightened.

He rewound the film, just enough to see the boy curled on the floor. He could see Isobel's shoes and her knees, legs bent ready to kneel beside her son.

He rewound the film again.

To the phrase 'And what did you actually see?'

'I was looking at the cliff, I heard noises. Robbie made a noise, crying. I saw Robbie on the ground and Warren had this stone, he was hitting him like this . . .'

'Then?'

'He looked up and saw me.'

'And?'

'I ran, he chased me . . . But he . . .'

The boy started to scream and howl.

The film broke, then restarted.

'But you and Callum got to Snooky Bay?'

On film, Jimmy nodded: a female hand was seen handing him a handkerchief. 'But Warren was faster – did you see him get to Callum?'

'I managed to get to the boat. He couldn't . . . I couldn't save him.' The cries became louder, the film stopped again.

Batten was now back in his own office at the university. He had been there all night, fuelled by strong black coffee and, if he was honest, a sense of guilt. He had got something very wrong. He was looking at things that were difficult to look at but were still easier than suffering the raw pain and anger in the main office at the station. He had left the team to lick their wounds. And assuage their guilt. Batten had seen many pictures of violence, death by violence, and it was never easy when it was children. Children killed in war zones, those images on the TV he could accept. But somehow children dying a violent death in their own home always hit him hardest. Something about that juxtaposition of them being killed in a place where they should feel at their safest, somewhere where a parent should protect them.

After watching the video of Jimmy's interview he turned to the post-mortem and the scene of crime DVDs. He started with Robbie, who was found dead on the highest part of the northerly bay, far from the water. He was lying on his back, the pale shingle underneath him clumped with blood, eyes closed, his left hand raised, right arm across his body. His injuries so much worse than the other boy. It had taken time, Batten thought. Was that rage on McAvoy's part because Jimmy had got away? Robbie had tried to fend off his attacker. His brown hair covered the site of the actual impact. They had not found the murder weapon, but the report said it was probably a stone from traces found deep in the wound. Callum's attack had been quicker, but just as fatal. McAvoy knew he still had to deal with Jimmy. Batten flicked over a few more photographs, trying to think like a ten-year-old boy on his holidays, on his adventures. Callum had been timid getting into the boat with the other three, maybe not keen to go with Warren. Yet in the film taken a few weeks before, Warren was filling the boy with confidence. Maybe the boy felt more confident with the others there; Jimmy, the older boy, and his pal Robbie. The three musketeers.

Psychology was a science and the rules of science were confirmed by the anomalies, but there were no anomalies here.

He flipped to the other folder with the pictures of Callum. Lying on his front, his hair parted at the site of injury. His left temple had been hit with a blunt instrument by a right-handed person. He was found on the beach near Snooky Bay. Batten kept flicking through. Not looking at the boys now but at the surrounding area, the landscape. There was something troubling him, something that somebody had said, but he was tired and couldn't connect the ideas. He stood up and slid his jacket on, bumping his head on the bottom of the bookshelf. He swore loudly and sat back down, rubbing his bald head as his fingers felt the blood. He looked at his crimson fingertips, scalp wounds always bled like hell. He got up and turned to the small sink in his office, sticking a white paper towel over the wound, then he sat back and watched the crimson stain spread. He thought about the ruffle of Warren's hand on the boy's head. That was the anomaly. Trust turning to violence so quickly, with no precedent. The precedent pointed elsewhere.

With his free hand he picked up the phone.

O'Hare was having his usual busy morning. His attention was currently on a young man, as yet unidentified, but as he had lots of distinguishing features it was just a matter of getting him on the database. He couldn't be any more than twenty-five and he was dead from a single punch. Unintentional, O'Hare was sure, nothing more than larking about by junkies with insufficient motor control to fall over safely. He waited until his assistant pulled together the fingers of the deceased left hand, to get the sense of the letters tattooed on each finger. H-I-L-D-A. He asked for a photograph, the camera flashed. Then O'Hare's phone rang. He muttered an obscenity. That would be somebody else telling him how to do his job.

Wyngate lifted the phone slowly when it rang. He couldn't take, or pass on, any more bad news. He swallowed hard then identified himself. He heard Vik's voice and listened in silence for a couple of minutes.

'Sir?' Wyngate called over to Anderson.

'If it's not good, don't bother.'

'It's good. It's Vik, something about an eyewitness who was staying at the Lodge on the Loch Hotel that night. The night the boys were killed.' Wyngate covered the mouthpiece, as the rest of the room fell silent.

Anderson took the phone.

A quarter of an hour later, Batten had arrived nursing a sore head and they were all sitting around the computer as the screen filled with darkness. They were on speakerphone to Vik's mobile at Inchgarten. The image swung back and forth, the light line of the opposite shoreline, a few islands dotted about. The camera moving so fast, Costello held on to the desk. It settled on a few dots, the focus changed, zoomed in, and then moving again.

'How long have you had this?' Costello spoke into the phone.

'Less than twelve hours.'

'And you got it enhanced, in that time? You're talking pish.'

'Not if you get a rich American to pay for a digital expert to get out their bed. He's only done half but you have to see this. Now watch and marvel,' said Vik, watching the same film in the lodge. 'See there, wait, he goes back over it. About thirty-four seconds in . . .'

'Hardly Steven Spielberg, is he?'

'Any more camera wobbling and I'm going to be sick,' said Costello. 'Couldn't watch that Blair Witch shite.'

'Just wait . . . There . . . Do you see that yellow dot in the darkness? I think that is the wee inflatable, dull yellow like the casing I found in the old boathouse on Inchgarten Island.' Elvie's voice loud and clear across the speakerphone.

'And there is somebody aboard rowing,' said Anderson, peering at the screen.

'Paddling,' corrected Elvie.

'Same thing,' muttered Anderson in bad grace.

'So he's moving away from the island, going . . .'

'North,' said Elvie, 'he's come off the top of the island. Then the image moves to the south, to the deer, the deer leaving the water.'

The film showed the beautiful, ghost-like forms, white in the dark air. Then the deer moved off to the north and the phone camera caught the yellow boat. There was a movement, then stillness and the camera moved away.

'You need to replay that bit, back to the deer,' said Elvie's disembodied voice. 'Then pause on the yellow object.'

'What is he doing?'

'Escaping. That is Warren McAvoy escaping.'

Anderson looked at the board then dropped his head on to the desk, feeling a sense of relief at something concrete.

'So he was heading off the island from the boathouse. Jimmy had some start on him; he had already pulled the Dreamcatcher far enough away for Warren not to catch him.'

'It wouldn't have taken him any time at all, young like that.' Batten showed a crumpled piece of paper on the screen. 'Here's a bad drawing of Inchgarten Island, cliff at the north end. Rocky beach at the east side, the side that faces into the narrows and over to the lodges. Nobody ever lands their boat there as the water is very unsafe, there's a big shelf under the water. Swim three feet from the shore and you are in three feet of water. Swim six feet away and you are in twenty feet of water. Round at the south side, the beach is sandy and sloping, so that is the preferred landing point, Snooky Bay. The handmade boathouse was here, on the west side. Robbie's body was found here, near the base of the cliffs at the north; Callum's was found here on Snooky Bay, the second boy to be killed. So Warren kills Robbie then chases Jimmy and Callum round the west side of the island, found Jimmy was getting away on the Dreamcatcher but attacked Callum on the beach. Then Warren goes back the way he came to the boathouse to try and escape on the raft. Can we prove any of that?'

'No,' said Anderson. 'But we don't need to. Technically, we are not investigating that, are we? We are investigating the deaths of Bella, Eddie, Bernie, Patty and Sammy. Now we know that Warren got off the island, we just have to find the bastard.'

Suddenly there was a voice from nowhere. 'No.'

They jumped as the single word floated round the room. They had forgotten about the couple at Inchgarten, listening in.

'Elvie? What do you mean, no?' asked Anderson, getting up, ready to ask Mitchum to launch a manhunt.

'The folly is in the way.'

'They must have climbed over it. Callum was found on the beach and Jimmy got away on the boat, both on this side of the folly.'

'The boys could have got through,' said Elvie. 'But Warren couldn't.'

'Well, you got over it.'

'On the way out, yes. But I couldn't get back that way. Nobody can. I had to swim the long way round. The wall is too high, too smooth to climb. The ground is lower on that side. The boys would have gone through the arrow slit.'

'But Jimmy did. Surely if Jimmy did then Warren did. The size of them . . .' Anderson was dismissive, but as the words left his mouth he thought about how tall Peter could grow in a year.

Elvie's voice was calm, patient. 'He wouldn't get through it now, he's too tall. But this was then, when he was smaller. He's lying. Warren could not have got back to Snooky Bay.'

*   *   *

Costello was running through the facts in her mind, thinking that the world had gone crazy. They had watched one half of a film that proved McAvoy's guilt. Anderson was now trying to get the second half enhanced, which might prove his innocence.

She took three Ibuprofen for her headache. Bernie's brother had been on the phone wanting answers as to why his brother wasn't better protected. Sammy's mother had collapsed at the news. The brutality of it was on the front of every newspaper. Mitchum was talking about taking them off the case, but that would be admitting errors had been made.

Somebody somewhere was laughing at them.

She washed the tablets down with a mouthful of tea and started nibbling a chocolate digestive. She opened the medical files of Robbie, Callum and Jimmy, part of a pile Batten had dumped in front of her, wee Post-it notes sticking out here and there. Batten had looked sunken cheeked as he had asked her to look at the injury history of the boys, and the dates.

To her eyes, Robbie Dewar's medical records were perfectly clear. A victim of violence. Fractures, marks, burns and bruises told their story. Most often they were present on the summer holidays when Warren was about at Inchgarten. Jimmy, the bigger boy, was maybe able to fight back and had suffered less.

It was all circumstantial. Everything was well explained: the burns while messing with the fire, the weals from branches and twigs whiplashing him as he ran through the trees. Happy boys, playing boys' games. Nobody ever got injured playing a computer game.

Why did nobody say anything? Perhaps it was a case of three boys trying to keep the peace. But one of them would have spoken out, surely? Had it gone from Warren killing the boys and now the guilty parents were fighting back? And Daisy raised the rain to help them? Costello was so tired, she would believe anything. But would they have kept quiet if it was a parent? The silence was more understandable then. Did the boys suffer when they were not in contact with Warren? She picked up her jacket and left, ignoring Anderson's warning about not going anywhere on her own.

Costello spent an hour talking to the guidance teacher at Jimmy's old school. She was in no doubt that the boy was troubled. Everything had been put down to what he had witnessed that summer's night twelve months before. As Isobel had admitted, he was both bully and being bullied.

Costello tried subtly to ask about his physical wellbeing and the teacher politely ducked the question. Then told her to speak to the PE teacher, Gareth Lamb. Ignoring her disgust of teenage boy sweat, the stench of hockey stick handles and rubber mats, Costello found herself in the PE department. Bad memories flooded back. She hated Gareth Lamb long before he walked out of the boys' locker room. Like most of her old PE teachers, this guy had an obesity issue.

'Yeah, that boy suffered bruises, odd cuts. Nothing too much. I tried to get him to talk about it but he would never engage. I know what the boy had been through and he was receiving counselling, so I presumed the abuse would come up in those sessions. They are trained more than we are for that sort of thing.'

'Surely there must have been times when he was not fit enough to do PE?' she asked.

But Lamb shook his head. 'Can't say that. He was always keen.'

She then drove out to speak to Isobel.

But Isobel was not for letting her in. Costello stood on her steps looking at the screw holes still empty where the former owners' nameplate had been. Isobel was still wearing her beige cardigan, even though it was a stifling day.

To Costello, Isobel looked like a closed witness. She had knowledge that she was not prepared to give them. No wonder, all victims of domestic abuse lived in a spiral of silence.

'So Isobel, the relationship between the four of you? It's not as simple as it seems. It's more than two couples who were friends, two couples with kids the same age. Kids that were very much wanted.'

Isobel Dewar looked at Costello as though she wanted to kill her. Costello waited for her to deny everything.

Then Costello said, 'It's never easy, Isobel, but you will have to tell the truth sooner or later. It was your son that died. We understand your anger.'

'My son . . .' Isobel took her hands out from behind the door to adjust the cuff of her cardigan.

'And who did that to your hand, Isobel?'

'I burned it on the iron.'

'Did you? Are you and Jimmy both accident prone? Was Robbie?'

She shook her head. 'I don't know what you're talking about.'

'You know, Isobel, I was very touched at the way you and Eoin hold hands, the way you support each other. But it's not that, is it? You sleep in separate beds. You are scared of him, aren't you?'

Isobel's eyes opened wide, an ugly deep breath. 'Leave me alone.'

'You're not doing him any favours. How did you burn your hand, Isobel?' Costello asked, her voice gentle.

Isobel shook her head in wry amusement, then spoke as though she was talking to a child, slowly, each syllable clear and spelled out. 'I burned it on the iron. It's the end of term and I have work to do. Goodbye.'

'See you tomorrow night, then,' said Costello. She put a copy of the paper, with its headline of 'Carnage', on Isobel's hall floor just before the door closed on her.

Saturday, 21 June
The Longest Day

Daisy was sitting at the water's edge on the Rocking Stone, her podgy fingers combing her hair. Mr Peppercorn was lying at her feet, after his usual 'somebody's coming' barking session. Daisy looked younger and slightly frightened. The big world had come crashing in on their idyllic home.

'Hello, Daisy,' said Anderson, casually dressed in jeans and fleece. 'Here for the big event, are you?'

'Indeed. Sorry business, but it has to be done.'

'If you say so.' She got up as if to walk away, slipping her Crocs on to her bare feet.

'We need to ask you something. What was Warren doing the night Grace was killed? We know he was not at Sammy McSingh's.'

She looked at Anderson suspiciously.

'Why did he not come forward?'

'I don't know. He wasn't here.'

'Have a guess.' He smiled at her, inviting a confidence.

'Flying.' Again she tried to walk away, this time prevented by Anderson's stretched out hand.

'Flying?'

'Flying. A little drink, a little smoke and he'd go flying. Like the witches used to.' She looked up to the hills, her face a picture of sad wistfulness. 'Good days, the best of days.'

Anderson recalled Elvie's warning about driving when he was feeling so chilled. And Elvie did not joke. 'Daisy, did you drug me the other day? In the gingerbread?'

'No, I gave you a herbal tea. It's relaxing. You were very stressed.'

'I was drinking coffee.'

Daisy looked out across the water, biting her lip. 'We were happy. It's all over now.'

'We are a murder squad, Daisy. I don't give a shite what you smoke.'

'I put something herbal in your coffee, nothing illegal. I could see your pulse in your temple, you needed to calm down. And before you ask, I never drugged the children. Neither would Warren. But he could go away for days, lying down, talking to the trees, mellow as anything. Sometimes, we fly. A wee bit of herb here and there, no harm done, consenting adults.'

Anderson thought of the warm fire burning in the summer heat. 'A wee bit of Mary Jayne. So do you all partake?'

'We all did a lot of things, DCI Anderson.' There was something in her tone but her attention had gone. She was looking up the loch with some concern.

That would be a huge deal for Isobel, if it got out. Instant dismissal from her job. How trapped had Isobel felt here? He looked up at the hills, the colours had changed again. He was thinking about another question when something stroked his cheek, like the caress of warm fingers.

'Did you feel that?' asked Daisy. Her face was calm now, resolved. She looked like a different person.

'Feel what?' Costello asked, joining them from the bonfire, and sitting down. Even Mr Peppercorn was looking out over the water, ears pricked, searching for a presence only he could sense. The air was warm but Anderson felt a chill down the back of his neck.

'The tears of angels. Oh, yes, this water will cry before the moon comes up. The loch will give up its dead tonight.' Daisy looked at the sky. 'You can feel it in the air – the rain is coming.'

Costello pulled a face, got up and walked away, but Anderson was transfixed. The water was unnaturally still, incredibly clear. Then, in front of his eyes, it started to dimple as if being spotted by fine rain. Anderson held the palm of his hands out, looking up, expecting to feel raindrops. The sky was clear.

Daisy placed a tiny spray of green leaves in his outstretched palm . . . 'For good luck, DCI Anderson.' Mr Peppercorn, sensing some distress, stuck his wet nose into Daisy's hand, for a lick of comfort. 'You have kids, don't you, Mr Anderson?'

Colin felt a little wary answering. 'Yes, I have two. I've been very lucky.'

'Yes, you are. You are very lucky indeed. Remember that. You're blessed. It is the angels who are talking to you.'

'Is that good news?' he asked in all seriousness.

'It means they are going to return one or take one.'

'One what?'

'Take a life or give up a body? Who knows? It's outwith your hands.'

Brenda got in the car, ready to drive off for her night out. She had replayed that conversation in her mind as she drove along the motorway. Helena had called her, thinking she was having a normal Saturday night at home, but this was her special night out with the new friends at work, her first one in . . . God knows how many years. So she didn't want Claire back, and Colin had left a message saying he would be held up at work. So Helena could babysit Claire, or the other way round if Helena was poorly again. Gallbladder trouble, she reckoned.

Funny how that circle of life had come round, another click on the cog. Her friends, not that she had many, thought she was crazy for not leaving her husband. Then crazy for allowing him to come back. Then crazy for allowing Claire to work with Helena.

They didn't know how hard it had been lying in their bed alone, without him, not knowing where he was. He had never lied to her. If she had asked she would have been told, but she never had. Life was something that was happening to her now. Gone were the days when her husband lived in a bedsit and she sat alone at home watching Jeremy Kyle.

His leaving was the spur to get up and get on with it. She'd got a job, got herself a life. Turned back into the girl he had met at university, the girl he had fallen in love with. The girl who had been allowed to tag along with the cool students to an outside performance of *Much Ado About Nothing*, only because her friend had fancied one of Colin's friends. On the coach going home she was left alone in a double seat, her friend having deserted her. Colin, carrying a bottle of beer, had climbed on the bus and slumped into the seat beside her. Tall, blond, handsome Colin Anderson. A bit of a catch. He had chosen her above all the prettier girls. Twenty-three years later they were still together. With only one small blip called Helena McAlpine.

Helena flicked through the mail she had picked up at the gallery without any real interest. The usual bills, enquiries, insurance going up, a few things that needed to be signed that she could not do by email. She slumped down on her stool, inhaling suddenly when she saw the black envelope. She felt its thickness, then realized that there were two slightly stuck together. She separated them, her fingers feeling clumsy. She opened hers and turned the black card over slowly. The Wheel of Fortune. She almost laughed, like they could do anything to scare her now. Then she looked at the second card. It was addressed to Claire.

That did scare her.

She sat down on her stool, trying to think. Brenda had said something about going out. She wasn't happy leaving Claire in the house alone, and she couldn't keep her here, not after what happened last time. Colin had said he'd be down at the loch, so she'd deliver Claire to him. He was doing background checks or something. She'd hang about with Claire until he had finished, they could rendezvous at Rowardennan. He'd be pleased to see them both.

She rubbed her temples, trying to think clearly. These cards were a threat, Claire needed to be with her dad. But she knew that she herself also wanted to see Colin. There was no eternity for them now, it was all numbered, all a countdown. Each moment to be savoured, there would be so few.

The small bonfire was lit, Tony taking a lot of time in fanning the flames and blowing air through the bottom of the pile of twigs and branches.

'Could never get the hang of that,' said Anderson. 'I failed the arson badge at the scouts.'

'Bloody scouts. All boys and toggles,' Costello mumbled.

'Woggles,' corrected Anderson. 'So, you know what you are doing?'

'I am standing here, observing. Vik is filming from the lodge steps with Walker. And Elvie is a free agent. Back-up will be in place at the field once all our guests have arrived. Secondary back-up is on the far side. In both cases arrival time to this spot is less than one minute.'

Anderson and Costello then stayed at the water's edge, observing. Eoin arrived with Isobel, hand in hand, his fingers entwined round hers, controlling her. A female police officer arrived with the diminutive figure of Ruth following her. The female cop was carrying a bag with a teddy's head sticking out. Eoin saw Ruth and immediately opened his arms. A genuinely affectionate greeting, a word spoken in her ear, in private. Isobel gave Ruth a functional hug, then Eoin lifted Ruth over the tree logs that acted as seats round the bonfire. Ruth took the teddy and kept it close as she sat down.

Archie Walker was in the shadows of the chalet. He had been told to watch Eoin. Vik was sitting on the steps of Eigg, with a video camera. Elvie was nowhere to be seen.

Anderson kept looking down the path, to the curve at Roonbay, waiting to see if Fergus would make it. Eventually there was a buzz of movement as one of the female officers got a message down her radio. Then she set off with purpose, meeting two colleagues who were helping a very frail-looking Fergus.

Anderson took the chance to leave the waterside and join Costello. 'God, he made it. That is determination,' he said in admiration, watching as Eoin greeted his friend before helping him to sit on a log.

Tony put more wood on the fire; Daisy appeared from between the chalets carrying something that looked like a casserole.

Costello gave herself a running commentary. 'So Isobel is on her own. Ruth has her son's bear. Daisy doing as Daisy does. Tony drifts around. Fergus and Eoin are chatting. They are waiting for the drink to come. It's like a bloody picnic.'

'Very good of you, to take me all the way out there.'

'No problem,' said Helena, concentrating on driving up Great Western Road. The light was failing. Her neck hurt, her back hurt. There was a persistent dull ache behind her left eye. The inevitability of what was going on in her body was ever present. But she had not been ready for the small increments it would take, bit by bit, bite by bite. How long did she have left driving? Her eyes seemed to take time to tell her brain about the distance between her and the car in front. Yet although her eyes were so tired, her ears seemed to have become super sensitive. She could hear the noise of the engine like an orchestra of internal combustion; every component, every instrument. She shook her head, trying to wake her brain up. It didn't work so she slowed down.

She concentrated on her lane position, flinching when the lights of the oncoming cars flashed in her eyes. She wondered if Claire sensed anything, but the girl was fiddling with the CD, humming along. Helena was concerned that the card had come to the gallery. How could that happen? It was tucked in the back of her jeans pocket, burning a hole. The Wheel of Fortune. She had Googled it. A load of crap about turning points, the poor becoming rich, the rich becoming poor, the living becoming the dead. But whoever was sending the cards knew where she worked. Where Claire worked. Somebody had made the connection between her and Colin. She wasn't taking the chance of what else they might know. What they might do. So she would deliver Claire to her dad.

She drove, not talking as Claire began to translate the sat-nav as they neared the road that would take them to Inchgarten Lodge Park. Fifty minutes door to door.

'The sat-nav says we have to go up here. Can that be right?' asked Claire.

'Yip, I think that is where we go. The postcode is for the lodge park and that is a bit further round.'

'Dad said they had to go the last bit on foot.'

Helena indicated, pretending to scratch her face. But wiped away a tear. The car was suddenly full of peat-scented air, wood smoke, faint petrol and something else. Something that provoked a memory of Alan coming in the door at three in the morning, straight to the drinks cabinet. Her subconscious grabbed a flashback of him sitting at the breakfast bar, a black coffee and overflowing ashtray beside him. She could see the tiredness in his eyes, the creases in his suit, thirty-three hours on duty, and the smell of sweat. Home for a drink and a shower before he was off again. How could she know that? The number of hours, something so specific? Why was she counting at the time? There must have been a reason. A missing person. A picture floated through her mind. A waitress. She had been so young. She had been dead by the time Alan found her. She had been one of his failures. And something that was not to be shared with her.

Did Anderson talk about such things? With Brenda? Another little stab.

'I think you might have missed the turn there,' said Claire.

She hadn't even seen it. Her mind was elsewhere. She blinked hard and tried to concentrate.

Back in the investigation room, Wyngate and Batten were researching the folly. It was a fake castle wall that effectively cut the island into two. It was recorded, probably erroneously, that two brothers had built it in Victorian times. The folly on the south-west and the cliffs on the north-east effectively halved the island equally, one half for each brother. They were still discussing the stupidity of folk who had too much money when O'Hare walked in.

'I want to talk to Anderson.'

'He's not here, he's at Inchgarten for the big showdown.'

'Shit.' He looked at Batten. 'Or maybe that is a good thing.' He sat on a chair, handed Batten two files and made himself at home. 'I want to run something past you. The medical history of the boys.'

'I've been through that, all three boys suffered abuse. The abuse is clustered temporally around the time Warren McAvoy had access to them.'

O'Hare nodded. 'I picked that up. The McCardle boy fractured his arm.'

'Fell out a tree.'

'The knee that needed a brace.'

'Fell over a tree root when not looking where he was running. They all have an excuse.'

'Yes, and Robbie is the same.'

'And so is Jimmy.'

'Is he?' asked O'Hare. 'Look at these. Jo had noted the anomaly at the post, but in the light of Jimmy's testimony she interpreted it wrongly.' He put the photographs of Jimmy taken by his dad in front of Batten. 'These were sustained running from Warren, that's all. Warren didn't ever get close enough to Jimmy to hit him, to cause any head injury, did he?'

'No.'

'OK,' said O'Hare, warming to his subject. 'A year ago Robbie was four feet four, Callum was four feet one. Warren was . . .'

They both looked at Wyngate, 'Five feet nine. We already know that Warren couldn't get through the folly wall, that's what we're doing here.'

The pathologist shook his head. 'This is something else, bear with me.'

Wyngate and Batten exchanged looks as O'Hare took out a tape measure and held it against the desk. He then piled up some books and placed Wyngate's own copy of *The Scottish Police Officer* upright on top.

'Right,' he said to Batten. 'Pretend you have a rock in your hand and you are going to hit that book in the middle. But stand up to do it.'

Batten did so, his arm at waist height, like he was hitting a volley from the baseline.

'OK. So now hit it without thinking about it. Just hit it.' Batten's arms went up and over.

'Exactly. We tried it back at the lab. As soon as we induce a height difference, it's easier to hit the object on top.'

Batten nodded. 'That's right. When Jimmy demonstrated, it was like an overarm bowl.'

'So why are there no injuries to the top of the skull? They are on the side; the fractures run inwards, not downwards, so the blows were horizontal. From someone roughly the same height. Not from someone much taller.'

Batten and Wyngate looked at each other.

'I don't think for a minute it will stand up to vigorous cross examination, but it's a starting point. This is a "definite" in a maze of supposition.'

'Wait a minute,' said Batten. 'Mitchum said it right at the start. Anderson has quoted it to me, "Jimmy's testimony never wavered." Word for word. *We took the boat up the shore. Warren pulled it high on the beach, in case the weather turned*, he said. And he repeats exactly the same words. The interviewer interrupts but Jimmy soon gets back to the agreed script. Until he gets to the bit where he pulls Callum up . . . *but I couldn't save him . . . I couldn't save him.* At that point he always dissolves into tears. Because at that point the story breaks down. I was looking for escalation from Warren. I was looking in the wrong place. It explains what happened to all those Dewar family pets. Cassie the dog, the mice, Petra the cat. I've read the emails from the vets. Chilling.'

'So these injuries happened when they were with Jimmy, not Eoin?'

'Just forget what you've been told and ask yourself who had injuries that were never that serious. Because they were self-inflicted. Who discovered Grace's body? Who got off the island? Who could get to the Dreamcatcher? Where is he now?'

'With his gran,' said Wyngate.

'Do you have authority to send somebody out to sit with him?' O'Hare asked.

'I'll try.' Batten looked at the clock. 'Wyngate, how long would it take you to drive us out to Inchgarten?'

O'Hare put his hands up. 'Count me out. I'm still suffering from the last time I was in a field with DCI Anderson.'

Batten stood up and tightened the thong round his neck. 'Might be best. It could get nasty.'

'Nasty? We are looking at a twelve-year-old triple child killer. How much more nasty can you get?'

'It's only half the story, isn't it? The boy is a psychopath, can't help it. But somebody is doing all this stuff with the cards. And that is evil.'

Anderson looked round, trying to gauge where everybody was. They had kept the news of the discovery of the life raft to themselves. He had kept the enhancement of the second part of the video to himself. Only Vik and Elvie knew. One firecracker to spark off a few memories.

'OK. So can you all remember where you were the night of the incident?' Anderson flicked a look at his watch. It was five past eleven. 'Fergus, you were sitting right where you are now. And Tony, you were over there?'

'Playing the pipes,' added Tony.

'Then you stopped. Did you put the pipes away up at the house, or in the Boathouse?'

Tony looked about. 'I just leaned them against the log there. I was passing some drink round and . . .'

'You were. Daisy was coming down with another bottle?'

'That's right. I was standing up, here.'

'For part of the evening I was standing here with my back to the fire,' said Tony.

'We have been over this a thousand times,' Isobel complained.

'So bear with me. Eoin was sitting beside you.'

'We were arguing about something, so what?'

'Well I joined in, we were arguing about wind farms,' said Tony. 'I was about here. Daisy at some point sat down in front of me, nearer the water, I mean.' He pointed and Daisy moved.

Isobel then added, 'I stood up and moved away over there.'

'Why?'

'Because the smoke was blowing this way.'

'You're right. I came round because the smoke was in my eyes,' said Daisy.

Costello circled the bay like a hyena, watching them. Anderson poked at the fire a little, sending out a rush of sparks. He looked at them through the smoke that burled into the night sky, a midsummer night. It was never really going to get dark.

He looked at the line-up sitting opposite him . . .

Isobel, Fergus, Ruth, Eoin, Daisy, and Tony standing slightly behind them, looking down over the water. He looked to the left, the small curve of Roonbay, the Rocking Stone. The dark mass of Inchgarten Island sitting low in the water. Through the smoke it looked ghostly dark and threatening.

'So at the critical time, what happened? It was Fergus who raised the alarm, wasn't it?' asked Anderson. 'Then Eoin saw Jimmy coming back. But it was Ruth who was looking out over the water.'

Ruth shrugged.

Costello pursed her lips.

'At some point I was sitting with my back to the fire slightly and didn't see. I wasn't watching. Not all the time. But I was right here.'

'No, I bet you were busy having a laugh with my husband. That's why you didn't see your own son, Ruth!' said Isobel. 'Your son!'

'And you?'

'I went to get a blanket. I was coming down the path when I heard,' spat Isobel.

Anderson noted the vitriol in her voice. 'And when you all saw Jimmy, what happened?' he asked calmly, daring them to look at each other as the terrible memories began to surface. 'So what happened then?'

'This is bloody worse than Agatha Christie,' muttered Isobel.

'I think I went over there, as Fergus was already on his feet,' said Eoin, pointing to the far side of the log. 'And when I got to the sand I noticed it was only Jimmy.'

'How far out was the Dreamcatcher?'

'Close enough for us to see that it was only Jimmy. Ruth grabbed my arm, she was shouting for Callum. I remember thinking that it must be OK as Robbie wasn't in the boat either . . .'

'OK.' Anderson picked a branch from the fire and waved it in

the air, sending sparks dancing in the gentle swirling wind, sending
a clear signal. He checked the time again; it was still earlier now
than it had been on the night the boys died. But even with this light
he would have found it difficult to see until the Dreamcatcher was
close. 'Were all the others up by then?'

'Yes.'

'All looking that way?'

'Yes.'

'Can you recall where you all were, even approximately?'

They shuffled into position, Tony giving Fergus a helping hand.
Daisy pointed out that Tony had stood on the log. All of them were
down on the bay side of the fire, all of them had a good view of
the water.

'And none of you saw anything? Although you were all looking?'
asked Anderson, incredulous.

'No, Fergus walked on to the shore. Eoin started to wade into
the water, he pulled his top off, and he started to swim. Daisy was
beside him. Then Tony ran for the Scoob . . .'

Daisy closed her eyes. 'The boy was screaming, Tony ran
back . . .'

Anderson recalled the original statement to the police. It all fitted.
Jimmy was rowing over. He was completely hysterical. They would
have been alerted by his screaming, the sound carrying well over
the water. A wee kid out on the ice-cold water alone. Eoin fit, able
to swim out to help. The pragmatic Tony going for the Scoob then
coming back as the Dreamcatcher approached. Eoin in plain sight.
Nobody saw the life raft. They were caught up in the terror of a
twelve-year-old boy.

'Fergus was standing, right there, in the water.' Daisy pointed.
'I was standing beside him.'

'Costello, can you be Fergus—' He was cut off by a scream, a
blood-curdling screech in the night air.

It was Ruth, shrieking, pointing. Out over the water.

'Jesus,' said Costello, clutching at Anderson, who told her to be
quiet.

'What the fuck!'

Anderson couldn't tell who said what as the Dreamcatcher floated
into sight, a lone figure paddling. The boat seemed to glide above the
water. Daisy nervously stood in her position, then reversed a little.

It was then that Anderson noticed Ruth was moving now. Ruth, the one who had recognized the sight of the life raft. So, on the actual night, where had she been? Surely, the concerned mother would have been on her feet, searching the skyline.

'Had you all had a drink by this time?' he asked, waiting for Ruth to do something. She didn't.

Anderson noticed that Tony had also not moved. He was standing biting his lip, his hand running up and down his arm. He was looking round the assembled company.

'We have seen a film, a film taken on the night the boys were killed, and on that film we can actually see the murder take place.'

'So you know who murdered the boys then?' Tony asked. His hands spread in wonderment. 'Jesus.'

'Not the murder of Callum McCardle or the murder of Robbie Dewar. But the murder of Warren McAvoy.'

There was an audible intake of breath then somebody, Fergus maybe, said, 'That's shite.'

'Oh no, you can see it clearly. He is on the raft, paddling with one knee on the wall of the inflatable craft.' The light of the flames moved around, creating shadows where there were none. The sky was grey, blending into the dark hills. Somebody moved – he didn't see who. 'Something hits him in the chest and he doubles up. He's in the water, he dies.' The night air had now closed in round the fire; the wind snatched at the flames, causing them to dance one way then the other.

'He died that night, trying to get off the island, trying to raise the alarm. He was shot while he was in open water by somebody here in Inchgarten Bay. The film is very clear, he grasps at his chest and is thrown into the water. Whatever hit him, hit him with great force. And you don't have any guns round here, do you, Tony?'

He shook his head. 'I certainly do not.'

'I've had enough of this.' Eoin was the first to break.

'Maybe a drink would calm everybody down,' suggested Fergus with some humour.

Daisy looked to Anderson for permission. He nodded.

'I'll give you a hand,' said Ruth, standing up.

'Thanks – that would be great. Come on then.' The two women walked up the slope to the Boathouse, Mr Peppercorn trotting behind them. 'It's good to see you, Ruth. It's good for you to be here, lay the ghosts to rest.' They hugged and walked off.

Isobel sat still, arms folded. She got up and walked slowly round the fire towards Anderson.

'DCI Anderson,' she said, her voice quivering. 'I don't think she was there. Eoin is lying. He's lying.'

'Who wasn't there?'

'Ruth.' Isobel's face crumpled. 'I never realized it until now. But I wasn't there when Eoin shouted. When I heard Jimmy, I was coming out the lodge. I went back in to get a blanket, I brought it down here. I passed Ruth when I was coming back. She was on her way up. She said something to me, something about Fergus being drunk again. And I know that I'm right because I went down to stand beside Eoin in the water.' She raised her arms. 'I was the one holding on to Eoin. She wasn't there.'

Anderson nodded thankfully, 'Thanks, Isobel. Can you sit down as you were and say nothing?'

Isobel looked very pale as she walked away, her eyes following the way Ruth had walked.

Anderson walked casually round to Costello who was still on the shore, looking across the loch. He explained what she had told him.

'So she was not here then,' said Costello. 'And she is not here now.'

'Eoin, where has Ruth gone?' asked Costello.

'She went up there somewhere. Behind the Boathouse, with Daisy,' his jaw fixed, a tic flicked on his cheek.

'Daisy's back. Where is Ruth?'

Eoin bit his lip. 'She's away because she is too vulnerable for this, too scared to face it. Of course she needs to get away.'

'Eoin? Come on,' pleaded Anderson.

Eoin's face froze, he looked haunted. 'Why would any woman return to the place where her only child was murdered?'

'No, none of that. You can stop this,' said Anderson, his hand out, warning Costello to be quiet.

'Yes, I can. If you let me.' He pushed Anderson out the way, charging up the path to follow Ruth.

Anderson moved his eyes to Walker and the two uniformed cops on the veranda of the lodge. 'If she is going to top herself then we are not going to help wading in, are we?' he said.

Costello looked out into the falling darkness, just able to make out outlines, shadows and shapes. 'If.'

'What do you mean, "if"?'

'It might be them. Two sets of footsteps in, only one set out. The way he lifted Ruth over the log. The easy way she allowed herself to be lifted. Ruth said she never saw Eoin these days. She's the one Sammy was talking to, passing on all sorts. And there is no way Ruth sat still while all that hell broke out last year. Daisy and Fergus would have blocked her view, if nothing else, especially Daisy. Need a wide angle lens to see round her.'

'Ruth and Eoin?'

'Bet my career on it. We have everybody here. So call in back-up and get those two picked up. What's that smell? Burning?'

'Something on the bonfire.'

But Tony was on his feet, sniffing the air. 'Something is on fire.' He was looking south towards the Roonbay. 'The smoke is drifting from over there. Oh God, the wood is on fire.'

'Well, Ruth went over there.' Anderson pointed in the opposite direction, but he could see clearly now the plumes of smoke rising, acrid and billowing. 'And a flaming arrow can set anything on fire.'

Smoke rose on both sides of the bay. And his heart chilled as he saw the flames licking at the Dreamcatcher.

They heard a rush of quick feet moving through the undergrowth, a shadow passed over the fire. A sudden scream chilled their blood, echoing round the night air. The echo continued as the scream was cut to silence.

'Who was that, Colin?'

'No idea.' But he started walking. 'I think we have fucked up big time. Isobel? Fergus? Get into the lodge. Vik, you keep them there.' Tony helped Fergus up, and a very pale Isobel hurried in, closely followed by Daisy. The breeze changed direction, causing the flames of the bonfire to swirl and flare. The crackles of the blaze in the woods were carried away and a stillness fell on the campsite. Once the door of the lodge had closed with everybody else inside, there was only the crackling of the bonfire.

'And now what?' said Walker, coming down the stairs, holding on to the handrail. He was shaking.

'We get our ducks in a row,' said Costello, looking at the sky that was starting to spot with rain. 'Back-up is parked round the corner.' She spoke into her phone, then swore. 'Well, keep trying. They can't get through the smoke, either way. Somebody has set their fires very carefully. We are cut off.'

Anderson watched the horizon. The air was still and deadly silent, broken by a howl. A primal wail that went on and on. Then stopped abruptly.

'What the fuck was that?' asked Walker.

Anderson was already pulling them both back into the cover of the trees. 'That, I fear, was Mr Peppercorn.'

'So what do we do now? We're trapped.'

'This is not a good situation,' said Walker.

Anderson put his phone away. 'I can't raise Cusack or Dempsey. We have been outmanoeuvred. We have water in front, a fire on either side and Eoin on the loose with Ruth under his spell.'

'Or vice versa?' said Costello. 'You got any ID . . .' At that moment something in the boat shed blew up. The pressure wave hit them in the stomach just before the sound wave rattled their eardrums. 'Walker, you get in the lodge, don't want to be responsible for you.'

'And you?' Walker asked. 'What about you?'

'I'm going after her,' said Costello.

'Her?'

'Oh yes, definitely her.'

'I suppose a joke about you knowing a mad woman would be inappropriate?' said Walker, trying a smile through his fear.

'As in takes one to know one?' Costello smiled back. 'Come on, Colin.'

They had had a daft moment, bumping along the track. Claire laughing as she was thrown about in her seat. Helena beyond caring.

'Yahhhhh hoooo,' shouted Claire, a kid again as the car hit a pothole in the track.

Helena had smiled and put her foot on the accelerator. It was all a bit Thelma and Louise. She started to shriek along with Claire.

Helena had noticed the smell of petrol in the air. She had stepped over dry grass on the path, cut dry grass, like somebody had been gathering it. Colin had said something about them having a bonfire here.

But now, walking along the darkening track with the swirling, deceitful wind . . . Claire was getting nervy.

'So why are you bringing me all the way out here?'

'I know you want to see your dad, Claire.' Helena kept walking, trying to stride out confidently. She was angry. Angry that somebody had threatened a child. Welcome to Colin's world. Was it not the death of a four-year-old that had sparked all this off?

'But he might not be here.'

'He'll be here.' Helena kept walking. She was part of this. Right at this moment Helena wished she wasn't, she wanted to stop to catch her breath for a moment, but Claire was now ahead of her, walking away confidently down the path to the holiday village, looking for her dad.

Helena heard an animal yelp, like it was in pain.

'What was that?'

'Nothing, keep walking. The country is full of things killing other things.' She could see the light smoke of the bonfire curling into the sky. The walk seemed to take forever. She slowed up. Claire would appear then disappear as the path twisted and turned in front of her, shouting bits of conversation over her shoulder, then too far ahead for Helena to hear.

Claire was already down at the lochside by the time Helena walked out from the cover of the trees. She was standing by the water in a perfect silhouette, looking at the top of the Ben, shrouded in clouds, Payne's, indigo, all kinds of blue and grey rolling in. She saw the smoke rolling in, crackling and gnawing.

Claire had her back towards the water, looking over Helena's head.

'Is that right?' she asked quietly.

Helena took her time to approach; it was rough underfoot. Every footfall jarred her back as she crossed the shore grass to the little bay.

Claire shouted something but the noise got confused in Helena's head. She looked at the shingle footmarks, at her own feet and then Claire's. There was another set, going into the trees. She turned and called out, no answer.

It was all very quiet here, just the popping and snapping of something coming their way through the trees.

'Claire? We need to find your dad. Come here,' Helena called out, watching as the draught of warm air, black specked, lifted the girl's long hair. She leaned against a tree catching her breath, still looking at the footmarks. She could hear the slap-slop of water. Somebody was swimming in the loch. There was somebody in the woods behind. The world was darkening, rumbling. She couldn't trust her senses any more. There was noise all around her. She started walking slowly across the rocks to Claire, telling her in a low voice to come back. Claire turned round to look at her. 'What's up?'

'We need to leave here, Claire. We need to go now.' She had to breathe the words in the air.

There was a loud bang, like an explosion. The smoke got thicker, drifting across them, keeping them hidden. Helena's eyes began to smart, then the smoke cleared.

Claire was talking to her. Helena could see her mouth moving but she was hearing another noise. A rustling in the woods. Something or somebody was in the trees. She was ten yards away from Claire. She moved with her arms out, making herself wider, opening the arms of her jacket. She tried to move quicker, holding her breath, ignoring the pain in her chest. Then Claire's eyes drifted from her face and focussed on the trees behind her, somewhere over her left shoulder. Her face drained of all emotion, her eyes open, her mouth almost a perfect O. Helena thought she might be screaming. She thought that she herself might be screaming. She turned round, looking through into the green, looking behind the curtain of lush, verdant leaves, focussing on where she heard the sound.

Helena saw the point of the arrow as it rose and retreated into the bushes. She knew what was coming next and took a step to the side.

Costello covered her mouth as the screaming went on and on and on – the howling of a fatally wounded animal that was taking a long time to die. Then the screaming lengthened into one word. 'Daaaaaaad.'

Costello set off with Anderson close behind. They ran down the path to the Roonbay, towards the smoke and the ever-increasing noise of the flames. The misty grey smoke now had an orange heart. The horizon was lost.

Claire came running out from the smoke. She didn't stop, and
ran right into her dad. Costello kept going, keeping to the side of
the path to get some cover from the bushes, her jumper pulled up
to cover her mouth. She was thumped in the stomach. She kicked
and screamed, a hand clasped over her face and she was dragged
backwards into the trees.

'Stop screaming, you dozy cow, it's us.' She didn't recognize the
voice, but she identified the scent as Batten's patchouli oil. She
opened her eyes and saw Wyngate putting his fingers to his lips.
He was pointing to a figure lying on the breach. A cloud of smoke
drifted past; black soot motes danced their way to the water's edge.
Costello walked forward, seeing the dark hair spiking on the ground
and a slow river of blood running over the shingle. A single arrow
stuck in the chest pointing at the sky. She shrugged Batten away
and dashed out, muttering to herself, 'Don't let it be, please don't
let it be.'

Helena was lying, eyes open, staring upwards. Costello felt for
the carotid artery. Nothing. Costello pulled the phone from her
pocket, struggling to get the words out. 'Oh my God, oh my God.'
But Helena looked at her straight in the face. There was a slight
movement in her eyes. Costello leaned forward, smiled at her and
lifted Helena's head a little to fold her hood under her hair. She
was comforted by the look of peace in the other woman's face.

'She's OK, Claire's OK,' said Costello, hoping it was true. 'She's
with Colin. Helena? Helena? Did you see who fired at you?' The
eyes closed over, shutters coming down. Long eyelashes wavered.
The eyelids slivered open a little. 'You'll be OK. The ambulance
will be here soon.' A slight smile touched the blue lips. Her eyes
rolled up and looked at the sky. Costello turned to look, the smoke
cloud moved on. The dark clouds parted and the moon came into
sight, bathing light on the top of the Ben.

'Beautiful,' Helena's eyes flickered, then closed.

Costello looked behind her. Anderson was hugging his daughter,
pressing her head to his chest and muttering something to calm her.
Claire's eyes were burning into the body on the ground. Costello
took her jacket off and placed it over Helena, then she took a picture
of the top of the Ben with her phone before the clouds covered
them over again.

Batten and Wyngate had followed her out, moving slowly on to the coarser sand. Wyngate kept his eyes on the water, Batten watched the shore.

The enemy was out there.

Then Costello heard, they all heard, somebody running fast through the copse of trees, fast and clumsy.

'Roonbay,' said Costello, feeling a faint brush of wind, or the heat from the blaze, kiss the skin of her face. Daisy's words fired into her head: *The loch will give up its dead tonight.* 'Colin, get Claire back to the lodge. Now.'

But Anderson had his eyes closed, holding on to his daughter as if she was the most precious thing in the world.

'Colin!' screamed Costello.

Anderson lifted his head and nodded slightly as Claire looked at the body on the ground and made a whooping noise: half sob, half scream. She put her fist in her mouth but held on to her dad, allowing herself to be pulled through the smoke, slipping and sliding in darkness.

Costello, Batten and Wyngate all moved back into the treeline. The smoke was a choking, dense blanket now. Costello leaned against a tree and listened to the wash of the small waves, the chatter of the wind in the trees and the crackle and spit of the fire. She was listening for footsteps on the shingle but she couldn't hear. She moved on, behind another tree, a smaller one this time. She should be close to the Roonbay by now. She closed her eyes as a thick bank of smoke enveloped her.

Then she heard one word.

'Hello.'

'Come out, come out, wherever you are,' called Ruth.

She was sitting cross-legged on the Rocking Stone. Her face was grey, black smears of soot, her eyes bright and vibrant.

Costello stepped out, slowly walking forward to get clear of the trees.

'What the hell is she doing?' asked Wyngate from his position behind a large Scots pine.

'Suicide?' said Batten, searching for something to cover his face with. 'If that mad bitch moves, you run for her.'

'Which mad bitch do you mean?' whispered Wyngate, aware that his feet were sticking to the ground. The warm ground.

Costello saw Ruth had something lying across her lap, something like a small harp. Fewer strings but more deadly.

Batten hushed Wyngate and listened to the conversation, watching the two women in their deadly stand-off from behind his own tree. The background of the flames fizzled and rustled, edging ever closer.

'Don't come any closer. I can kill you from here very easily.'

'Yes, I know.'

The wind seemed to push the flames a little nearer. Costello could see them now. She could hear the deep waves slap and break against the stone, as if trying to get to Ruth, but not quite reaching.

Costello looked out across the loch.

'Smoke on the water,' said Ruth. 'The most famous guitar riff ever.'

'I prefer "Black Night". *It's a long way from home.* And so are you, Ruth.'

'That's good, keep it personal,' whispered Batten.

'I'm not; this is where my boy died. And where I will die. Just wondering how many of you I will take. You and your two pals, hiding behind the trees. They can either burn there or be shot by an arrow.'

Wyngate and Batten exchanged a glance, both aware how hot it was getting. Wyngate pulled the neck of his sweatshirt over his nose and mouth. Batten held his own arm up, breathing into his elbow.

Costello kept her eyes on the water. She was less than twenty feet away from Ruth but edging closer.

Batten watched, muttering, 'Don't, don't, don't.'

'Oh, this? You're looking at this?' Ruth lifted the bow.

Batten winced and pulled his head back behind the tree.

'It was the one question you never asked. The one fact you did not release to the press. If you had said how Patricia died then Isobel would have told you. Fergus, Daisy, any of them. They could have told you how good I am with this, how accurate.'

'True,' said Costello.

Batten could see Ruth face on, but only the back of Costello, who had now stopped walking. But was not retreating.

'Eoin wouldn't have told us, though.'

'No, not Eoin.' Ruth laughed, the bow lifted slightly.

Costello winced as she heard the Tinkerbell chime of Sammy's charm bracelet, hanging from Ruth's wrist.

'Sammy, Bernie. All that was revenge?'

Don't be confrontational, thought Batten, debating whether to step out and join the chat. But two against one might make Ruth feel more threatened and that would be dangerous. This way they still had the advantage of surprise.

'Not revenge. Grief. Let them live without the ones they love. Let DCI Anderson get on without his Helena, without his Claire. You have no idea how much I wanted my boy. My boy. Only to have him taken.'

'But by who? Not by his dad, his real dad, I mean. He was innocent. Or was he guilty of becoming what you were scared of – Callum's real dad?'

'He was mine,' hissed Ruth.

'But not Fergus's?'

'He was not Warren's to take,' Ruth's eyes narrowed.

The smoke passed again, Costello took a step forward. 'Warren was not yours to kill.'

'He so was, it was the will of the Gods. We got all of them except Lexy.'

'Give her her moment, Costello,' Batten whispered, the words choking his burning throat. 'Let her talk about her grief, her pain. Empathize.'

'You're so full of shit, Ruth.'

Batten cursed.

'It wasn't Warren. Eoin played you and your grief. It was Jimmy who killed your precious boy. He hated Robbie. Eoin should never have had Robbie. Jimmy preferred to be an only child. Have one. That one is not good enough, so Eoin went shopping for another. That sucks.'

Wyngate looked at Batten. 'What the fuck is she talking about?'

Batten placed a finger over his lips.

'So you were blessed by Callum, but cursed by Robbie.'

'Careful, Costello,' muttered Batten as the bow moved.

'And Bella was a mistake.'

'It still hurt, though,' Ruth insisted. 'Hurt Elizabeth, knowing her friend died instead of her. And that gave us more hope. Kill those close to our victims. Make them suffer. Like I am suffering.'

'So not grief, then. It is revenge.'

'Careful,' warned Batten.

'Got you, though, didn't I?'

'Not yet.'

'I'm not done.'

'Oh, you are,' Costello's voice was deadly.

Batten rolled his eyes heavenward.

'But you are in front of my arrow.'

'So?'

Batten heard the confidence in Costello's voice, Ruth heard it too.

Then Wyngate nudged him, 'Look.' Batten looked out but saw nothing except Costello and Ruth in silent stand-off, smoke blowing between them, sparks flying. He stifled a cough.

'So do you want us to say how clever you have been, Ruth?'

'Cleverer than you, obviously.'

'You won't get out of here.'

'I never intended to.'

Batten closed his eyes, both in prayer and because the smoke was burning. Ruth was playing her end game and that made her dangerous. He was about to step out and start to negotiate when Wyngate stopped him. The constable shook his head. 'Look.'

The wind was moving the trees now. Ruth lifted the bow slightly; it looked very comfortable in her hands.

Batten heard the crack in Costello's voice, each nerve twanging. 'Do you feel that wind? Do you feel it, Ruth? Do you know what that means?'

Ruth was confused as well, the bow lifted, the arrow came up.

Costello started quoting Daisy. 'The tears of angels. Can you feel it?'

'It's the fire.'

'No, it's all over the water.'

'You won't get me to turn round.'

'Don't. But the loch will give up its dead tonight. And you put Warren in the water.'

'It's not raining.'

'Warren will come after you.'

Ruth went quiet, something like fear flickered across her face.

'What the fuck is she going on about?' Then Batten saw something rise from the darkness behind Ruth. He saw the shimmer of dark wet hair, ebony eyes shining in the night, the flash of green, the white of a necrotized flesh. Two arms rose from the black water beyond the Rocking Stone, white water splashed as two strong arms closed round Ruth and pulled her backwards into the dark water. There was a silence, then white bleached bones danced in the surface as the waves closed over, rippling to stillness.

Sunday, 22 June

Vik looked out the window at the devastation around him. The weather was glorious again. He felt shell-shocked. Inchgarten Bay looked like London after the Blitz. The lodge had remained untouched, thank God. He had spent two hours that morning in his initial debrief. A DCI Turner was taking charge, going over Anderson's mistakes, Bernie's mistakes and no doubt coming out squeaky clean himself. From the tone of the meeting, Colin was number one fall guy. He had believed Eoin, he had empathised with him. That was his big mistake. It was nothing to do with Colin, the way Helena and Claire had appeared at the scene, but it didn't look good for him.

Still, there was Helena.

Colin had bigger things to worry about.

Vik looked round. It was still better than home. Roonbay was in full view now that the trees had been razed to the ground, a stark, grey, smouldering landscape. It looked post-nuclear. The remains of the boatshed were still smoking, burnt out, stinking. CSIs this way, photographers that way. Elvie and Daisy at the end of the jetty. They could have been sitting in the sun on holiday, the scenery behind them, Inchgarten Island, chocolate box perfect. Daisy had been very upset that the big apple tree had been charred. But had been consoled it had survived for a hundred years, and would survive a hundred more.

So beautiful out there.

And evil all around. He reread the email conversation, the last thing on Elvie's laptop.

Hello

Hi, Amy Lee. How are you? How is the project going?

I'm not Amy Lee. My name is John Wark, RCMP. Amy Lee seems to have disappeared. We are going through her contact box to see if anybody knows what has happened to her. Can I ask you what your relationship was, when you last saw her?

I have never met her. I was helping her with the Scottish part of her ancestry. Where is 'Grandpappy'?

Why do you ask? He was the last one to see her alive this morning. Who are you?

My name is Elvie McCulloch. I work for Parnell Fox Investigations, Glasgow, Scotland. I was researching her family history for her.

OK, Elvie. I think I have some bad news for you.

Mulholland read on, kicking himself as he did so. He had been a detective for fifteen years and shit like this still passed him by. Wee Amy Lee had been found strangled.

Just like Angela eighty years ago, when Robert's childlike hands had been mistaken for those of his mother. Amy Lee had been killed by those same hands. Was he another psychopath, like Jimmy, unable to bear the birth of the younger child? In Robert's case, the mother was willing to hang so her child could go free. Eoin's actions had been little different. Did either of them realize the monster they were setting loose? What would Jimmy have matured into? Didn't bear thinking about, but they didn't have to think about it; James Dewar was incarcerated and receiving treatment. He wouldn't get the chance to grow into a Robert Cohoon.

Elvie was gunning to fly out there. Vik had insisted on using more official channels but he didn't know who to go to. He was content to know that whatever luck had kept Robert Cohoon at liberty for all these years, it was over now.

He watched Daisy flinging stones into the water, and wondered what conversation was going on out there. The CSIs were clustered far beyond the Boathouse, where Eoin had been found with his throat cut, and around the Roonbay, where Helena McAlpine had had her life cut short, if only by a few months.

A policewoman sweating in her uniform came into view of the lodge window, Costello walking behind her. Trousers and a blouse, an official visit then. Who was escorting who? The uniform tried to guide Costello up to the Boathouse where they had eaten and where Turner now had his office. But Costello went down the jetty, waving the uniform away. Words were said. There was an argument. The uniform didn't win.

He wondered what Costello was in for. A medal for bravery? Or was the whole epic failure going to be her fault? Knowing Police Scotland, it could be both.

Vik picked up his crutch. He needed to be in on this conversation.

*   *   *

'How's Colin?' he asked, clonking his way along the wooden jetty. Elvie trotted off and returned with a plastic crate for him to sit on.

'How do you expect?' said Costello. She had black bags under her bloodshot eyes. 'He's not good. Claire's not good. Helena knew she was very ill, but to witness somebody sacrificing themselves to save you, that's some burden for young shoulders to carry.'

'Her decision. A very sensible one, if she was terminal,' said Elvie, looking out to the islands.

'Tony?' asked Daisy.

'He'll be out later, just a little smoke inhalation. Batten and Wyngate are with him, all talking in strange, husky voices.'

'And how are you?' Daisy asked.

'I'll survive,' Costello said.

'You might not survive the inquest,' Mulholland pointed out. 'Not with DCI Turner.'

'Well, he can wait. Walker's report is complimentary.'

'And Warren? What about Warren?' asked Daisy. 'I saw the bag, on the stretcher?'

'The prof has him now, what's left of him. The water has had him for a year. It will come out that he died going for help. He had taken a few blows to the head and still managed to get off the island. His dad will be proud of him.'

'How are we going to explain Elvie to Turner?' asked Mulholland quietly.

Costello noted the protective tone in his voice. 'Geno was paying her.'

'He can't threaten me with anything,' shrugged Elvie.

'No, but they will threaten Colin.'

'It was my idea for you to be here, Elvie.' Costello put her head in her hands. 'For God's sake, you swam up behind Ruth and pulled her off that rock. Before she could kill me, Batten, Wyngate or all three of us. I thought you had drowned her.'

Elvie shook her head. 'Only punched her unconscious.'

'I really thought you were Warren, then I saw those bones.'

'I think he was trying to help. From beyond the grave.' Daisy nodded. 'That would be him.'

'Or would that be the wind, the peculiar tide at the solstice? The wind that brought the rain which hampered the progress of the fire, Daisy, not witchcraft?'

'The tears of the angels, like I said.'

'But are you a witch, Daisy? How did these women get pregnant?' asked Costello.

Daisy opened her mouth then closed it. 'I suppose it is all over now.' She looked around.

'It is, Daisy. It's all going to come out and I think that is wrong. People don't need to know. We can just not say.'

Daisy looked over at the burned-out shell of the boatshed.

'Blue-eyed parents with brown-eyed children. For different reasons, Eoin, Fergus, Adam all had their infertility. Warren was a healthy young man . . . Tony knew how sperm donation had tumbled after the law was changed. Sperm donors could be traced, chased by the CSA. It left people desperate. Warren cared nothing for money. He had none. He believed that life was life.'

'Did money change hands?'

'Not really – they paid for the lodges. Kept us going. They came back, we saw them grow up.' She started to cry. 'Lovely children.'

'Conceived by . . .?'

'Turkey baster, aided by horny goatweed, apples. All aid fertility. Tony knew that.'

'But Jimmy found out. Found out his parents had deliberately sought a second child, Robbie. That pushed the little psychopath over the edge. He killed their pets, killed Grace, tortured his mum. He saw the way Warren looked at Robbie, the way Warren looked out for Callum. Isobel admits that she was scared of him. That's why the attack on Robbie was so savage. Jimmy is being assessed by the head shrinkers.'

'Did he know about Angela? The case has so many similarities.'

'He did know. Eoin knew everything of the history of this place.'

'So did Tony. We talked about him, Jimmy would have known,' added Daisy.

'Batten says he's never been so scared of or so seduced by a boy of that age. Can't help but feel sorry for Isobel; she got so caught up in protecting what she thought was right. Scared of losing her job, her child, her marriage.'

'Her job?' asked Elvie.

'If she was discovered up here, pot smoking, drinking illegal whisky, of course she'd lose her job. And she needed that income.'

'Do you think Warren was starting to see his boys through an adult's eyes?' asked Daisy.

'Ruth saw the writing on the wall years ago. Warren might want some involvement in the boys' lives, his sons. Batten had noticed the way Warren stroked Callum's face. Very telling.'

'Yet her narrative of Warren being the murderer allowed Eoin not to face the extremely unpleasant truth about Jimmy,' said Vik. 'Where is Ruth?'

'Held at a secure unit for the moment.' Costello swallowed hard. 'She's not insane; she's an evil bitch. Making us look stupid.'

'She didn't need any help with that, Costello.'

'You're right,' said Costello. 'Drugging Eddie with her own medication that she didn't take. She told us about the confusion of neighbours going in each other's houses – we didn't pick up on that. She said the death of her son was something that she couldn't accept, we ignored that. She said she couldn't live with the fact the killer of her child was out there, walking around. We misread that. Killing Warren was a decision made in a heated moment, but her own heart had already written the story as soon as she found out Taylor and Lexy had lied about Warren's alibi. Therefore Warren murdered Grace.'

'She was accurate with a bow at that distance?' asked Elvie.

'She was then, obviously,' said Costello.

'But not now, otherwise Mr Peppercorn wouldn't have survived. Moving target, thank God,' said Daisy, biting back a tear.

'How did Ruth find out about that alibi being false?'

Costello shrugged. 'A wee chat around here? In the hairdresser's? Doesn't matter. But as soon as Jimmy came back screaming, in that split second she had Warren tried, judged and executed. She was a remarkable woman.'

'I thought it was weird that she watered her plants, at odds with the disarray of the rest of the house. And when she shook my hand, I felt how rough her skin was. How does a woman who does nothing all day have skin that rough? She must be doing something. I never asked what. Archery. I'm from Mosspark, I know the council let out garages. Turner has already found one of Eoin's old Berlingo vans with a fake council logo in a garage near Ruth, but it was listed in the neighbour's name.She even told us the dog next door was black. She more or less told us!'

'What has a dog got to do with anything?' asked Mulholland.

'Rereading the notes, I think we will find a woman with a black dog appears somewhere. Outside Bella's. At the Boden Boo. But it really only clicked when Eoin picked her up, so easily. I saw it in my head, him carrying her out the field away from Eddie's body.

'I think Bernie had worked it out in the end. He wasn't looking for Warren, he had guessed something had happened to him. Crecy was his codename for Ruth, so he knew about her archery. But he was playing it too clever, being clandestine, phoning her and texting her. He thought he was keeping tabs on her. But she was playing him. Then Ruth tipped off Karen Jones. He sealed his own fate when he phoned her about Eddie's body.'

'And the way he behaved here with Sammy . . .' Daisy shuddered. 'Still, it was a terrible way to die.'

'What was the point?' asked Vik. 'All that tarot card stuff. Was she telling us that she was in the know, that she was the powerful one?'

'She ran rings round us, Vik.' Costello stood up and looked out over the loch, the island, the glimmering water. The click of efficient heels approached behind her. 'She's coming to take me away. I can always say my throat is too sore to talk.'

'DI Costello? DCI Turner wants to speak to you. Now.'

Costello turned to Daisy. 'You are lucky, you know, living here. No matter what has gone on, you're really lucky.'

'The door is always open. Good luck.'

'I'll need it.'

Epilogue

Costello closed the car door quietly and took a long look at the house. If she had to pick out a house from the street, *which one of these houses do you think belongs to an anally retentive shit of a fiscal with OCD?* Yip, she would have picked this one.

A hyper-neat bungalow, a lawn that looked as though it had been trimmed with nail clippers, and two topiary bushes cropped within an inch of their lives. The gravel in the drive showed lines of a recent raking. The chipped path was the same. Absolutely perfect. Costello walked on the path, taking delight in squirming the soles of her boots in, leaving an untidy pattern behind her. Simple things.

The front door was a modern plastic one with false stained glass patterned in some abomination of the Rennie Mackintosh rose design. Cheaper taste than she would have expected from him, although maybe it was *her* taste, the taste of the wife he claims he doesn't get on with. The taste of the wife he doesn't bring out with him because that would interrupt his love life too much.

Well, the wife's taste in husbands wasn't very impressive.

She pressed her finger on the doorbell for slightly longer than was polite. She'd teach him about what happens to married men when they play away. Not that she was going to do anything, just a warning shot across his libido.

The procurator fiscal was a long time in answering. Through the glass panel she saw an internal door open and close, a figure walking to the door, three bolts sliding back, the key turned, the handle twisted, the door opened.

Archibald Walker's eyes opened in horror.

'Hello,' she said sweetly, pulling the word into three syllables. 'Hope you don't mind me standing on your doorstep.' The answering glower proved that he very much did. 'But Colin has gone to the trouble of typing this up. I thought you might like a flick through the final version before he makes it official . . .'

Walker's face didn't move.

'You know, before he signs it all off, in case there's something there that you wish to keep under the official secrets or something.' She made a joke of it but Walker's face was poker straight. She showed him the folder but made no attempt to hand it over. She wanted to meet the wife; she wanted to put him on the spot. And see him wriggle.

Eventually he remembered his manners. 'Oh, there was no need to come out here. How is Colin?' he said, smiling a smile that warmed his lips but hardened his eyes.

'As you would expect. His daughter is in a bad way, emotionally.'

Walker nodded. 'It was a terrible thing for one so young to witness. You really shouldn't have come all this way.'

'No problem. There was every need, Sir. DCI Bernie Watson was a two-timing shit of a police officer.' She smiled as Walker had the good grace to blush. 'So best that I come out and show you this, make sure that the force is not going to be embarrassed by the activities of any of our officers.'

He put out his hand. She reluctantly handed over the folder. Walker turned round at the sound of a door opening behind him.

'Darling, you stay . . .' But she had broken through, the wife who did not understand him.

'Is that one of your colleagues, Archie? Invite her in, for God's sake, don't leave her on the doorstep. Come on in.' The small lady with a neat grey bob opened the door fully. On first glance she was a lot older than her husband, in her sixties, maybe. Archie Walker – fiscal and toy boy?

'Thank you.' Costello smiled as she passed them going into the hall. On closer look the age was only an impression given by the elastic waisted trousers, the washed out woollen jumper . . . the beads round her neck . . . lots of beads round her neck. Was this why Walker never allowed her to come out? Was she too much of a fashion frump?

She smiled at Costello; her eyes were sparkly and friendly and her face full of laughter lines.

'Do come through. Archie, put the kettle on. Oh, look at him standing there like a useless article.' She bustled her way through into the front room that looked as though it had just been emulsioned with brilliant white. There were vacuum track lines on the plush red carpet, like a ploughed field.

'I'm sure DI Costello has better things to do than join us for afternoon tea.' He looked meaningfully at Costello and even more meaningfully towards the door.

'No, I don't,' Costello said airily.

'Oh, you sit down, dear. Archie, put the kettle on.'

The procurator fiscal tootled off in the direction of a highly glossed door, leaving it open as he went through. Costello noticed the sliding bolt at the top of it.

'Do you like my beads?' Mrs Walker asked, placing herself delicately on an armchair.

'Yes, they're lovely. Don't wear much jewellery in my job, I'm afraid.'

'And what is it you do, dear?' She leaned forward, her eyes keen and intelligent.

Costello paused; maybe she was deaf . . . 'I'm a police officer, I work with your husband.'

'Archie, yes. He's a fiscal.'

'Yes,' said Costello, aware of a slow sinking feeling in her stomach.

'Do you like my beads?'

'Pippa, don't annoy DI Costello.' Archie came through carrying a tray with three mugs on it. He caught Costello's eye, that look was there again. 'I've stuck the file in the study. I'll try and have a look at it tonight.' He put the tray down on the coffee table. 'Pippa? Our friend is going to join us for a cuppa, do you want some tea?'

Pippa nodded enthusiastically and sat back, beaming at Costello but speaking to her husband. 'Is this the new cleaner?'

'She'd be crap, I've seen her desk,' muttered Archie. Then said loudly, 'No, she's having a cup of tea.'

'That's nice, dear. Does she like my beads?' And Pippa started taking them off, strand after strand. Dangling then carefully over her wrists. She did this with great care, having forgotten her audience.

Archie held out a mug. 'There's your tea, dear.'

'Oh, no, thanks,' she said, brushing it away, trivia she had no time for.

Archie put the mug down then carefully slid the beads from her wrists and placed them over her head again. This was clearly a routine they had been through many times before. 'Are you happy with these ones or do you want some more?'

'I'm fine, where's my tea?' But she made no attempt to reach for the mug, though she was staring straight at it. 'You are a lovely girl,' she said to Costello.

'Lovely beads,' was all Costello could manage.

'Some days we do quite well,' Archie said as he handed Costello her tea. 'Some other days are a bit more of a challenge.' He sat down on the sofa, almost collapsing into the cushions. He looked exhausted. He closed his eyes, grateful of a minute's peace.

'Archie? Can you get me my beads?'

'In a minute, darling.'

Pippa smiled.

Silence hung in the room like a funereal veil.

'That's a nice name, Pippa. Short for Philippa?' asked Costello.

'Sorry, who are you?' Pippa asked.

'Just a colleague from work.'

Pippa stared at her. 'Really, are you leaving now? Do come again . . .'

Costello picked up the slight aggression in her tone. 'Do you want me to go?'

Archie gave her a half-hearted smile. 'I'd like you to stay but you had better go.'

'I'll see myself out.' She stood up. 'Bye, Pippa.'

'Bye,' said Pippa, bored.

As Costello closed the front-room door she heard Pippa say, 'Who was that dreadful woman? I think she stole my beads.'